# 4 PUZZLING COZY MYSTERIES

# MISSING PIECES

CYNTHIA HICKEY
LINDA BATEN JOHNSON
TERESA IVES LILLY
JANICE THOMPSON

T0054203

BARBOUR
PUBLISHING

*Elvis Has Left the Building* ©2022 by Cynthia Hickey
*The Puzzle King* ©2022 by Linda Baten Johnson
*A Puzzling Weekend* ©2022 by Teresa Ives Lilly
*Puzzle Me This* ©2022 by Janice Thompson

Print ISBN 978-1-63609-289-8

Adobe Digital Edition (.epub) 978-1-63609-288-1

Cover Art: Chloe Dominique / Bright Agency

Published by Barbour Publishing, Inc., 1810 Barbour Drive, Uhrichsville, Ohio 44683, www.barbourbooks.com

*Our mission is to inspire the world with the life-changing message of the Bible.*

Member of the
Evangelical Christian
Publishers Association

Printed in Canada.

# ELVIS HAS LEFT THE BUILDING

*By Cynthia Hickey*

# CHAPTER 1

"Elvis is in the building!" Or he will be. I, Celia Adams, better known as Cee Cee, waved a sheet of paper in front of my friend Annie's face. "We have our impersonator. Not only that, but I found an exact replica of Elvis's pink Cadillac."

"See? I told everyone you were the perfect pick to host our first annual themed jigsaw party." Annie grinned. "I do hope you'll wear a poodle skirt."

"Wouldn't dream not to." I'd also managed to borrow a puzzle the King of Rock 'n' Roll had been rumored to put together himself. A self-portrait. I'd leave that as a surprise for the attendees. No sense inviting thieves beforehand. Which reminded me I'd need a couple of security guards for the event. I reached for the phone and called the local police department.

"Apple Blossom P.D.," a cheery woman answered.

"This is Cee Cee Adams at the library. I'm wondering whether I can get a couple of officers to attend the jigsaw party. I'll have a couple of artifacts that will need guarding."

"I'll run it by the chief and get back to you." She hung up, leaving me to turn to the next item on my list.

Find a band, vendors, and folks with vintage cars. Why had

I agreed to run this party with only a couple of weeks before the date? Because someone backed out and Annie volunteered me. I glared her way.

She grinned, totally unashamed at what she put me through. "Chin up, Buttercup. You're doing great."

I sent a classified to the paper about the event and sent a second one asking for people to bring their vintage cars. A few days ago, I'd posted in the papers of neighboring towns. Now, to visit some of the local diners. "See you tomorrow. Can't have an event this big without food and drink available for purchase."

"I'll work on getting us some tents to use in the parking lot. I'm anticipating a crowd way too large to hold inside the library."

"The high school gym?"

She shook her head. "Everyone would have to take off their shoes in order not to ruin the wood floor. I know someone who can build us a dance floor. I've hired some muscle to move the library tables outside for the puzzles. It's all coming together."

It truly was. Knowing we had most everything under control, I grabbed my purse and headed down Main Street. First stop, Have a Hole, our town's doughnut shop.

A bell jingled as I pushed the door open. "Hello, Sadie." I smiled at the middle-aged woman behind the counter. "I'll take a plain glazed, please."

"Howdy, Cee Cee. Bet you're here about the party."

"I am. Interested?"

"Sure. I'd love to set up a table to sell my goods. Who else you got?" She handed me a doughnut wrapped in waxed paper. "On the house. We all appreciate you taking over this event after Mrs. Woodworth dropped out. Not only will it be a great time, but it'll draw people to our town. Why, they might even decide to stay."

Apple Blossom did have several homes for sale. Maybe a Realtor could have a table set up. It wouldn't hurt.

Happily munching on my treat, I moved through the adjoining door to the coffee shop. Millie and Sadie refused to combine their two businesses but did agree to the opening between their shops.

"I heard." Millie turned from a large carafe. "I'll be glad to sell my coffee. I'll set up right next to Sadie. Coffee and doughnuts go great together." She leaned her elbows on the table. "Old Man Stevenson used to run the county fair. I bet he has a cotton candy machine and a popcorn machine."

"That's a great idea." I wiped the last of the sugar from my lips. "Can you call him and let me know?"

"Sure thing." She flashed a grin and turned to a customer coming through the door. "Welcome back, Dane."

I gasped and turned. It couldn't be. It was. Dane Dixon stood grinning at me like a goon as if he hadn't broken my heart ten years ago. Man, he looked good. Muscles, that cleft in his chin I'd once drooled over. Hazel eyes to melt a girl's heart. . . No, I would not look at him that way ever again. "Hello."

"Cee Cee. You haven't changed a bit."

"Well, it's good to see you, but I've got to run. Lots to do." I ran out of there as if chased by bats. Outside, I leaned against the building and tried to still my racing heart. Of all the people to return to town, why did it have to be him?

I whipped my phone from my purse and called Annie. "Did you know Dane is back in town?"

"Everyone knows."

"I didn't."

"Are you still upset that he went away to college? Seriously,

Cee, you're the one who dumped him. Remember that mug you threw at him? I bet he still has the scar."

"He promised to never leave." And yes, I'd noticed the tiny scar on his eyebrow.

"Now he's back. Focus on the party and stop acting like you're still in high school." *Click.*

Ouch. I pushed away from the wall, realizing my best friend was right. High school was a long time ago, after all. I rarely dated, but life felt complete working at the library and helping with the youth at church. I doubted my path would cross with Dane very often.

I headed to the diner, received a promise to sell burgers and fries, then the ice cream parlor. If Millie secured the cotton candy and popcorn, there would be plenty of food to choose from.

A puzzle. I'd forgotten to purchase a puzzle. The one thing people were required to bring, and I didn't have one. I rushed to the bookstore.

"Help me, Lucy. I need a 500-piece puzzle. Something very Elvis."

She blinked at me from behind thick glasses. "There are a few in the corner. Take a look. People have been buying them like crazy because of the party. I had to run to the city to restock."

"Thank you." Bless her for selling a few items that weren't books. I found a puzzle of Elvis singing on stage in a white rhinestone jumpsuit. I would have preferred a younger Elvis, but one couldn't be picky when they waited until the last minute. I doubted I'd have time to sit down and put it together, but at least I wouldn't show up empty-handed.

Seeing Dane headed my way, I crossed the street and ducked into the corner drugstore.

"Who are you hiding from, young lady?" Mr. Rogers came from behind the counter.

"No one." I smiled. "Can I put a flyer about the party in your window?"

"Absolutely."

I dug one from my purse and handed it to him. "I hope you'll come."

"Girl, I was a teen in the fifties. The wife and I can't wait to jitterbug again." He glanced past me. "Oh, I see. You're running from your past."

I frowned. "No."

"Say what you will, but it's time to let bygones be bygones. Dane will be an asset to this town."

"How so?"

"He's one of our new police officers."

*Great. He's bound to be one of the guards for the party.*

Since I'd completed my rounds quicker than I'd thought, I returned to the library, dropping off flyers in every shop I passed. Remember the 50s Jigsaw Party would be the biggest event in this town for a long time to come.

"You look happy." Annie glanced up.

"Things are coming together." I sat down at my desk.

"I've got the tents rented and the cotton candy and popcorn. Mr. Stevenson said he's more than glad to pull them out of storage and make a few bucks. Oh, and the Rowdy Recruits will be the band."

"Can they play that era? I've only heard them do bluegrass." I raised my eyebrows.

"Said they could."

"That's it. The last on our list." Feeling rather pleased with myself, I started entering newly arrived books into our inventory.

Our library might be small, but folks donate books in good condition on a regular basis, allowing us to have a large inventory. When I'd finished, I browsed the internet for an authentic-looking poodle skirt and saddle shoes.

I purchased a black top and a pink skirt with a black poodle appliqué and gauzy slip underneath. Bobby socks, shoes, and a matching hair ribbon completed the ensemble. Now to relax for two weeks.

After work, I stopped by my parents' house for supper. Tonight was spaghetti night, and my mom made the best sauce. The aroma greeted me the instant I opened the front door. "I'm here."

Mom greeted me with a hug. "I know you're too busy to eat with us most nights, Celia, but you never miss Wednesday night supper. If you did, I'd have to alert the authorities."

She refuses to call me Cee Cee. Says she preferred the name she gave me at birth. "Need any help?"

"You can get your father from his shop. Everything is ready."

I set my purse down and stepped out the back door. Dad's cement block shop takes up half the yard. Mom complains about the ugliness of it, but the shop is his happy place. "Dad?" I entered the dim building. "Supper's ready."

"Oh, good. I just finished my project for your party." He held up a life-size silhouette of a couple dancing. "I'll paint it black and mount it on your dance floor."

"Annie roped you into building it, didn't she?"

"I don't mind. Keeps me busy." He propped the wood piece against the wall. "How's everything?"

"Ready to go." I looped my arm with his and walked back to the house.

As we ate, I told them about all Annie and I had done to make the event a success. "Did you get your puzzle? Remember, it has to be a minimum of 500 pieces."

"Yes, one with vintage cars." Mom passed the bowl of garlic bread.

"And I'm waxing the Buick," Dad said. "You know how I like to show her off."

"Get there early to get a prime parking spot. Maybe you can get close to the pink Cadillac. Everyone will be wanting to look at that car."

"So, why the puzzles?" Mom asked.

"I think it's a way of drawing people together. There's a prize for whoever finishes theirs first." A bobblehead Elvis. "I didn't plan that event, Mrs. Woodworth did. Maybe it started as an event for senior citizens but ballooned into something else."

"That makes sense." She handed me the grated Parmesan cheese.

"Now to pray that everything goes as planned." I did not have good luck on big projects. *Please, God, let this time be an exception.*

# CHAPTER 2

Tonight was the night. Excitement fluttered through my stomach like a hummingbird.

I smoothed my poodle skirt, checked the bow in my hair, and skipped down the stairs. "See you at the party," I called out to my parents. As the one in charge, I needed to arrive early. Way early to make sure vendors, the band, the cars. . .everything got set up on time.

Oh, the pink Cadillac. I reached across the red velvet rope keeping people from getting too close and stretched out my hand. My ponytail flopped forward, slapping me in the eye.

"Please, don't touch." Dane, looking handsome in his police uniform, grinned. "I just waxed her."

"This is yours?" I widened my eyes and stepped back.

"A hobby I picked up. I've got a Model-T in my garage at the moment. Still needs a lot of work." His eyes narrowed at something over my shoulder. "He belong to you?"

Elvis staggered toward us, a crowd of vendors and owners of vintage cars trailing behind. "Yo." He gave a lopsided grin.

"You're drunk." My breath came in gasps. One of the star attractions of the party could barely stand up. The crowd behind him snickered and pointed. I poked him in the chest. "If you ruin this evening, you'll regret it, that I promise you. Find a way to sober up in the next two hours or I'll clobber you."

He blinked like a sleepy owl. "I only had a sip." He continued his lumbering walk toward the vendor booth selling coffee.

I doubted any amount of java would fix him. "What do I do?" I turned to Dane.

"Pray he sobers up enough to do his job." He shrugged.

"You're a policeman. Do something."

"He hasn't done anything wrong."

"Yet," I snarled and checked on the tables set off to one side for folks to work on puzzles. On the makeshift stage, the band set up. Hopefully, nothing else would go wrong.

By seven the party was in full swing. People danced, laughed and chatted over puzzles, took pictures by the Cadillac, and strolled among the vintage vehicles. With no sign of Elvis.

"Have you heard?" Annie waved an electronic tablet in front of my face. "A puzzle went missing from Elvis's estate. A collage of all his movies."

"Really?" I quickly scanned the article. What were the odds a puzzle disappeared the very night of our party? "Why a puzzle?"

She tapped the screen. "Signed by Elvis himself."

"That'll be the main topic of conversation tonight." I glanced to where Dane strolled among the attendees.

The police department had sent only him to keep a very large group of people under control. So far, so good. He smiled and laughed at something a young woman said. My heart did a somersault.

"You still like him," Annie said.

"I never stopped." With a sigh, I watched as my still very

in love parents danced to a slow tune. I wanted what they had. God might have other plans though. "What do you think of our Elvis?"

"He's a disgrace. You said you hired an impersonator, but I had no idea it was Billy Baron. He spends more time sleeping off a drink than anything else." Her face hardened. "Don't you remember how he used to bully us in school?"

"Oh." I hadn't put the slightly overweight impersonator together with Billy. "I guess I was only thinking about checking another item off my list."

"The worst person you could have hired."

Loud voices drew me away from the dancing. I glanced at Dane. Seeing him busy consoling a child who had gotten separated from her parents, I went in search of the voices.

Billy and a man with his back to me exchanged heated words. All I could tell about the man was that he was bald and big. "I said I'd get it to you," Billy said. "I'm a little short right now."

"If you'd do what I hired you to do," I said, crossing my arms, "you'd have some money. No work, no pay."

The other man marched away without turning in my direction.

"I'll go pose for pictures." Billy didn't stagger quite as much but still leaned a bit to the side when he walked.

"You're supposed to put on a show at eight." I jogged to keep up with him. "Are you prepared?"

"Yep. Practiced with the band last night." He smoothed his pomade-covered hair. "Relax, little lady, I got this."

He'd better. I glared at his back then went to get a cup of coffee. Styrofoam cup in hand, I watched the clumsy Elvis climb onto the stage and grip the microphone stand as if it would keep him on his feet.

"At least he's up," Dane said, joining me.

"Barely." Fortunately, the guy could do a very good imitation of the King of Rock and Roll. He belted out "Jailhouse Rock," complete with hip moves. Those watching cheered and clapped. Some of the tension left my shoulders.

"You've done a good job here, Cee Cee."

"Thank you." I cut Dane a glance. "You didn't want to be a cop when you left here. Didn't you go to college to be an architect?"

"I did, but my roommate was jumped and killed one night walking home after a late class. They never found his attacker. So I quit and went to the academy to try and keep other murderers from getting away with their crimes."

"Not a lot of crime in Apple Blossom." I took a sip of my drink, my heart aching at his loss. I would have gladly consoled him if he'd asked.

"Maybe, but I wanted to come home."

I wanted to ask why a small-town boy with big-city dreams had wanted to return to the very place he couldn't wait to leave. Instead, I kept my mouth shut, excused myself, and strolled among the tables of puzzle workers.

"This is the most fun I've had in a very long time," Millie said. "Who thought putting together puzzles could be this entertaining?"

"It helps to get friends together," Sadie replied, placing a center piece of Elvis's face in place. "Good music doesn't hurt. You did good, Cee Cee. I hope you're managing to have some fun."

"I'm enjoying the night very much." I smiled, surprised at how true my statement was. Now that Billy was cooperating, the event was going very well.

After the Elvis show, the band picked up the pace and folks

took to the floor to jitterbug. I laughed as Mom and Dad owned the dance floor. I clapped and hollered along with everyone else.

From the corner of my eye, I saw Billy plop on the steps of the library and wave away someone wanting to take a photo. I'd give him fifteen minutes to rest, then back to work. He'd wasted enough time at the beginning of the evening. As I walked closer, I saw that the man did not look well at all.

I went to sit next to him. "Feeling poorly?"

"Haven't had anything in my stomach but alcohol and coffee." He put his head in his hands.

"How about I buy you a sandwich and a soda?" I might be angry with him, but seeing how bad he felt tugged at my heart.

"That would be great. Thank you. Thank you very much."

I choked back a laugh at the famous Elvis saying and went in search of food. I returned a few minutes later with a Coke and burger and fries. "Hopefully, this will give you the energy to take some photos with people."

"I'll do my job, don't worry. We still have two hours before this gig is over."

After a quick pat on his shoulder, I continued my patrol, smiling and stopping to chat on occasion. I had to squelch down the pride that rose each time someone told me how well I'd done with the party. While the accolades were appreciated, I'd done it because no one else would. Maybe I had a knack for event planning.

"Hey." Dane snuck up on me. "Saw you being nice to Elvis."

"I'm not an ogre."

"I've seen your temper in action." He brushed a finger across his eyebrow.

"That was a childish tantrum." One I'd always felt horrible about.

"If I wasn't in uniform, would you dance with me?" A dimple winked in his cheek.

I stared into his eyes, doing my best to decipher why he'd bother with me after all these years. "I'm working."

"I said 'if.'" He tapped a finger on my nose and melted into the crowd.

"Uh-oh." Annie smiled as she passed. "Looks like he's flirting with you."

"Hush." I bit back a smile and glanced at the library steps.

Elvis was nowhere in sight. I decided not to worry about him. He'd performed well. It would be enough to satisfy the partygoers. I'd choose the entertainment more wisely next time and get references rather than hire from a video online.

Nine o'clock, and while a few folks had gone home, most had stayed, moving from one puzzle table to another. Exhaustion settled on my shoulders. My feet ached. Four hours with another to go, then tear down and clean up. I'd sleep like the dead tomorrow.

I eyed Dad's Buick, wishing I could crawl in and take a nap on the backseat. No rest for the weary, they say. I took a deep breath and purchased another two cups of coffee. Dane didn't look tired, but he'd been here as long as I had.

"Thank you." He took the cup with a smile.

"How's the patrolling?" I peered over the rim of my cup.

"Two skinned knees, one child who lost sight of Mommy, and a dropped wallet that was promptly found. Busy night." He chuckled.

"That's about the extent of crime here. Oh, you'll get the occasional transient, vandalism, stolen bike. . ." A few drunks needing a night to sleep it off.

"You've never gotten bored?"

I frowned. "No. I don't crave danger. That's a strange question from someone who came back."

"I got smarter in my old age." He winked.

"Ha. That remains to be seen."

How I'd missed joking around with him. Funny, handsome, kind, everything a woman wanted in a man—except that he'd gone away.

"You got sad. What's wrong?"

"Nothing." I forced the smile back to my face. "Just tired."

"You have a reason to be. Why not take a few minutes to sit down?"

"You haven't."

"Sure I have. All under the pretense of working. I sat when I consoled the lost child, sat and talked when I returned the wallet. No one will fault you for taking a break." He led me to a table with an empty seat. "Fifteen minutes to find fifteen pieces. Y'all don't let her leave until she does."

"Will do, Officer." Mr. Stevenson slid the wooden box over to me.

*Wooden* box? I glanced at the puzzle. Elvis Presley's famous signature scrolled across the bottom right corner. "Uh, Dane?"

"Yeah?" He faced me.

"I think this is the puzzle stolen from Graceland this morning."

His brow furrowed. "Are you sure?"

"Unless someone made a replica, which I doubt, then yes." I pointed out the elaborate box the puzzle came in and the signature.

"You mean we've been playing with a stolen, priceless puzzle?" Mr. Stevenson's eyes widened. "I'll be gobsmacked."

"Did you bring this puzzle, sir?" Dane's cop face slipped into place.

"Nope. Finished mine ages ago. Saw this one sitting here, and me and Frank decided to give it a go. Good quality."

"Was anyone at this table before you?"

"Didn't notice."

My heart threatened to beat out of my chest. This type of thing didn't happen in Apple Blossom, Arkansas.

"The two of you stay here. Cee Cee, please see that they do. I need to call the station." He took two steps.

A scream erupted from the opposite end of the parking lot.

# CHAPTER 3

N one of us listened to Dane. We sprinted after him, straight to the pink Cadillac.

"Oh, my." I covered my mouth with my hand.

Slumped over the steering wheel, a huge gash on his head, sat our Elvis impersonator. On the seat next to him was a brass bust of an open book that normally sat on a shelf in the library.

"Stay behind the ropes, people," Dane ordered. "No one leaves here." He assigned a couple of men to guard the exit to the parking lot.

Not that it would help much. Despite the tables and vendors set up all along the perimeter, forming a funnel at one end, there were plenty of places folks could slip out. Although, right now, they seemed more interested in the dead man than leaving.

"What can I do?" I tapped Dane on the shoulder.

"No offense, Cee Cee, but stay out of the way. You're a suspect." He plucked a long dark hair off Elvis's shoulder and dropped it into a bag he took from his pocket.

What? I wasn't the only one there with dark hair or the only one who had been by the Cadillac or Billy. I glanced around the crowd.

Lots of people in town had a beef with Billy. At least as far as I knew. I hadn't recognized him. Time had not been good to the man, and our paths hadn't crossed. Church and the library took up most of my time, both places he didn't frequent.

"This will definitely be a night folks will remember." Annie stepped next to me, eyes wide.

"Dane thinks I'm a suspect."

"We all are until cleared. Some people have already left. Guess he'll want a list of those in attendance. I'll get that."

"Thank you." I studied the faces in the crowd, looking for the man I'd spotted Billy arguing with earlier. My gaze landed on Mr. Stevenson. The puzzle!

I whirled and raced back to the table. The puzzle and its box were gone. Dane would strangle me.

By now, the other five police officers had arrived and began separating people into smaller groups. One of them motioned for me to sit where I was and wait to be questioned. If someone attended alone, they sat alone. Families sat together.

A rivulet of sweat trickled down my spine, causing my sweater to stick to my skin. I'd never been a murder suspect before. Anyone who knew me knew I wasn't capable of murder, right? I've learned to control my temper, mostly, over the years. Maturity and God have helped. It wouldn't bode well for me having been heard telling Billy he would regret it if things went bad for the event.

I groaned and put my head in my hands. I was doomed.

An officer placed Annie, who carried a clipboard, at a nearby table. "No talking to anyone."

Annie nodded, but the moment he stepped away, she looked at me. "I scanned the list, and I'd guess at least twenty people are already gone."

"That'll make things harder for the police."

"That's their problem. If I were you, I'd be more worried that I heard someone telling one of the officers about you yelling at Billy."

"Too late for that."

"No talking." An officer scowled as he passed. "Wait to be called on."

I sighed and continued watching the officers work, my mind spinning over the night's events. Surely my taking pity on Billy and getting him food and a soda would work in my favor.

After about an hour, Dane sat across from me. From the grave expression on his face, he wasn't there as a friend or past boyfriend. He exhaled slowly. "This doesn't look good, Cee Cee."

My blood chilled. "I didn't kill him."

"You were seen arguing with him. Some said it sounded like a threat. Your hair was on his costume—"

"Hair *like* mine. Only DNA will tell for sure."

He nodded. "He'd vomited up what looks like a burger. You were seen taking him a burger and a—"

"See? I'm not that bad of a person."

"We suspect the burger was poisoned. Either that or the soda."

My stomach dropped. "Maybe someone gave him something besides what I did."

"It's possible." He tilted his head. "We don't know at this time whether he died from poisoning or the bash to the head. Only an autopsy will determine the cause of death. The library was left open, so anyone could have gone in and taken that brass book."

"That's not much of a defense for me, is it? But I'm not the only one here who didn't like Billy Baron."

"So, you admit to disliking him?"

"You know what kind of person he was. That doesn't mean I'm capable of murder."

"Maybe you got angry." He rubbed a finger across the scar on his brow.

"Seriously, Dane. That was a long time ago. You know me better than that."

"Do I?"

I blinked back traitorous tears. I would not show fear or weakness. "If I'd bashed him, wouldn't I have blood on my clothes?" I stood and turned in a slow circle.

"Not necessarily, but we will need your clothes to inspect."

For crying out loud. "Want me to change right here in the parking lot?" Anger replaced worry. I took a deep breath, squelching it deep inside.

"Sit down, please. I'll have an officer escort you home so you can change."

I plopped into the chair.

"Did you see anyone else arguing with the deceased?"

"Yes. A large man I don't know accused Billy of having something that belonged to him. I interrupted and told Billy to get back to work."

"Any idea where the puzzle I told you to guard is?"

I didn't think I could slump any lower in my seat. "No. After seeing the body, I raced here to retrieve it, but it was already gone."

"Yes, you were seen returning here, which also makes you a suspect in the disappearance of the puzzle."

The tears I'd fought to suppress fell. "I didn't kill anyone or steal anything."

His features softened. "I have to ask these questions."

"Okay." I sniffed. "When can I go home?" I wanted to curl into a fetal position and sob.

Over his shoulder, I saw another officer questioning Annie. I bet he wasn't accusing her of murder. She handed him the pages from the clipboard, stood, and headed for her car, mimicking for me to call her.

If I ever got away from there, I would.

Dane glanced over his shoulder. "Don't be discussing this with her, Cee Cee. Let's not make this look worse on you than it does."

I hitched my chin. "I'm innocent, and I intend to prove it."

"Oh, boy." He slid a notepad and pen across the table. "List everyone in attendance you think might have a grievance against the deceased."

I wrote down *strange man*. Under that I wrote, *everyone who went to school with him*. I slid the notepad back. "That's it."

He shook his head. "You aren't helping here."

"I don't know anything. If I did, I would tell you."

Two paramedics loaded Billy into an ambulance. I might not have liked him, but he'd pulled through as the night's entertainment. Not even a bully and a drunk deserves to be brutally murdered. "Will you let me know what actually killed him?"

"I can't discuss the case with you." Dane stood. "You'll have to read about it in the paper like everyone else. Go home. I'll have Officer Snowe escort you and bag those clothes." He gave a slight smile. "You look real cute tonight."

Didn't make me any less hurt at being a murder suspect. "I can't leave until I clean up."

"Everything here is part of a crime scene. It stays the way it is."

I frowned and marched to my car, the officer who'd questioned Annie following. As soon as I turned the key in the ignition, I called Annie on the Bluetooth. "They sent me home. What's up?"

"Girl, we have to clear your name. People were tossing it around like you're a famous serial killer."

"How do you suggest we do that?" Not that I hadn't already decided to start my own investigation.

"The list of attendees. I kept a copy."

"How do you feel about slipping under crime scene tape?"

"Well, I don't relish going to jail, but we could always go around back to get in the library. Use tape to lift a fingerprint. There'll be that black powder everywhere. My cousin Leroy will help us. He works at the crime lab in Ashford and owes me a big favor."

"I like the way your mind works." I pulled into my driveway and stopped. "I'll pick you up at eight in the morning."

"Be careful, Cee. Billy had some rough friends. Same ones he went to school with."

I shuddered then jumped and yelped as Officer Snowe tapped on my driver-side window. "Gotta go." I turned off the car and shoved open my door. "Let's get this over with."

Inside the house, Mom wrapped me in a hug. "We'll get you through this, sweetie."

"Please wait until she's changed," Officer Snowe said. "You've just contaminated evidence."

Mom whirled on him like a terrier. "Excuse me? I know your mother, young man. You will not speak to me in that tone."

He stiffened. "Yes, ma'am."

"It's fine." I shot him a glare and headed to my room. I couldn't get out of the costume fast enough. The poodle skirt would only hold bad memories for me from now on. After changing into jeans and a T-shirt, I carried the fifties-style clothes to the officer.

He dropped them into a bag. "Don't leave town, Miss Adams."

"I haven't left town since birth." I crossed my arms. "Why start now?"

Stone-faced, he let himself out.

I collapsed onto the sofa. "They think I killed Billy."

"Is that who played Elvis? Well." Mom sat next to me. "He got a little. . .fat. And wrinkly for someone your age."

"Hard living, I guess." I leaned my head back. "I threatened him, Mom."

"I know." She patted my hand. "Lots of people heard. Lots saw you give him food. While that was a very nice gesture, it might be the straw that broke the camel's back. Don't worry. Your father and I have some money set aside. We can bail you out of jail."

I bolted upright. "I'm going to jail?"

"Only if you're arrested," Dad said. "We'll hire a good lawyer. Let's pray for a quick resolution." He took our hands and prayed. When he'd finished, he grinned. "That ought to take care of things."

I wished my faith was as strong as his. While I believed in God, I also believed in a person taking initiative. I'd be working on clearing my name while waiting for God to do His thing. "I'm going to bed. Lots to do tomorrow." I kissed them both on the cheek and went to my room, where I closed the door and the window blinds.

I didn't know why Billy's friends would come after me, but I wasn't taking any chances. He'd run with a group of rough people, but they didn't seem like bosom buddies in high school. Just someone to hang with. Maybe things changed when they became adults.

Just as my eyes drifted closed, my phone buzzed on my nightstand signaling I'd received a text. I didn't recognize the number but opened it and read, "Watch your back and no nosing around."

Why would someone think I'd start nosing around unless they knew me and my personality?

# CHAPTER 4

The next morning, I stared at the myriad of fingerprints where the brass book had sat. Why don't people pay attention to "Do Not Touch" signs?

"So, where do we start?" Annie crooked a brow.

"I'm going to spend the next hour at my desk researching crime scene investigation. Then, we go out the front door. No tape there. They just circled the parking lot. We might find something the police missed." I told her about the text I got.

"Did you show it to Dane? That proves you didn't kill anyone. And. . .I'm sure Dane will consider the library a crime scene same as the outside. We risk being seen if we go out."

"We have to start somewhere." I wasn't against playing dumb if it kept me out of jail. "No, I didn't tell him. I haven't seen him this morning, not to mention I'm peeved at being a suspect."

"He's only doing his job." She headed for her own desk.

"Why are you taking his side?"

"I'm not. I'm being reasonable. You should try it sometime."

I rolled my eyes and sat down at my desk. She wasn't wrong, but I'd have to work on not taking the questioning personally. I looked up every book we had on crime scene investigating then pulled them from the shelves and moved to a table. Minutes later, they lay spread across the surface, and I started studying while Annie reshelved.

The clearing of a masculine throat had me out of my chair. My face and neck flushed. "Good morning."

Dane did not look pleased. "May I ask why you entered a crime scene?"

I did my best to look innocent. "There wasn't any tape on the back door. We always enter that way first thing."

His brows lowered. "Don't play stupid."

"You didn't say we couldn't come to work."

His gaze flicked to the books. "Since when are crime scenes part of your job?"

"Since she got a threatening text," Annie called from the other side of the room.

I closed my eyes and took a deep breath. "I got one last night. Here." I opened my phone and showed him. "I don't recognize the number."

"Then how did this person get your number?"

I shrugged. "They must know me."

Worry shadowed his face. "Have you stuck your nose where it didn't belong before?"

"It's not like this happens to me a lot." I crossed my arms. "The only nosing I did in the past was when I worked for the school newspaper." I'd aggravated a lot of people back then, exposing those who cheated on tests, had a crush on so-and-so, etc., but I'd done nothing of the kind since. "It has to be someone from school. I also think this proves I'm not the killer."

"Not unless we discover who sent you the text. You could have bought a burner phone and sent it to yourself."

"Dane." All my frustration came out in that one word.

"I'm not saying you'd do that, but a good prosecutor would." He handed back my phone. "I've forwarded the text to my phone and made a note of the number. I'll see what I can find out."

"Thank you." I lowered back to my seat.

"Don't get involved, Cee Cee. Let me and the other officers handle it. It won't help us if you get yourself killed."

I glanced at the books in front of me. I didn't want to lie, so I said nothing. I couldn't sit back and wait. The more time that went by, the bigger the chance of me going to jail.

"You're as impossible as ever." Dane marched out the front door.

"That went well," Annie said, laughing. "I think he still likes you as much as you do him."

"Absolutely not. Stop dreaming, and let's find out who killed Billy." I tapped one of the books. "Find out from Leroy the time of death. That will help me pinpoint where I was. Ask about the autopsy. Since we're not a big city, maybe it won't take as long. When you've done that, let's go over the list of attendees and start questioning people."

Annie grinned. "You sound like a real detective. I'll call Leroy now so he can be finding those things out. I doubt he'll know much so soon." She returned to her desk.

When she returned, she set the list in front of me. "Counting us, the townspeople, vendors, and entertainment, there were over a hundred people. Also, Leroy said he should know something in a day or two."

"Wow." The event had almost been a success. "Somebody on this list killed Billy. Let's find out who." Before whoever sent me that text discovered my snooping. Of course, I might call

31

them, not knowing, and give myself away. "Maybe I should do this alone. No sense putting you in danger."

"Absolutely not. We're in this together." She handed me half the list.

First on my list was Millie. I dialed the coffee shop. "Good morning, Millie, this is Cee Cee."

"Girl, you're in trouble."

"I know. I'm trying to find out who killed Billy and who took the puzzle. Hear anything?"

"A lot of folks couldn't believe you hired him, but they said he did a good impersonation of the King."

"Any of them have bad things to say? Had a grievance against him?"

"Honey, lots of people." She chuckled. "The man owed folks money, for starters. Why, just the other day, he ran his car through Mr. Stevenson's white picket fence. Almost hit the house. That didn't go over well at all."

I could imagine. I jotted down that information. "What about this morning? I bet the coffee shop is overflowing with gossip."

"You betcha. Everyone says they can't believe feisty but sweet Celia Adams is a killer."

"I'm not!"

"Of course not. Nobody really believes you are. Isn't that what I just said?"

"Okay. Keep me informed if you hear anything." I hung up and called Sadie.

"I heard you talking to Millie. Only her side of the conversation, of course. Let me add one more to your list. There's a newcomer in town, big man, not very friendly. Which around here is a red flag in itself. His name is Ronald. Don't know the last name. Comes in every morning for a jelly-filled doughnut then heads next door for his coffee. Always complains that he can't get both in one place."

"Lots of people feel that way."

"This is how we've always done it. See no reason to change now. Anyhoo, the first day, he asked if I knew where Billy lived. I said everybody knew he lived in the trailer park right outside of town."

I hadn't, but definitely wanted to visit his trailer. "Where is this Ronald staying?"

"We only have one motel, Cee Cee. If you're going to solve this, you'll have to start thinking."

I rolled my eyes and added the name Ronald to my list. "Thanks. Let me know if you hear anything else." I hung up and drummed the end of my pencil on the desk.

Did Dane know this information? If I shared it with him, he'd know I was snooping around. If I didn't share, I could be considered interfering in a police investigation. After weighing the pros and cons, I called him.

"Officer Dixon."

"It's Cee Cee."

"Everything okay?"

"Right as rain. Can you stop by?"

"Sure. I'll bring lunch. See ya." *Click.*

My mouth dropped open then snapped shut. *Please don't let him think I asked him on a lunch date.* Nothing could be further from my mind.

Next call. . .Mr. Stevenson.

"Sure, I had a beef with Billy. He never did pay for the fence he ruined. I'm on a fixed income. I don't have that kind of money.

But I ain't never killed anything I wouldn't eat. I definitely would not eat Billy Baron."

"That's good to know." I bit back a laugh. "What about the puzzle?"

"Someone stole it."

"I know that. Did you see anything?"

"Nope. Took off running toward the scream same as you and Ed. Didn't know it'd been stolen again until the police told me."

I sighed. "I was hoping you'd seen something."

"Saw lots of things, some I wish I hadn't, but none that will help you, girlie." He proceeded to tell about some unruly teens making out behind the library.

"You wouldn't know their names by chance?"

"Of course. I wanted to let their parents know what they were up to." He rattled off their names. "I changed my mind, though. I was young once too."

"I'm only going to ask them if they saw or heard anything. Not snitch."

"Good girl. I gotta run." *Click.*

Hopefully, he'd let me know if he learned anything new. Gossip runs rampant in small towns. Someone would eventually hear something to help me, but I had to put out enough feelers for that gossip to get back to me. Mom always tells me there's an element of truth in every bit of gossip. I prayed that was true.

By lunchtime, I'd acquired a fair number of notes to share with Dane. He arrived with sub sandwiches and sodas.

"This isn't a date," I said after thanking him for the food.

"That breaks my heart." He put a hand to his chest and grinned. A dimple winked. "No, really. I figured you'd found out something."

I breathed a sigh of relief. "I have." While we ate, I told him what I'd learned.

"What I didn't know was this Ronald guy's name." He set down his sandwich. "You aren't going to leave this alone, are you?"

"I can't." I gave him an imploring look. "If it's any consolation, Annie is helping me."

"Great. Of course that doesn't relieve anything. At least take your daddy's gun with you whenever you go anywhere."

"You're giving me permission to keep investigating?" I tilted my head.

"I am not." He returned to eating. "But if I feel it's gotten too dangerous for you, I'll put a stop to your snooping."

"I think Billy was killed because of the puzzle. What if that's what he had that the other guy wanted?"

"I've considered that. He stashed it somewhere in the library and an unsuspecting attendee thought it belonged on one of the tables. Then, when everyone gathered around the body, the suspect took off with it."

"Any evidence of that?" Hope leaped.

"I'm not sharing any information." He popped a potato chip into his mouth.

"I shared with you."

"You aren't an official investigator on this case. While I appreciate anything you can give me, I cannot return the favor." He reached across the table and put his hand on mine. "You understand, right?"

Electricity pulsed up my arm. My traitorous skin remembered his touch and warmed. "I'll let you know if Annie learned anything. She had some errands to run after her phone calls."

"Have you been in the parking lot?"

I shook my head. "Haven't discovered anything to lead me out there yet." Although I did want a closer look at the Cadillac. That would have to wait until nighttime.

"It's good to spend time with you again." He withdrew his hand and picked up his sandwich. "Even if it is because of a murder."

I wasn't sure if I agreed. He'd broken my heart a long time ago. Was I willing to resume a friendship with him? I decided to focus on my food rather than dwell on something I didn't have an answer for.

"Have you made it through all the attendees who left before you ordered everyone to stay?" Bringing attention back to the crime seemed the wisest choice.

"Mostly families with young children up past their bedtime. I don't think any of them killed Billy." He wiped his mouth with a napkin and stood. "Here's my cell phone number. Call me if you need me. Be careful, Cee Cee. I don't want anything to happen to you."

Him and me both. I was completely out of my element.

# CHAPTER 5

Since Dane hadn't ordered us to leave the library, Annie and I completed our workday. I'd phoned Mom to tell her I'd be eating out and now sat at the local fifties-style diner across from my friend.

"So, after we eat, we hit the trailer park and the motel if we have time, then after dark the scene of the crime?" I studied the menu although I always order the same thing. A bacon Swiss mushroom burger.

"It's as good a plan as any." She closed her menu. "How was your lunch with Dane?" She wiggled her eyebrows.

"He won't share information but didn't order me to stand down. Only to be careful." Not to mention his threat to stop me if I got in too deep. I set my menu on the edge of the table. "I gathered they don't have any solid evidence. Hopefully, we can remedy that."

She narrowed her eyes. "Are you sure we won't get arrested?"

Shrugging, I averted my eyes. "What Dane said was that he wasn't giving me permission, but if I insisted, I should take Daddy's gun."

"Are you armed?"

"No." I met her gaze. "If I went home, my parents would ask too many questions."

"You really need to get your own place. You're twenty-eight."

"I know, but why? They like me there, I like it there, we do our own things, and the rent is cheaper." I grinned. I did pay them rent, but it was paltry compared to what an apartment of my own would cost. "And the food is good."

"You are so spoiled." She laughed.

The waitress arrived, and we gave our orders, both requesting the same thing. While we waited for the burgers, I studied those inside the diner. Was I looking at the person who killed Billy? No one seemed to pay me and Annie any attention other than a hello when they passed the table. A few stopped to say how much they'd enjoyed the other night's event. A few expressed sympathy over Billy. None seemed to think me capable of the violent act, which made me feel better.

"How's the food?" The owner, Mrs. Lewis, smiled down at us.

"As good as always," I said. "Business looks good."

"Could be better. Times are hard. The Elvis event was a nice distraction though. I love Elvis. Enjoy."

After we ate, I drove us to the only trailer park in Apple Blossom, noncreatively called Apple Blossom Trailer Park. "Do we know which one was Billy's?"

"No." Annie pointed to one with a MANAGER sign out front. "Let's ask there. Or we could drive around and see whether there's any crime scene tape fluttering in the breeze."

"I like the manager idea better. They might have some information about Billy that would help us." I cut the ignition and opened my door.

A woman with a cigarette hanging out of her mouth and

a wire-haired terrier at her feet greeted my knock on the door. "We're full up."

I smiled. "We're here about Billy Baron."

"He's dead is what I heard." She put the cigarette out in an ashtray on a table right outside the door and stepped onto the stoop, closing the door behind her. "I don't believe he'll be missed much. His trailer is a dump. Neighbors complained a lot, but he wouldn't clean up no matter what I said."

"Did he own his trailer?"

"Free and clear. Came into a bit of money a few weeks back and paid it off." She glared. "You the police?"

"No, ma'am. Have they been here?"

"More than once. Some in uniform, one not."

I widened my eyes at Annie. "Can you describe the man not in uniform?"

"You sure ask a lot of questions. You a reporter? A private investigator?"

I shook my head. "I organized the Elvis puzzle event at the library where Billy was killed. Did you attend?"

"Don't have time for such frivolous nonsense." She laughed then coughed. "I guess you must be Celia Adams out to clear your name. I don't mind helping. The man you're asking about was big, bald, and mean looking. Hold on. I've got a key to Billy's place." She returned a few minutes later and led us to a trailer.

We had to maneuver around the beer bottles and garbage on the lot. I'd hate to have to be the one to clean up the place. "Did you let him in?"

"Nope. He couldn't show me any identification. I let the handsome cop in though." She unlocked the door and waved us inside. "Knock yourselves out. Lock up when you're done."

I doubted Dane had missed anything, but since there wasn't any crime scene tape to cross, it didn't hurt for me and Annie to take a look.

The inside of the trailer looked far better than the outside. Guess Billy didn't want to live in the filth so he kept it outside. "I'll take the bedroom."

Annie nodded. "I'll start in the kitchen. We can work toward each other."

I headed down a short hall past a bedroom and a bathroom to the bedroom at the end. Wow. An Elvis-style dressing room. Imitation costumes, framed prints, a couple of wigs, even a life-size cutout of the King himself. Billy hadn't only impersonated Elvis, he'd idolized him.

After a few minutes carefully rummaging through the items in the room, I found a photo of the stolen puzzle taped to the bottom of a shoebox containing rhinestone-covered boots. I snapped a picture of it with my phone in case Dane didn't have the shoe obsession I did and hadn't looked at the bottom of the box on the top shelf of a closet.

"Find anything?" Annie called from the other room.

"Just a picture. Still looking." I moved to the room where Billy slept.

This room was a little messier but not nearly like it was outside. Finding nothing of interest, I did a speedy check of the bathroom then moved to a bookcase in the front room. I pulled a photo album from the bottom shelf.

Inside were multiple photos of Billy as Elvis. I'd found his scrapbook. Even better, in one photo, I found his arm around a big bald man who could have been the one arguing with Billy at the party. "Look, Annie."

ELVIS HAS LEFT THE BUILDING

She came and peered over my shoulder. "They seem pretty chummy."

I snapped another picture with my phone. "And they're smiling, which might mean that when this photo was taken. . .a month ago by the date stamp, they were friends."

"Friends can kill on occasion."

I put the book back in the case. "Doesn't he seem too obvious though? I mean in every book I've read, it's the least obvious person."

"This is real life, Cee Cee. Not fiction."

I made a face and sent the two photos to Dane via text.

He immediately responded. "I missed those boots. Thanks."

Feeling quite proud for finding something he hadn't, I suggested to Annie that we head to the motel. "It's only eight. We'll still have time to visit the library if we hurry."

"Sounds like a plan."

I locked the door and pulled it closed behind me. Visiting Billy's trailer hadn't been dangerous, but snooping around where our only suspect was staying could be. I sent up a quick prayer for protection and climbed into the driver's seat.

The motel took less than five minutes to get to. I parked in front of the manager's office. "Here's hoping it's someone chatty on duty tonight."

A bored young man blowing bubbles watched a sitcom on a television near the desk. "Want a room?"

"No, thank you. We're looking for Ronald."

That got his attention. "What for?"

"That's our business." I stood as tall as my five-foot-three inches would let me.

He leaned closer. "I wouldn't mess with him. I think he might be into something illegal."

I widened my eyes and fought the urge to look at Annie. "Why do you say that?"

He lowered his voice. "People come and go from his room at all hours of the night. That ain't normal."

"What room?"

"I reckon I shouldn't tell you. Confidentiality, you know?"

"Give him a twenty," I told Annie.

She scowled and fished a bill from her purse. "What room?"

"Two-oh-three." He grinned and pocketed the twenty. "You two don't look like druggies to me, but whatever."

Druggies? That was a new concept. One I hadn't considered. "You think he's a dealer? Ever seen Elvis here?"

"I hate to tell you this, but Elvis died a long time ago." He turned his attention back to the television.

"An impersonator." I shook my head and moved back outside.

"Are we sure we want to do this?" Annie asked. "The police have most likely already been here."

"True." I stared at the second floor and the door to 203.

A pickup on big wheels pulled into the parking lot. A man in jeans and a cowboy hat hopped down and headed to the second floor. He knocked on 203 then entered.

"Come on." I rushed up the stairs and stopped at the window. "Let's just listen."

"I'm telling you the old woman has it," a man said.

"How do you know that?" another asked.

"I saw her grab it at that stupid party. Ran off like an old banty hen. I couldn't get through the crowd fast enough to catch up with her."

"An old lady would be too weak to lift that brass book."

"Maybe she had help. Someone to create the distraction she needed."

I glanced at Annie. This was good stuff. *Come on, give us a name.*

"Break into her house and get it. If we don't pay for the stuff, we'll get the same thing Billy got."

Footsteps approaching the door had me and Annie dashing for the alcove holding the vending and ice machine. I peered around the corner to see Mr. Cowboy Hat leave room 203 and head for his truck.

"We need to follow him."

"How?" Annie frowned. "He'll see us coming, not to mention we have to pass 203 on the way to the parking lot."

"Let's wait and see if Ronald leaves. Maybe we can follow him." We'd never catch up to the truck peeling out of the lot. "Let's take the back stairs to my car."

We thundered down the metal stairs, climbed into the car, and slouched down in the seats. While we waited, I sent a quick text to Dane about the mystery woman.

He replied THAT DOESN'T NARROW IT DOWN MUCH.

DOING THE BEST I CAN. I clicked off my phone's light as the door to 203 opened and Ronald stepped out.

He hurried down the stairs to a sedan with a rental car sticker on the window. I took a picture of the license plate and jotted down the rental car company's name. I quickly sent both to Dane.

Once he backed from his spot, I turned the key in the ignition and followed. On the highway, I kept a car between us like I'd read in books.

"What are we going to do if he goes to someone's house?" Annie asked.

"Observe. Maybe take some photos and send them to Dane." I grinned, enjoying myself. My normal life had gotten anything but.

Ronald turned onto a residential road and parked on a tree-lined street of older homes. He sat there for a few minutes before exiting his vehicle, a black cap on his head.

I stopped a couple of houses down and turned off my lights.

He glanced both ways then jogged across the street to a white clapboard house with a wraparound porch. No car sat in the driveway. No lights shined through the windows. If this was the mystery woman's house, she was either asleep or not at home.

After trying the front door and finding it locked, Ronald headed around back. The sound of shattering glass reached my ears.

# CHAPTER 6

"We have to see what he's up to." I reached for the car door handle.

"Wait." Annie put a hand on my arm. "It could be dangerous. Let Dane know where we are."

"Whoever is in that house could be in danger." I texted Dane then exited the car and dashed across the street, staying behind the houses.

Despite her reluctance, my friend followed, running into me when I made a sudden stop next to a rhododendron bush. "Hmmph." I stumbled, righting myself. "Careful."

"Don't leave me," she hissed. "Safety in numbers, you know."

"Then keep up." Since no screams came after the breaking of glass, I figured no one was home in the white house and rushed forward.

A glass pane in a back door had been broken, allowing the intruder to reach inside and unlock the door. The door hung open, allowing Annie and I easy access.

Avoiding the glass on the floor, I stepped inside and listened. Sounds of a search came from down a short hallway. Dare we go any farther, or should we wait to see what the man emerged with?

What if he had a gun and shot us? We could be taken as intruders same as him, right? At the sound of footsteps, I yanked Annie into a walk-in pantry. The frosted glass of the door didn't provide much protection from being seen, but something was better than nothing. We stepped back as far as we could.

The man's shadow moved past the pantry. He paused as if he sensed us before continuing outside.

"Did he have something in his hands?" Annie whispered.

"I couldn't tell. Shh." I slowly inched the door open. Not seeing Ronald, I waved Annie forward. "We have to hurry or we'll lose him."

"We're still going to follow?"

"If we don't, we've wasted our time." I had no plans on stopping now. Not until I found out exactly what this man was up to. That he searched for something, most likely the puzzle, was certain. Whether he killed Billy was unknown. Now, another suspect loomed on the horizon. . .an old woman. Too many questions, not enough answers. We had to see this through and clear my name.

The sound of a starting car engine had us sprinting for my vehicle. I turned the key in the ignition as taillights turned the corner up ahead. I pulled away from the curb and sped after Ronald.

"Where is he?" Annie leaned forward and peered through the windshield.

"I don't see him." I turned another corner then headed for the highway.

Headlights beamed to life behind us. Ah. We'd been fooled. "I think he's behind us." Who else would it be? Sneaky man had lain in wait with his lights off until we passed.

"What do we do now?" Annie tightened her seat belt.

"Try not to get into trouble." I increased the car's speed and prayed God would get us out of the situation I'd gotten us into. Maybe I should have prayed before heading out on this stupid adventure. "Sorry for roping you into this."

Annie cut me a look. "You didn't. I came willingly. I might be scared spitless, but it's also the most fun I've had in ages."

I laughed. "You're as crazy as I am."

My laugh was cut short as Ronald rammed us in the rear.

I tightened my grip on the steering wheel, fighting to keep us on the road. I pressed the call button near my right thumb. "Call Dane."

"Calling Dane Dixon," the electronic voice said.

"Hello?" His voice sounded groggy.

"I'm sorry. Did I wake you?" I glanced at the clock. Ten p.m.

"Cee Cee? Yeah, but no worries. It's been a long day. What's up?"

"I'm in trouble." I glanced in the rearview mirror.

Ronald rammed us again.

Annie screamed.

My head whipped forward.

"Where are you?" Dane sounded fully awake now.

"Highway 65, exit 94, heading east. Someone is chasing us and hitting the back of the car."

"I'm sending help. Whatever you do, do not stop and do not get out of the car." *Click.*

I sure hoped help came soon because each time we got hit, it became harder to keep control of my car. "Come on, girl, go faster." I pressed the accelerator past the point I'd ever pushed before. The speedometer inched toward ninety.

Annie leaned over and gasped. "If we get hit at that speed, we'll never recover."

"If I slow down, he'll catch up with us."

"I'd rather take my chances of him hitting us than a head-on collision with someone else."

Good point. I slowed down to eighty and braced for the next impact. Ronald did not disappoint. His next hit was the hardest yet, sending us into a spin toward oncoming traffic.

Horns blared.

I whipped the wheel to the left, or should it have been the right? We continued spinning, ending up almost on the car's side in the ditch. Sorry, Dane. We stopped.

"You okay?" I glanced at Annie as I shoved the airbag out of my face.

"Just shook up. He's coming, Cee."

I followed her gaze to where Ronald's car had stopped on the shoulder. "We've got to go. Get out however you can." I powered down the passenger window and gave her a shove.

Once she was free, I clambered over the center console and heaved myself out the window. Ronald had started sliding down the steep embankment.

"Run, Annie. Into the trees." I reached back into the car for my purse and followed at a full-out run.

It didn't take long for the aches and pains of a car crash to catch up with me. My sternum hurt from the force of the seat belt. Powder from the airbag made my eyes gritty. My knee ached, slowing my pace.

Annie didn't seem to be faring any better, if her limp was any indication. We were doomed if help didn't arrive quickly. *Dane, where are you? Don't fail me again.*

ELVIS HAS LEFT THE BUILDING

"Stop." Annie bent over, gasping for breath. "I'm done."

"No, he'll kill us." I gripped her arm and forced her on.

My cell phone rang. Digging it out of my purse as I ran was no easy task. Finally, I succeeded. "Hello?"

"What's happening?" Dane's voice brought hope.

"We were run off the road and now we're running for our lives through the woods off the highway. Aren't you coming for us?"

"Yes. What was the last mile marker you passed?"

"I don't know. I was trying not to crash." I leaned my back against a tree and peered behind us. "He's coming, Dane. You'll see his car on the shoulder. My car is in the ditch. Run straight into the woods from my car. Hopefully, you'll catch up with us." Unless we'd veered off. I didn't want to think about that.

"Can you see a house anywhere close? Someplace to hide?"

"It's very dark out here." That could work to our advantage, right? "I need to stop talking. He's getting closer." I slipped the phone into the pocket of my jeans, leaving it on so Dane could still hear.

A stand of saplings rose on our right, as thick as jail cell bars. I slipped through them, Annie following, and hunkered down. There were advantages to being on the thin side. Ronald's large bulk would never fit.

He sounded like a bull charging through the woods. He skidded to a halt on the leaves covering the ground and glanced around. "You've got to be close by, ladies. The white shirt one of you is wearing shone like a beacon until the clouds covered the moon."

I glared at Annie and shoved her flat on the ground.

She handed me a thick stick, and I tossed it across from our hiding place.

Ronald moved in that direction.

I used the noise of his footsteps to pile leaves over the upper half of Annie in hopes of hiding her shirt before the clouds moved away. I kept my gaze on his shadow, pausing in my work whenever he did, resuming only when his movements covered the noise of my actions.

"You two need to stay out of this," Ronald said. "Especially you, Celia. You've been a nosy busybody your whole life. This is way above your head. Stick to your books or you'll be sorry."

I frowned. How did he know me? I really needed to get a better look at his face. Ronald had to be one of Billy's friends from high school. I couldn't judge who he was based on his size. They'd all been big enough to play football, but grades had kept them from participating. So they'd turned their attention to drinking and bullying. Not much had changed.

"Come out, come out, wherever you are. I won't hurt you."

Right. Heard those words before. Like a curtain had been lifted, I whispered, "Ronnie Delray." The worst of the bunch. Lack of hair and weight gain had kept me from recognizing him.

In a split second, I found myself thrust back to high school and being shoved into a locker by Billy and Ronnie. I hadn't been found until the next break between classes. I hated the dark to this day.

My fingers curled around a fallen limb the size of my wrist. What I wouldn't give for a chance at revenge. I took a small step forward.

Annie clutched my wrist. "No," she said softly.

No way could I win in a hand-to-hand fight with the man. I kept a tight grip on the stick as a weapon of self-defense rather than a plan of attack.

Sirens wailing in the distance brought tears to my eyes. The cavalry had arrived.

Ronnie cursed and sprinted away from the highway, shouting over his shoulder that Apple Blossom was a small place and he knew where I lived. Wonderful. I'd have to leave town.

After I could no longer hear the pounding of his retreat, I helped Annie to her feet. "Let's get back to the highway."

"Best thing you've said all day."

Staying still had stiffened my body. We leaned heavily on each other and limped toward safety.

On the highway's shoulder stood a man. One whose shadow I'd recognize anywhere. "Dane!" I let go of Annie and hobbled toward him like a twisted form of a romance scene where the hero and heroine run to each other.

He slid down the embankment and darted toward me. "Cee Cee." He gathered me in his arms, lifting me off my feet. "I've never been more scared in my life."

I buried my face in his neck. "Imagine how we feel."

He put an arm behind my knees and cradled me against his chest. "There's an ambulance waiting at the top. Let's get the two of you looked at. Annie, wait here. I'll come back for you."

"Not on your life. I'll hobble the best I can. I will not be left behind."

His chest rumbled under my cheek. "I'll send another officer to assist you."

Once we reached the ditch, he relinquished his hold on me, putting me in the care of a waiting paramedic. The man took my hand and helped me to the road.

"Dane, it was Ronnie Delray."

"Are you sure?"

"Positive." I'd never forget his singsong taunt. "He broke into a house. I think it belongs to the mystery woman. I don't think she was home. We followed. He must have suspected then circled back and followed us. He said he knows where I live. Will you send someone to watch my parents?"

"I'll do that immediately. Your family and Annie will have to be placed in protective custody." His features hardened. "I told you if this got too dangerous, I'd have you stop. Now, stop."

I couldn't agree more, but it might already be too late. Ronnie wasn't one to let bygones be bygones. He'd wouldn't like that we were witnesses to his breaking into the house.

# CHAPTER 7

After the paramedics cleared me and Annie, Dane insisted we stay at his house until the department found better lodgings for us. He drove us to Annie's house first. She packed a suitcase, then we headed to my house to break the news to my parents.

I barged in the door, banging it against the wall. "Mom? Dad?"

"In here, dear." Her voice came from the kitchen.

"You two are up—" I widened my eyes at the sight of the puzzle almost complete on the kitchen table. "Where did you get that? Put it away. Now." I started scooping pieces into the wooden box. "This puzzle was stolen from Elvis's estate. The real Elvis." My heart beat so hard I could barely breathe.

"Lock the front door, Annie." A muscle ticked in Dane's cheek. "Mr. and Mrs. Adams, where did you get this?"

"The flea market. Most of the used puzzles from the other night went there. They have tons. We bought several." Mom paled, her hand fluttering around her neck. "We had no idea it was stolen."

"I'm sure you didn't." Dane explained the need for us all to go into protective custody while I cleaned up the puzzle. "If you could pack a suitcase quickly, please, we'll get y'all out of here."

I thrust the puzzle box into his hands and rushed to my room. How could a simple night of putting together puzzles and dancing lead to my family having to hide away? This wasn't one of the novels I liked to read. This was now our reality. *Lord, help us.*

After quickly packing a few days' worth of clothing and some personal items, I rejoined the others in the living room, where Mom grilled Dane on whether he had enough room for all of us. "As I remember it," she said, "the house you grew up in only had three bedrooms."

"Which is plenty." His brow furrowed. "Cee Cee and Annie can share. Rather than argue, we really need to get going. I've got a security system at my house and a big dog."

"Well, I feel safer already."

"Mom, Dane isn't being difficult. He's trying to keep us safe." I shook my head and moved to the door.

"I'll go out first." Dane stepped in front of me. "Wait until I call you."

The rest of us huddled together like lost sheep until he called out that it was safe. "I'll follow you to my house."

Dad nodded and ushered us to his SUV. Once on the road, he drove like a NASCAR driver until Mom put a stop to his speeding. "You'll kill us before Ronnie has a chance."

"Sorry, sweetheart." He slowed a margin, getting us to the house I'd once spent so much time in.

I never thought I'd step foot in it again. Yet here I was.

Dane rushed us inside where a very large mixed-breed dog greeted us. "Say hello to Brutus."

"Hello." I held out my hand for the beast to sniff.

He did, then licked it, his tail thumping against the wall. I hoped he was as tough as he looked and not this friendly if a bad guy came inside.

"Make yourselves comfortable," Dane said. "I've got to get this puzzle to the station for safekeeping. I'll be gone no longer than half an hour. I'm setting the alarm, so do not go outside." He punched numbers into a keypad on the wall and left us alone.

The four of us stood and stared at each other.

"I can't sleep now," Mom said, "no matter how late it is. Why don't y'all get settled somewhere and I'll find the coffee?"

Sounded good to me. Since I was familiar with the house, I led Annie to the room Dane had once used as his. Nope. I went to the guest room. Mom and Dad could have Dane's old room. "Home sweet home." I dropped my suitcase on the queen-size mattress.

Annie perched on the edge of the bed. "You do realize we won't be able to go to work, right? We'll be prisoners here until Ronnie is caught."

"I have no intention of staying in this house until then." I plopped next to her. "Who do you think put the puzzle in the flea market? Ronnie seems to think this mystery woman has it."

"I had Mrs. Olson clear the tables right after the police got finished questioning everyone." She flopped onto her back. "Wherever that puzzle was hidden, she found it."

"Then she's the next person we need to talk to."

"How do you propose we get out of here without setting off the alarm?"

I grinned. "I watched as he punched in the code."

She laughed. "That man is too trusting around you. Big mistake. How does it feel to be in his house?"

"Weird."

"Coffee!" Mom's voice rang through the house. "Decaf."

Never could understand the use for decaf. I pushed off the bed and joined my parents in the kitchen. "Maybe I'll just have some water."

"There's orange juice. Drink what you want. I'll send your father to the store tomorrow to replace whatever we use." Mom jerked her head toward the refrigerator.

"I don't think you realize the severity of our situation." I removed the juice. "Dane won't want any of us to leave this house."

"Ridiculous. He can't keep us locked up here. We'll watch our backs and live life the best we can." Mom set a cup of coffee in front of Dad.

"Have you forgotten an attempt was already made on my life?" I arched a brow.

She waved a finger at me. "Do you mean to tell me you don't plan on leaving this house?"

I sighed. I never could lie to my parents very well. "No. I'm going to continue to try and clear my name."

"It's clear." Dane spoke from the doorway. "You will not leave this house."

"I'm clear?" How had he snuck in so quietly?

"The chief doesn't think you would run yourself off the road, although he was a little suspicious that the stolen puzzle ended up in your house." He declined a cup of coffee. "We'll find Ronnie. Until then, no one goes anywhere."

Protests rose from the rest of us like helium balloons released into the sky. Dane would not be swayed and threatened to lock us behind bars if he had to. "If I'm not here, there will be an officer parked out front."

"With orders to shoot?" I glared and crossed my arms.

He rolled his eyes. "I'm going to bed. Brutus, door."

The dog obediently blocked the front door as Dane headed to his room. Fine. The back door was still available. So was the trellis outside the room Mom and Dad slept in. Dane had used it multiple times during his teen years.

Sleep was a long time coming, and the sun rose far too early. I groaned and tossed off the thin sheet I'd covered up with and padded to the bathroom. It seemed as if every muscle in my body ached. I felt marginally better after a shower. Annie went in as I came out. We grunted a greeting, neither of us morning people on a good day.

The other three chattered away in the kitchen as if they'd had a full night's sleep. I frowned in their direction and made a beeline for the coffeepot. After a few sips, I realized Dane and my parents were discussing how to find Ronnie.

"His family owned a mountain cabin, last I heard," Mom said. "If the scoundrel isn't at his parents' house, you might want to check there."

"Which mountain?" Dane sat back in his chair. "We're surrounded."

She shrugged. "Guess you'll have to figure that one out. You're the law enforcement here."

I hid a smile by taking another sip. Mom wasn't the only one who knew secrets about the people of Apple Blossom.

"What do you know?" She narrowed her eyes. "I recognize that gleam in your eyes."

My shoulders slumped. "I know where his cabin is."

"How?" all four said in unison, Annie entering just in time to hear me.

"Vacation Bible School camping trip. Ronnie's mother volunteered the cabin for a weekend when I was twelve."

"Where is it?" Dane leaned forward.

"Take me with you, and I'll show you. I don't know how to get there other than turn here and go there." The scenery would have changed a bit, but I was sure I could find the place.

"Wouldn't that be too obvious?" Annie poured herself a cup. "Surely Ronnie isn't that stupid."

"I bet he is." Considering how he was in high school. Nowadays he wasn't proving himself any better.

"It's a lead that needs to be followed up on." Dane got to his feet. "I've got some things to do, but I'll come and get you, Cee Cee, when I'm finished."

I grinned and nodded. I'd have to spend the day with Dane, but at least I'd be out of the house. Oh, who was I kidding. I could act as injured as I wanted to, but spending time with him was not a hardship in any way. I still had feelings for him. Feelings that had come back full force when he returned to town.

Mom cooked eggs and bacon. After scarfing his down, Dane set the alarm again and left.

Since I'd be leaving in a few hours anyway, I decided sneaking out would do me no good. I parted the curtains, noted the squad car at the curb, and stepped back. What would I do with my time until Dane returned?

Mrs. Olson. Of course my mother knew her phone number. I called her on my cell phone.

"Hello?"

"Mrs. Olson, this is Cee Cee Adams. Do you have a minute?"

"Of course. I'm an old lady. I've always got time to talk."

I sat in Dane's leather easy chair. "Annie said she had you

gather up the puzzles after the event. Do you remember one in a wooden box? It had Elvis's face on the front?"

"I do. I marveled at the fact it didn't come in a cardboard box. Wanted to keep it for myself, but I'd promised to donate all of them to the flea market that helps underprivileged children."

"Do you remember where you found it? It wasn't on one of the tables, was it?"

She clicked her tongue for a minute. "No, it wasn't. When I went into the library to find some boxes to put the puzzles in, I saw it on the cart with books that needed to be reshelved. I grabbed it, found the boxes, and carried them to my car. Did I do something wrong?"

"Not at all. We thought it was misplaced is all. Thank you so much." I hung up.

Billy went in and out of the library a few times that night, but Mr. Stevenson was putting the puzzle together when Billy was killed. Why would someone take the puzzle off the table and stash it in the library?

Because they hadn't been questioned yet. Whoever took the puzzle stayed until the very end.

I tapped my finger on my lips, trying to pull up the faces of all those still there at the time of Billy's death. "Annie, we need to make a list."

"Let me find some paper."

A few minutes later, I joined her and my parents at the kitchen table. Between the four of us, we came up with a long list of people we remembered circling the pink Cadillac. All people we'd known for years.

"Do you think Billy's death and the puzzle are actually related?" I asked. "Do we have more than one criminal here?

We've got a mystery woman and Ronnie. Ronnie is looking for the puzzle. Someone took it off the table and hid it. The mystery woman might not be strong enough to bash someone in the head with the brass book."

Annie's phone buzzed. "It's Leroy." She swiped the screen and read the text. "Billy didn't die from the bash on the head. He was poisoned."

# CHAPTER 8

Why would someone poison him *and* bash him over the head? It made no sense.

"That isn't all," Annie said. "Leroy saw a paper on Dane's desk. Ronnie was adopted."

I shook my head. "I don't see how that matters. It's never been a big secret. People always speculated because he didn't look like either of his light-haired parents."

"I thought that was kids being mean and teasing him." She shrugged. "Anyway, you're right. Probably doesn't mean anything."

The front door opened, and Dane entered. He turned off the alarm. "Let's pack a lunch, Cee Cee. It's going to be a long day."

"I can take care of that." Mom bustled to the pantry. "Give me fifteen minutes."

I hurried to my room to change into a good pair of walking shoes. If I remembered correctly, the road stopped at the bottom of the hill, and a person had to walk up to the house. I've always wondered why the drive didn't continue. It seemed as if the owner wanted to know who was coming up the road. I mentioned that to Dane when I joined the others again.

"Then we'll circle around and approach the house from a

different direction." He took a sack from Mom then tossed me a water bottle.

As I clicked my seat belt into place in Dane's truck, I asked, "Does it mean anything to the case that Ronnie is adopted?"

His attention snapped to me. "Where'd you hear that?"

"Common knowledge." I shrugged.

He narrowed his eyes. "Do you have a spy at the station or the lab?"

"I do not." A twisted truth, but to be honest, Leroy was Annie's spy.

"Uh huh." He turned the key in the ignition and pulled out of his driveway. "Which way?"

"Right to one-oh-five. It'll take about forty-five minutes to the next turn. You'll see an abandoned school bus. Turn right there."

"You actually think it's still there?"

"I'm hoping it is, although it might be hard to see." A lot of mountain folk aren't known for clearing away their debris. If the bus was gone, I'd have to rely on my navigation skills, which have never been very good. "Couldn't you find a deed or something for the property?"

"Yes, but the physical address changed so much no one is certain what it is. I wrote down all four of the last known addresses. They're on that piece of paper on the dash."

I snatched the paper. Why did the county keep changing routes? "They aren't making it easy for us."

"Murder cases are rarely easy."

An uncomfortable silence hung in the air, full of words unspoken years ago. I fiddled with a loose thread on the pocket of my jeans. I'd always known Dane wanted to go to college. That hadn't been the problem. The trouble arrived when he didn't want to attend one close to home. Heartbroken, I'd retaliated in an immature way and broken up with him, avoiding him whenever he returned to Apple Blossom for visits. What could have been if I'd accepted his decision and waited for him?

I cut him a sideways glance. We could be married with children by now.

"Want to talk about it?" he asked softly.

I chose to pretend to not know what he meant. "How did the puzzle get stolen?"

Pain crossed his features. "It was on tour with some other Elvis pieces. The guard was knocked over the head and the items stolen. A framed record, a photo album, the puzzle, all small things. Now that we have the puzzle, everything has been retrieved."

"How much is it worth?"

"That's the weird thing. Only about five hundred dollars. Except for the record, nothing was of great value."

"Then why take them?"

"Someone needed a quick couple of thousand dollars, I guess."

"Any other suspects?"

"Your mystery woman."

We fell into silence again, except this time, he reached over and held my hand. I wanted to talk about the night before he left but didn't know how to begin. So I told him of my conversation with Mrs. Olson then pulled the list Annie and I had made from my pocket.

"Read the names to me. We can cross off the ones I've already questioned." He passed a slow-moving truck pulling a camper.

"I haven't questioned Mrs. Lewis yet or Mr. Stevenson outside of the event," he said. "I've also contacted the adoption agency, but it'll take a day or two to open the files. Once we have them, we'll know who the birth parents were and maybe get some answers. There are a few more names of people I don't know. Circle those, please."

I smiled. "Sharing information about the case?"

He laughed. "Nothing that will jeopardize it." He squeezed my hand. "You've been a big help, Cee Cee."

The words warmed my heart. My face flushed as he touched a bruise on my cheek.

"I'm sorry you were injured."

"No big deal. Have you ever been injured in the line of duty?"

"Got shot once. I'll show you the scar sometime." His grin widened.

"Where is it?"

He put a hand over his heart. "Barely missed it."

He could have died, and I would never have had the chance to tell him how sorry I was for that night. I opened my mouth to say something when a dark green truck sped past us. "That's Ronnie."

Dane held back a bit but kept the truck in sight. "We don't want to spook him. Maybe he'll lead us straight to the cabin."

"I thought you said nothing was easy."

"Sometimes we get a break." He patted my hand then put both of his on the steering wheel. "Since there aren't a lot of places to turn off this road, it shouldn't be suspicious that we're staying behind him. I doubt Ronnie knows my truck."

No, it was me the rat wanted to see in a ditch.

Ronnie turned right, exactly where I remembered. Amazingly, the school bus was still there. Weeds grew up around it, a tree sprouting through one of the windows.

Dane continued past the turn then off the road and into the

trees. "We hoof it from here. How far?"

"A mile maybe? I was just a kid. Distance meant nothing to me." I shoved open my door.

"We'll have lunch after we find out what Ronnie's up to." Dane locked the truck, leaving the food behind the driver's seat. "Ready?"

"As ready as I'll ever be." I wanted it to be over. If that meant hiking through dense foliage, then that's what I'd do, while keeping an eye out for snakes.

Thick briars blocked our way, making me glad I'd worn long pants. Dane went first, moving them aside the best he could. The nasty little things still snagged my jeans and pricked my hands and arms. I bit my bottom lip to keep from complaining and urged myself on.

Finally, the cabin came into view. Dane continued in the trees until we came to the back side, where a door hung open. He put a finger to his lips then motioned me forward.

Staying low, we darted toward the cabin then stood, backs plastered to the wooden walls, under an open window.

"I don't know where she is," Ronnie said. "The police squirreled her and her family away."

When no other voice could be heard, I figured he was speaking on the phone.

"The puzzle is still missing too. I've got a contact at the station. He's looking into it. I said I didn't know where she was hiding. I'm at the cabin." He cursed and muttered something about having to repeat himself. "Finding you was a big mistake."

Footsteps pounded. The back door, inches from us, slammed shut. Then the front door, and a few seconds later, the roar of an engine.

"Now what?" I asked after Dane tried the door and found it locked.

"We find a way inside." He straightened and stepped back, staring at a window a few inches above his head. "You're small enough to squeeze through there. Here." He cupped his hands. "I'll give you a boost. Hopefully, it's unlocked."

"Isn't this illegal?" I stared at his hands in shock.

"Look who's talking. Come on."

Heaving a sigh, I put one foot in his hand and squealed as he lifted me, too fast for my taste, toward the window. It was unlocked, and it took several attempts before I could pull myself to a position on my stomach. "I'm stuck." I wiggled, trying to get my hips through.

"Rock back and forth. Do you want me to give you a push?"

"A push how?"

"Uh, I'd have to, uh. . ."

No thanks. I was embarrassed enough without him shoving me through by putting his hands on my backside. I sucked in my breath, ducked my head, and kicked.

That did the trick a bit too well. I dropped onto the toilet and rolled to the floor. As I lay there trying to get back the breath knocked out of me, Dane kept calling for me to open the door. By the time I could get up, I wanted to throttle him.

I ran to the back door and yanked it open. "Patience, sir."

He laughed. "This is just like old times, isn't it?"

"Hmmph." Glad someone was enjoying himself.

"Let's find something to help us nab this guy." Dane moved past me. "I'll take the bedroom."

After a quick search of the bathroom, I moved to the living room/kitchen. Since the cabin was used for vacations and rentals, the sprawling room held the bare necessities. It didn't take long to realize Ronnie was living here though. Dirty dishes in the sink. Canned food in the cupboards. A few things in the fridge.

"Find anything?" Dane called.

"Not yet." I continued opening cupboards. "He must be moving back and forth between here and the hotel."

I turned in a slow circle, finally spotting a cardboard box under the plaid sofa. I sat cross-legged on the floor, pulled it out, and unfolded the flaps. Clothes, a couple of books, ammo, and a framed photo of current-day Ronnie standing with his arm around Mrs. Lewis, the owner of the diner.

"Dane."

I held up the picture when he joined me. "Do you think she's his birth mother?"

"It's a good guess, but I don't like guessing. This was taken by the lake. See? This is where we used to go parking."

My face heated again. That was a long time ago. "What do we do now?"

"You do nothing. I question Mrs. Lewis." He put the photo back in the box.

Tires crunched gravel outside.

I quickly closed the box and shoved it back under the sofa.

Dane grabbed my hand and rushed me to the back door. "Lock it. You have to go out the bathroom window."

"I'll never make it."

"Hurry." He raced outside.

I slammed the door, locked it, and sprinted for the bathroom, closing the door behind me. Hopefully, Ronnie wouldn't see me struggling to escape before I actually could get out the window.

The closed toilet seat sank under my weight. I gripped the

windowsill and hauled myself through, squirming like an eel. Thankfully, Dane stood ready to catch me rather than let me fall to the ground.

He set me on my feet, gripped my hand, and pulled me into the trees. We knelt behind some thick brush and watched the house.

Ronnie, a beer in one hand, exited the back door and stared in our direction. His gaze dropped to the ground then back to the trees before moving to stare up at the bathroom window.

I studied the ground. Dane and I had left a nice trail of footprints for anyone to follow.

# CHAPTER 9

"Let's get out of here." Dane took my hand. "We need to get far enough ahead that he doesn't follow us to my house."

I didn't need to be told twice. I dashed for the truck faster than I'd approached the house. Once inside the vehicle, Dane sped us down the highway toward town.

"At least we know Ronnie is involved in some way with Mrs. Lewis." I cut Dane a sideways glance. "Any idea how?"

"Yep."

"Mind sharing?"

"Yep."

"Does that mean yes or no?" I frowned.

"I'm not sharing my speculation. Use your head, Cee Cee. You saw the photo, same as I did. Put the pieces together." He glanced in the rearview mirror. "You like puzzles."

I closed my eyes and envisioned the photograph I'd found as pieces began to snap together, starting with the corners. The lake. Mrs. Lewis lived by the lake, I remembered. I continued with the imaginary pieces until I got to their faces. Same eyes, same smile. I punched Dane in the arm.

"No wonder you didn't want to guess. You knew as soon as

you saw that photo that Mrs. Lewis has to be Ronnie's birth mother."

"Watch it. I'm driving." The corner of his mouth quirked. "I did, but it's more fun to see you work through it yourself."

"Don't go to the house. Head to the lake."

"I'm not taking you with me. It's too dangerous."

"But you'll have me to climb through windows." I crossed my arms and glared. "You can't pick and choose where and when I help you."

"Yes, I can." He glanced in the mirror again. "Company."

I turned to look behind us. Ronnie's old truck came up fast on our bumper. "Can you outrun him?"

"Most likely, unless he's got a souped-up engine in there."

Considering he and his buddies back in the day did a lot of that to their vehicles, he most likely did have a fast engine. I didn't relish ending up in the ditch again. I ran my fingers over the bruise on my collarbone left by the seat belt.

Dane rocketed past the city of Apple Blossom.

Ronnie followed.

"Where are we going?" I kept my attention on the truck behind us.

"I'm going to try and circle back around and head to the police station. He won't follow us there."

I swallowed past the boulder in my throat. "He knows I'm with you. He'll go to your house if he can't find us. My parents. Annie."

Dane groaned and pressed a button on his steering wheel. "This is Officer Dixon. I need the Adams family and Annie Jones at my house removed and brought to the station. Their lives may be in danger. Please take Brutus too. After that, find Mrs. Lewis and take her to the station as a person of interest in the murder of Billy Baron and the theft of the puzzle."

When he disconnected the call, he patted my knee. "That's all I can do right now. Let's concentrate on staying on the road."

"Sounds like a plan."

A few minutes later, Dane's phone rang. "Dixon."

"Elvis has left the building," the person on the line said. "As in, Mrs. Lewis has flown the coop. Didn't show up at the diner, and her neighbors haven't seen her all day. The woman is an Elvis fanatic. Velvet posters on her walls, a pile of puzzles on her coffee table, you name it, she has it. Weird."

"Thanks." Dane hung up again. "Guess her running shows she's involved."

"And she collects Elvis memorabilia. Why kill Billy though?"

"When we find her, we'll ask." He took us down an exit ramp, across a bridge, and back to the highway in the way we'd come.

"We lost him." I sagged in the seat. "I sure am glad you're driving."

He chuckled. "Me too. What an adventure we've had together."

I'd like more adventures with him—without the threat of getting killed.

A few minutes later, he pulled into the station parking lot. "Let's find out where we'll all be staying for a while."

I nodded, wanting to see with my own eyes that my family was safe.

Mom jumped to her feet the instant we stepped through the door. "You're okay." She wrapped me in a hug.

"Of course. I was with Dane." My gaze locked with his over her shoulder.

"We packed as fast as we could when Officer Johnston told us we had to leave quickly," Annie said.

"What now, Dane?" Dad asked after he hugged me.

"I'll find us a safe house. Excuse me." He gave me a soft smile then marched down a short hallway.

"Sit." Mom led me to a chair. "Who knows how long we'll be here. Are you hungry or thirsty?"

I nodded. "We didn't have time to eat. In fact, the lunch you packed is still in the truck." I moved for the door.

"Oh no, you don't." Dad stopped me. "Ronnie could be waiting out there to take a shot at you. Send an officer."

Officer Johnston agreed to retrieve the lunch and returned a few minutes later with the bag. "Let the receptionist know if you need anything else. You might be more comfortable in the conference room." He held the door open for us.

The padded chairs were definitely better than the plastic ones in the reception area. I pulled out my lunch and set the rest aside for Dane.

"Tell us what happened." Dad folded his hands on the table.

"We found the cabin. I climbed through a bathroom window to unlock the door so Dane could get in." I unwrapped the ham and cheese sandwich. "We found a photo of Ronnie and Mrs. Lewis. We're pretty sure she's his biological mother. Anyway, he returned, saw that we were there, and chased us back to town. He now knows we're with Dane." I took a bite. "Also, Mrs. Lewis has skipped town."

"Gotta go." Dane burst into the room. "Now."

"Why?" I quickly took another bite of my sandwich.

"The puzzle is missing from the evidence room." He shoved

the bag containing lunch into my hands.

"So. . .oh." I raised my eyebrows. "We've got a rat."

"Yep." He rushed us back to the reception area. "I'll pull the truck as close to the front doors as I can. When I do, all of you run out and get in. I'll find us a place to stay." He slammed the door open and darted out.

I met Annie's startled gaze. "Leroy?"

"No, he'd never betray me that way. We've been friends forever." She pulled out her cell phone. "I'll text him to keep his ears open."

I eyed the receptionist. She'd stopped typing, watching us instead. I approached her desk. "What do you know?"

"Nothing." Her heavily made-up eyes widened.

"Do you know Ronnie Delray?"

"Who doesn't?" She gave a one-shoulder shrug. "The man's brought in here for disorderly conduct a lot."

"He seem cozy with any of the officers?"

She lowered her voice. "Look. I have to work here. If I get caught telling you confidential information, I'll lose my job."

"Someone has been killed. . ." I glanced at her nameplate. "Nancy. Do you want to be responsible for someone else dying?"

She paled under her makeup. "Ronnie seems to be buddies with Officer Johnston."

The very officer sent to fetch my parents? "That doesn't make sense. Who else?"

Dane honked outside.

"Gotta go, sweetie," Mom said, tugging on my arm.

"In a minute. Nancy?"

"Officer Rickson."

"He's ready to retire, isn't he?" My mouth dropped open.

"Next week."

"Cee Cee!" Mom yanked harder.

"Thank you, Nancy." I made the motion of locking my lips and rushed after the others.

Dane peeled out of the parking lot. "Took you long enough."

"What do you know about Officer Rickson?" I fastened my seat belt.

"Not much. I'm the new guy, remember?"

"If he's getting ready to retire," Dad said, "he might be in need of some fast cash."

"The puzzle isn't worth that much," Dane replied.

"No, but I bet that isn't the only thing these thieves have stolen. Find out why they killed Billy, and we might have some answers."

"Good point, Dad." I grinned. "Dane?"

"Billy's last known address was the trailer park. I didn't find anything there." His fingers drummed on the steering wheel. "He was poisoned, most likely by the burger you gave him."

"Which I got from Mrs. Lewis," I pointed out. "I told her I needed something for Billy. Who can you call to find out if any other items were stolen?"

Dane sighed. "Since I don't know who I can trust around here, I'll see if anyone from Little Rock can help. Mrs. Lewis has flown the coop, so let's head to her place and do some digging. Mr. Adams, are you armed?"

"You betcha."

"Good. You're on guard duty." Dane turned off the main road, drove through a subdivision by the lake, and slowed in front of a redbrick house with a wraparound porch. "I'm bending all kinds of rules here, so try not to break anything."

Dane parked in back of the house. The back door hung open. Had Mrs. Lewis left in a hurry?

Dad moved through the house, taking Brutus with him, and stood inside the front door so he could have a clear view of the driveway. His right hand clutched his gun.

"Look for anything that might tell us why Billy was killed and whether anything else was on Ronnie and his mother's radar to steal," Dane said. "There's a clue here somewhere. All we have to do is find it."

We split up, me taking the kitchen. I opened and closed cupboards, looking in every closed container. I did my best to think like a crook, using what I'd read in crime books to help me along. The cupboards revealed nothing. "Are you sure we'll find something? Mrs. Lewis would have been stupid to leave anything important behind when she fled."

"She might have missed something," Dane called from the other room. "Most crooks aren't that smart. That's why they get caught."

Okay. I moved to the refrigerator and opened the freezer. I'd heard of people freezing credit cards so they couldn't be used. Maybe Mrs. Lewis had done the same with a clue. I found nothing other than some freezer-burnt steak.

*Come on, Lord. A little guidance, please.*

I opened the door to the walk-in pantry. Every shelf was jam-packed with food. Mrs. Lewis believed in being prepared. I knew where to go if food shortages threatened.

Where would I hide something important? Spotting a small folding stool, I used it to reach the top shelf lined with plastic containers of cereal. I pulled one down and shook it. Something glittery winked then disappeared.

I removed the lid and plunged my hand inside. My fingers wrapped around something hard. I pulled out a diamond ring. "Dane."

"Yeah?" He poked his head into the pantry.

I dropped the ring into his hand. "Help me open all these containers." I handed them down one by one, and he set them on the kitchen table.

A few minutes later, we'd uncovered jewelry, cash, an autographed photo of Elvis, the puzzle missing from the station, which I'd found behind a stack of aluminum pans, and an envelope. "Do you think these are her personal belongings?" Except for the puzzle, of course.

He shrugged. "I'll take photos and send them to the lab. If anything here was reported stolen, they'll know. This adds up to quite a large amount dollarwise." His phone buzzed. He glanced at the screen. "Uh, that's not the original puzzle."

"What do you mean?" I jerked to face him.

"The original is at Graceland. That's a clever knockoff."

"Sweet." Guess I was wrong about someone being able to make a replica. It did seem a bit far-fetched that someone could get close enough to Elvis artifacts in order to steal them.

I grinned, opened the envelope, and pulled out a sheet of paper.

"It's a letter. 'I know what you've been doing and want a cut. If you don't include me, I'll alert the authorities to what you and your little gang are up to. Me and Ronnie have been pals since grade school. He won't leave me out. I ain't joking. See you at the puzzle party. I expect your answer then. Billy.'"

"Well." I slipped the letter back into the envelope, my smile fading. "I guess he got his answer." We knew now why Billy was killed and had a pretty good idea who killed him.

# CHAPTER 10

"Squad car," Dad called. "It's stopping."

Dane's features settled into hard lines. "Get these items out of here. I'll handle whoever's out front. Put the containers back and get in the car. Make it fast." He marched out the front door.

"He's going to be in trouble, isn't he?" Annie asked, scooping the items we'd found into a plastic grocery bag.

"Probably. I don't know much about law enforcement. He is assigned to this case, so that will help." I hoped that would keep him out of hot water. I put the containers back into place and headed for Dane's truck, the others on my heels. "Try to look like we've been sitting out here for a while." I climbed into the front passenger seat, leaned my arm on the open window frame, and did my best to look bored.

But my brain was whirling. Mrs. Lewis killed Billy. Possibly with the help of Ronnie and a police department rat. What if the rat was in the squad car out front? What would I do if I heard a gunshot? Oh, this was ridiculous. How could I sit here and do nothing? I reached for the door handle.

"Settle down." Dad put a hand on my shoulder. "You'll distract him, and that could get him killed."

With a sigh, I plopped back in my seat, resigned to wait. Movement in the trees behind the house had me sitting back up. I narrowed my eyes, trying to determine what I saw. "Anyone see that?"

"Get down!" Dad pushed my head down as shots rang out.

I peered over the door frame as Dane and an older officer sprinted from the front of the house. They stopped at the tree line, guns at the ready. When no more shots came, Dane returned to us in the truck.

"Aren't you going after the shooter?" I asked.

"No." He turned the key in the ignition. "I'll leave that up to Rickson. I used getting y'all to safety as an excuse."

"Did he seem like a rat to you?"

"No." He was a man of few words at the moment and drove around the house, past Rickson, and onto the road.

"Aren't you going to tell us what you talked about?" I glared.

"I'm processing."

I glanced over my shoulder at those in the backseat. Annie shrugged.

"Where are we going?" I turned back to Dane.

"Not sure yet."

Ugh. I hated indecision.

We left Apple Blossom in our rearview mirror. Boredom really did set in, and I dozed, opening my eyes when the truck slowed.

Dane parked in front of a rundown motel in the middle of nowhere that reminded me of Bates Motel. I shuddered. "This place doesn't look hygienic."

"We haven't gone inside yet." He opened his door and got out. "Stay here."

"That man has something on his mind," Mom said. "He's worried."

"I wish he'd tell us what about." I kept my gaze locked on the manager's office door. "What are we going to do about food while we're holed up here? I'm hungry, and we can't locate Ronnie and Mrs. Lewis if we're hiding."

"We can eat vending machine food," Dad said. "You loved that when you were little, and we won't solve anything if we're dead."

"I can't believe we're hunting for people with an Elvis obsession. Don't most crooks simply make one big heist rather than a bunch of small ones?" I drummed my fingers on the door.

"Maybe they thought the risk of getting caught was smaller," Annie said. "It took time to get this much stuff." She patted the bag in her lap. "Maybe they knew the police wouldn't pay as much attention if it was just one small thing after another here and there."

"Why wasn't it in the paper?"

"The *Gazette* already came out this month," Mom said. "I bet it'll be in the next issue."

I reached for my phone to call the *Apple Blossom Gazette* but stopped when I spotted Dane returning, keys in hand. "Connecting rooms. One for the ladies, one for the guys." He tossed me a key. "The door between the rooms stays open, though, so Brutus can alert me if anyone tries to get into your room." He drove to the end of the L-shaped building then around the corner.

"You think someone will find us out here?" I arched a brow.

"Not taking the chance."

The rooms were identical, from the stuck-in-the-seventies olive green and gold right down to the shag carpet. Brutus roamed the room, nose to the ground, then glanced at Dane as if to say, "We're staying here?"

Dane chuckled and patted the dog's head. "Just for a night or two."

I sat on the hard mattress. "Ready to fill us in?"

He sat in the gold chair in the corner. "I don't know what to think about Rickson. He's happy to retire, that's understandable, but he didn't ask too many questions about why I was in the Lewis house. Didn't ask whether I was alone."

"Maybe he couldn't see the truck." I bounced a bit, trying to soften the mattress.

"It was like he already knew we were there." Dane pursed his lips. "He did ask if I'd found anything he might have missed."

"He was the officer who was sent to find Mrs. Lewis?"

Dane nodded. "Said he did a cursory search of the house, but since nothing seemed out of the ordinary other than doors left open, he left."

"That seems. . .contrived," I said. "The open doors should have been a red flag to a cop."

"He reported her missing and questioned the neighbors, but since no missing person's report was filed, he did nothing else." His brow furrowed. "I asked a few questions about his plans for retirement. Said he planned to catch up on all the traveling he never had time for."

"Which will need money." Mom gave a definitive nod. "We've figured out that this bag of goods is stolen."

He glanced at her as if she'd sprouted a horn. "Of course they are. Been happening for weeks." He held up a hand to stop my protests. "Before you get upset, remember, you aren't law enforcement, and it didn't concern you."

"We're all in this together now." I glared.

"Which is why I'm telling you this."

"Now what?" Dad asked.

"I'm going to do some digging into Rickson's career. See if anything suggests he's capable of becoming dirty." He stood and headed to the other room.

"What are we supposed to do in the meantime?" I lay back on the bed.

"I'll hit the vending and ice machines." Gun in hand, Dad headed out the door.

Dane rushed back into the room. "Where's he going?"

"To get food and ice," I replied, staring at a watermark on the ceiling that looked like the state of Texas. "We can't stay here and starve."

"Annie, Mrs. Adams, will you excuse us so I can speak with Cee Cee alone?" A muscle ticked in his jaw.

Uh-oh. I'd made him mad. I sat up as the others left. "Sorry I'm surly. I don't do well with inactivity or someone coming after me."

He sat next to me. "I'm trying to keep you safe and do my job at the same time. I've already broken quite a few rules. I could get fired from a job I've had less than a month."

I put my hand over his as guilt ripped through me. "I'm sorry. I really am."

He brought my hand to his lips. "We're all on edge. I've got people on the lookout for Ronnie and Mrs. Lewis. Someone else digging into Rickson. We have to be patient."

Electricity shot up my arm at his touch. "I'll try," I said softly.

He released me and stood as my father reentered the room. "Don't leave without me again."

"You're needed to keep my girls safe." Dad locked the door behind him. "There's a man in the manager's office who looks a lot like Ronnie. I couldn't see his face because of the hat he's wearing, but the build is right." He tossed me a bag of chips. "Didn't take him long to find us."

Dane heaved a sigh. "There aren't that many motels around here. We've got to go."

"He'll see us." I popped a chip into my mouth.

"If we stay, we're cornered." Dane rushed into the other room. "Ladies, got to go."

"I wish we'd find a place we could stay until this is over," Mom grumbled. "I'm tired of driving around willy-nilly." She accepted a snack from Dad. "Let's confront these fools and get this over with. A good old-fashioned shootout, figuratively."

"That's it!" I jumped to my feet. "A trap."

"We'll discuss it when we're out of here." Dane pulled his weapon and peered through a crack in the curtains. "Whoever that man is, he's still in the office. Let's go."

We raced outside and around the corner to the truck. I agreed with Mom. I was tired of driving around. The problem was we had nowhere to go and night was falling.

"I'm calling Johnston," Dane said.

"Can we trust him?" Dread filled me.

"He guarded y'all in my house with no issues. I have to trust someone. He may know of a place we can hole up." He pressed the call button on his steering wheel. "Pray we don't regret this."

I put my hand over the back of the seat where the others linked theirs. Dad prayed for safety, guidance, and a quick end to solving the murder of Billy.

Some of the fear clogging my throat trickled away. God was

far bigger than Ronnie or Mrs. Lewis. We'd find a way to bring them down and see that justice was served.

"We need a place to hide out," Dane told Johnston. "You can't let anyone know I've called or where we're going."

"I got just the thing. I'll text you the address to a local storage place. In lot thirty-two is a twenty-seven-foot RV that belongs to my parents. The key is in the spare tire. Leave your truck there and drive the RV to a camping site. I think your truck is bugged."

"What?" Dane's eyes widened. "I've got you on speaker, man. What makes you think that?"

"Because I found some how-to instructions on installing bugs in vehicles in the break room garbage can. The force usually hires out to do that sort of thing. Someone wanted to do it themselves."

"Why throw them out where someone could easily find them?"

"They weren't. I dropped my spoon and had to go digging. Found the instructions at the bottom. I'd hurry if I were you. The storage place closes in thirty minutes, and if whoever bugged your truck heard me say where you're going, you need to beat them there."

An RV? Our adventure took a turn I'd never have expected.

We arrived at the storage lot with five minutes to spare. The key was right where Johnston said it would be.

"Stay here." Dane drove the truck to the other end of the lot and after a few minutes that seemed like hours ran back to us. "No bug that I could find. Johnston must have been mistaken, thank goodness. Everyone in."

Thank goodness whoever tossed the how-to instructions in the garbage hadn't been able to listen to Dane's conversation with Johnston. I climbed the two steps of the vehicle.

The inside of the camper greeted us with tones of tan and brown. A bedroom with a queen-sized bed was at one end. A bathroom with a shower divided the bedroom from the living space. A sofa folded out into another bed and the table folded down to yet another. Plenty of space for however long we needed it.

I doubted anyone would think of looking for us at a campsite. We could settle in and plan how to set a trap to catch a few rats.

"What do we do with these?" Annie held up the bag of stolen items.

"Hold on to them," Dane said. "If things get really bad, we might need them to bargain with."

After half an hour of driving, we settled into the campground on the other side of the town's only lake. I held up the infamous puzzle. "Anyone care to have a go?"

# CHAPTER 11

"Bored already?" Mom asked, tilting her head.

"No, but I need something mindless to do to clear my head so we can figure out the trap we want to lay." I dumped the pieces on the table.

"You women play." Dad reached for the door. "I'm going to sit outside and keep an eye out."

"I'll go with you." Dane followed him outside.

"Gives us more elbow room." I started separating the edge pieces while Mom and Annie sorted the rest by color. "Any ideas on how to lure Ronnie and his mother into the open?" I snapped two pieces together.

"We could use you as bait," Mom said, "but I'm not partial to that idea. Until Billy was killed, I had no idea you were a magnet for trouble."

"That's because you don't know all she did as a kid." Annie laughed.

"Hush." I inserted another piece. "This isn't the world's easiest puzzle, is it? Too many different colors."

"Shh. I'm concentrating. It's obvious you don't do puzzles often. More colors makes it easier." Mom separated a few pieces then formed them to show Elvis's feet. "Jailhouse Rock."

"I could go for a stroll." I arched a brow. "Have Dane hiding in the bushes."

"Here?" Annie frowned. "No one knows where we are other than Johnston."

"Not here, silly. By the lake."

"How will Ronnie know you're in the open?" Mom shook her head. "You'd have to let it slip to someone with loose lips. Maybe that girl who works at Lewis's Diner? I bet Mrs. Lewis checks in on occasion."

"I can hear that conversation now. Hello, Sally, this is Cee Cee. I'm going for a walk around the lake in case anyone asks." I smirked. "Silly idea."

"Do you have a better one?" Mom glared.

"Not yet."

"If you two could stop bickering for a minute, you might want to take a look at this." Annie tapped the pieces she'd put together. "It's Blue Hawaii. Look at the beach."

I leaned across the table. "Yeah?"

"Look closer. At the X."

"As in X marks the spot?" I didn't remember a treasure in that movie. I rubbed my finger over the pieces. "Permanent marker?"

She nodded. "The only beach around here is the lake. We're at the lake, only the side we rarely go to. This looks like it might be past the swimming area near the showers."

"It's by a palm tree."

She huffed. "I know that. Look at the distance. Use your imagination to fill in landmarks from around here. There's a building here, and the only building around is the showers."

I moved to the door. "That makes sense. I think we should

check it out. Dane? You might want to see this." I turned back to the others. "We'll go when it's fully dark."

"I'll go alone," Dane said once we explained our theory. "Your father will stay behind to protect you."

"Who's going to protect you?"

"Brutus."

"I'm going with you." I stomped my foot and whirled. "Someone will need to check the women's showers. You aren't a woman." I marched to grab a towel and shampoo from the bathroom in case I needed a cover for being there.

"Might as well give in," Dad said. "You will eventually anyway."

"No, I won't." Dane glowered.

"Sure you won't." Dad laughed.

Half an hour later, Brutus trotting along beside us, I walked alongside Dane, who carried a small hand shovel, toward the showers. I ducked my head to hide a satisfied smile.

"Think you're something, don't you," Dane said.

"Nope."

He made a noise in his throat. "When this is all over, you and I need to have a serious conversation."

"About?"

"Us."

The windows in the shower building glowed in the night. On the puzzle, the X was placed at the rear of the building. Dane headed to the back.

"Keep watch," he said. "If someone comes, create a distraction. Oh, and stay out of poison ivy. This area is covered."

Wonderful. The stuff usually seemed to jump from whatever tree it climbed to land on me. I'd break out into horrible, itchy hives. I stayed well away from the trees and took my chances on the sidewalk under the glow of the light from a window, close enough Dane could come to my aid if needed.

A few other late-night strollers passed us. A family split off and entered the showers, each person sending me curious glances.

"Are you almost finished?" I hissed. "I'm attracting attention."

"Because you're standing there clutching a towel like a life-line. Digging with this little shovel isn't easy." The shovel clanged against something.

"Found it?"

"Hit a rock."

I groaned and leaned against the building. If we didn't find something soon, I'd be reported as a suspicious lurker. I'd have a hard time explaining to a park ranger what I was doing there.

"Check inside. I don't think there's anything out here," Dane said. "The X was on the outside of the building, approximately where the women's toilets are."

The second I entered the women's restroom, the mother ushered her child out, sending me a look that clearly said she thought I was a child snatcher. "I got tired of waiting for my friend," I said, trying to give her a reassuring smile.

She glared and shoved the door open.

I slung my towel over one of the stall doors and stared at a toilet without a tank. Nowhere to hide anything. I studied the concrete block walls, hoping one would be loose. Nothing. I started to think I wasn't cut out to be a sleuth.

Not expecting much, I headed to the first of the two shower stalls. A big, hairy spider, well, maybe not too big or hairy, but too big for me to want to get closer, scurried across the floor. I jumped back, more than willing to give it space.

I bent and scratched my ankle. Once the spider had moved on, I entered the dressing area of the stall. A metal bench provided a place to set clothes and sit down to put on shoes. I peeked underneath it. Nothing but spiderwebs. I shuddered and moved to the next stall.

A peek under that bench revealed a metal box held in place by magnets. Bingo. I snatched the box, yanked my towel from the door I'd hung it on, and rushed to Dane. "Found this." I handed him the box.

"Great. Let's get this back to the RV before the ranger comes." Dane snapped his fingers for Brutus to stop sniffing around the trees and led us at a quick walk back to the camper.

Once inside, he opened the box to reveal a jump drive. "Anyone have a laptop?"

"I do." Annie pulled her laptop bag from a cupboard.

Seconds later we were looking at a list of all the stolen items we'd found in Mrs. Lewis's pantry. At the very bottom, it said, "This is Billy Baron. If something happens to me, I really hope the clue I left in the puzzle can be figured out. Rickson, Lewis, and Delray are crooks. Rickson and Lewis had a fling that resulted in Ronnie."

I glanced at Dane. "Why didn't he just mail this to the police station instead of having us run around in circles trying to figure it out?"

"My guess is he wanted in." Dane pocketed the jump drive. "When they wouldn't let him, he threatened to turn them over to the authorities. They killed him to shut him up. I've got to get this to the station. Y'all stay put. I'll be back in an hour." He narrowed his eyes at me. "I mean it. Do not leave this camper. I'll call for a ride."

"No problem. I'm going to bed." I smiled because I was telling the truth. The clock approached midnight, and I'd had way too many late nights. "We'll lock up tight."

When I woke the next morning, Dane hadn't returned. Fear clogged my throat. I grabbed my phone and called Johnston. "Did Dane drop off anything at the station last night?"

"I wasn't working, but let me check. Hold on." Elevator music started playing. A few minutes later, Johnston returned to the line. "He didn't come here last night. How's the camper?"

"Good. I think something might have happened to him. He left here a little before midnight with a jump drive from Billy Baron listing Ronnie Delray, Mrs. Lewis, and Rickson as the thieves." My voice broke.

"What did he leave in?"

"I don't know. I went to bed. He said he'd find a ride. I thought maybe Uber?"

"Stay put. I'll call you back." *Click.*

I stared out the camper window. *Dane, where are you?* I couldn't stay there, but I had no idea where to look for him. I glanced at the completed puzzle, wishing for another clue to jump out at me.

A long half hour later, my phone rang. It was Johnston. "Uber gave him a ride to the station. Said they dropped him off in the parking lot. Night duty officer said he never saw him. I'm sending a squad car to pick y'all up."

Someone had grabbed Dane right outside the station. "Don't bother. Dad will drive the RV to you."

"Don't dawdle. Your lives are in danger."

Thank you, Captain Obvious. I hung up and relayed the conversation to the others. We immediately started breaking down camp. I helped Dad outside while Mom and Annie secured things inside.

"Don't worry, sweetheart. He'll be fine." Dad put a hand on my shoulder. "He's smart and strong."

"I know." Tears sprang to my eyes. Dane couldn't leave me again. He couldn't.

He wrapped his arms around me and cradled my head to his chest. "Our main concern right now is finding somewhere safe."

"There isn't such a place. Everywhere we go, these people find us."

"They don't know we're right here. We can leave, go to the next county—"

"And leave Dane?" I pulled back.

"Johnston will find him."

"You don't know that. It's me they want." I slapped my chest, more than happy to exchange myself for him if the situation arose. "Let's set that trap, Dad."

"How?"

"I think those three are close. Most likely on the other side of the lake. There are campsites over there for tents. I'm going for a jog."

"No. Absolutely not. You will mind me on this, Daughter." His face darkened.

"Ugh." I whirled and stomped back to the camper, where I closed myself in the bedroom and threw a hissy fit to beat all hissy fits despite it only lasting a few minutes. When I had composure again, I joined the others. "I'm ready now."

"Good. I think the people in the next campsite were ready to call the ranger." Mom's lips thinned and she shook her head. "Temper tantrums never solve anything, Celia."

"It allowed me to release some pent-up frustration." I buckled myself into one of the captain's chairs.

Mom took the one up front with Dad, and Annie the other chair near me. "Let's get out of here," Mom said.

"Easier said than done."

"What do you mean?"

"We have company." Dad pointed out the front window.

I leaned forward to see around him. Ronnie's pickup truck blocked our exit. The big goon grinned and pointed a gun at the camper's front windshield.

"How'd they find us?" Mom asked. "I know Dane would never have told."

"I think we're about to find out." I widened my eyes as the passenger door of the truck opened and Officer Rickson climbed out.

# CHAPTER 12

D ad reached for the gun in the center console.

Ronnie fired a shot through the camper windshield, barely missing Mom's head.

Dad froze.

Rickson tapped his handgun on the driver-side window and motioned for Dad to roll it down. "I'm going to take over driving this rig now, Mr. Adams. Your daughter will ride with Ronnie."

"Why?" My stomach dropped to my knees.

"Call it insurance." He grinned. "Now, Miss Adams will move to the truck. Mr. Adams, move so I can slide into the driver's seat. Don't make me ask again. I'm a much better shot than Ronnie is. I won't miss your wife's pretty face."

I clambered out of my seat and out the door of the RV amid protests from the others. Not knowing whether Dane still lived, I wasn't adding the worry of something happening to my mother to an already heavy burden.

I took Rickson's place in the truck. "Now what?"

A grin spread across Ronnie's face. "Guess that depends on you. Right now, we drive."

"Where's Officer Dixon?"

"You'll see him soon enough." He backed from the spot and led the way to the highway.

I glanced over my shoulder to see the RV following behind us. My parents are resourceful. I knew they'd find a way out of this predicament. Plus, Johnston would start looking for us when we didn't arrive at the station soon. All we had to do was not get killed in the meantime.

"Is he alive?"

"Still have a thing for him, huh?" Ronnie shrugged. "Women are strange creatures. You should have gone out with me. We'd be married by now, maybe a kid or two, and I'm going to be stinking rich soon."

"You never asked me out."

"Because you were hanging on Dane's arm. No one would dare take away his girl."

As if anyone would've had a chance. No, my heart had, still, belonged to Dane.

"You must be happy to have reunited with your birth parents." I cut him a sideways glance.

"Ha. They serve no other purpose than to get me what I need." He looked startled as if he'd said too much. "No more talking."

"Is it a long drive? We'll need some way to pass the time. Why not talk?"

He clamped his mouth shut, his grip tightening on the steering wheel.

I sighed and stared out the window, taking note of any landmarks. I'd been in Apple Blossom my entire life but didn't know the woods and mountains as well as some. I'd need to know how to get to town if I found myself free from Ronnie.

After a while, the thick silence got the better of me. "Tell me more about your parents. Why'd they give you up?"

He shot me a hard look. "Rickson was married."

"How was I supposed to know that?" I glared. "I didn't hear any rumors other than that you were adopted. Not who your biological parents were."

"Because you were so wrapped up in your perfect little life." He slapped the steering wheel.

Time to change tactics. "Who does the stealing in your little group of criminals? We found all the stuff in your mother's house."

"Don't call her that. She's Mrs. Lewis." He chewed the inside of his cheek for a minute. "I knew she'd stashed it away, wanting to keep it all to herself. You should have seen the fight between her and Rickson. Epic. They hate each other." He laughed. "Doesn't matter though. I've got plans to take it all and go to Mexico. You can come with me."

"No thanks." I turned my attention back out the window.

"Suit yourself. You probably won't live to see tomorrow otherwise."

I'd take my chances. "You'll be the one to regret this day if you hurt anyone I care about," I mumbled.

"What's that?"

"Nothing."

He turned off the highway and drove up a curvy mountain road. I knew this mountain. Cobalt Mountain. It overlooked the lake where he'd taken us from. I glanced back at the RV. Smoke poured from under its hood. "You might want to slow down. Looks like they're having trouble back there."

"I'm surrounded by idiots." He slammed on the brakes, reached into the glove compartment, and withdrew a set of handcuffs. He cuffed me to the door handle. "Only Rickson has the key."

"Make sure you bring it back with you." I glared.

He patted my cheek a little too roughly. "You bet. Can't have anything happen to my little hostage."

I yanked against the cuff until my wrist ached. I couldn't free myself, so I watched the proceedings behind me.

Rickson and Ronnie tinkered under the hood for several minutes before Ronnie trotted back to the truck. "I've got to drop you off and come back with water and antifreeze. Who owns that piece of junk anyway?"

I smiled. "Officer Johnston. He won't take kindly to it being stolen."

"That's the least of my worries." He dangled the handcuff key in my face then freed my hand. "Not too much farther."

I watched the RV grow smaller as we continued up the mountain, finally losing sight of it as we rounded a corner. *Please, God, let my parents and Annie find a way to escape. Please don't let me arrive at our destination to find Dane dead.*

Believing him still alive was the only thing that kept me from dissolving into a puddle of hysterics. Sure, Ronnie had said I'd see him soon, but that could mean in heaven.

"Why the Elvis obsession?"

"That's Mrs. Lewis's thing not mine."

"Who bashed Billy over the head?"

He laughed. "That was an accident. He was already dying from the poison. I was goofing around with that brass book, telling him he ought to try reading sometime. It slipped." He sobered. "Billy was my friend."

I nodded. "For a very long time."

"Yeah, but he got greedy."

"We put the puzzle together. What's at the X?"

"You didn't find it?" His brow furrowed.

I didn't say anything, hoping he'd take that for a no. Did this mean Dane had a chance to hide the jump drive before being taken? Hope leaped in my heart. This gave us leverage over these people.

"Mrs. Lewis and Rickson were sure y'all had found whatever it was Billy hid. Who would have thought that dumb Elvis impersonator had something upstairs?" He tapped his head.

I ducked my head to hide a grin. Ronnie had no idea of the evidence against him and the others that was on that drive. "Y'all had everyone thinking the puzzle was authentic. The whole town was in an uproar over it. Quite clever of you, actually." While all along they were nothing but thieves, robbing their neighbors.

"It did provide a distraction." He laughed and slapped his knee. "Billy wasn't the only one with brains. I know a trick or two."

"You definitely made the Fifties night one people won't forget." I caught a glimpse of a rusty metal barrel on the side of the road.

The farther up the mountain we went, the more debris I spotted. "Are we going to a dump?"

"No, but it looks like one. The old man who owned the place hoarded just about everything you can imagine."

I widened my eyes. "Did you kill him?"

"Nah, he died last year. No one has been in his cabin since. At least not until we chose it as our hideout."

"Where's Mrs. Lewis?"

"At the cabin."

Around another corner, and an old-fashioned log cabin with a sagging porch greeted us. Rusty vehicles, farm equipment, and barrels littered the yard. "The inside is worse," Ronnie said. "You'll have to climb over stuff to get to the one room we managed to clear."

Awesome. The day got better and better.

Once we were out of the truck, Ronnie gripped my arm and marched me through the front door. "I'm back." He gave me a shove toward a pile of clothing and magazines. A clear trail of others having climbed over it before made the way easy to see. "Got the girl."

I climbed up and rolled over the top, landing in a heap on the floor. I stared into the amused face of Mrs. Lewis.

"You'll get used to it, Cee Cee." She pulled me to my feet then led me to a straight-backed chair. She plucked a nylon cord from a table overflowing with newspapers and secured my hands behind my back before turning to Ronnie. "Where are the others?"

"RV overheated. I got to take them some water. I saw some antifreeze in the shed out back. Shouldn't take too long." He barely spared her a glance as he exited through a door opposite of the way we'd come.

"Sorry it's come to this." Mrs. Lewis pulled up a chair. "I've always liked you, but you don't seem to know when to mind your own business."

"Where's Dane?"

She jerked her head to a corner behind her.

I peered around her to see Dane, gagged and hands and feet tied like a Thanksgiving turkey. His left eye was black and blue and swollen almost closed. A crusted-over gash painted his right cheek. His one good eye gazed at me with what looked like regret.

Whipping my attention back to the woman in front of me, I narrowed my eyes. "Was beating him necessary?"

"He wouldn't cooperate." She shrugged. "Although I do believe Rickson enjoyed the task a bit too much."

"I'm thirsty and need to use the restroom."

She sighed. "You really don't want to. The plumbing hasn't worked in who knows how long. You'd have to go outside."

"Fine. Take me outside."

"You're going to cause trouble, aren't you?"

I smiled and arched a brow. "Well?"

She snatched a gun off the table and untied me. "Try to run and I'll shoot Officer Dixon. His fate is in your hands."

I tossed Dane a worried glance as I passed. I had thought of trying to run for help, but I couldn't leave him to get shot. Mrs. Lewis had already killed once. She wouldn't hesitate to do so again if it suited her purposes.

Outside, I took care of business and studied my surroundings. Thick woods surrounded the overgrown plot of land the cabin sat on. If I did run, I'd get turned around for sure. The only way out was the road. The road where a plume of dust signaled Ronnie's return—without the RV.

"Of all the imbeciles. . ." Mrs. Lewis prodded me to the front of the house. "Where are the others?"

Ronnie dragged Rickson from the vehicle and shoved him forward. The older man sported a few bruises of his own with a good-sized goose egg turning purple at his hairline. "They overpowered him and got away. Dumped him on the side of the road like garbage and drove the RV down the mountain. I doubt they'll get far. It'll overheat again. Want me to go after them?"

"Want me to go after them?" Mrs. Lewis mimicked in a high

voice. "Of course I do. If they get away, we're all doomed."

"Why not take the two hostages and go?" Ronnie marched toward the cabin with the bag of stolen goods in his hands. "They left this with him. We have what we need."

"Give me that." His mother held out her hand.

He gave her the bag.

She peered inside. "Did you even look?"

He shook his head.

"It's nothing but empty soda cans and garbage. You've been had." She tossed the bag onto a pile of rubble. "We have to go after them. Leave Rickson behind to guard this one and Dixon." She glared at Ronnie's father. "Try not to mess up again, or you'll suffer the same fate as Billy. I don't have time for this."

# CHAPTER 13

Once inside, I immediately removed Dane's gag. "Are you okay?" I ran my hands down his arms then gingerly touched his face.

"Yes." He glared at Rickson. "I can't wait to see him behind bars. He's a disgrace to his badge."

Rickson laughed. "We'll see about that. Once Betty and Ronnie get back, you two are toast, and we'll be headed south."

I hadn't known Mrs. Lewis's name was Betty. I sat next to Dane and contemplated a way out for us, absently scratching my arm. "She was going to get me some water."

Smirking, Rickson left the room and returned a few seconds later with a bottle of water. He tossed it to me. "Make it last."

"What about Dane?"

"Share."

I uncapped the lid and held it to his mouth, leaning close to whisper, "He looks to be in bad shape after the beating my family and Annie gave him. I have an idea. First, we have to get you untied."

"There's no feeling in my hands and feet." He took several sips of water. "Find something sharp. I'll figure it out while you keep him distracted."

Right now, Rickson seemed more concerned with cleaning his fingernails with a pocketknife than in what we were doing. I shoved my hand under a pile of garbage, trying not to think about what might be in there, and fished around for something sharp. Dangerous, but I had to be sneaky. Couldn't very well start pacing the room in search of something to cut Dane's bindings with.

I faked a cough to hide the sound of my rummaging, not that Rickson bothered to look up. My fingers closed around a picture frame. I felt around and smiled to discover the glass was broken.

"What's wrong with you?" Rickson narrowed his eyes.

I froze. "What?"

"You're all blotchy."

Oh, no. Poison ivy. No wonder my body itched like I'd stepped in a patch of nettles. I glanced at Dane.

"Your face, neck, arms. . ."

"Find a bit of kindness in your heart, Rickson, and see if there's some calamine lotion somewhere."

"It's more fun to watch you squirm." He got to his feet and left the room.

I started sawing away at the twine around Dane's hands. If I could free his hands, he could work on his feet. It might go faster if I didn't have to stop and scratch every couple of seconds. Why did this have to happen now?

When Rickson returned with a bottle of the pink stuff that had to be way past its expiration date, I slid the piece of glass under Dane's leg. Rickson handed me the bottle and a couple of cotton balls. "Thank you."

He grinned and resumed his seat across from us. "You're going to be polka-dotted in a few minutes. Who thought a life of crime could be this entertaining?"

"Why'd you do it?" I started dabbing my blotches. "You're retiring this week." Well, not anymore. Now, he'd go to prison.

"That's exactly why. Didn't manage to save enough money to live comfortably, and business at Betty's diner has slowed down. Got back with Betty, found my son, and voilà. Sending the other police officers on a goose chase looking for a stolen Elvis puzzle was a genius idea. Mine, of course."

I laughed. "Show's what you know. Ronnie plans on running off with the loot himself. No honor among thieves and all. I'm sure you've heard the saying."

His face darkened. "He can try. Once Betty finds your folks and gets back what they took, we'll be outta here. Sorry to say, the two of you will die in this old cabin."

Not if I could help it. When he returned to cleaning his nails, I scooted in front of Dane and put my hands behind me, cutting through the last of the twine around his hands. He took the glass from me and started on his feet.

"Hurry," I hissed.

Rickson had folded and pocketed his knife and now stood on a pile of rubbish to see out the small amount of window not blocked by clutter.

"Hands are still a bit numb. I'm doing the best I can. It'll take a few minutes to get circulation back in my feet. You got a plan?"

"Yes." I'd been staring at a pile of books and magazines next to us. *Let's see who really gets the cabin as a coffin.* "I'm going to need you to do a little playacting. When I call him over, play dead."

"Won't be hard." He chuckled then groaned.

"You're hurt worse than you're letting on." I narrowed my eyes over my shoulder.

"Couple of cracked ribs, maybe."

Enough stalling. Dane needed medical attention. "Rickson! Help. He isn't breathing."

Dane flopped over like a fish.

Rickson glanced our way. "So?"

"Please." I put on my most imploring face.

Rickson sighed and came toward us. When he reached the tower of books, I leaped up and shoved. The pile teetered then fell, taking him down with it.

"Come on." I grabbed Dane's arm and hauled him to his feet. "He won't be down long." The pile hadn't been as heavy as I thought.

Shouted curses followed us as we lumbered toward the back door, Dane leaning heavily on me. Progress was slow since we had to skirt piles of stuff or climb over things that had fallen. The kitchen door shined like a beacon, moonlight showing us the way.

I snatched a couple of water bottles from the counter and stepped outside. "I hope you know the way."

"I do. Head for the trees then circle left." Dane pressed an arm against his side. "Hopefully, we run into your family and not Rickson's."

As we ran—more like lurched—I prayed for God to show us the way. For my family's safety. For Dane's injuries. Praying kept my mind from dwelling on the what-ifs that would choke me if I allowed them to.

Something thrashed in the bushes behind us. Dane and I hunkered down. A possum waddled by, its eyes eerie in the moonlight. It wasn't four-legged critters that scared me.

"Come on." Dane pushed to his feet, his breathing ragged. "If

I can't make it, you'll have to leave me behind."

"I won't leave you." I gripped his hand. "We aren't separating again. Ever."

"You stubborn woman." His teeth flashed. "Hold on to that thought for when we get out of here."

Still holding my hand, Dane continued through the thick forest to where he said the road would be. I'd have gotten us lost and turned in the other direction. "Remember the moss, Cee Cee. Always grows on the north side of things."

Oh, right. I remember my father telling me that once.

We stopped as headlights broke the darkness and passed us, heading for the cabin. Betty and Ronnie had returned.

Dane increased our pace, moving to the road, where progress was easier. "Once we get to the highway, we can flag down a ride. Do you have your cell phone?"

"Sorry. Left it in the camper. If I had it, I'd have made a call by now."

"You wouldn't have had service until the highway."

"See? That's why I need you around. You know stuff." I grinned.

"Is that the only reason?"

I started to answer but dove into the bushes as the car that had passed us returned. Dane followed, lying in the dirt like a wounded deer.

"That hurt." He groaned and wrapped his arms around his midsection.

After a few minutes of rest, we continued but then stopped at the sight of Ronnie's truck blocking the end of the road leading to the highway. My shoulders sagged then lifted at the sight of two squad cars, lights flashing, stopped next to the truck.

Rickson fired the first shot followed by Ronnie. The police followed suit.

Dane and I huddled together behind a large maple tree and tried not to get hit by a wayward bullet. It felt good to be wrapped in his arms despite the circumstances. I didn't want to be anywhere but with him ever again.

The gunfight didn't last long. Rickson and Ronnie lay in the dirt, Betty having taken refuge in the truck.

Dane and I, hands up, stepped from the trees. "Glad to see you guys," Dane said.

"You both okay?" Johnston stood over a cursing Rickson. Both looked our way, then Johnston looked back down at Rickson. "Shut up. You ain't dead."

"You shot me in the leg."

"I was aiming for your head."

I glanced at Ronnie as we headed to a squad car. He'd live too. The shot to his shoulder wouldn't kill him. "Where's my family?"

"Waiting at the station." Johnston grinned. "They've got quite the tale to tell, same as you, I expect. Let us get these three squared away, and I'll give you a ride to the hospital. Looks like Dixon is in need of medical attention."

An hour later, I glanced up from my chair next to Dane's hospital bed to see my parents enter the room. I jumped up and into their arms. "I was so worried about you."

"You should have seen your father." Mom's grin couldn't get bigger. "He took that wooden puzzle box and whacked Rickson right upside the head. Then we all took a turn letting off some frustration before hightailing it toward town. A trucker picked us up."

"That's more creative than my toppling a tower of books

onto him." I wouldn't have minded a kick or two at him myself. "Annie?"

"Home sleeping. Said she's had enough excitement to last a lifetime. She's got Brutus with her."

"My big dog wasn't much help, was he?" Dane said from the bed. "He only looks ferocious."

"Oh, and Annie said she's going to put the Elvis puzzle behind glass for folks to gawk at," Mom said. "Once this story hits the paper, everyone that worked on it the other night will want another look."

"The stolen items?"

"We took those with us." Dad patted my shoulder then went to shake Dane's hand. "Thank you for watching out for my baby girl."

"She actually saved me." His gaze warmed as it settled on me.

"Try not to let her get away this time." Dad motioned for Mom to follow him outside.

I returned to Dane's bedside. "How about that conversation? I'll start. I am so sorry for acting childish and resenting your dreams all those years ago." I took his hand, brushing my thumb across the back.

"I should have taken you with me."

"I didn't want to leave Apple Blossom." My throat clogged.

"I should have convinced you. I could be an architect any-where. Of course, I changed careers and came back. Seems like God had other plans for us." He raised the head of the bed to a better sitting position. "You're the reason I never married, Cee Cee. No one could compare to you."

"Same here. Ronnie asked me to run off with him after he took me from the camper." I smiled. "Seems he's always had a thing for me."

"I'll kill him." Dane's eyes twinkled.

"I let him down gently."

"Good, because I'm going to marry you."

"Oh?" I arched a brow. "Is that a proposal?"

"Yep." He pulled me close. "What's your answer?"

"I'll take some convincing." I bit my lower lip, my gaze locked on his.

He pulled me closer. "I think I can manage." His hand released mine and cupped the back of my head. His lips pressed against mine.

This was no high school kiss. This was one of promises and the fulfillment of dreams.

"To think Elvis brought us back together," I whispered. "Thanks to you bringing that pink Cadillac to the puzzle party."

"Sweetheart, this town isn't that big. I'd have come knocking on your door." He kissed me again. "I'm still waiting for your answer."

"Silly man. Of course it's a yes."

Multi-published and bestselling author, CYNTHIA HICKEY, has taught writing at many conferences and small writing retreats. She and her husband run the publishing press, Winged Publications, which includes some of the CBA's best well-known authors. They live in Arizona and Arkansas, becoming snowbirds with two dogs and one cat. They have ten grandchildren who them busy and tell everyone they know that "Nana is a writer."

# The Puzzle King

By Linda Baten Johnson

# CHAPTER 1

I swiped my hands on my shorts then wiped my brow. "Donna, I'm sweating through my clothes even though it's only eighty degrees. Do the wet spots in my armpits show?"

"No, they don't, but that's because your whole top is damp." Donna nudged me, attempting to garner a smile. "I'm sure all the other competitors are as nervous as you are."

"I'll be so embarrassed if I'm the last one to finish. Why am I doing this?"

My older sister shrugged. "I have no idea!"

Donna never cuts me any slack, even though she serves as my most enthusiastic cheerleader in whatever I attempt. "Jane, you thought the competition would be fun. It wouldn't be for me. But you're good at puzzles, and look at the support you have."

I followed Donna's arm sweep at the people milling around the North Dakota Red River Fairgrounds. The state jigsaw championship drew a large crowd, and many individuals sported the bright aqua "Jigster Jane" T-shirts my sister designed. In addition to family and friends, many of our church members agreed to wear them on my big day.

"I'm afraid I'll disappoint them and myself. I only got into the final competition because the qualifier occurred on the same day as a whiteout blizzard."

"Which you insisted on attending. No more whining. This is your chance. Carpe diem. Seize the day, Sis." Donna took my shoulders and turned me to face the Mansions on Red River, a hotel situated across the street from the fairgrounds. They'd changed the venue so the contestants could stay and puzzle in the same hotel, and this year's field came from twelve different states.

"You know I probably don't deserve to be here." I was killing time to avoid future humiliation and hoping for her reassurance.

Donna gave me a gentle push. "I send you into battle. You have a lunch break between practice rounds and finals, and I'll be waiting right here with a healthy salad."

"Could you make it a chicken waffle on a stick?" I knew my sister would ignore my futile request. As a nurse, she good-naturedly nags everyone about nutrition and exercise. Fortunately for me, Donna's kids and husband keep her too busy to meddle in my eating and exercising habits—most of the time. I'm lucky to live in the same town where I grew up with my parents and sister. Fargo, North Dakota, is a great place, although most outsiders identify our city with the unusual and somewhat disturbing movie *Fargo* made by the Cohen brothers.

"Go!" This time, my sister's gentle push morphed into a forceful shove.

I exited the fairgrounds for the competition I'd dreamed of winning for the past four years. After learning about the state event, I'd become obsessed with increasing my speed at jigsaw puzzle assembly. The prizes aren't exceptional, and the entry fee of forty dollars makes winning a wash—if you rank a victory by dollars alone. For me, brandishing a trophy and wearing a blue ribbon stokes my competitive juices. I told myself I had a real shot at annihilating my fellow puzzlers with my keen color insight and nimble fingers. But my personal pep talk didn't calm the jitters dancing in my stomach or give me confidence. I rubbed my itchy neck and wondered if the rash showed yet. The hotel ballroom, set with round tables placed in rows of three, provided a space for the event moderators to walk between the contestants. During the competitions, some people sit when puzzling but most stand. I prefer standing because the perspective gives me an overall view of the completed sections. Clusters of similarly clad persons occupied various tables. Those were the team competitors. The event offers prizes for individuals and teams, and some talented puzzlers compete in both.

A long table with coffee, juice, pastries, and fruit was on the right, and I gravitated toward it, staying alert for an empty chair. I spotted a lone person in a bright red shirt seated at a table near the back and scurried to snag a spot.

"I'm Jane Dahl, a first-time singles contestant. Mind if I share this table?" I tilted a chair against the round table's edge before he answered.

He examined my shirt. "Be my guest, Jigster Jane. Are you getting something from the breakfast bar?"

"I am. Can I get you something?"

"Coffee, black. You can refill my cup. Together, we'll help save a tree and maybe some work for the custodian."

My table companion's shirt had DISSECTOLOGIST #1 printed in bright white letters across his chest. I gasped as I realized the seat I'd selected was next to the Puzzle King, Steven Grazer. He'd captained the team winners for the past two years, the Dissectologists, and also taken the top spot in the single-person competition. My legs felt a little rubbery as I moved toward the buffet. *Keep calm. He's just a man who solves puzzles. You have a lot in common. You can talk to him without being nervous.* I ignored the attractive pastries and settled on tea instead of acidic coffee.

When I returned to the table, a long-legged brunette engaged Steven in an animated conversation. Not a tendril or wisp of black hair escaped from her severe upswept style. Her face—with a broad forehead, penciled eyebrows, and regal nose—was pale, even by North Dakota standards. She acknowledged me with a glance but didn't speak. Her light blue eyes seemed anxious, and her hands worked nervously in her lap.

"Coffee, black," I announced cheerfully and placed the disposable cup in front of the master puzzler.

"Thanks. Jigster Jane, this is my wife, Marta. She doesn't love puzzles like we do. She doesn't even like them at all unless they're over a hundred years old. She plans on antiquing today instead of cheering for me to win again."

Marta gave a slight nod and resumed the conversation with her husband. "Steven, I heard about a dissected puzzle at the antique mall. It's a world map from the late 1800s. You'd like it, wouldn't you? If you don't want it, I could resell it—if not in my shop then online."

Steven grabbed a bottle of water from Marta and turned to me. "Do you know what Marta's talking about?"

"Uh, well, I know the first jigsaw puzzles were maps on wooden boards that were sawed into pieces."

Steven Grazer grinned and made a thumbs-up gesture. "Impressive, Jane. Those maps were dissected into irregular shapes by hand with a fret saw. People categorized the puzzles as educational as well as entertaining. And that's the reason for my team name. Dissectologist is the official name for a jigsaw puzzle solver."

Steven had left off the "Jigster" part of my moniker when he spoke, so I considered that a mark of respect.

I addressed Steven's wife, who seemed to cower in his presence. "Marta, I've never seen a dissected map. If you manage to buy one, I'd love to see it. I'll put my phone number on the back of my business card." I rummaged through my bag and fished out my card showing I worked as a technician in a dental lab. Ironically, my curiosity about the rare item seemed to sway Steven's viewpoint about his wife's outing.

He turned to his wife. "Marta, you don't have a shop. Now I'm permitting you to look, but don't spend more than I said you could."

"I won't." Marta stood and kissed his bald head.

Even though he'd spoken unkindly, Grazer's dark brown eyes seemed to soften as he waved his wife off on her mission. He had a round face with high cheekbones, thin lips, and a broad nose. From watching videos of past championships, I knew he was probably about five feet eight or nine, and I judged Marta to be a few inches taller.

Still watching his wife, Steven addressed me. "My wife often forgets budget practicalities."

"I see." I did see one crucial thing. I understood why Marta appeared flustered and nervous. I'd hate to be married to someone so controlling.

"I'm head custodian at a high school in Minnesota, and Marta trades junk, which she calls antiques. She's nagging me to rent a stall space in the Fargo antique mall, but we're not rich. We don't have much in savings." He seemed both bashful and prideful as he disclosed the information.

"Does your wife have a knack for finding treasures? When my sister and I visit the antique mall, we just buy things we like. We never plan to resell."

"Marta considers it a job, but it doesn't bring in much money. I suspect she hides the amount of her profits. I never bug her about her hobby, and she doesn't bother me about the hours I spend working jigsaw puzzles."

I didn't pursue the topic. "I'm single, so nobody minds if I stay up until three in the morning to put in the final piece."

"Here comes trouble." Steven dipped his head toward three people clad in red shirts with the numbers 2, 3, and 4 after the word DISSECTOLOGIST, indicating they were Steven's teammates.

Dissectologist #2 ignored me and launched into a grievance. "Steven, the three of us agree that I should be the tactile person today. Your dexterity is slipping. The team thinks I should put the pieces together. You can be the sorter."

Steven, who'd remained seated when his teammates arrived, waved to the two empty chairs. When I stumbled to my feet, Steven wagged a finger in my direction. "Stay, Jane. Jon can find another chair."

The man who wanted to be the team's tactile person dragged a chair from the perimeter of the room. "As I was saying—"

Steven held up a hand, which I saw as a move to assert his authority. "Let me introduce Jigster Jane Dahl. This is her first competition. No squabbling in front of a newbie."

Dissectologist #2 touched his forehead in a salute rather than shaking my hand. "Jane, I'm Dr. Jon Schott. I teach biochemistry and molecular biology at Minnesota State University Moorhead."

Steven winked at me. "Are you impressed, Jane? Jon, who's probably not much older than you, delights in sharing his credentials at every opportunity. But I'm a school custodian and number one, while the good doctor is number two."

Dr. Schott's color changed, and he muttered something under his breath.

Steven ignored him and continued with introductions. "These two ladies are the amazing Zacho sisters. Vera, our number three, is a hardy woman who leads backcountry camping in the Boundary Waters of Minnesota, and Alma, number four, is a guidance counselor at the high school where I'm employed."

In an attempt to diffuse the palpable tension, I spoke to teammate number four. "What is your role on the puzzle team, Alma?"

The overweight woman with short reddish hair wearing tortoiseshell-framed glasses looked nothing like her tall, lithe sister.

Alma seemed eager to dampen the tension. "Me? Oh, I have the easiest job. I put the border together. After that, I start working on a specific section of the puzzle. I find it easier to work with shapes rather than color."

Alma's round face didn't exhibit the raw competitive spirit Dr. Schott and Vera Zacho radiated.

I continued the conversation with her. "I watched your team from the sidelines last year. Your time of forty-one minutes set a tournament record. Want to share any secrets?"

Dr. Schott laughed. "You know the old saying. If we tell you, we'll have to kill you, and there's only one person at this table we'd all like to bump off."

Steven leaned into Dr. Schott's face. "I invited you to be a part of the group, and I can kick you out. This is my team. If you forget, well, I'm sure you don't want to think about what might happen to your career."

The professor glared at Steven. If looks could kill, the team leader would've been a dead man. Jon Schott resembled my idea of a professor. He was tall and wore a neatly trimmed beard to offset the lack of hair on his head. For glasses, he'd chosen the round-wire frames made famous by John Lennon decades ago. Tanned legs showing from beneath the cargo shorts suggested regular exercise. For footwear, he chose leather deck shoes sans socks. But right now, he looked more like a furious child on the brink of a temper tantrum than a university educator.

I was uncomfortable with quiet, so I spoke to the woman with the friendly face again. "Alma, do you want to share any secrets?"

"No," she said quickly then stammered, "Oh—oh, you mean a secret about puzzle techniques. I'm sure you have your system, Jane."

Alma's regal-looking sister, Vera, leaned forward. "Jane, you do know that Puzzle Twist is providing the stock for this competition. Their signature 'twist' is that the picture on the box doesn't look exactly like the finished product. The items and colors may differ from those shown. One year the cover picture showed snowmen, but there were cats in the finished puzzle. In another match, the fuchsia flowers were lemony yellow. That's my secret to share."

"Thanks for the tip." The friendly banter felt forced.

Vera pulled her long brown braid over her shoulder and offered me a Cheshire cat smile. "Steven is our captain, so we have to put up with him. But why are you sitting here?"

"It was the only table with an open seat."

A squawking overhead speaker announced practice rounds for the team competition would start in five minutes.

I popped up, eager to escape. "Good luck. I'll sit in one of the perimeter chairs."

Dr. Schott politely rose when I stood. "No one cares about practice rounds. We're here for the finals. And good luck to you in the singles competition, Jane."

Steven Glazer, who had no friends at the table, blew me a kiss as I left.

# CHAPTER 2

I stumbled to a chair by the wall opposite the buffet table, mumbling to myself about the tension I'd seen at the Dissectologist table. In my opinion, working puzzles, even in a competition, should be fun. Most other team participants wore amiable expressions on their faces. Perhaps the Dissectologists didn't fit together. I grinned at my joke and waited for the team practice bell to ring.

Suddenly, striding past me was the man I watched every night on the six o'clock news, Daniel Elver. I sucked in my breath and ended up having a coughing fit. People waved and greeted him, but he was focused on the red-shirted crew at the table I'd just vacated.

Elver ranked first in the news-viewing audience polls for the Fargo-Moorhead area. Men remembered and respected him as a fierce competitor on the football field before a knee injury sidelined him. Women appreciated his good looks, self-deprecating humor, and confident manner. He'd started his rise to television fame by interviewing sports figures, then he graduated to sports announcer and finally news anchor. At six foot four and devilishly handsome, he commanded the attention of the whole room.

I punched in my sister's number. "Donna, guess who's here."

"Uh, Snow White and the seven dwarfs. Jane, you know I hate it when you do this. Who are you with?"

"Daniel Elver," I whispered. "And he's wearing a lanyard indicating he's in the singles competition."

"Go introduce yourself. He's agreed to be the celebrity emcee for our church's Harvest Home Festival, and you're on the committee," Donna said.

"Good idea. Maybe I'll grab a cup of coffee, make the meeting seem casual. Uh-oh."

"Uh-oh, what?" Donna asked right before I ended the call, slipped the phone into my pocket, and approached the table.

In front of me, Daniel towered over Steven, who had not moved from the seat where I'd first seen him when I arrived. Daniel's face had reddened and contorted into a scowl, and he'd balled both hands into fists. Steven looked up at him with a glazed expression, grinning like a kid at a birthday party.

I placed the coffee on the table and extended my hand. "Mr. Elver, I'm Jane Dahl from the First Community Harvest Home Committee. We're so appreciative of your offer to emcee the event."

Daniel tilted his head as if trying to remember me, while the Dissectologists relaxed at my intervention.

"Jane, Jane," Steven crooned, "I've had more than enough coffee today, but because it's from you, I'll drink it." He sipped from the cup I'd placed on the table before I could tell him I'd gotten it for myself.

Daniel stared at me, Steven sipped the coffee, the red-shirted team members seemed mesmerized by the tabletop, and I rambled on about our local mission projects as I shifted my weight from side to side. *Awkward Moment* would have been the ideal caption for our tableau's snapshot.

The event monitor broke our pose when she placed a box in the center of the table. "Puzzle boxes remain facedown until the bell rings." She turned to Daniel and me. "If you two aren't a part of a team, you must move to the observation area."

As Daniel and I turned to leave, Marta rushed toward her husband and knocked me into Daniel. We both fell against another table, which skittered that team's puzzle to the floor. The monitor gave us the evil eye and pointed toward the exit.

"Guess we better go," Daniel said. "My teacher in second grade had that same look, and she terrified me. Are you staying to watch the team practice session?"

"I'm not sure," I said.

"I'm going to look around the fairgrounds. It's always fun to see how many different fried foods can be served on a stick. Want to come with me? You can remind me what I agreed to do for your church and when."

I glanced back and saw Steven's pale wife holding open a bag in front of him. He reached inside as if to check the contents then nodded. He held out his hand, and Marta placed something in his palm.

The overhead speaker screeched, then a garbled announcement requested participants and observers to silence cell phones for the practice rounds and refrain from talking or cheering during the session. A countdown began, and the bell rang as the minute and second hand on the clock pointed straight up.

Our path through the fairgrounds reminded me of the Pied Piper's magnetism. Children and adults followed in our wake at a respectful distance, but I could hear the whispers. Daniel acknowledged those brave enough to call out or reach for his hand, and I wondered how the man tolerated the constant stares and comments.

Daniel spoke as if there were no listeners around us. "Since you have your personalized logo shirt, I know you're a contestant. You must be in the singles category with me. Tell me how you earned your invitation."

I babbled about the qualifier where I'd received my entrance ticket for the tournament finals and my sister and her family making the T-shirts. I explained about the importance of my church family, especially the singles class. And I told him about my eagerness to move somewhere else as well as my fear and reluctance to leave my family safety nets. He asked about my relationship with Steven Grazer and the other Dissectologists.

Later, I struggled to pinpoint the precise wording of the questions Daniel asked and suffered a blank. I'm sure Daniel asked me questions, because I'm not one to spew information, especially personal tidbits, to anyone except Donna and my parents.

An announcement overpowered the amusement rides' music, barkers hawking merchandise, and squealing children who had overeaten sugary products. "The jigsaw team practice round has concluded. All singles competitors should report to the Mansions Hotel Ballroom for their practice session."

Daniel tilted his head toward the exit. "That's us."

My heart thumped. I scratched my neck and started gulping air.

"Nervous?" Daniel asked.

"I shouldn't be. Maybe it's the word *competition* that trips me up. The great thing about jigsaw puzzles is that you compete against yourself." I looked into Daniel's blue eyes for confirmation and saw a twinkle of. . .what? Pity? Sympathy? Condescension?

"We're all here to win, Jane. The title of the event is the North Dakota State Jigsaw Championship. My goal is to take down Steven Grazer." The acrimony in his tone surprised me until I remembered the furious expression on his face when I'd seen him with Steven earlier. During our foray around the fairgrounds, I'd talked nonstop and hadn't asked about his confrontation with Steven.

Three of the four Dissectologists—the college professor, Dr. Jon Schott; the naturalist, Vera Zacho; and the school guidance counselor, Alma Zacho—chatted by the ballroom door.

"Did you win the practice round?" I asked.

"No." Dr. Schott pointed to four people sporting Viking horn hats with yellow yarn braids hanging over their ears. "A Minnesota team won. We never had a chance working with three members instead of four."

Vera gestured to the table they'd abandoned. "Steven napped through the whole session. He doesn't believe in practice rounds, but it's an insult to the other teams to behave as he did."

Steven's head rested on his folded arms.

"Aren't you going to wake him?" I asked.

Alma shrugged. "You can wake him. We're going to lunch. I'm sure Steven will be geared up for the finals, with detailed orders and directives for each of us."

The trio brushed past Daniel and me.

I glanced at the sleeping man. "Daniel, should we wake him?"

"You can. I don't care if the master puzzler ever wakes. See you later, Jane. Maybe we can get a deep-fried pickle after the practice."

My mouth watered, and I puckered my lips at the thought of eating one of the fair's star staples. I gave the news anchor a thumbs-up before threading my way through the aisles.

I reached Steven's table and jiggled his shoulder. "Hey, you can't sleep through the singles session too."

He didn't lift an eyelid, move a shoulder, or flinch at my touch.

"Steven, wake up." This time I called a little louder and nudged the man.

Nothing.

When I shook him harder, he rolled off the chair and fell onto the floor, his head banging off the carpeted surface with a resounding thud.

"Steven!" I screamed. I knelt beside him and gave him a vigorous shake. I put my head on his chest, hoping to hear him breathe.

My yells triggered a swarm of people who circled us. Instead of shrieks at the sight of the immobile man, I heard muffled mutters and the clicking of cell phone cameras, indicating the documentation of the scene by the gawkers. Their pictures would show me leaning over Steven, whose wide-open, brown eyes stared vacantly at the overhead ceiling fans.

"Call for help. Call 911!" I ordered.

"No need. I've called our chief security officer, and you should move away from him." The woman who served as the head monitor for the jigsaw puzzle championship elbowed me aside, checked the artery in Steven's throat, and shone a penlight into his unflinching eyes.

"Is he dead?" I knew the answer but lingered, unable to turn my gaze from Steven's face.

The official competition monitor nodded in my direction and put a silver whistle to her lips. After an ear-splitting shrill, she bellowed, "Monitors, man the exits. No one goes in or out until the authorities arrive."

# CHAPTER 3

Wide-hipped, tight-lipped Sara Bergensen waddled into the hotel ballroom and headed in my direction. Technically, she marched toward the lifeless body, but her demeanor whooshed me back to my high school days when she attempted to educate me about the finer points of government and economics. She'd failed with me but succeeded with the voters when she ran for sheriff against an unpopular incumbent and won. Her clothing color penchant hadn't changed when she shifted from the classroom to crime scenes, and today she wore a khaki-colored skirt and shirt with a black-and-white striped scarf around her neck. The scarf reminded me of the prisoner clothing on the Monopoly game's get-out-of-jail-free card, and I wondered if her accessory choice was deliberate. The color of her short hair could also be described as khaki, and the steel rims on her glasses completed the picture of boring until you noticed those grayish-green eyes.

Toggling back to my memories of the teacher in the classroom versus the woman in front of me, I calculated Ms. Bergensen had added twenty pounds to her hefty physique. For shoes, the recently elected sheriff chose masculine-looking lace-ups designed for comfort and support not style. She's about the same age as my parents, goes to our church, and participates in Bible studies with my mom and dad. They frequently mention her insightful comments. Even though I'm an adult, Ms. Bergensen still intimidates me.

Daniel Elver, microphone in hand, played to a news camera that magically appeared on the scene. He wore a serious face not the smiling, confident one he used for the evening news. "We have a tragedy at the North Dakota State Jigsaw Championship. A man scheduled to compete in both the singles and team competition has died. We are live at the Mansions on Red River, where I qualified to compete in the singles division." He held up his lanyard showing a smiling photo and the card identifying him as a jigsaw singles competitor. "The deceased, an acknowledged king by fellow puzzlers, sat in this room." Daniel directed the photographer to focus on the empty table.

I sidestepped, avoiding the TV camera and hoping to avoid Sheriff Bergensen's notice. I was successful with the former but not the latter.

The sheriff zeroed in on me. "Jane Dahl! What's your relation to the deceased?"

"None. I don't know anything about him." I felt like I was melting into the floor, but in truth, I stumbled backward and plopped down on a chair.

"The medical team said you found Mr. Grazer." She signaled for the EMS crew to remove the body. "Inform the doctor that Mr. Grazer was from the Sioux tribe in case he has trouble tracing the deceased's medical records."

I watched as Ms. Bergensen flipped through the cards in Steven Grazer's wallet and wondered when she'd slipped the wallet from the dead man's belongings. "Is his wife here?" she asked me.

I scanned the area. "Marta was here earlier, went to find an antique puzzle, and came back to show Steven her purchase before the team practice round started."

The sheriff snorted. "You claim you didn't know the deceased, yet you know his wife and her shopping goals. Did you happen to see what she bought?"

"No, but I assume it was a dissected puzzle. She'd asked Steven about buying one."

"Did you see it?" Ms. Bergensen persisted.

"No, but we'd talked about how the team got their name and the history—"

Ms. Bergensen waved her hand like a windshield wiper in front of my face. "If you didn't see it, Jane, the answer is 'no.'"

"No. I didn't see the package contents." Her badgering unsettled me, but I vowed to remain calm to prove I was not the same irresponsible teen I'd been in high school.

She flipped open a small device. "I'm recording. The subject is Jane Dahl. Jane, why were you with Mr. Grazer?"

For some reason, the recorder stuck in my face generated an involuntary shiver, and I cringed, even though the temperature registered in the hot category, and I had nothing to hide.

She repeated her query. "Jane, why were you with Mr. Grazer?"

"I wasn't with him. I was looking for an open seat, and he was sitting at a table by himself. Of course, when I got there, I recognized him as the puzzle king. He's the reigning champion of both the singles and team competitions. The name on his shirt confirmed it for me. You know, sometimes you see someone who looks like someone else, but then when you see them up close, you realize they're not the person you thought they were, but Steven was. He's jigsaw royalty, and he was wearing the

Dissectologist team shirt. He has the number one on his because he's the captain. Even if I hadn't recognized him, which I did, I would've known the man was Steven Grazer. Both Mr. Grazer and his team are famous in puzzle circles."

"Try to give succinct answers, Jane."

"Yes, ma'am." I stared at my feet.

"Had you met Marta before today?" She poked the handheld device toward me again.

"No. Marta stopped by to ask Steven about purchasing an antique dissected puzzle. She'd heard about one that was for sale in the antique mall. After she left, Steven's three teammates arrived. I offered to leave, but Steven told me to stay. They started to talk strategy, so I left. Oh, and Daniel Elver stopped by for a short time. I wasn't there at that time, but I saw him with Steven. He's going to be one of the celebrity emcees for Harvest Home—but you know that—anyway, I'm on the committee, so I thought I'd introduce myself and say thank you. I didn't want to barge in, so I picked up a cup of coffee to seem more casual, you know. I put it on the table and he picked it up. I didn't want to—"

Sheriff Bergensen interrupted me. "Succinct and brief, Jane." She nodded toward Daniel, bathed in a bright spotlight, who spoke directly into the camera. "For the record, you saw the television news anchor approach the deceased?"

"Yes." I remembered the sheriff's mandates, but she didn't seem pleased with my short response this time.

She bumped the recorder closer to me, suggesting I say more. "Did they appear to be friends?"

I pondered my answer. "The two men looked angry. Well, Daniel did. Steven looked, maybe amused? I'm not sure. I didn't really know the man."

"So you keep saying," Sheriff Bergensen said. "Did the deceased drink the coffee?"

"He drank a little. Then the official monitor shooed Daniel and me out. We're both in the singles not the team competition. We went across to the fairgrounds to see the exhibits before our practice round." I stopped my monologue. "I know, succinct. Yes, he drank the coffee."

Out the corner of my eye, I noticed Daniel edging closer to us. "Excuse me, Sheriff Sara Bergensen, Daniel Elver with First News. Do you have a statement for our viewers?"

Ms. Bergensen lifted her chin. "I have no statement at present."

"Our cameras saw the EMS crew removing what appeared to be a covered body on a gurney. Can you confirm whether there's been a death at the jigsaw championship?"

Ms. Bergensen preened and adjusted her black-and-white scarf. "The public looks forward to the puzzle event each year, but we must consider the feelings of the bereaved family."

Daniel nodded knowingly at the camera before turning back to Ms. Bergensen. "So you can confirm a death but not the person's name?"

The sheriff clamped her lips together and narrowed her eyes. "This office will issue a press statement at a later time."

"Of course, we at First News would not want to intrude on a family grieving the untimely death of a loved one."

Sheriff Bergensen placed her hand over Daniel's and pulled the microphone directly in front of her mouth. "And, if the untimely death was not from natural causes, this office will not rest until the guilty person is behind bars."

Daniel ran his tongue across his lips as if tasting the sweetness of a tantalizing story. "So you're not ruling out murder?"

"Our city has an excellent forensics team."

"Do you have any persons of interest? Suspects?" Daniel asked.

"I want to thank the voters for electing me to serve as sheriff. My officers aim to comb through every case carefully, not just this one but the cold and old cases, the citizen complaints, and all those in active status."

I stifled a grin. Should I interrupt what was sounding like a reelection speech with a "succinct, please" request? The crazy interview aroused my interest. Who would want to kill the puzzle king? He was just a man who loved putting together jigsaw puzzles.

Eager to see if my sister had seen our former teacher and fellow church member on television, I pushed in Donna's number again. "Are you watching television?"

"No, I'm at the fairgrounds with my husband and kids. We're here to support my sister in the jigsaw competition."

"Donna, you know Steven Grazer, the team leader of the Dissectologists? His moniker is the Puzzle King because he's won both the singles and team competitions for the past two years. Well, Steven is dead."

"How awful!"

"I discovered his body."

"Oh, Jane. Want me to meet you?"

"I can't leave yet. Sara Bergensen thinks I might be involved."

"Sara Bergensen?" Donna covered the phone then spoke in her firmest parental tone. "Boys! Don't go there without your dad or me."

I waited until she indicated I should continue. "Yes. Ms.

Bergensen is our newly elected sheriff, remember?"

"I'd forgotten."

"She acts like I'm a suspect!"

Donna laughed. "You? That's ridiculous. Oops, gotta go. Peter is trying to get on the roller coaster by himself. Call me later."

As Donna ended the call, Sheriff Bergensen returned to my side. "Good speech for the television audience," I said. "Do you really suspect murder?"

"Because Mr. Grazer was a young man and apparently healthy, an autopsy is a precautionary step."

"If it's murder, you have to find out who did it."

"Glad you think so, Jane, because you're a suspect."

"Me? I just met him today," I said.

"And supplied him with not one but two cups of coffee."

"But I just met the man," I repeated lamely.

The sheriff gave me an enigmatic smile. "So you say."

"It's true!" I bit my tongue to keep from repeating the phrase a third time.

When I was younger, I daydreamed about doing life-changing, essential things, but after the accident, I'd burrowed in the soft comfort of my family and an isolated job. How could anyone believe I might be capable of murder?

# CHAPTER 4

The Mansions on the Red River didn't accurately describe the quality of the rooms in the hotel where the contestants stayed for the jigsaw tournament. When Marta Grazer mentioned she didn't want to be alone, I invited her to share my room, which had two queen beds. To my surprise, the Zacho sisters, Vera and Alma, occupied the space next to mine, and Dr. Jon Schott's was two doors past theirs. Despite their hostility toward Steven, I noticed they gravitated to his gentle and skittish wife.

When Marta brought her belongings to my room, we watched Daniel relocating to a ground-level suite close to the rest of us.

The Mansions Hotel and Conference Center stands near the Red River, which separates Fargo from Moorhead and also North Dakota from Minnesota. Its location gave my hotel room a musty, mildew scent, and the decor featured my least favorite color, brown. The carpet was brown. The drapes were a lighter shade of brown, and the pattern on the two beds featured geometric shapes in golds, russets, and dark greens. Fall foliage prints repeated the color scheme. I found the overall ambiance depressing. The good thing was that the room was suite style and included a sofa, two chairs, and a desk. I was thankful I didn't have to sit on the bed.

Sheriff Bergensen invited the key witnesses, aka suspects, to the ballroom, where we should've been competing in the finals of the singles and team competitions for the jigsaw tournament. She informed us she'd conduct interrogations at the hotel rather than the precinct and exhorted us to make ourselves available. The timeline worked, as most contestants had packed for two nights, expecting to return home after the competition.

She laid out her ground rules. "I'm going to isolate you as best I can. I've asked the manager to disconnect the television service from the rooms."

"What?" Daniel practically shouted.

"Elver, don't be melodramatic. You just want to see your face on screen." Dr. Schott didn't sound like he'd be organizing a Daniel Elver fan club anytime soon.

The sheriff shushed the two men. "Although the autopsy remains incomplete, Mr. Grazer's death appears suspicious. In the postmortem, they'll check for poison but not a typical poison. Most cause an extreme reaction, like strychnine, which causes twitching, arching the back, and extreme discomfort. Everyone thought Mr. Grazer had fallen asleep, so this poison caused him to slip into unconsciousness before he died."

"Then his death was peaceful?" Marta Grazer looked for confirmation from the sheriff.

"Yes, Mrs. Grazer, I think his passing would've been peaceful. The autopsy can determine the exact cause," the sheriff said.

Marta plucked at her tissue, shredding it into confetti. I put an arm around her thin shoulders, startled that she felt as fragile as she looked.

"Is there something I should be doing?" Marta asked. "About funeral arrangements?"

Her plaintive query generated a modicum of sympathy from our sheriff, who handed her a couple more tissues from the box on the table. "You don't have to worry about anything right now. Do you have family members to call? Is there someone you'd like to be here with you?"

"I don't have anyone." Marta started ripping up another tissue. "Could you call Steven's parents? His family never accepted me. I'm not a tribal member."

"We'll notify them," Sheriff Bergensen said.

Marta switched from shredding to rolling the tiny bits into a ball. "Thank you. Ma'am, you should know that Steven wasn't close to his family, except his dad."

I filed Marta's comment away. Did the man have anyone who cared about him? Dislike is one thing but murder? My knowledge of what natural causes might kill a person was woefully inadequate, a field where I didn't wish to be an expert. But I felt protective of the delicate Marta.

I said, "Sheriff, why are you so certain it was murder? Couldn't it have been a heart attack or, I don't know, a breathing problem, or maybe a blood clot in the brain?"

Before the law officer could answer, we heard the honeyed voice of Daniel Elver, who stood against the wall of the ballroom, microphone in hand.

"We just learned that Sheriff Bergensen considers the jigsaw competition death a murder, possibly by poisoning. Stay with this station for the latest updates. This case is similar to a jigsaw puzzle where Sheriff Bergensen must find the missing piece to complete the picture of an attack that left an individual dead."

Daniel's somber tones and concerned facial features switched to cheerful and excited when the camera was off. "Have them do a breaking news spot with that broadcast. This is going to be a fantastic story!"

I squeezed Marta's shoulders, noting her face had turned even paler than her natural hue.

Sheriff Bergensen stalked to where Daniel stood. "You're here as a suspect not a newsman. There will be no more live broadcasts about my investigation." She signaled a uniformed officer at the door to escort the video crew out of the room.

"If I don't report, our rival stations will. You can't keep this quiet." Daniel's sculpted chin with its signature dimple jutted forward as he protested.

"That's fine, but you can get your facts like the rest of the media, Mr. Elver, during my press conferences. Do you understand?"

Conflicting emotions danced across Daniel's expressive face before he acquiesced. "Yes. But I have the right to interview your possible suspects."

Sheriff Bergensen raised one eyebrow, just as I'd seen her do so many times in civics class, and said, "Daniel, you're one of my suspects."

When I giggled, she turned to me. "Don't laugh. You, Jane Dahl, are number one on my list."

"You can't be serious," I protested. "I'm not a murderer."

"You sought out Mr. Grazer. You brought him two coffees and discovered his body. Interesting, don't you think?"

Marta drew away from me as I stammered a reply to the accusations. "But I never met the man before this morning. I had nothing against him."

The sheriff looked over the top of her glasses. "So you keep saying. If you have any secrets, I'll find them."

I did have some secrets, but they didn't involve poisoning a championship puzzler. I was no longer a fifteen-year-old kid intimidated by her stern looks, but did she believe I could kill? If she genuinely considered me a suspect, I needed to launch an investigation of my own.

The sheriff promised to start the interviews after she'd notified Steven Grazer's family and met with the medical examiner. I did not doubt that she'd assign her junior officers to unearth details from our private lives, starting with mine.

Other competitors and contest officials, also suspects, selected lunch tables away from ours. The six of us, Daniel, Dr. Schott, Vera, Alma, Marta, and I shared a round table, which proved conducive for conversation. To my surprise, I emerged as the facilitator, or peacemaker, generating exchanges on small-talk topics. My goal was to learn about the others without addressing the elephant, or corpse, in the room. Steven could have died of a heart attack, a blood clot, or any other malady. However, if the autopsy did show he had been poisoned, perhaps the killer sat at this table. I shivered. The idea astounded me, as my tablemates all seemed so amiable.

Dr. Schott, who'd suggested we address him as Jon, brandished his cell phone. "Our jailor is out of touch with reality. Disconnecting television service is ridiculous when we all use these. I asked a colleague to cover my classes for Monday and Tuesday."

Vera nodded. "But you'll get paid. I had to hire another guide to take my wilderness trip this week. That's money out of pocket. Money we need."

"I can help," Alma told her sister.

"We're not desperate, Alma. You know I'd ask if we needed money." Vera turned to the rest of us. "My husband was mauled by a bear when leading an adventure outing. He's in a wheelchair, which makes me the primary guide for the business."

"How did it happen?" The question came from Daniel.

Vera pursed her lips and shook her head. "I don't want you parading my life on the six o'clock news."

An awkward quiet settled over the table as Jon, Vera, Alma, and Daniel fiddled with the remainder of their food.

"I make teeth," I blurted, and the statement elicited laughs and grins.

"Really?" Jon's smile, with his evenly aligned teeth, altered his appearance. "Tell us more, Jane."

My face felt warm, and I knew my cheeks were flushed with embarrassment. "It's true, but I don't know why I said that."

"Is that your job?" Alma asked. "I'm a guidance counselor, and your unusual occupation might appeal to some of my high school students. What training is involved?"

The focus had turned toward my life, not ideal for my role as an amateur sleuth. I needed insight into their lives.

I explained. "The job requires an associate's degree in dental lab technology. I fashion crowns, bridges, and implants. I think that's why I'm good at jigsaw puzzles. I have excellent hand dexterity and a good eye for color. Every tooth is different in shading and shape. The skill is matching both precisely so the new crown or tooth looks natural."

"That might be a good option for students who don't want to

go for a four-year degree," Alma said.

Daniel tilted his head. "I'd guess that you have to work with potent chemicals, maybe even poisonous ones in your line of work."

"No! Well, yes, I do, but I didn't give Steven any poison. I only met the man this morning. I'm going to my room." I stood, momentarily forgetting my purpose in finding out the secrets of others at the table.

Marta, my recently acquired roommate, said, "You go ahead. I'll be there shortly."

I had the unpleasant feeling that the murdered man's wife—my new roommate—now suspected me.

# CHAPTER 5

"Donna, do you know what Sheriff Bergensen said?" I blurted the words before my sister said hello.

"Uh, that you have a charming sister?"

"Donna, this is serious. She said I'm a murder suspect!"

"That's ridiculous, Jane."

"You know Ms. Bergensen never liked me in high school."

"Not many teachers did. You weren't the poster child for good citizenship," Donna reminded me.

"And Marta Grazer suspects me too." My attempt at a laugh came out as a cough. "She's sharing my room."

I heard the sound of a key card unlocking the door, so I said a quick goodbye to Donna and plastered on a smile for Marta, who hesitated before stepping through the door.

"I didn't kill Steven," I said.

"I know." Marta sank into the chair closest to the door.

I moved to the identical companion chair. "I'm so sorry." I waved as though I could erase the statement. "That's a lame comment. Is there anything I can do?"

She shook her head. "Do you think I'll have to see him?"

"Do you want to?"

She shook her head again. "I thought I might have to, oh, I don't know, go identify him or something."

Comforting people is not a natural act for me as it is for Mom and Donna. Both are good at it and serve as grief counselors at church, but I didn't get that gene. Around sick people and at the few funerals I've attended, I usually huddle quietly in the back of the room. Instead of talking to Marta, I jumped up, grabbed some tissues, and pressed them into her hands.

"If you have to do that, I could go with you." I covered my mouth, wishing I could stuff those words back in.

She dabbed her eyes, which didn't appear to be wet. "I told the sheriff I didn't have anyone to call. I do have a sister, but we don't keep in touch."

"My sister's my best friend. Donna's the greatest, married to a good guy, and they have two mischievous boys. My dad was military, so we moved frequently, but Donna and I always had each other. She's three years older..." I trailed off in my personal story when I saw Marta wasn't paying attention. I recalled Bergensen's mandate about succinctness. "Does your sister live here?"

Marta shook her head. "She married to get out of the house, just like I did. She lives in Louisiana. My dad was a mean drunk and bashed anything or anyone in his path. Our house overflowed with broken furniture and bruised people. Steven lived a few houses down and knew what went on behind our front door. Well, the whole neighborhood knew."

"I'm sorry." I reached out, wanting to stroke Marta like you would a sick or injured pet.

"When Steven asked me to marry him, I agreed. I didn't love him, and he didn't love me."

"I'm sure he loved you," I said.

She shook her head again. "Our marriage insulted his Sioux parents. They wanted him to marry someone from the tribe. When Steven took me to meet them after we married, they barely spoke to me. We left after about fifteen minutes."

"I'm sorry." I clenched my teeth after my third "I'm sorry." Why couldn't I think of anything else to say?

She shrugged, crossed to the dresser, and opened the top right drawer.

"I put my things on that side, but we can switch if you prefer."

She closed the drawer and grinned. "You have plenty of dental care items."

"Guilty," I said and mentally noted her two front teeth had a slight gap and her incisors were more pointed than rounded.

"Have you ever arranged a funeral?" Marta returned to the chair and placed her head in her hands.

"No, but I'll check my phone. You can find anything on the internet." I typed in "death arrangements" before she could dissuade me.

"Steven told me the Sioux prefer burial not cremation. They view the earth as our mother, so burial in the dirt reconnects the body and frees the soul. I don't know what we were talking about when he said that, but it stuck with me." Marta picked at her nails.

"Here are some lists." I offered her my phone.

She waved it away. "Maybe Steven's family would like to arrange things."

"I remember my parents saying that you need several death certificates. As his widow, you'll have to switch things to your name."

Marta walked to a spot between the beds. "Which bed is yours?"

"The right," I said.

Marta moaned. "I'm not sure how I'll get by."

I didn't know what to say to this woman I'd only met—I glanced at the nightstand clock—four hours ago. So, I did what I always do when in uncomfortable situations. I changed the subject.

"Marta, did you find the dissected puzzle?"

Her eyes had a haunted, unfocused look, but she became animated when she moved to her belongings piled in a heap on the couch. "Yes. It wasn't a world map, but a map of New York by the McLoughlin Brothers. The seller offered a discount because it's incomplete."

She cradled the box with the pride and delight of a new mother and kept her baby out of my reach.

"Is McLoughlin a famous maker?" I knew they were, but that was the extent of my knowledge.

Marta's facial expression seemed reverential. "Oh, yes. This is not as valuable as a Spilsbury, but still a prize. John Spilsbury created dissected maps in the 1700s, and King George III had a cabinet of Spilsbury's works to teach his children geography. McLoughlin Brothers is an American company, and their puzzles date to the 1880s. Many have scenes on both sides. This one lacks a piece, but it's rare to find one intact. And this is in the original container."

Her passion for vintage puzzles gave free rein to her tongue, and she spoke with vibrant energy.

My hands itched to grab the box, but I restrained myself. "What will you do with it?"

"Sell it," she replied immediately. "I'll put it together, using gloves, and then post the photographs. I should triple my investment."

"May I see it?"

Marta took a piece of cloth to cover her fingers as she removed the lid. Her body language shouted "Look with your eyes and not with your hands."

"The company name and the date are shown on the puzzle itself, which increases the value. Fortunately, the missing piece is an edge part."

I remembered my last glimpse of Marta and Steven together. She'd shown him something in a bag, and he'd held out his hand. "Did Steven see it?"

"He did. This morning I told Steven I could get it for under five hundred, and I got it for two."

"So, when you sell it, you'll make a good profit." Did she expect to impress me with her business acumen?

"Steven doled out money only when I gave him details of how I planned to use it. When I found an exceptional treasure and resold it, he put the profit into the bank account and gave me a percentage for my efforts."

I didn't want to get in the middle of a marriage squabble, especially when one party had just been murdered, but... "Maybe your husband worried about paying the bills. He mentioned he worked as a school janitor."

Marta's grief, if that even existed, seemed to have passed. I suspected this woman was smart and savvy, despite her subservient and meek demeanor.

"He worked as a custodian, but he got cash regularly from another source. Every month, he'd show me a stack of money and say the 'private ATM' paid out again."

"But didn't you see the entries on the bank statements?" I asked.

"Like I said, he gave me money for 'justified' expenditures." Marta closed the box and reverently returned it to the bag.

"As his widow, I assume all his money will go to you." I said the words slowly, watching for a reaction.

"I suppose." She shrugged nonchalantly, but I thought I saw a spark of avarice in her eyes.

"Unless he has a will and it says something different," I added.

Two questions niggled at the back of my mind. Could Marta have killed her husband? And where was Steven getting his windfalls?

"Jane." A man's voice called my name after three raps on the door.

I lifted the edge of the light-blocking drape to see the visitor. After all, a murderer ended Steven Grazer's life, and I intended to be careful.

"It's Jon Schott," the professor said from the other side of the door. "I have an idea of how we can kill some time. Is Marta with you?"

Even though killing anything, even time, sounded malevolent, I opened the door. "Marta's here."

"Good." He nodded to the widow, who was hanging her clothes in the tiny closet.

"What's your plan?" I motioned toward the brown couch.

"The Jigsaw Championship Committee canceled the competition, but I thought we might stage our own event," Jon said.

"That's a great idea. A contest will keep us busy when the law isn't grilling us," I said.

Jon turned to Marta. "How do you feel, Marta? Maybe we

could call it the Steven Grazer Memorial Championship."

Marta rolled her eyes. "Play your games, Jon. I might compete in the singles event myself. No reason to sit in the room all day."

"I didn't know you were a puzzler." Jon tilted his head.

"We all have secrets, don't we?"

Jon's tone turned icy. "What are you saying, Marta?"

"Just stating facts. Steven always kept two puzzle tables set up in our house. Maybe his skills rubbed off on me."

"What about your team, the Dissectologists?" I asked.

"Would you join us? Everyone else is already on a team." Jon's face colored as he realized his error.

I grinned. "You want me to join the team because you've already asked everyone else."

He began to mumble, but I stopped his apologies by extending my hand.

"I'd be honored. Do you think I could get one of those shirts?" I pointed to the red Dissectologist shirt Jon wore.

"I'm sure Alma or Vera has an extra. I'll see about getting the tables set up and registering contestants."

After he left, I turned to Marta. "Steven said you didn't like his hobby."

"As I said to Jon, we all have secrets."

# CHAPTER 6

A s Marta and I edged forward into the hotel ballroom, a vivacious Jon Schott welcomed all the competitors.

"He's quite different from the man I met yesterday," I said.

"He's not in Steven's shadow anymore." Marta pointed to an isolated table. "I'll grab a spot in the back. I've heard all the 'sorry for your loss' comments I can stand."

I filed away her statement about Steven overshadowing Jon and headed toward the only other people I knew, the Zacho sisters, Vera and Alma.

"Jon said you agreed to complete our team," Alma said.

"You're pros, so now I'm nervous about the competition *and* the murder inquiry," I said. "Sheriff Bergensen insists I'm her top suspect."

"Don't worry. Steven was the only one who took puzzling seriously." Vera looked over her shoulder. "Just checking to see if Marta's nearby. You can be certain that before the investigation ends, the law officer will find plenty of suspects, including the wife."

"Really?" I didn't relish that option, since Marta now shared my room.

Alma claimed a table. "This diversion will help all of us. I'm glad Jon suggested it. But you're not the only one on the suspect list. I'm there, as well as Vera and Jon."

Her comment offered consolation, and I concentrated on the upcoming event. While watching family members and friends work jigsaw puzzles, I've learned things about each person I didn't know before. My cousin has a natural eye for color. My mother is good with shapes, while my dad homes in on small details. Some individuals take a scattered approach, working on the border then switching to color shadings or textures. Other people work with deliberation and patience. Had Steven's murder been deliberate or spontaneous? This informal tournament offered a chance to learn something about the suspects by watching them work puzzles.

Vera grabbed my hand before I could put it to my neck again. "Jane, you have hives. Those bright red welts are spreading. Did you eat anything different?"

"No, it's nerves. I get them when I'm uncomfortable. They always show up on the first day of any venture, such as opening day of school, visiting somewhere new, a first date. My scratching usually guarantees there isn't a second date. Being considered a murderer is stressful. I'm sure that's why I've blossomed." My attempt to make light of my red neck didn't work.

"Come with me. I have some salve that'll soothe it." Vera grabbed my hand and dragged me from the ballroom.

I said *dragged*, not led, because her legs were considerably longer than mine, and Vera intended to care for the hives before the contest commenced. Perhaps she thought my compulsion to scratch might distract the team from setting a completed puzzle time record.

Back in the hotel wing, the Zacho sisters' room suffered

from a split personality. A clear line of demarcation separated the flawlessly organized half from the explosive, chaotic section and Vera's belongings from Alma's. Vera opened the top drawer on the left, removed an extra-large first-aid kit, and retrieved a green tube of salve.

Noting her container included several vials and syringes as well as assorted bandages, creams, and tinctures, I had to ask the question, "Are you a nurse?"

"No, but as a wilderness guide, I'm prepared to address life-threatening events."

I tried to read the labels surreptitiously. "Are any of these poisonous?"

Vera removed gauze from the kit. "Most counteract poison, and some mitigate extreme pain."

"Do you have to use them much?" I hoped she believed my interest was casual and not because she was now on my suspect list.

"I had to use one on my husband when the bear mauled him." Vera's tone switched from conversational to rancorous.

"I'm sorry." I should make a recording of the phrase instead of parroting it repeatedly.

"My husband loves the Boundary Waters as much as I do. He doesn't want me to give up the business, but we may not have a choice. If the sheriff is looking for someone with a motive for bumping off Steven, I had one."

"You do? I mean, you did?"

"Steven booked the camping event where my husband was permanently injured. It turned out to be a bachelor's party that got out of hand with too much drinking and disregard for our company rules, such as lofting food so animals can't get it, respecting quiet hours, and collecting all garbage to take out with us. We finally told the men we were cutting the trip short and returning to headquarters just before the bear arrived for a meal. My husband moved in front of the men, but the bear had a goal in mind. He swatted my husband against a tree with such force that it shattered some vertebrae, and the claw marks caused excessive bleeding. We used the emergency pager after we scared the animal off with generous doses of bear spray. We don't blame the bear. We were in his territory, but that one booking changed our lives forever."

"Was Steven with them?" I asked, trying to fathom why she blamed Steven.

"No. But he knew the men planned a drinking week, which is not appropriate for wilderness camping. Then, for the past six months, Steven's hinted that the group plans to sue us for reckless endangerment. He showed me the list of names and addresses."

"That's mean. Why did you continue to compete with him?"

"He promised to intervene with the men on our behalf if I continued. In my opinion, being the puzzle king was Steven's only triumph in life, and he didn't want to lose his crown. Rather ridiculous, isn't it?"

I didn't comment because my participation might seem insignificant, even ludicrous to others, but to me, it was vital. Just as the wilderness adventure had altered Vera's life, the car accident transformed mine.

Vera continued, "Steven considered me essential to the team because I have an exceptional eye for color due to my life in the outdoors. All shades have subtle tones, which I'm able to discern." She closed the first-aid kit.

"Steven didn't have many friends," I said.

Vera laughed. "That's an understatement. I can't think of a single one." She studied my neck. "If you'd like, I can clean the area before you apply the salve. It's spread to the edge of your hairline."

I followed her to the bathroom—which had the same irreconcilable differences between order and turmoil as the hotel room—and sat on the toilet seat while Vera performed her cleansing ritual. I felt the same shame and humiliation I'd experienced as a second-grader when my mother combed through my hair, checking for lice after a school outbreak of the good-for-nothings.

Fortunately, the magic cream provided instant relief. "Thanks, Vera. Since I won't have to think about the itching, I might help the Dissectologists."

"We'll adopt a different name. Dissectologists was Steven's idea." She eyed my Jigster Jane T-shirt. "Maybe we could be the Jigsters. Would you like that?"

"Of course." I'd daydreamed of hearing "Jigster Jane Dahl" announced as the singles' champion, but I probably had a better chance at fame with three skilled players on the Jigsters team.

Vera replaced her case in the drawer, which also held a sewing kit and a nail kit. She flipped her single braid over her shoulder and shook her head. "Alma looks good when she walks out the door, but what she leaves behind looks like straight wind damage."

"The difference is surprising, since you're sisters." My comment didn't seem to ruffle her.

"Some people ask if we really are sisters, and our parents always reassure them we are." Vera's smile showed nice, even teeth. "I'm tall and lean like my father. I followed him into the woods as soon as I could walk. I've always loved camping, hiking, shooting a bow and arrow, and learning to live in harmony with nature."

"And Alma resembles your mother?" I asked.

"In every way. They're both short and a bit plump, share the same strawberry blond hair color, and fair complexion. Both have big hearts. Alma loves cooking and taking care of people. That's why she's a good school counselor. She goes the extra mile to help her students get into good colleges."

I gazed at the room. "Her job must require order and structure."

She laughed again. "Alma knows where to find things in the mess. You ask for an item, and she'll retrieve it in a flash. Mom's the same. Our house looked like a disaster zone, but chaos stopped at the garage entry. That was Dad's area and neater than a hardware store. Everything had its place. I followed his example."

I glanced at the nightstand clock and saw we had nearly an hour before the competition began, so I probed further. "How did the Dissectologists get started? Even an outsider could sense the tension in the group was more than competition jitters."

"Steven pulled each of us into his web and didn't plan to let us escape. We're all free now. I doubt there will be many tears at his funeral—if anyone attends."

"Surely there was some decency in the man." The picture painted by his wife and teammates didn't match the cordial, friendly man I'd met.

Vera chuckled. "If there was, I didn't discover it, and I tried because I'm an optimist."

# CHAPTER 7

Although I hated the sensation of wanting to claw my skin off, the opportunity for the magic salve interlude in the hotel gave me insight into a fellow suspect. Vera could be a murderer but said she'd looked for the good in Steven. That didn't sound like a cold-blooded killer to me. I mentally checked the three main categories for a would-be killer.

Motive? Yes, I could understand Vera's reason for disliking Steven.

Means? She knew about poisons, maybe things in nature that could kill a person, and she had syringes.

Opportunity? We were all near Steven. Give everyone a checkmark in that category.

I needed more information from Sheriff Bergensen. She'd suggested poison but hadn't divulged the type, when it had been administered, or how. She harped on my bringing him coffee, so maybe she believed Steven drank or ate something lethal immediately before his demise. But perhaps he had come in contact with something toxic in the janitorial supplies where he worked. I liked that idea. Then, none of my new acquaintances would be guilty.

"Excuse me," I said as I bumped into someone. I looked up to see Daniel Elver's amused expression.

"You were in a fog. I planted myself in your path, and you never even looked up. Want to have dinner tonight? I assume we'll be stuck with the hotel's restaurant, so the deep-fried dill pickle I promised is out."

I peeked behind him. "No microphones?"

"No microphones, now or at dinner. We can talk about your church's Harvest Home event. I like to be well prepared." Daniel flashed a bright smile.

My occupation making dentures and implants made me hyper-aware of the shape, size, and color of teeth. Because Daniel's could be labeled B-1, I wondered if he had bleach work done recently.

"Well?" he asked.

"Yes, I'd love to have dinner."

For a fleeting moment, I worried about my roommate. Despite my initial impression of her fragility, I'd learned that Marta didn't need coddling. She seemed pretty capable of taking care of herself.

Daniel motioned toward the exit door. "Shall we meet there at seven? I'm going to compete in the team event. It was a last-minute thing. I was talking with three other singles, and we decided to sign up." He looked apologetic for not including me.

"The Dissectologists asked me to complete their group, so we'll be working against you."

"You agreed to take Steven Grazer's spot? Don't let any of his personality traits rub off on you," Daniel warned.

"I'm going to ask for clarification of that remark over dinner.

I only met the man in person today and found him charming. See you at seven." I hurried to join my teammates at a table near the front.

Jon assumed the mantle of leadership. He assigned me the role of "islander," which meant I'd be working on specific puzzle segments such as a house, a horse, or a vase. We'd all turn pieces upright and slide the edge pieces to Alma. He continued with instructions, more for my benefit than for Alma's or Vera's.

When the Puzzle Twist representative issued contest specifics, the room hushed. I sat on my hands to keep them from straying to my neck, which erupted again with the itching sensation. Occupying a dead man's position felt strange to me, but my three companions seemed oblivious to the oddity.

A bicycle-style horn announced permission to turn over the box on the table and begin. I considered myself adroit, but the fingers of the other three at the table fairly flew. Alma had the top border of the puzzle completed before I'd decided on two island objectives—a yellow kite and a black cocker spaniel. Remembering what I'd learned about the Puzzle Twist jigsaw creations, I knew I couldn't depend on the kite being yellow or the dog being black or them being a kite or a dog at all.

Subdued murmurs broke the hush resting over each table like a cushiony cloud of quiet. The footfalls of the monitors created a steady rhythm marking the passing minutes. Alma, finished with the border, whispered to me that she'd work on the garden gate. I'd managed to finish the dog—a golden retriever instead of a black cocker spaniel—and the kite, which transformed into a lone dress on a clothesline. Since I'd only done a couple of this company's puzzles, I kept looking at the picture on the box for clues and found none.

Alma knew there was a gate because Vera had assembled the stone fencing. The team coordination amazed me, and my three companions slid pieces to each other without studying the box. I wondered if I was a hindrance or help. Observing their focus now, I assumed they'd worked with this same intensity during the practice event, and I wondered if Steven participated at all. Vera said he'd slept through the practice. Had he begun work on the puzzle before resting his head? My intuition told me the answer was central to the timeline.

The bicycle horn sounded, and the earlier practice winners, the team with the Viking hats and long blond braids, claimed victory again. A huge Viking horn appeared from under their table, and a resounding blast let everyone in the room know that the Minnesota Manipulators were the champions. We still had a whole section unconnected.

"Those Puzzle Twists are challenging, aren't they?" Jon asked.

"The different elements don't change my approach, since I'm sorting by shading," Vera said. "It's the island people who struggle."

I lifted my fingers to my neck and dropped them when Vera wagged a forefinger in my direction.

Alma began placing pieces in the box. "That's the first competition I've ever enjoyed."

I expected the three to be upset at not coming in on top, but they all smiled and exchanged remarks with people at other tables as if this was just a friendly afternoon activity.

"Shall we celebrate our new union over dinner?" Jon asked.

"I have plans, but thanks for asking." I decided to ask the question niggling in my mind. "I'm curious. Did Steven participate in the practice round at all?"

Alma shook her head. "He gave us orders, as he always did, but as soon as we opened the box, he put his head on his arms. That was it."

Jon snorted. "We moved the puzzle work area toward the top of the table since Steven had his head down and ignored our requests to help."

Vera nodded. "We thought it was Steven being Steven. I told the sheriff he never yelled or called out, but we were focused on the puzzle."

"He never said he wasn't feeling well, complained of tiredness, nothing," Alma added. "That annoyed me. The rest of us would have had the common courtesy to explain why we couldn't participate."

Even after his death, his teammates didn't seem sympathetic. I'd spoken to Vera privately. How could I finagle a private conversation with Jon or Alma? I checked the time. I wanted to freshen up before meeting Daniel for dinner so I stood and thanked them for including me in their group.

Vera grabbed my wrist to stop my departure. "Was this our last team competition?"

Jon shrugged. "I'd like to keep competing. Jane, are you interested?"

"I'm not sure I'll be here next year," I said. "And since the sheriff has us ranked on her suspect list, one of us might be on trial for murder or in prison."

Alma frowned. "That's a bit melodramatic, Jane. Can you see one of us killing Steven? I'm sure it will turn out to be natural causes."

I wanted to believe Vera, Alma, and Jon were innocent, but I also liked the two remaining suspects, Marta Grazer and Daniel

Elver. Of course, I didn't put my name on the list as a possible murderer.

Daniel had switched his attire from casual to his professional look. Our hostess fiddled with the menus and became tongue-tied when asking where we'd like to sit. As she led us to a corner table, heads turned to watch as we passed. I wore a colorful sundress and heels, but I had no illusions the gawkers were ogling me.

"Do you ever get used to it?" I asked as the hostess handed us the menus.

"I think they were looking at you," Daniel said. "Would you like something to drink before we order?"

I shook my head. "I don't drink alcohol."

"Neither do I," Daniel said, "although photographs might indicate differently. At public relations events, I carry a glass so I don't keep having to refuse. Do you have a reason for not drinking?"

I did, one that harkened back to my teens, but not one I shared. When I changed clothes for dinner, I promised myself that I'd ask the questions tonight. He'd learned plenty about me this afternoon during our walk around the fairgrounds.

I smiled as I looked up from the menu. "Personal choice. How about you?"

"I was an athlete before I got on the communication track. I didn't believe alcohol or tobacco was good for physical performance, so I steered clear. Plus, our parents hounded us to make good choices."

"How many in your family?"

"Two, like you. An older sister, like you." Daniel's comment reminded me of his questions earlier today. He remembered my answers.

"Does she still live here?" I planned to turn the tables on him tonight.

He shook his head and looked back at the menu. "I'm having the pork medallions. What sounds good to you?"

"The fish special the waitress mentioned, but you don't get off that easily. I told you about my sister, Donna. You have to give me some information about your sister. Are you close?"

"Not the way you described your relationship with Donna. My sister is three years older, and she tried to ignore me rather than mother me."

He signed an autograph for a couple who approached the table then posed for a photograph with them, which I took with the woman's phone.

"Since Steven was murdered, I'm curious what you two were discussing earlier this morning. You looked angry to me."

"Is that what you told the sheriff?"

"If she asks, I'll be obligated to tell the truth, won't I? Jon, Vera, and Alma heard whatever you discussed with Steven. They'll also have to tell Sheriff Bergensen if she asks. I only saw you together. I didn't hear anything."

"Saved by the medallions and your fish. Please, Jane, let's have a pleasant dinner without any mention of murder."

The waitress placed the entrees, and a second waiter offered us warm bread from a basket. This was my first date with a man in at least two years, if it could be considered a date. I should enjoy the evening, but I kept wondering if the man sitting across from me and artfully buttering his roll might be a murderer.

Out of the corner of my eye, I saw Jon and Marta huddled at a corner table, heads close together. Marta said Jon had lived in Steven's shadow, which hinted she had insight into her current dinner companion's feelings and emotions. The proximity of their bodies indicated they might share more than a passing acquaintance.

However, my emphasis tonight was on Daniel Elver. After small talk about the food, I zeroed in on my research topic.

"Where does your sister live?" I asked him a second time as we neared the end of the meal.

"Better meal than I expected. I'm usually not a fan of hotel fare. When I have to travel, I try to find something typical of the local cuisine." He signaled for the waiter and turned to me. "Coffee? Dessert?"

"I'm a sucker for sweets, but the coffee will have to be decaf," I said.

The waiter arrived and listed the delectable choices. I chose the cheesecake, and Daniel opted for the Double Chocolate Lava Cake.

"Why don't you want to talk about your sister?"

"Personal reasons, like yours for not drinking. Why don't you talk about that?" He concentrated on his extravagant dessert, which could have served four people.

My intuition told me his sister had something to do with his animosity toward Steven Grazer. I sucked in a deep breath and launched into the story I rarely shared with people.

"My best friend in high school crashed her car when we'd had too much to drink. I emerged without a scratch, but she wasn't so lucky. Shattered glass messed up her face, and she uses a cane. She blames me for her altered looks and physical limitations. Noreen says I pushed her to do things she never would have done on her own. That night changed my life."

Daniel leaned forward, his dessert and coffee ignored. "I wasn't there, but it doesn't seem like you were the only one at fault."

"I think I was. I was brash and cocky in high school. Thought I was invincible."

Daniel dabbed his mouth. "Most teenagers feel that way."

"I convinced my friends to do things they wouldn't normally do."

"You're not that way now." Daniel slid the dessert plate away.

"No. After the accident, I became tentative about everything. I always dreamed of exploring the world, but instead, I camped out in my parent's walk-out basement until they 'helped' me find my own apartment. I work in a secluded lab and go straight home every night."

"But you're here," he said. "And you don't seem like the reclusive type."

"I'm acting," I confessed. "This competition was a giant step for me."

"A step toward what?" he asked.

"I told myself if I got through the competition, I'd move out of here to a place where my parents or Donna couldn't be a constant crutch. If I succeed at that, I plan to find Noreen."

"And?"

"I haven't thought past contacting her, and I may not do that if Sheriff Bergensen has her way. She keeps reminding me I'm at the top of her list." I pushed the empty cheesecake plate away. "Your turn. Tell me about you and Steven Grazer."

"Steven and my sister dated in high school. He was toxic

back then too, and he ruined her life. I wanted to hurt him for what he did, so I researched him. Being the puzzle king seemed his only point of pride. I wanted to dethrone him in honor of my sister."

"Did she approve of your scheme?"

"I didn't ask her. You haven't told me about your church's mission projects."

"The fund-raiser is for local needs. Our church supports a prison ministry and a senior work care group. They're amazing. They install ramps, grab bars, do minor plumbing and electrical work, even do yard and garden clean-up. They need funds for their projects because they don't charge. I could email you the complete list of programs and the summary of their work."

"How about if I put my contact information into your phone? I like to study before I show up at an event."

I handed him my phone, and he entered his information into it before returning it to me and picking up the check from the table. "Ready? We can take a walk around the hotel parking lot." He offered his hand to help me stand then continued to hold mine as we walked through the restaurant.

"Sounds divine, and thank you for a wonderful dinner, especially the cheesecake. I should probably do an hour on the treadmill rather than a parking lot lap."

As we left the restaurant, still holding hands, I wondered if Daniel's grudge against Steven was powerful enough for him to resort to murder.

# CHAPTER 8

The message light flashed on the bulky phone. Marta and Jon must still be out. I followed the prompts to retrieve the message, and the voice of Alma Zacho resonated in the room.

"Marta, this is Alma. I need to talk to you about a flash drive Steven has. He pocketed it by mistake at our last practice and promised to bring it to the competition. The drive has personal information about my students on it. Could you check his belongings for me?"

I replayed Alma's words a second time, without feeling the remorse I should for eavesdropping on a private conversation. Alma's voice sounded shaky, and I doubted she believed Steven snagged her computer stick accidentally. This was a clue.

I opened the room's closet where two bags sat, the pink one begging me to look inside. The click of the doorknob saved me from my darker impulses. I shut the closet and plopped on the bed.

"Hey, saw you and Jon at the restaurant. I thought the food was good. I had the fish special." I sprawled on the bed in what I hoped looked like a casual and innocent pose.

Marta nodded. "You were with the newsman. What did you tell him?"

Her accusatory tone startled me.

"Nothing. We talked about puzzle things, our families," I said.

"Did he mention Steven?"

"Why would Daniel mention Steven?" I asked.

"Daniel came to our house once. He ranted about how he planned to get even. If I had to guess who killed my husband, my chief suspect would be Mr. Elver. The man hated Steven, blamed him for getting his sister pregnant, which he didn't. And the great news anchor's sister now lives in a Minnesota facility for those not in touch with reality." Marta jerked open the drawer and threw her pajamas on the bed.

"He didn't say his sister was pregnant," I assured Marta.

"Don't let his good looks and charm fool you. Be careful."

Marta's spirited responses shocked me, but she'd opened the door for me to probe further. "What happened to the baby?"

"I don't know. Rumors said his sister gave the child up for adoption. She never named Steven as the father and never asked him to marry her. Her going away to stay with an aunt was the talk of the school. Daniel was a freshman, so he was in the same school. He was embarrassed by the gossip and angry because of the snide remarks about his beloved sister."

"You knew Steven and Daniel in high school?" I pulled an eye makeup remover sheet from my cosmetic case and worked on my upper eyelid.

"I told you about my family life. I wasn't in the social circles at school, but you'd have to be blind and deaf to miss the gossip of the Elver girl's humiliation. She was in the popular group, pretty, proper, and condescending. School opinion split between the sympathetic and those delighted she'd been caught in a scandal." Marta took her pajamas and toothbrush to the bathroom.

"Which was Steven?" I asked.

"Don't know. We didn't know each other then. Steven moved to our street about two years later. We never talked about her, but Steven might have known who the father was. He knew things about people, bragged to me that he was privy to people's hidden skeletons, even in high school." The buzz of the electric toothbrush prevented further conversation.

That remark triggered what Vera said earlier. She mentioned Steven knowing the camping group who booked their services when the bear attacked her husband. She also said Steven told her he could keep them from suing. The phone message from Alma indicated Steven knew something about her private or professional life too. The dead man knew other people's secrets but also had some of his own.

When Marta emerged from the bathroom, I pointed to the phone on the nightstand between the beds. "Message for you."

"Was it Steven's father? Was it about the funeral?" She stared at the phone.

"No, Alma Zacho called. Steven had a flash drive of hers, something from school. Once I started listening, I listened to the whole message. I'm never sure if you can get back to them once they've played. She and Vera are only a few doors down the hall if you want to check with her."

Marta recovered the message while I was yakking about it. After listening, she pulled the pink roller case from the closet and opened it on the foot of the bed.

"Pretty color," I said.

"Steven and I both packed in my bag. Pink's my color not his." She actually smiled.

Marta stacked the contents on the bed, felt in the side pockets, and unzipped each closure. "Nothing here. Guess he didn't bring it with him."

Despite the emptiness of the suitcase, a slight bulge appeared underneath the lining. If Marta noticed, she didn't react.

"Are you and Jon friends?" I asked.

"He invited me to dinner because he knew I'd be alone. I wouldn't call us friends, and he didn't consider Steven a friend."

"They shared a two-year-old affiliation as the Dissectologists," I said.

"Solving jigsaw puzzles together doesn't generate friendship. I think the group stayed together because they were successful and because Steven wouldn't let them quit."

I laughed. "How could Steven force them to stay on the team?"

"Perhaps with a missing flash drive or some photographs. That's what Jon pumped me about over dinner tonight. He wanted to know if I had access to Steven's picture file."

I grabbed my pillow and hugged it. Jon's obsession sounded like another clue. "Can you open Steven's computer?"

"Probably not. People think because we were married, we shared everything. We didn't."

The lump in the suitcase lining resurfaced in my mind. Should I mention it to Marta? Should I mention it to Sheriff Bergensen? The law officer had warned us not to make plans for tomorrow morning, and the thought of a full interrogation left me queasy. Even though I had nothing to hide, Ms. Bergensen had the most daunting stare in the world.

"Did you hear anything from the coroner?" I asked.

"Only that they couldn't release the body yet. I talked to Steven's father earlier today. He wants to do a traditional Sioux funeral, and I agreed. He thanked me for being cooperative and said he'd let me know about the arrangements."

"The coroner didn't mention the cause of death?" I pushed.

"No. I guess the sheriff will inform us tomorrow morning. I'm sure she suspects me. In murder cases, they say it's usually the spouse."

"Ms. Bergensen told me I was on her list because I brought Steven coffee."

Marta smiled for the first time that evening. "I know you didn't do it. I hope we still get to have the puzzle contest for singles."

"Have you been practicing? You seem confident about being a contender," I teased.

"I don't think I'll embarrass myself," Marta said. "I'm going to get some sleep."

"I'm going to call my sister. I'll step outside so I won't disturb you." I grabbed the room card and my phone.

Marta's assertion that she knew I hadn't killed Steven felt oddly comforting until I considered another avenue of thought. What if she knew I hadn't killed him because she had? The moon sliver gave little illumination, but the evenly placed stanchions provided enough light for me to feel comfortable.

"Mmm, hello?" Donna sounded groggy.

I pulled the phone away from my ear and looked at the time—eleven twenty-five. "Donna, I'm so sorry. I didn't look at the time. Go back to sleep. I'll call you tomorrow."

"Talk, Jane. I'm awake now, and I have a busy day ahead. What's up?" Donna didn't seem very alert, but I didn't want to annoy her further by calling her in the morning before breakfast.

"I feel like a real detective. I wanted to tell you what I've uncovered. Sheriff Bergensen will be back tomorrow morning for official interrogations, but I've been talking to some of my fellow suspects, and do you know what I've discovered?"

"No. Stop asking me questions I can't answer. Why did you call?" Donna sounded exasperated.

"Okay. I'll give you the list and why I think each person wanted Steven Grazer dead. Marta, the wife, didn't love him. He gave her an allowance. She wanted to be free, and she might get some insurance money to start anew."

Donna yawned and summarized, "Marta. Wife. Insurance."

I continued, "His teammates all have a reason to want him out of the picture. Vera Zacho's husband suffered a spinal accident in a wilderness excursion, and the clients, who were referred by Steven, threatened to sue Vera and her husband for endangerment. Isn't that ridiculous? Anyway, if the case should go to court, it could destroy Vera's business and leave them no money for her husband's care. Alma Zacho left a message asking Steven to return a flash drive that contained information about some students at the school. She sounded desperate. Donna? Donna?"

"Yes, Vera has financial problems, and Alma is terrified the flash drive might fall into the wrong hands," Donna summarized.

"Two more to go. Marta told me the professor, Jon Schott, begged her to find some pictures Steven had of him. What kind of pictures do you think he has? My mind has been racing in several different directions. Plus, I think the suitcase has something hidden under the lining."

"Oh Jane, your imagination is running amok. Tell me about the last one," Donna said.

"Daniel Elver. He thinks Steven ruined his sister's life, and he's close to his sister. We had dinner together. I don't think he could murder anyone, although he definitely disliked the man."

"You had dinner with Daniel Elver? Spill."

"He's just a nice man blessed with good looks."

"I'll need more details later, Sis. Back to the suspect list. Are you still on it?"

"Me? I didn't have any reason to want Steven out of the way."

"Right, Jane. So don't worry about the interrogation tomorrow."

"Don't hang up, Donna. Could you research poisons for me? What kind of poison makes you sleepy, something where you lose consciousness and die?"

"Why can't you?" She gave an overloud sigh.

"No computer, and my phone coverage is intermittent."

"I'll see what I can find. Let's both go back to sleep."

"I wasn't asleep. I'm in the parking lot," I said.

"What?" My sister sounded alert and alarmed. "Go to your room and lock the door. Anyone could've overheard what you were saying."

"I don't see anyone." I looked over my shoulder, a bit nervous now that my big sister seemed panicky.

"Keep talking to me until you get to your room," Donna ordered.

I went back inside the building and started down the hall. "I'm outside my room. Sorry I woke you. Go back to sleep."

"Next time, check the time before you call. Love you," Donna said.

I slipped the phone into my pocket and reached for the key card when I sensed someone behind me.

# CHAPTER 9

The key panel flashed red. I swiped again. Red. I slapped the card against the reader a third and fourth time. I heard someone breathing, and then a strong hand closed over mine.

"Let me try."

Uncertain of whether to jerk my hand away from the man's grasp or punch him in the nose, I slowly pivoted.

Jon Schott took the card, slid it over the slot, and the light turned green. He turned the knob but blocked my entry into the darkened room. "These things can be temperamental. I had to get mine replaced in the front office and saw you outside. Jane, may I remind you that the police think Steven was murdered? What were you doing alone in the parking lot?"

"Talking to my sister." I giggled self-consciously. "I woke her up. She wasn't too happy. I should've checked the time."

"Must have been urgent." Jon didn't move.

Mom raised us to be polite, but I think she'd understand my curtness with a possible killer. I ducked under his arm and scooted inside. "Thanks for helping me with the door, Jon. See you tomorrow."

"Jane, the next time you want to go out in the middle of the night, knock on room 118. I'm only a few doors down."

Inside, I leaned against the door, with my heart pounding, and listened to his receding footfalls on the carpeted hall. How absurd I'd acted. We'd been teammates earlier in the competition, and just now, Jon behaved like a gentleman concerned for my safety.

The bathroom light provided an illuminated ribbon, and I closed the door to do my nighttime routine. The mirror showed my hives were back, no surprise. I did gentle yoga breathing to relax myself when I got into bed, but sleep didn't come. The firm mattress caused me to toss and turn until I finally dozed off. I slept until I sniffed the intoxicating aroma of coffee and opened my eyes.

Marta emptied her pockets of creamers, sugar, and sweeteners. "Didn't know how you took yours, so I brought a little of everything. Two cups for each of us."

I pushed up on my elbows and squinted at the clock. "What time did the sheriff want us in the ballroom?"

"Nine. You have an hour." Marta, dressed, hair done, and makeup complete, thumbed through the *USA Today*. "Saw the rest of the group at breakfast. You'll have to hurry if you want something before the breakfast service closes."

I held up the coffee cup. "This is all I need. You're a lifesaver. I'll get some crackers from the vending machine. Wait! It's Sunday. Do you think we'll be allowed to attend church services?"

"I don't think the sheriff will allow us to come and go at will."

I reached for my devotional book. "How about if I read today's meditation and scripture out loud?"

Marta nodded, and I began with a prayer.

The ballroom, blocked off in sections, had long drapes, round tables, padded chairs, and the faint odor of floral cleaner. The Puzzle Twist representative stood next to a rectangular table, guarding his wares.

Marta led the way to the others. As relaxed as she'd been with me earlier, her demeanor changed to standoffish and wary when we joined Jon, Daniel, Vera, and Alma. Daniel appeared to be in reporter mode, speaking into his phone and describing the room and its occupants.

Sheriff Bergensen plodded from table to table, saving ours for last. Hands on hips, she addressed us. "Don't understand why, but the puzzle competition officials requested completion of the singles event. I'll interview hotel staff, food service, and anyone who came in touch with the deceased while you aficionados play your little games. The person providing the puzzles says the competition should finish within three hours. I'll interrogate you then."

Daniel produced a microphone and stuck it in front of the sheriff, asking her questions, which she deflected.

Jon whispered to me, "I think the sheriff raised her eyebrows to alarm us."

"It worked. Ms. Bergensen taught at our high school, and I feel like I'm back in economics class. She's served on almost every committee in our church, so I know she's a God-fearing woman, but she still intimidates me."

"If you're innocent, you have nothing to fear," Jon said. "You are innocent, aren't you?"

I rolled my eyes. "Haven't you heard of wrongful imprisonment?"

"I have, but I wouldn't worry about that if I were you. For the contest, the monitors allow two people to a large table. Want to share?"

"I came with Marta."

"She doesn't like puzzles," Jon said.

Marta, who overheard our conversation, rose. "I'm entering this competition. The coordinator waived the registration for me. You two sit together. I'd rather have a table by myself."

Jon and I picked up our belongings and said goodbye to Vera and Alma. We watched as Daniel, trying to obtain a scoop, danced alongside the sheriff as she marched toward the front of the room.

"I think I frightened you last night," Jon said.

"You did. Marta said you wanted some pictures Steven had. I'm curious why he would have anything of yours since you didn't seem to like him." Surrounded by at least fifty people, I felt at ease questioning a murder suspect.

"The pictures aren't mine. Steven took them or had them taken." His tone sounded acerbic.

I plunged ahead. "What kind of pictures?"

"Pictures of me with the dean's wife. We both serve on the same community service boards, such as the Youth Hockey League and Toys for Tots, and we attend the same faculty gatherings."

"Were the pictures altered?" I asked.

"No. The pictures show us with our heads together, smiling, and in one group shot, I have a hand on her shoulder. The photograph cropped the picture so it looks like we're alone."

"Wouldn't the dean's wife confirm the innocent nature of the shots?"

"She would, and so would her husband, but even the

implication of impropriety can wreck a person's reputation, and the timing is awful. I'm up for tenure this year. If the pictures appeared on the desks of the review committee members, they'd probably pass over me." Jon appeared dispirited.

I tried to reassure him. "I'm sure they'd listen to your explanation."

"They have plenty of candidates this year. Eliminating someone from consideration would speed the process." Jon twisted his neck from side to side, which emitted cracking sounds. "Steven could be mean and vindictive. He liked playing the tune and watching people dance."

Our discussion ended when the Puzzle Twist rep distributed the boxes and issued tournament guidelines. Then the competition administrator squeezed the bicycle horn, and thousands of pieces rattled onto tabletops.

The puzzle pieces seemed to magically slide into their spots today. I'd experienced the same sensation in the dental lab when coloration, contour, and shaping seemed to come together with minimal tweaking. My stomach began to growl, and my breathing quickened. Only a few pieces remained. I worked with both hands, fitting them into the remaining slots.

HONK. My hands flew from the pieces, and I craned my neck to find the origin of the horn's blast.

The competition coordinator began the applause, and we all joined. "We have a winner! This year's singles champion is Marta Grazer. As you know, Marta's husband, Steven, was known as the puzzle king, and she's the new puzzle queen. Well done."

Jon looked at my puzzle with two pieces left. "You were close, Jane. I could see a judge watching you. Can you believe Marta won?"

"Did she ever practice with you?"

"Never. Steven brought her to a few strategy sessions, but she sat in the corner like an obedient child," he said.

"Their marriage is an enigma." I glanced at Marta, whose pale face seemed flushed.

"To you and everyone who knew them. Should we rejoin the Zacho sisters?" Jon transferred the pieces back into the box and stood.

"I'll join you later. I'm going to congratulate Marta." I waved goodbye and headed toward Marta, who was speaking with the competition coordinator.

"Marta, congratulations." I gave her a hug where she sat. She remained stiff and didn't relax. "Are you feeling okay? Should I get you some water?"

She nodded to me and signed one of several papers the contest coordinator placed in front of her, and I rushed to the beverage table. I pushed the spigot of the container with lemon slices floating in the water and filled a glass for each of us.

Marta downed the water in one gulp before I sat.

"Take mine. I'll get another." I retraced my steps and found Alma Zacho.

Her apple cheeks grew rounder as she smiled in greeting. "Jane, Jon told us you only had a couple of missing pieces when the horn sounded. None of us can believe Marta won. That's bizarre. We all thought she hated jigsaw puzzles. You never know about people, do you?"

"She said she might surprise us, and she did. Alma, are you interested in lunch? I'm starving. I missed breakfast."

"Sure. I don't think Vera and Jon will go. Both are health nuts who love their kale, quinoa, and almonds. But I'd love a juicy hamburger with a side of greasy onion rings from the fairgrounds."

I groaned with pleasure. "With fried ice cream for dessert?"

"Absolutely."

"I should tell Marta." When I turned, I saw the boxy silhouette of Sheriff Bergensen blocking the view of where Marta sat. "On second thought, Alma, let's go. I want to delay my confrontation with the law."

Like schoolgirls skipping class, we hurried from the ballroom to the fairgrounds gate across the street after dutifully telling Jon and Vera of our destination.

We selected a food vendor booth proclaiming both burgers and dogs and a wooden picnic table with fewer flies than the others. Alma toyed with the idea of a chili cheese dog before we ordered burgers, onion rings, and milkshakes that were so thick we had to use spoons.

"Alma, I only met Steven once, but no one seems to have liked him. Did you?" I pegged Alma for a chatterer and hoped my instincts were correct.

Alma sucked on her straw. "It's not very Christian of me, but no. I didn't like him. He worked at the school for several years. Teachers and staff endeavor to get on the good side of the custodians. They can make life in the classroom easy or hard."

"And Steven?" I squirted a liberal amount of ketchup on my onion rings.

"Steven bargained, always expected compensation for his services. Teachers liked him when they first arrived, and then after six months, they avoided him." Alma took a big bite of her burger.

"Do you know why they changed their attitude?" I asked.

"Custodians have access to trash cans, desks, and closets.

From what I've heard, Steven's daily examination of the rooms made many uncomfortable. They'd find things in the drawers out of place, moved around. A janitor has no reason to open desks or look inside closets."

"Why didn't you like him?" I wondered if she'd confide in me.

"I'm the guidance counselor. I help students get into college or special programs after they graduate."

My plate had only a bit of greasy residue left on the surface when I pushed it away. "I remember those scandals of celebrity parents paying extravagant amounts of money to get their kids in the right schools."

"I didn't do anything like that. Couldn't afford it."

"Were you able to help in other ways?" I pushed.

"I learned over the years how to help students prepare better college packages by focusing on their strengths and downplaying their weaknesses."

"Doesn't every applicant do that?"

"They should. I kept the documents on a flash drive in case the college checked with me about the student's application." She took a sip of her soda. "The students trust me. Some of the information on that flash drive is highly confidential. It disappeared one day when I was at lunch."

"Are you sure he took it?"

"He told me he had. That's what he held over my head. Among other things, Steven could have torpedoed students' applications by exposing innocent indiscretions or immature behavior."

Suddenly we heard the whine of an ambulance, and we spotted an emergency vehicle turning into the hotel lot.

"We better head back. Don't want to be caught AWOL," Alma said.

I chucked our trash in the bin, and we jogged toward the exit. Our hurried pace didn't last long.

Alma bent over, breathing hard. "You go without me. No reason for both of us to be in trouble."

The sirens whined above the Ferris wheel's carnival music. Alma and I exchanged looks.

"Let's go," Alma said. "I want to find out what happened."

"I hope it isn't anyone we know." My stomach felt queasy, but I attributed the feeling to our greasy lunch.

# CHAPTER 10

To avoid the sheriff, we slipped through the hotel's front door then sauntered toward the ballroom, where a uniformed man guarded the entrance.

"What's going on? We heard the commotion," I said.

"Room's closed on sheriff's orders. No one goes in or out. She's conducting an investigation."

I offered an apologetic expression. "We went to get some lunch after the jigsaw competition. What happened in there?"

My attempt to charm the door protector didn't work. "You left the room? Sheriff Bergensen won't be happy. Names?"

Alma and I supplied our names, and he relayed the information over his handset. He didn't have to convey his boss's response because Sheriff Bergensen's orders squawked over the box as clearly as if she were next to us.

"Put Jane Dahl in handcuffs and bring her to me."

I protested, "You're handcuffing me for sneaking out for lunch?"

Ignoring my question, the officer slapped cuffs on me and marched me into the ballroom. Now I knew how Daniel Elver felt anytime he went outside. Like fans following a tennis match, heads pivoted to follow my "perp walk" toward the waiting sheriff. My gait wasn't stately or dignified. I stumbled a bit because arms help with balance, and mine were manacled behind my back.

The man rested his hands on my shoulders, indicating I should sit in the chair facing the sheriff.

"Jane, why did you run off?"

"We were hungry and didn't want hotel food. Alma and I just walked across the street for some fair food."

"I told you to stay here." The set line of the sheriff's mouth reminded me that she had no tolerance for people who didn't do what she said.

"We're back now. Have you interviewed the other suspects?"

"No. I planned to start with Marta, but I couldn't. Do you know why?"

Now I understood why Donna hated it when I asked unanswerable questions. I offered the sheriff a smart-mouth response. "Did she sneak out for a corn dog too?"

"Not funny! The medics took her to the hospital. When I went to her table, her head was down like she was taking a nap. Does that sound familiar? Marta wasn't sleeping. She was barely conscious. Good thing I approached her when I did, or we might have a second fatality on our hands."

I gasped. "Is she okay?"

"She was alive when the EMS crew arrived. Strange that you gave her a drink of water and then left. You also gave Steven a cup of coffee and left. After you served drinks to Steven and Marta, they both became very sleepy. Steven never woke, but I think we saved Marta."

"I didn't do anything to either of them! Should I pack some things for her? We're sharing a hotel room," I said.

She seemed surprised. "You told me you didn't know either of the Grazers until yesterday."

"I didn't. But Marta didn't want to stay alone, and my room had a second bed. I offered, and she accepted."

The skeptical look on the sheriff's face told me she didn't believe me.

"Do you think I should pack Marta a bag for her hospital stay?" I asked.

"No. You won't be going back to the room. You'll be going to jail until I sort this out. The evidence is mounting against you, Jane. I don't know why you did it, but I will figure it out."

A vision of the slight bulge in the bottom of Marta's suitcase blossomed in my mind. "If I'm going to jail, could I pack a bag for myself? I take thyroid pills, vitamin D, a multivitamin, and I just started on a blood pressure med."

The sheriff waved her hand, and a female officer joined us. "This is Officer Kelso. Give her your room key and tell her what you need. And Jane, we'll examine the pills and make sure they are what you claim they are. When Officer Kelso returns, she'll take you to a holding cell."

Officer Kelso, a tall woman with reddish-brown hair and a face smattered with the same shade of freckles, looked broad-shouldered in her uniform, but judging by her neck and wrist size, she probably had a slender frame. I guessed her to be about my age, late twenties, and wondered if we'd been in high school at the same time.

"Did you go to school in Fargo?" I asked.

"No. Let me know what you'll need, and I'll get it for you. Key card?" She held out her hand.

She didn't want to chitchat, so I told her my belongings were in the drawers on the right side and described my toiletry items.

While I waited for Officer Kelso to return, the sheriff moved up to a front table where Daniel Elver waited for his interrogation. I searched for Jon, Vera, and Alma, but they had their backs turned to me. I didn't know if their positioning was on purpose or by accident. I felt like a leper in biblical days with everyone shunning me.

Just like on television, Officer Kelso placed her hand on the top of my head as I struggled into the backseat, hands still bound behind my back. Also, like on the cop shows, people lined the sidewalks to watch my dramatic and disgraceful exit. I hoped the departure wouldn't be on the evening news. What would my family, church friends, and coworkers think?

My hope was in Marta's pink bag. Surely that case held Steven's blackmailing secrets hidden under the lining and not just lumpy padding from its old age. But I'd never know, since the bag would be in the hotel and I'd be in a jail cell.

The screeching sirens secured a clear path for us. People in cars pulled over, hoping to catch a glimpse of a villain, but I was the only one in the backseat. Instead of taking me to the Fargo jail, the officer detoured.

Officer Kelso looked over her shoulder. "Taking you to a smaller facility near the sheriff's office. Got word the reporters and lookie-loos are lined up by the jail entrance. Sheriff Bergensen doesn't want you to suffer that humiliation."

That action seemed out of character for Ms. Bergensen, but I appreciated the change of venue.

"Have you heard anything about Marta Grazer?" I asked.

"Still alive, last I heard." The officer pulled into a small parking lot behind the county court building. "We'll go through those doors. Looks like we have company after all."

The company she referred to was Daniel Elver and his videographer. I wished the waiting reporter had been someone else. Last night, Daniel and I held hands after a lovely meal. Today my hands were cuffed, and his would be pressing a microphone toward my face.

With Officer Kelso holding my arm, I hurried inside, head down, avoiding Daniel's face and ignoring his words. A new paint smell lingered in the empty and quiet corridor. There were no clicking computer keys, phone conversations, or people walking and talking.

"Awfully quiet. Am I the only one here?" I asked.

"The sheriff thought this would be safer and more isolated than the regular jail. You should thank her for not sticking you in the tank." Officer Kelso fished out a key and opened my room.

The single bed suggested this was solitary confinement. If this scene were playing out on the movie screen, there would have been ominous music and perhaps manic laughter from the guard. Instead, Officer Kelso pointed out the room's features, an unnecessary monologue taking less than a minute: bed, sink, toilet, shelves for belongings.

My sleuthing and looking for clues started as a frivolous activity, but the stark reality of this room reminded me of the seriousness of my plight.

"Excuse me, do I get my phone and my bag?" I asked.

"You may have *a* phone, but not *your* phone. The tech team is tracing your past calls, texts, checking your pictures, items stored in its memory."

"They won't find anything. I'm a boring person."

"I wouldn't say that." Officer Kelso smiled for the first time. "Anyone who gives two different people a beverage before they fall into a stupor is fascinating."

"How about my Bible? A jigsaw puzzle? Paper and pencil? My clothes? How long am I going to be in here?"

"Can't say." Officer Kelso pulled the door firmly. "Oh, we read you your rights, but you didn't say if you wanted us to call a lawyer."

"Can you call my sister?" I pictured Donna's face. She would not be happy to see me in a cell, even if it was a nice one.

"Is she your lawyer?"

"No, she's my sister," I said.

"I'll ask the sheriff. She wants to keep you away from other people."

"Even my sister?" I asked.

"Sheriff said no visitors for you. A lawyer would be the exception. I'll bring your food about six." Her footsteps echoed down the tiled hallway.

I walked the room's perimeter and counted thirty-two steps. A digital clock over the door told me the time was two forty-five and the day was Monday. As Marta guessed, we'd not been allowed to go to church services yesterday. But Sunday worship started my week on a positive note and helped me get through the rest of it. It wasn't only the preaching and the music, it was also being in the company of fellow believers that refreshed my soul.

I had nothing to do, nowhere to go, and no one to visit except my heavenly Father, who was always with me. I knelt on the cell floor beside my bed. "Father, I thank You for the many blessings You've given me, my family, my church family, my health, and the glorious beauty You provide for us every day. You know that today my heart is filled with chaos and confusion. I really need the strength and peace that only You can give. I also pray that You surround Jon, Vera, Alma, Daniel, and Marta with Your comfort. I need Your strength to reach out in love to them."

I prayed for a few more minutes, and when I stood up, I felt better able to face whatever might come.

Before Officer Kelso returned, I'd lapped my cell ten times clockwise and ten times counterclockwise. Pacing calmed me, and God had taken away my overwhelming fear.

The officer unlocked the door. "We inventoried the items from your bag. Here's your clothing. The lab boys have your meds. You'll get them when they finish. Brought your Bible and a notepad and pen."

I reached for my Bible as if it were a lifeline. "What about the bag?" I asked.

"You'll get it back if you're released."

I inhaled sharply. "*If* I'm released? May I have my phone? Can I call my family?"

"This isn't a hotel."

After placing the items I'd received on the two shelves, I plopped down on the bed. With Marta's bag at the hotel, I might never know what the puffy section behind the lining contained.

# CHAPTER 11

When stuck in a cell, time passes at a turtle's clip. I went over the suspects, their motives, and what each stood to gain. From my vantage point, I was the only person the sheriff should not target as responsible for the murder of Steven Grazer. Daniel, the broadcaster, wanted vengeance for his sister. Jon, the professor, wanted tenure, which required an unblemished reputation, so he needed the photographs showing him with the dean's wife. Vera, the outfitter and guide, needed financial security for herself and her disabled husband. She wanted assurance they wouldn't face a catastrophic lawsuit that could destroy them. Alma, the guidance counselor, needed the flash drive with her students' confidential information on it.

Pacing the perimeter of my quarters helped me concentrate. I understood why each wanted Steven out of the way. But why attack Marta? She probably didn't even know she possessed Steven's blackmail stash. I didn't know myself, because I couldn't access Marta's bag. My assumption might be crazy conjecture. My mind leapfrogged from a bump in a bag's lining to contraband material.

Ponderous footsteps sounded, a key turned in the lock, and Sheriff Bergensen stuck her head inside the door. "Come with me, Jane."

"Should I get my things?" I asked.

"Leave them." She marched ahead of me to a room with basic furniture but no personal touches.

"How's Marta?" I sat, expecting a lengthy interrogation.

"The hospital released her."

"That's good news." I sighed and relaxed.

"Not all good." Ms. Bergensen peered at me over the frames of her glasses. "Marta reported her hotel room had been ransacked. Strange, isn't it?"

She expected an answer, so I agreed.

"Marta said her pink bag was missing while your black one was still there."

"If mine is at the hotel, maybe the officer packed my belongings in her bag. Steven blackmailed people, and I think the Grazers' bag has something in it he was hiding. If we examine it together, perhaps the evidence will tell us who the murderer is."

"Jane, you're not a detective."

"Please look in the bag." I yammered on about the bulge in the lining, the photos Jon Schott wanted, the flash drive Alma needed, the list of people and addresses Vera wanted. I told her about Daniel's sister and his animosity toward Steven.

"Jane, you're rambling. Be succinct."

"Can we check it?"

The sheriff lumbered to the door and asked Officer Kelso to fetch the bag they'd brought from my hotel room.

"I didn't have anything to do with the death of Steven Grazer. And I didn't harm Marta," I said.

The sheriff nodded to the officer and waited until she came back with the pink bag. She placed it on the desk and motioned for me to open it. "Is this your bag?"

"No. It's Marta's. It's natural that your officer assumed a pink bag would belong to me and the black bag to Steven and Marta."

"Well?"

I unzipped the bag and saw no puffiness in the lining. I slapped the surface on all sides, feeling nothing but the metal ribs underneath. "It's gone. Something was in there. I know what I saw. Ms. Bergensen, I shape and contour false teeth and dentures, so my eyes gravitate to irregularities. I noticed it as soon as Marta opened the bag. When I heard about the blackmail items, the hiding spot made sense."

Ms. Bergensen ignored me and focused on the bag, running her fingers around the edge of the suitcase, tugging gently until a section peeled back at her pressure. "I can see someone cut the lining and tucked the frayed ends back into the frame, but no proof of hidden items. Jane—"

I held up my hand to stop her. "I should have told you about my suspicions."

"Now your safety is a problem. Marta told everyone in earshot that you intentionally took her bag. So, whoever tore the room apart believes you accessed the bag's contents. Do you see where this leads?"

"Yes. If the murderer thought the contents were a reason for killing Steven, I could be next on the list, and Marta is still in danger. My sleuthing boomeranged."

"I could keep you here," Ms. Bergensen said.

"What if I went back to the hotel? If the killer doesn't think you blame me, he or she might make a mistake. But I don't know what I'll tell Marta. I don't want to tell her that you looked through her bag."

"You never had trouble coming up with outlandish concoctions in high school," she said.

"I made a lot of mistakes when I was younger," I admitted.

"You did, but you were always inventive and creative until the accident. Teachers see many students pass through their classes, and some seem destined for a promising future—you were such a person. Jane, you need to forgive yourself for what happened. Noreen was the driver not you."

"Noreen never talked to me after she got out of the hospital, but she wrote me a long letter saying she blamed me for convincing her to go out that night, encouraging her to drive too fast and drink too much. She wrote that I'd destroyed her life."

"And you let her accusation destroy yours." Ms. Bergensen arched an eyebrow. "When was the accident?"

"Ten years ago."

"Jane, were you at fault?"

"I've asked myself that a million times." I shook my head. "I don't know."

"Sabotaging your life, hiding out in your parents' basement for five years, then in a dental lab, and denying yourself a social life doesn't change your friend's situation."

"How do you know what I've been doing?" When I looked into Ms. Bergensen's eyes, I saw genuine concern and compassion.

"Your parents and I have attended Bible studies together regularly for the past ten years. They've shared their concerns about you. Many church members have been praying for you."

"They have?"

"Yes. I care about all my students, but your reaction to Noreen's unfounded deceits broke my heart. You should go see her," Ms. Bergensen said.

"I don't know where she is."

"I do. I've kept in touch with the family."

My jaw felt like it dropped to the basement on a fast elevator. Ms. Bergensen kept in touch with Noreen? She thought I was creative and inventive? Well, she'd done a terrific job of fooling me in high school.

"Jane, you can focus on resolving your issues with Noreen later. Now, we have to catch a killer."

"Right. What can I do?" I asked.

"Tonight, the prime suspects will check out of the hotel. You gleaned plenty of information about them before. Could you try it again? But you must put my number on speed dial, and don't let anyone get you alone."

I grinned at the invitation to be a valuable sidekick to Sheriff Bergensen. "I can't see any of the puzzlers as a murderer. Have you looked at other people? How about someone from Steven's family? Steven disappointed them, and they didn't like Marta. That might explain the attack on both of them."

"I considered it, but the why doesn't make sense. The Grazers were married for eight years. If Steven's family wanted to express disapproval, they would have done it earlier, don't you think?"

Flattered she'd asked my opinion, I responded with the succinct style answer she preferred. "Yes."

"I'll explain to Marta about the bag mix-up, but I'd like you to concentrate on Daniel Elver. He has a way of deflecting all questions, even mine," the sheriff said.

"Since you knew about Noreen and me, do you know what happened to Daniel's sister?"

"She got pregnant and was convinced to give the baby up for adoption. Her mental state has been delicate since then, and she's been in and out of clinics and hospitals."

"Daniel believes Steven was the child's father. Was he?" Since Ms. Bergensen seemed to be an authority on happenings at the high school over the past decade, I hoped she'd know.

"Gossip fingered Steven, and he didn't deny it. In fact, he reveled in the attention, but I think the father was our school's valedictorian, who had received an appointment to the naval academy. The whole community cheered about his success."

"Nate Wilkins? He died, didn't he?"

"Yes, in the service, less than a year after his graduation."

I sighed. "Daniel's sister had a double loss. The baby and the boy she loved."

The sheriff pushed the lining back under the suitcase frame. "You try, Jane. Your hands are smaller than my mitts."

When we finished, I replaced my belongings in Marta's suitcase for the return trip to the hotel. "Why don't I suggest a farewell dinner at the hotel? I could share my lockup experience," I said. "Sheriff Bergensen, who do you think killed Steven and tried to kill Marta?"

"If I tell you, you'll act differently when you're with that person, and I might be wrong. I need any facts you can gain to prove me right or wrong."

Initially, I thought her idea of using me as bait was a joke. Now I realized she was deadly serious.

# CHAPTER 12

The sheriff marched me into the hotel as if we'd never shared a confidential moment. Stone-faced, she requested the manager ask Jon, Daniel, Vera, Alma, and Marta to report to the lobby. When I attempted to begin a conversation, she glared and stepped away from me. I got the point, and we waited in silence for the others to arrive.

With all suspects accounted for, Sheriff Bergensen explained my return. "We've released Jane Dahl. We now have evidence she was not involved. Both Marta and Steven received Rohypnol, enough to render them unconscious, but that's not what killed Steven. We will continue to investigate, but I can't hold you. I thought we might have a farewell dinner, compliments of the department, before you go home."

Marta dashed toward me. "You took my bag! Why?"

"It was a mix-up. The officer who packed my things assumed the pink bag was mine. The sheriff said someone ransacked our room. Were you there? Are you okay? What did they take?"

"I didn't find anything missing, and you'd left with *your* stuff and *my* bag."

A second bag comment. I glanced at the sheriff. "Since my

things are in Marta's bag, may we go to our room and switch them?"

Marta waved a room key. "They changed the code."

I followed Marta across the lobby and down the hallway on the right. The entry worked flawlessly.

"What happened to you? They said you passed out, just like Steven. Everyone was frantic. We didn't know if you'd live or die."

Marta's rigid posture relaxed. "I was lucky. Someone gave me enough Rohypnol to make me unconscious."

"The date rape drug," I said.

"Yes. It's usually administered in a drink, and you brought me water. That's why the investigators suspected you."

"I would never—"

She indicated for me to switch my clothes to my black bag.

"Marta, they didn't even give me the bag in jail. The officers thought I might find something in the bag to use to harm myself. They even took my shoelaces. How can you harm yourself with shoelaces?"

Marta zipped her bag closed. "I can't wait to get out of this place, but then I have to go home."

"Marta, I don't know anything about Native American funeral customs, but if you need help, call me."

My offer caused Marta's eyes to fill. "His parents have the burial scheduled for Thursday. It's private, but I'd like someone to talk to when I get home."

The room phone rang, and Sheriff Bergensen reminded me they were waiting for us in the lobby.

"You want to put your bag in my car? I don't know when the sheriff will let us go."

I opened and closed every drawer, checked the closet and

bathrooms to confirm we weren't leaving anything behind.

After stowing the luggage, we walked to the ballroom to meet the others.

"You're here." Sheriff Bergensen announced the obvious. "After we interviewed the other contestants and puzzle officials, we let them go. After supper, you may leave the hotel, but don't leave the area. We may need to follow up with you." We lined up like second graders and followed her into the dining room, where the hostess led us to a large booth in the back. We scooted around the horseshoe banquette. Officer Kelso and Sheriff Bergensen took chairs on the opposite side, partially blocking the aisle and preventing anyone from making a hasty departure.

The sheriff delayed her statement until we all had drinks and meal orders submitted. Although she didn't stand, she lifted her shoulders and inhaled, which created the perception that she was standing at a podium.

"Here's the scuttlebutt about Steven's death and the attempt on Marta's life. Both received Rohypnol, which caused them to lose consciousness. Then Steven received a second and deadly poison. We saved Marta because she only had Rohypnol in her system. I don't have enough evidence to make an arrest, but if anyone needs to leave the Fargo-Moorhead area, let my office know."

Although the sheriff didn't single anyone out, I watched my table mates squirm, fidget, and cast distrustful glances at each other. The arrival of the food forestalled questions or comments.

In an aside, I asked Marta if she'd like the others to come to her house for a meal after the graveside service on Thursday. She shrugged, which I took for a go-ahead.

I tapped my glass to get everyone's attention. "Steven's family has arranged the service and burial for Thursday. I plan to go to Marta's after the service and take a deli platter in case neighbors stop by to pay respects. Would any of you like to come?"

Daniel nodded. "Could I go to the funeral with you?"

"No outsiders. Sioux tradition," Marta said.

I'd thought Daniel so charming, but that question squashed my interest in him. He wasn't thinking of Marta. He was thinking of getting another story for the six o'clock news.

"Jane, I could ask the station to cater a meal at Marta's house. How many people do you think will be there?" Daniel asked. "If you don't mind, I'd like to include my crew."

Vera looked up from her vegetarian plate. "If Marta doesn't mind your crass suggestion, I do. Daniel, a man was murdered. Don't use a burial as your personal sideshow to increase viewership for your station."

"I agree with Vera. Jane, we can all contribute. I'll bring a casserole and some fried chicken," Alma said.

Jon and Vera offered to fill in with sides, salads, and rolls. Then Daniel piped up and offered desserts.

"Sweets will be great, but please don't bring your microphone, Daniel." My comment generated a few laughs and a half-hearted smile from Daniel.

"Steven's parents said the service will be at eleven. Jane, I'll leave the house open if you want to come early." Marta looked at the others. "Thanks. I know none of you liked my husband."

"Not liking Steven is no excuse for bad manners toward you, Marta," Jon said.

The table talk slanted my opinion on both men, and Jon's last comment elevated him in my books.

Marta's house occupied the fourth spot in a row of carbon-copy structures, only distinguished by differing paint colors. The Grazers' home was the dingy gray with peeling paint. All front yard depths consisted of three concrete slab widths from the sidewalk to the front stoop. I made a show of opening the front door after noting an audience of children who'd stopped their games to stare at me and adults who hid behind lifted curtains and doors slightly ajar.

I placed my deli platter on the kitchen's Formica counter. The L-shaped room had cabinets with chipped white paint on two sides. The gas stove was on the wall with the entry door, and the fridge was on the remaining wall. A tall café table for two provided the only seating. Most of the linoleum's pattern had disappeared due to years of use. The apple motif curtain theme reappeared in the toaster cover and the potholders. We couldn't set a serving line in the kitchen. I checked the plates and glasses and decided to ask someone to bring paper goods rather than clog up the kitchen doing dishes after the meal.

The living area had two card tables with half-finished jigsaw puzzles. Other puzzle boxes ringed the room, stacked in columns and sorted by the number of pieces. That area was out for serving. We could use the small dining room by moving the table against the wall to serve as a buffet. This option left space for visiting. I pictured the room in an hour, with people elbow to elbow in this tiny home, and wondered how many of the Grazers' neighbors would show up. I wasn't sure whether Marta had told them about funeral arrangements or if they only knew what they'd read in the papers or heard from the television.

I called Jon about getting paper goods and ice for the drinks before allowing my nosy bent full rein. I checked the two bedrooms, and both looked obsessively tidy. The medicine cabinet told me Steven took a high blood pressure medicine and a thyroid tablet. I tucked one of each into my pocket. I'd mention the prescriptions to Sheriff Bergensen and give her the pills to analyze. What better hiding place for Rohypnol than a prescription bottle in the victim's home?

Marta said the service started at eleven, so she wouldn't be home for at least an hour. I had time for sleuthing. If I were a blackmailer, I'd want a hard copy as well as a digital one, so I started with the office desk drawers. Nothing. Neither the house nor the shed out back yielded any clues. When my phone dinged with Jon's message saying he was five minutes away, I abandoned my search and went out front to wait. Parking would be a problem.

When Jon arrived, he handed me an aluminum foil pan of green bean casserole and placed two bags of paper products on the counter. "Bought a Styrofoam cooler for the ice. It's in the trunk." Jon looked grim.

"Glad you thought of that. We can put the cooler in the kitchen. I thought we'd set up the food in the dining room," I said.

"Jane, I got another blackmail note. I thought it would end with Steven's death."

"Oh no! Jon, you must tell Sheriff Bergensen." I opened the door and stood in front to let Jon pass.

"I don't think I'm going to pay this one. When I knew it was Steven, I imagined negotiating and getting the photographs. With another person pulling the strings, well, there's no end to it. I'll not only lose my chance at tenure but probably my university position if the pictures are made public, and the dean's wife would suffer needless humiliation." Jon put the cooler on the floor.

"I'm so sorry." I sensed his distress and hugged him.

He shook free of my embrace. "I wouldn't have come if you hadn't called and asked me to pick up the plates and napkins. Why are we paying tribute to a man we despised?"

"We're doing it for Marta. I don't think her life with Steven was easy," I said.

"Steven made everyone's life miserable. I have tea and soft drinks in the car." Jon walked out without a backward glance.

Sheriff Bergensen hadn't known about the blackmail scheme until I told her. She needed to be aware that the puzzle king's tentacles extended beyond his grave.

# CHAPTER 13

When Marta arrived at her home after the funeral, she seemed antsy and surprised by the number of people who congregated in her dining room. I considered it odd that none of the neighbors embraced her or offered to help in the kitchen. In a sleeveless black dress without adornment, the widow welcomed guests who shook her hand or spoke a few words. The five of us from the puzzle tournament seemed to be Marta's closest friends, and we barely knew her.

Alma replenished the dining room table, and Jon scooped ice into cups and helped with drinks. The food and guests were gone within an hour, except for the puzzle people and Sheriff Bergensen.

"Marta, sit. You look exhausted. We'll clean up." Alma indicated one of the tall kitchen chairs.

Daniel pulled out the other. "Marta, how was the service?"

"Daniel, stop being a reporter for five minutes," Vera said.

"I'm curious. Was there an indoor service or just the one at the graveside?"

Marta shook her head. "Steven's parents arranged everything. You should talk with them about the traditions."

I pointed to the items on the counter. "I jotted down the names and addresses of those who brought something. Most were in disposable containers, but a couple brought their own dishes."

"I don't know these people," Marta said.

"I guess neighborhoods turn over all the time, don't they?" I said.

"This one does. I'd say every house on the street is a rental except ours. People move in and out every weekend. Steven and I went to work and came home. We didn't mingle," Marta said.

Her comment triggered something her husband said the first day I met him. Steven said his wife didn't have a job, just traded junk at the antique mall.

Daniel leaned toward Marta. "Did you know Steven when he was in high school? My sister and Steven were in the same class."

Sheriff Bergensen's phone shrilled, and we all got quiet.

"I'll be right there." The sheriff slapped the phone back into its holster. "Lab has the toxicology report. I have to leave, and Daniel, perhaps you should leave too. I think you've badgered Marta enough."

Reluctantly, Daniel vacated his spot opposite Marta and followed the sheriff out, quizzing her about the toxicology screen.

"Thank you for doing this. Why don't I order pizza? I know you didn't get much to eat. I never expected so many neighbors," Marta said.

Alma, Vera, and Jon demurred, collected their belongings, and left. But because Marta's big eyes seemed so sad, I caved.

"I could stay," I said.

"Could you spend the night?" Marta asked. "We can return the dishes, and maybe you could go with me to the bank tomorrow."

"I don't have to work until Monday. I can stay tonight."

Marta sighed. "Thanks. I'll make you a bed on the sofa, and I can give you an oversized T-shirt for sleeping. I also have a new toothbrush and floss from my last dental appointment. I know how important oral hygiene is to you."

Later, when Marta went to pick up the pizza, I called my sister. "Donna, do you know where I am?"

"In Disney World? No, Jane, I don't know where you are, and you know I hate you asking me these inane questions."

"Sorry. I'm spending the night at Marta Grazer's house."

"The widow of the murdered man?" Donna asked.

"Yes, she doesn't have any friends. I'm like her bestie now. I feel sorry for her."

"Can she hear you?" Donna asked.

"No, she went to get pizza for dinner. The other puzzlers and I put together a lunch for her after the funeral, and the neighbors who showed up were more curious than sympathetic. They didn't seem to know her at all, but they were good eaters. Cleaned us out. Oh, I hear her car, gotta go."

"Jane, you don't know this woman. Isn't she a suspect too?"

"Bye, Sis." I slipped my phone into my pocket as Marta entered, carrying the pizza and a bottle of soda.

The coffee scent woke me, and I inhaled and stretched. I heard the rattle of a garbage can from the back of the house before Marta appeared.

"Oh, I didn't mean to wake you. I couldn't sleep, but I tried to keep quiet. Coffee?"

"Please. I take mine black." I remembered that Steven also took his coffee black as I moved into the kitchen and sat in one of the chairs.

"Breakfast? I have eggs," Marta said.

"No, thanks. I'm not a breakfast eater. I usually grab a fruit cup or some yogurt midmorning."

"I'll treat you to a late breakfast after we go to the bank. I found the account numbers and a key to a safety deposit box." Marta handed me a mug with a high school emblem in gold and green.

"Is this mug from the school where Steven and Alma worked?"

"Yes, we have a set," Marta said.

"Oh, you might add the school to your list of things to do. Steven may have things stored there too. I know you have a million things on your mind, but that popped into my head when you handed me the mug," I said.

"We could go there before stopping by the bank. They're holding summer sessions, so I know they open early. How soon can you be ready?"

That comment was a definite hint not to linger over my coffee but jump up and use the toothbrush she'd provided. The bathroom mirror didn't offer a sharp reflection because of its age, which I considered a plus. I slipped back into the black slacks and patterned top I'd worn yesterday, finger-combed my short hair, and removed my phone from my pants pocket. Dead. Marta's phone was the rival brand, and my car charger was in Donna's SUV.

"I'm ready. Want me to drive?" I offered.

"No. My car is old but reliable, and I know the way. I wonder if Steven had an insurance policy through the school or some sort of savings. I know he's due a paycheck. I'll ask in the office when we pick up his belongings." Marta locked her house and followed me toward the dented Kia.

Marta's gray car meshed with the fading gray exterior of the Grazer home. As I fastened my seat belt, I noticed a camera in the backseat.

"You still use a camera? I thought those became obsolete along with calendars and calculators when smartphones arrived."

"That one gives me close-up details, perfect for my antique business." Marta zigged through back streets, and soon the high school was visible. Instead of parking in the lot, she pulled into the circle, leaving enough space for another car to pass.

"Want me to come with you?" I knew she expected this to be a quick visit, or she would've parked in a legitimate spot.

"No, I'll get some bags from the trunk and get his stuff. Steven never kept much here, and the office staff won't be able to tell me anything this soon, so it'll be quick. I want to get to the bank."

While she was inside, I took a better look at the camera. A telephoto lens lay beside it. I associated that lens style with distant nature shots, not close-ups of an antique vase or cabinet.

Marta flashed a smile when she emerged from the building with a bag over each shoulder and carrying a box. "Could you pop the trunk, please?"

I leaned across the front seat and pulled the lever. Before I could get out to help, she'd slammed the lid and opened the driver's door.

"They said each employee has a small insurance policy, but the company won't pay the claim until the court addresses the cause of death. His salary went directly to the bank. I need cash. It's all working out."

She seemed almost giddy. Before today, she'd never shown more than a hesitant smile, and her attitude had always been cautionary and tentative. I repeated a question I'd asked her yesterday and this morning. "Do you truly need me to go to the bank with you?"

"Steven never took me to the bank. The tellers won't recognize me, and you probably know how banking things work better than I do." She drove faster than I liked, particularly as she glanced my way when talking.

She wheeled into a front spot. We'd arrived before the bank opened, but I didn't suggest a second cup of coffee. Marta seemed determined to get inside the bank as soon as possible after her husband's internment. Even though I'd met the Grazers only a week ago, I knew Steven controlled the purse strings, and Marta seemed eager to grab them for herself.

She got out of the car and waited for my exit before clicking the remote lock. Cupping her hand over her eyes, she peered inside. "People inside, but they'll make us wait until it's ten sharp."

Even though we only had a few minutes to stand outside in the July heat, I felt the perspiration building on my forehead. "The bank was established in 1913. I hope they've added air conditioning." I pointed to the etching in the plaque by the door.

Marta stepped back when an employee opened the door to

admit us. "I'd like to see someone about my husband's account. I'm Mrs. Steven Grazer."

A man in a tan jacket with a bank logo printed on the pocket heard Marta's request and hurried to meet us. "Mrs. Grazer, I'm Nathan Loomis, the bank manager. May I offer you my condolences? I saw the news about your husband in the paper. He was our customer for over fifteen years. Come into my office and tell me how the bank may help you. Coffee?"

"Please, black is fine," I answered before Marta because I was desperate for caffeine. The half cup I'd managed to swallow at Marta's didn't equal my typical intake of two large mugs each morning.

Mr. Loomis picked up the handset and asked for coffee for all three of us. The employee who opened the door brought in coffee on a tray with creamer packets, sugar, and stirring sticks. When Marta saw how greedily I grabbed the small paper cup, she suggested I drink hers as well.

Marta placed the piece of paper with the account numbers and the safety deposit key on the edge of the desk. "As you can imagine, Mr. Loomis, I'm a bit short on funds. I'd like to get the bank account transferred into my name so I can pay some bills we have. I'd also like to get into the safety deposit box."

"I can only help you with one account," the bank manager said.

"How many did Steven have?" Marta leaned forward, and I heard the incredulity in her voice.

"He had three. He listed your name on one, but the other two have the balance of his funds. He had a joint account with his father. The other is in your husband's name only. We can't disburse those funds until we receive instructions from the

217

court. I believe Steven used that account primarily for rental property transactions. He made a wise investment by buying up the properties on the street where you live. Those houses stay at ninety percent occupancy. Never could convince him to move out of that neighborhood. He said he liked keeping an eye on his tenants."

I rose and placed the empty cup in the trash receptacle. "Would you like me to wait outside?"

"No." Marta turned from me back to Mr. Loomis and waved the distinctive key. "What about the safety deposit box? I have the key. I would guess the deeds to the rental properties and our home will be there. I would like to retrieve the contents."

"I'm sorry. The safety deposit box is attached to the joint account Mr. Grazer had with his father. Only your father-in-law can access the box now."

"What about the account in my name?" Marta asked.

"That money I can give you. But we would love for you to continue being our customer," Mr. Loomis said.

"How much?" Marta's voice no longer sounded cordial.

"Five thousand."

"Five thousand? I worked for that man for eight years in addition to cleaning his house, cooking his meals, ironing his clothes, putting up with his insults, and having to beg for money. Can you believe he left me a measly five thousand when he has rental properties and two 'substantial' bank accounts?"

"There are legal requirements on the bank holdings of a deceased. We must receive an executor letter to close the account, unless—"

Marta held up a hand to stop him. "You can give me the whole five thousand, right?" She stood. "I'll wait."

I wished I'd followed Marta in my car, but I hadn't, and now I'd be stuck with her, a woman scorned and insulted by her husband from beyond the grave. I'd just witnessed a display of her anger at being under Steven's thumb for eight years. Could that anger have festered enough for her to hatch a plan to murder her husband?

But she couldn't be involved. She'd been an attempted murder victim too.

# CHAPTER 14

**M**r. Loomis counted out the five thousand dollars in bills of hundreds and fifties and placed them in an envelope. Marta watched the counting and reached for the package with zombielike movements.

I tentatively placed a hand on her shoulder and guided her toward the exit. Without speaking, she gave me her car keys. I opened the passenger door and waited until she reached for her seat belt before closing it. Watching Marta's robotic movements hit me in the gut. I remembered the devastation I'd felt after the car accident, leaving my friend Noreen in intensive care and her face permanently scarred. I'd had no one to prop me up during those dark days. Donna and her husband had just moved to North Carolina, and phone calls didn't make a dent in my anguish and remorse. My parents expected me to know that I wasn't at fault, but my heart was in the hospital bed with my best friend, who refused to let me visit.

"Okay if I stop at that sub shop and get sandwiches for lunch?"

Marta nodded but continued staring out the window.

"I get the steak and cheese. What would you like?"

"That's fine," Marta said softly. "After we eat, I want to go home and empty the whole place."

I accepted the sandwich meals from the drive-through window server and passed the bags to her. "Marta, I'm not sure of the best way to get to your house."

My ruse worked because she sat up, focused on her surroundings, and gave me directions. We soon parked on her street with the houses lined up like spice cans on a shelf.

Marta looked down the row after unlocking the front door. "No wonder the neighbors didn't act friendly. Steven never fixed up our own house, so I'm sure he limited repairs to the rentals."

"I'm famished. I should change my habits and start eating breakfast." I jabbered to fill the silence as I distributed the chips, wrapped subs, and drinks on the kitchen table for two.

Marta poked her straw through the crisscross cut of her drink lid. "I'm going to get rid of everything in this house. I'll sell what I can at the antique mall—I've got some items here that qualify as antiques—and I'll give the rest to charity if I can find anyone who wants what I have."

"You'll need some things," I ventured.

"The house, like everything else, is probably in Steven's name. So I'm going to sell this junk before someone tells me I can't and then leave this place," Marta said.

After lunch, Marta began dragging out boxes and bags. I didn't remind her that the sheriff had specified we not leave the area.

I took another tack. "Where will you go?"

"New Orleans or Canada. We'll start in the living room. I know a shop where I can sell Steven's huge jigsaw collection. Tape those puzzle boxes and stick them in the leaf bags," Marta ordered.

The strangeness of her relocation choices baffled me. "Why New Orleans? Why Canada?" I sealed the boxes with tape and put them in bags. After doing a rough count in my head, I surmised the room held over three hundred puzzles. I set aside some for my own purchase.

"New Orleans is warm, with antique shops on every corner, or so I've heard. As for Canada, starting a new life in a new country is appealing, and I could use the private ATM until I can establish myself."

I shivered. A "private ATM" was the term she'd told me Steven used for his sudden influxes of money. I paused in my repetitive tasks. Jon told me he'd received another request for money. Had it been from Marta, or was it a delayed demand from Steven? Had Marta known about the blackmailing scheme? The camera and lens in her car might signify her involvement.

"Marta, did you know that Steven's teammates were being blackmailed? They all told me that was the main reason they participated with him in competitions."

She ignored my comment, folded the two card tables that had held unfinished puzzles, and pointed to the last stack of boxes in the corner. "Almost done in here. We should tackle the dining room, office, bedroom, and then the kitchen. That room will be the hardest."

Her demands stuck in my craw. The woman expected me to work side-by-side with her until she cleaned out the whole house. The place was small, but I hadn't signed up for a cleaning, packing, moving gig. Still, my curiosity trumped my good sense, so I rephrased my unanswered question.

"Jon told me Steven had some pictures of him with a married woman. Do you know what he was talking about?"

"Sure. I took the pictures. They were of Jon and the dean's wife. I even got one with his hand on her shoulder. Steven gave me a pitiful amount to follow his teammates around, even the newscaster after he showed up at our house. He told me what he wanted, and I did it. He said we would have a huge payday. But now I understand what Steven meant was *he*, not *we*, would get money. Let's pack the dishes from the china cabinet. That piece of furniture might be worth something."

We moved to the dining room and placed the dishes and serving pieces on the table for easier access.

"But you knew," I said softly.

"I knew what Steven was doing. I expected to get my half and leave him, but that didn't happen. He strung me along, just like he did all the others."

The truth hit me with the clarity of a crisp fall day. The pain in my stomach caused me to wince and lean over. Did she realize what she'd said?

"You knew you'd never be free unless you acted." I let the unthinkable wash over me. "But Marta, you almost died," I said.

"Hardly. I gave myself a half dose of the Rohypnol, enough to make me sleepy. Steven got those pills from a high school kid. He threatened to report him, so that boy did lots of favors for my husband."

She wanted me to admire her cunning plan, so I obliged.

"Taking the drug yourself was smart. No one suspected you."

"Yeah. I guess I pointed the finger at you. I took the water you gave me, dropped the pill in, and tossed it back before I lost my nerve." She surveyed the dining room. "Look at what we've accomplished. This room's done. On to the office."

"So you have the blackmail files?" I asked, reluctant to ask about the murder of her husband. So far, she'd only admitted to giving her husband a potion that put him to sleep.

"I do." With pride, she led me to the bathroom, emptied a tissue box, and removed a flash drive from the bottom. "Steven placed all the files on Alma's drive. My pictures of Jon, the history of Vera's Boundary Waters trips and client complaints are right here. Vera and her husband didn't have many negative comments so Steven coerced a couple of teachers to take a trip with them and stage problems. Got out of hand."

Marta's comment that it "got out of hand" meant that a man had been permanently crippled. Even then, Steven had held a lawsuit over their heads, all for the glory of being a puzzle king. My dumbfounded stare stimulated her to elaborate.

She led me back to the office and indicated the drawers I should pack. "People love money, don't they? Steven suggested comments Vera's clients might include in their letters, and now their business is hanging by a thread."

"You helped Steven with everything?" I slowed my packing.

"Of course. He promised me half. I was going to use my part to leave him and start a new life. Today, Mr. Loomis says the money went only into Steven's account. Jane, I had to hold my hand out and hope he'd give me money. I could've been a great antique dealer. I have a gift for finding treasures."

"Steven should've appreciated you." I praised Marta, who obviously wanted recognition for her achievement, but her triumph was blackmailing and damaging lives not as an outstanding antique dealer.

"The dissected puzzle was the last straw. The sale coincided with the state tournament. Steven understood the value, but when he made me beg, I admitted to myself he'd never change.

I decided on a double play—breaking free from my chains and preventing him from winning another championship, which was the only thing that truly mattered to him."

"How?"

"Gave him the Rohypnol, which he kept stashed in a high blood pressure prescription bottle. He kept his real pills in a shoebox and refilled the weekly pill containers. Having the date rape drug in plain sight amused him. He used it on his puzzle teammates too. Gave them enough to loosen their tongues. Of course, I recorded everything, but Steven said he did it by himself. Same with Daniel Elver. He came to our house ranting about his sister. I calmed him down, gave him some doctored coffee, and Steven learned secrets about his sudden rise to the industry's top, secrets the handsome news anchor would not want his adoring public to know."

"But how did you manage to kill Steven? The Rohypnol didn't do it," I goaded.

Marta laughed. "Steven was a snake, so I gave him a taste of his own medicine."

"Snake venom?"

Her eyes had a strange glint. "Steven secured the poison when he planned to destroy Vera's business but didn't need it after the bear episode."

Did Marta realize she'd just confessed to being a murderer?

"Marta, I'm getting a headache. Mind if I grab some leftover pizza?"

"Help yourself. I'll get you some Tylenol. Does that work for you?"

Tylenol worked for my headaches, but how would I know she wouldn't be giving me a unique remedy of Rohypnol and snake venom? That would alleviate any headache permanently. When she left to get the Tylenol, I grabbed her cell phone from the pocket of her purse and punched 911.

"911. What is your emergency?"

"Can't talk. Tell Sheriff Bergensen that Marta is the killer and to get to Marta's house ASAP."

I slipped the phone back into the compartment and opened the fridge, praying Sheriff Bergensen would get the message and I'd be alive when she arrived.

I heated the pizza on a leftover paper plate, got my water from the spigot, and vowed not to take my eyes off it for a second.

Marta returned brandishing two bottles. "How bad is it? Regular or extra strength?"

"Maybe I was just hungry. I think the pizza took the edge off."

She placed the two bottles on the table. "Food usually does the trick for me too. Pizza smells good. Did you leave some for me?"

"You have your choice, supreme or sausage and pineapple."

She microwaved a supreme slice and slid into the chair across from me. "Grabbed some lip balm when I was in the medicine cabinet because I noticed your chapped lips. The summer weather is awful, isn't it? Both brand-new. Which flavor do you prefer, lemon or mint?"

"Mint. Thanks." I licked my cracked lips and applied a generous coating of the lip balm. Then I heard the pounding of my heart in my head.

Marta's smile was the last thing I remembered.

# CHAPTER 15

When I felt the slap, I fought to lift my eyelids and focus.

"Do you know what she gave you?" The voice sounded like it came from the bottom of a well. "Jane, help us."

Someone propped me up and held water to my lips. The liquid dribbled from my mouth and onto my blouse.

Sheriff Bergensen supported me with one strong arm and tilted water toward me again. "Do you know what she gave you?"

"Snake venom." My words sounded slow and soft even to me. "In lip balm. She gave it to Steven too."

"Load her up. Tell the hospital to have the antivenom waiting. Same poison discovered in Steven Grazer's body. I'll take Marta."

Even with the screaming ambulance sirens, I drifted into a fitful slumber, the bumpy ride feeling like trampoline bounces on fluffy clouds.

Donna bustled around the hospital room, lecturing me as she packed my suitcase. "Do you know how worried I was?"

"Donna, that's typical of *my* unanswerable questions, and the answer is, 'I don't know.' How worried were you?"

"I was frantic. You weren't answering your cell, and then the police told us you were in the hospital after being poisoned by a murderer." My sister, who'd protected me since we were kids, recited a list of concerns, which boiled down to saying she loved me.

I stopped her midstride and threw my arms around her. "You're the world's best sister, Donna."

"I am, and you should appreciate me." She swiped at her eyes. "I brought two outfits for you."

"Which one will you insist I wear?" I asked.

Donna laughed and offered me the blue one. "This one will look better when you face the television cameras."

I was lucky to be alive, lucky to have great parents and a super sister, whose husband understood the unbreakable bond Donna and I shared. I'd banked on the jigsaw championship proving I could do something on my own. Instead, I'd learned how much I depended on others.

Sheriff Bergensen tapped on the hospital door. "Press is waiting."

"I'd rather face the newspeople than spend another day in the hospital," I said.

Donna waggled my suitcase. "Mom's planning a celebration dinner. See you tonight at six."

Sheriff Bergensen and I stepped out of the entrance together to the shouts of reporters demanding answers.

Daniel Elver jabbed his microphone forward. "Will you have any long-lasting effects from the poison Marta Grazer gave you?"

"No, nothing physical, but I'll see life differently from now on."

Sheriff Bergensen stepped forward. "Jane Dahl is a resourceful and caring person who helped solve what the press dubbed the Puzzle King Murder. We at the sheriff's department wish to acknowledge her assistance. I'm happy to announce the case is closed, and please remember me when you mark your ballot for my reelection."

"Do you have plans for competing in any more jigsaw competitions?" Daniel asked.

In the audience, Jon, Alma, and Vera all wore green shirts with THE JIGSTERS printed on them. Jon held a similar shirt above his head and pointed to me.

I nodded to them and turned to answer Daniel. "Definitely, but before any competitions, I plan to visit a high school friend I haven't seen in years."

Daniel pulled a finger across his throat to indicate the end of the interview and lowered the microphone. "Want to go out to dinner, Jane?"

"Hey, I was just going to ask her that." Jon handed me the Jigster team shirt.

I savored the sunshine on this perfect July day and wondered if one of these two men might become more than a friend. I lifted my face to the sun's warmth and offered a prayer of thanks that I'd lived to have options. My first jigsaw competition showed me that my own life was like a Puzzle Twist puzzle. Not always what I expected but sure to be perfect with all the final pieces fitted into the frame.

I couldn't wait to see what my future picture revealed.

**LINDA BATEN JOHNSON** is an avid puzzler and game player, but she's never entered a jigsaw puzzle competition. She loves reading and writing mysteries because she enjoys the challenge of following the clues to arrive at the right answer. Linda grew up in a small Texas town, where she won blue ribbons for storytelling, and she still loves telling tales. A tornado destroyed her hometown when Linda was young, and watching faith-based actions in rebuilding lives and homes after the tragedy influences her writing. In addition to cozy mysteries, her historical fiction books for young readers and her squeaky-clean romances are available in print, e-book, and audio.

# A Puzzling Weekend

By Teresa Ives Lilly

# CHAPTER 1

Standing on the front porch of the Pumpkin Patch Bed and Breakfast in the freezing cold wasn't my idea of fun. When Officer Jace Miller pulled his police car in front of the house, rolled down the window, and waved at me, I wanted to duck my head and run back inside. I was sure my nose was as red as my hair.

Unfortunately, all I could do was raise my mitted hand and wave back, hoping Jace wouldn't get out of the car and come any closer, but at the same time, wishing he would. I'd met him a few times in the singles group at my church and noticed he'd begun sitting next to me during the singles sessions, but I didn't know him very well yet. Like most single women in town, I wanted to get to know the good-looking officer better, but I hadn't expected it to be when I was standing on my front porch with my teeth chattering from the cold. I'd been hoping to invite him out for coffee but hadn't gotten the opportunity yet.

"You okay there, Tabi?" he called out. Only in a small town like Pumpkin City, Pennsylvania, could you find a policeman who stopped to check on a woman standing outside in the cold for no apparent reason.

I nodded, trying to think of something interesting to say, but my mouth just opened and closed. No words came out. I was both thankful and disappointed when he turned his attention to his squawking police radio. A few moments later, Jace glanced back at me, shrugged his shoulders, and waved goodbye. I suddenly felt as if I'd missed my chance to make an impression and could only hope I'd get another, hopefully next time without the red nose.

As he drove off, I realized he had called me by my nickname, which was a good sign. Although my name's Tabitha Jenkins, my friends and family called me Tabi, but not because I reminded them of a cat. I'm anything but catlike, a bit clumsy, in fact. Instead of having sleek, silk-like hair, my head is covered in a mass of orange curls, which go any direction they want. I try to straighten them to no avail.

My mother always tells me I have lovely auburn hair. Whenever I look in the mirror, though, all I see are orange curls surrounding a face gently speckled with freckles. I feel fortunate my freckles never turn very dark. If I don't want them to show, I use a bit of cover-up. I'm usually a plain-Jane-type woman and don't wear any makeup at all.

I've lived in Pumpkin City my whole life. I even won the contest for Miss Pumpkin Patch my senior year of high school. Not because I was a beauty queen but because I looked best in the orange dress all the contestants had to wear to enter. I'm not sure how a girl with orange, unruly curls and freckles could look good in an orange dress, but I did.

That's been my biggest claim to fame my entire life. There aren't many ways to stand out in a small town like Pumpkin City unless you go off to college and become a lawyer or a doctor or run away and become a famous actress.

I did none of those things. I graduated from high school in 1980, stayed in town working at the Piggly Wiggly, and saved money toward my dream. It took ten years of scrimping and pinching pennies, but I finally saved enough to approach the bank and get a loan to open a bed-and-breakfast.

I had my eye on a quaint but run-down, shall we say, "mansion" at the corner of Main and Seed Street. Yes, the street is named Seed. All the streets around Main are named after things related to pumpkins, which was something our mayor initiated in his first term to inspire tourism.

When I was a young girl, Mrs. Abigail Adams lived in the mansion. It was old then but not so run-down. She watched me after school twice a week for five years, and I loved her home. It had three stories and a huge wraparound porch, and the attic boasted two glorious gables. I loved playing hide-and-go-seek in the ten-bedroom house, and the scrumptious aromas drifting from the kitchen, where Mrs. Adams made her famous pumpkin pies that she sold to local restaurants, still fill my memories.

The day Mrs. Adams died, I knew I wanted to buy her house. At age sixteen, I hadn't heard of bed-and-breakfasts, but I knew whatever I did with it, I'd have to make money to pay for the upkeep. I was well aware that working at the Piggly Wiggly wasn't going to do it. So even back then, I was researching and making plans for the day I could own the mansion.

Mrs. Adams had no relatives, and there wasn't anyone else in our little town who wanted the house, so it sat empty for thirteen years, deteriorating as I scrimped and saved, working weekends and overtime until I came up with the down payment, got the loan, and purchased it. Luckily, I'm pretty handy, and my father is a retired carpenter. He was able to help me restore the house and repaint the white wood with the dark green trim.

There were many antiques left behind I was able to sell off to help pay for some of the major repairs. In the huge attic, I found plenty of lovely vintage furniture in perfect condition to furnish all the rooms. It took a bit of elbow grease to buff them to their original beauty, but it was so worth the effort. Other than that, all I had to do was purchase new towels, bedding, and a few tablecloths to ready the house for my paying guests.

Five years after I purchased the mansion, I'm doing very well as the proud owner of the Pumpkin Patch Bed-and-Breakfast. Because Pumpkin City doesn't offer many other places for visitors to stay during our quarterly town festivals, my place stays booked many weekends. Of course, picking up on the pumpkin theme helps. The rooms are all decorated in orange, white, and green, with pictures of pumpkins on the walls. Glass miniature pumpkins are scattered throughout the house. I've purchased almost every book with the word "pumpkin" in its title, and they fill the mansion's bookshelves.

The mayor added photos of the house and rooms to the town's local visitor guide both online and in print. We felt it would help pull in a lot of outside guests.

There are down times, though, when the town is quiet. When the streets are covered with scattered snow, and no one comes to visit. During those times, I have to get creative to keep revenue coming in, and this particular weekend was the result of one of my greatest ideas.

I was hosting a Mystery Jigsaw Puzzle weekend. I planned a great adventure. First, my guests would each be given one of the Alphabet Murder jigsaw puzzles to put together over the weekend.

Each puzzle comes with a short story inside, a mystery of sorts. The solution to the mystery is found in the completed puzzle.

The first guests to complete and solve their mystery puzzle would win a prize basket. I still planned to offer our pumpkin-themed meals, which are usually part of our festival packages. All together with the jigsaw puzzle theme, I thought it made for an interesting weekend event. I didn't even have to advertise it on the website because the slots all filled up with local women within an hour of opening the reservations.

Keep in mind, I live in a small town. There isn't much to do, so anything allowing women to get away from their homes for a night or the whole weekend, without having to travel, is always a big hit.

There I was, standing on the front porch wearing my heavy fleece brown coat decorated with a pumpkin patch scene across the back, waiting for my guests. I was actually excited for two reasons. First, I had some local friends who were signed up for the weekend. I usually didn't have time to visit with them because of being so busy with the Pumpkin Patch. Also, I planned to participate in the activities myself. I hadn't put together a jigsaw puzzle in about ten years, but back then I was pretty good at it.

Usually, I did the hosting and all the cooking, but I felt I'd earned a little break. So I hired Monica Carsly, a woman in town close to my age, who was known to be an excellent cook, to do all the cooking for the weekend. When I first saw her during our brief interview, I recognized her face. She actually went to my high school but left before graduating. I never knew why, but there had been stories, none of which swayed me from hiring her for the weekend. I hadn't seen her since high school, and that was a long time ago. I suggested she stay in one of the first-floor guest rooms instead of traveling back and forth to her home, which was several miles outside of town.

She arrived early on Friday morning and was eagerly going over the recipes I'd found in an old cookbook that once belonged to Abigail Adams. There was one problem with hiring Monica. Actually, two. She insisted on bringing her two beagles, Bonnie and Clyde. She assured me they were two little angels and would stay in the back room off the kitchen. Not knowing what else to do, I agreed.

Monica planned to spend the day cooking the evening meal and prepping the other meals we would have over the weekend. I'd already started to defrost a small turkey for Saturday night's meal that would include pumpkin rolls and pumpkin mashed potatoes.

I heard a horn blasting. I looked up to see a garish red sports car pull up in the driveway. The door opened and a tall, slender woman slid out of the car. She reminded me of a sleek cat. It was Scarlett Star, our very own local actress. She graduated from my high school two years before me and immediately moved away to become an actress. At least, she appeared in a few episodes of the town's favorite soap opera. Her acting career was short, however, and she returned to take over the local playhouse. Her name wasn't always Scarlett Star, but I couldn't remember what it used to be.

"Yoo-hoo, Tabi, I'm here!" She waved at me. The faux fur coat she was wearing probably wasn't warm enough for the thirty-six-degree weather, and her stiletto heels were not great for the snow. I was glad I'd gotten out early and shoveled the sidewalk.

"Is it okay if I park right here?" she asked me. She'd pulled into space number one, which actually belonged to another guest, but I didn't think it would really matter which slots the guests parked in. They all had equal access to the front porch.

"Sure, Scarlett. Need help with your bags?" I was already moving that way. I was sure she would.

"Oh, wouldn't that just be wonderful? I wasn't sure what to bring. I've never participated in a puzzle mystery weekend before, so I brought several outfits." She popped the trunk open with her key fob, revealing three large suitcases.

I had to smother a giggle. I don't think I own enough clothes to fill even one suitcase, and here she brought three. I wasn't sure why she thought she'd need different outfits. I planned to wear my most comfortable jeans and a nice sweater, although I wished I could just wear sweatpants and a flannel shirt all weekend. As the hostess, I supposed I should look nice.

Scarlett reached into the trunk and pulled out the smallest case, leaving the two larger ones for me. I eyed them unhappily but lifted them out and trudged behind her as she slowly made her way to the porch, taking tiny steps.

"I'd hate to slip or twist an ankle and ruin the whole weekend. Not to mention, I am the leading lady in our next production at the playhouse. 'Gone with the Wind.' It starts next Friday. At first, I thought you'd planned this event on the same weekend as our premiere, which would've been a disaster for you. No one would choose this jigsaw puzzle thing over seeing our production! I'm glad you chose wisely and held it this weekend instead." Her words stung me, but I kept reminding myself I was a Christian and needed to turn the other cheek. I had a feeling my cheeks were going to be smarting pretty badly by the end of the weekend. The crazy thing is, she was probably right. The whole town usually shows up for the playhouse performances on opening night. I made a mental note to check playhouse calendars in the future when planning any Pumpkin Patch Bed-and-Breakfast events.

"I'm not sure what this weekend is all about, Tabi, but you know if there's any skits or acting parts, you can count on me." Her voice trilled up and down enthusiastically. I decided I better think up a skit for the weekend, or Scarlett would never be happy. I knew her recommendation would go a long way in our little town.

# CHAPTER 2

Usually I greet my guests, give them the key to their room, and allow them to head up the stairs alone, but I wasn't sure that was the best thing to do with Scarlett Star. I had a feeling she'd be the type to go peeping into the other guests' rooms, and none of them were locked. If I allowed that, she might ask to change rooms, which was out of the question. Once the others arrived and were able to secure their doors, I wouldn't have to worry so much about Scarlett.

I set her suitcases down in her room, hoping to get away before she started another conversation. A note was on the front door instructing guests to enter and wait in the hallway. I heard some voices downstairs and was pretty sure my friends Cathy and Barb had arrived.

When Scarlett turned her back, I quickly slipped out of the room and jogged down the stairs. I was right. Cathy and Barb were standing in the front hallway. They both glanced up at the sound of my footsteps, smiles on their faces.

It amazed me that we'd all stayed friends for so long. In high school, Cathy was always popular. Her senior year, she was head cheerleader and Barb was her faithful sidekick. Whenever I wasn't working at Piggly Wiggly, they'd let me hang around with them. Cathy and Barb went to college after we graduated. Two years later, Cathy married Tim, her high school sweetheart. He was tired of waiting for her, so he'd given her an ultimatum—move back home and marry him or lose him. Cathy moved back home. Barb wasn't far behind. It seemed she only went to college because Cathy had gone. Barb, like me, still didn't have a boyfriend.

"Hello, girls." I reached the bottom floor. "So glad you're here." I gave Barb a hug, then Cathy.

"Are we the first ones?" Barb asked, her eyes scanning the big front room to the right where I'd set up tables for the puzzles.

I shook my head, held a finger to my lips, and waved for them to follow me up the stairs.

Barb shook her head. "I need a ladies' room first."

I nodded in the direction of the hallway beside the kitchen, and Barb slipped away.

"I'm excited about this weekend. I haven't had a real getaway as long as I can remember," Cathy exclaimed. "I thought we'd never get here though. We were stuck behind several Amish buggies."

Pumpkin City is close to Lancaster, which is known for the Amish who live there. We often see their buggies in town.

When Barb returned later, her cheeks seemed a bit flushed.

"Everything all right?" I asked.

She nodded, and we all promenaded up the stairs. I'd barely opened Cathy's door to show them her room when Scarlett looked out her door.

"Hi there," she called out. "Aren't you all excited? This should be a pretty interesting weekend."

Cathy and Barb looked at me, aghast. They both knew

Scarlett, and I was pretty sure neither of them liked her very much. Barb, always a peacemaker, regained her composure first and gave Scarlett a friendly wave. "Yep, it's gonna be great."

After we entered Cathy's room and I closed her door, she turned to me, real anger on her face. "What is she doing here?" she hissed.

"She signed up. I can't turn down guests just because she and my best friend dated the same guy in high school."

Cathy looked like I'd slapped her.

"I'm sorry, Cathy. I shouldn't have said that. I didn't know Scarlett was coming until yesterday. She just signed up."

Cathy looked at Barb. I expected Barb to say something calming, but she didn't seem to be paying attention to the conversation.

Cathy straightened up. "Whatever. I mean, we're all adults now. Besides, he broke up with her before he started dating me, right?"

Roger Steubing was the best-looking guy in high school our freshman year. Scarlett was dating him at the beginning of the year, but he broke up with her and started dating Cathy. However, he was also dating a few others at the time, though Cathy always considered him *her* boyfriend. She just didn't want to face the fact that he was seeing anyone else. She was really heartbroken when Roger dropped out of school a few days before prom and disappeared.

I kept a smile plastered on my face as I showed Barb her room. I hurried through her orientation, feeling I needed to get back downstairs to wait for the next guest. "You get settled. The itinerary is on your desk."

Before she could say anything, I closed the door behind me

and headed back to the stairs. I had to keep in mind that Scarlett was one of my paying guests. I couldn't get myself caught up in a gossip session about her. And gossip was one of the issues I felt God had been working on in my life lately.

I'd barely reached the bottom step when the front door opened again, a swoosh of cold air striking my face.

Two more ladies stepped in, Dawn and Jennifer. These ladies were older than I, probably in their midforties. I knew them both from church. We all attend our local nondenominational church. Everyone in town just refers to it as "the church."

Both ladies were dressed in their Sunday best, which caused me to frown. I'd really hoped to have a casual dress code for the weekend, but these two might end up setting the tone.

"Hello, ladies." I met them at the bottom of the stairs. Dawn was writing her name in my guest book, which I didn't mind. However, for locals, I don't think it's necessary. I like to have my out-of-town guests put their addresses in the guest book in case I ever lose my files on the computer.

Jennifer is soft spoken, which always surprises me. I'm amazed that she can keep her five kids in line with such a quiet voice. "Hello, Tabitha."

I cringed at my full name. I wasn't sure if they had some kind of biblical rule against using nicknames or what.

"Hello. Do you have any more bags you need help getting from the car?"

Both women shook their heads.

"Okay, follow me upstairs. You did say you wanted to share a room?"

Both women nodded. They were best friends, and I think just coming to the Pumpkin Patch was the most adventurous thing they'd ever done. I imagined they'd stick together pretty much most of the weekend, and I didn't plan on trying to split them up. I knew that would make them too uncomfortable.

They followed me up the stairs. I had given them the largest room, which overlooks the back garden. The walls are painted white, and I'd hung a few pictures of local pumpkin patches around the room. The quilt on the bed is covered in very fragile-looking vines. Not too overdone or underdone. It's my favorite room in the house.

"My, this is lovely, Tabitha," Jennifer said.

Dawn's head just moved up and down in agreement. She whispered, "Lovely."

"Okay, you two get settled. There's an itinerary on the table over there. We'll have dinner at six then meet in the front room at about seven to begin our mystery jigsaw puzzles." I slid out of the room and closed their door, wondering if Dawn ever initiated a conversation herself.

I hurried away, determined to do better with my inner opinions as well. So far, since opening the Pumpkin Patch, I'd seen God working in many ways, helping me get through all the city ordinances and finding great help. All along, though, I could feel Him tugging on my heart to get deeper in my relationship with Him.

I'd been reading a devotional each morning but knew God wanted me to start reading the actual Bible more often. Plus, as I already mentioned, I could feel His nudging about not getting involved in any gossip. Being the owner of a bed-and-breakfast, I have a lot of opportunity to hear all kinds of garbage about all kinds of people. This was going to be a really difficult weekend because I knew all these women, and most of them knew about a million secrets about everyone in town.

I suddenly realized I'd been standing at the top of the stairs, just lost in thought. A bell ringing finally pulled my attention. Someone was pressing the front doorbell. I moved rapidly, thinking by the end of the weekend I would've put in about fifty thousand steps if I had to keep going up and down the stairs.

I rushed across the hallway. I could see a man standing at the door.

I opened it. "Yes, may I help you?"

"I'm the driver for Mrs. Royal. I just wanted to assure myself this is the right place. *This* is the Pumpkin Patch Bed-and-Breakfast?"

The man said the words as if they were something dirty.

"Yes, it is."

He frowned then glanced at the walkway. "I suppose it's not too icy. Do you have someone who can carry Mrs. Royal's bags? I will have to escort her in."

I wanted to giggle. The man was so stoic. Surely anybody who wasn't disabled could walk from the car to the front porch without an escort, but I gulped down my thoughts and nodded. "Sure, I can get her bags."

His frown deepened as he turned in military style and strode back to the car, which I realized was a limousine. He opened the passenger side back door, and I watched as a truly beautiful woman, with silver hair piled atop her head, got out. This woman's fur coat made Scarlett Star's look like faux fur off a bolt at Hobby Lobby. Because of her silver hair, I thought she might be over sixty, but her youthful skin made me wonder.

The driver opened the trunk, and I moved closer. Glad to see there were only two bags, I reached in and pulled them out. I followed behind as the driver allowed the woman to lean on his arm.

Personally, I felt she could drop his arm and jog up to the porch. She was walking so quickly beside him, he was barely keeping up with her. When we all finally reached the porch, I pressed by them, opened the front door, and moved so they could step in.

*Patience,* I kept telling myself over and over.

Once inside, I set the two bags by the stairwell. I was sure I'd be the one hauling them up, but that could wait until later. I turned with a smile I'm not sure I actually felt.

"Hello, Mrs. Royal. So glad you could join us this weekend."

The woman eyed me up and down, and I could tell she found me wanting.

"We have an interesting itinerary for the weekend. Do you want to sign the guest book? Then I can show you to your room." I pointed at the bureau behind her where the guest book lay open. She moved over to it, seemed to read all the names, then turned back without touching the pen.

"George, you can sign me in." She glared at me. "I'd like to see my room. I hope it lives up to my expectations. So often pictures on the internet are not true reflections of reality." Her voice was a bit husky. For just a moment, a memory flashed through my mind. Had I heard her voice before? Did I know her? She didn't look familiar.

With a shrug, I lifted her two suitcases and began to climb the stairs again. Her voice stopped me.

"Upstairs? I wasn't aware I'd have to be upstairs. I prefer rooms on the first floor."

I cocked my head sideways, wanting to huff with irritation. "No, sorry. All the rooms are on the second floor, except our accessible room, which is reserved this weekend for a guest who uses a wheelchair. Other than that, only the kitchen, dining, and living rooms are on the first floor." I turned and began my trudge again. I heard her muttering something about why I didn't give her the first-floor room, but I didn't have time to argue with her about the arrangements. The website clearly notes that all rooms for people without disabilities are on the second floor and that there is no elevator. I doubted the authenticity of her surprised reaction.

When I reached the tenth step, I heard her begin to follow me. She called over her shoulder at George to keep his phone on at all times in case she needed anything, then I heard the front door open and close.

It was going to be hard enough to deal with Scarlett Star for the weekend, but I was beginning to wonder if Mrs. Royal might be the worse of the two.

I stopped outside her door and allowed her to enter before me. This room was painted a light green color. The bedspread is a quilt made from different fabrics with pumpkins on them; something I had found at the local Patchwork Pumpkin Quilt store at the other end of Vine Street. I'm pretty sure it was handmade by an Amish woman. On the walls are pictures of pumpkin-themed quilts I found at a quilting show last year. The furniture in this room was very elegant, old wood, painted over with a whitewash.

I watched Mrs. Royal's face and could see she was pleased, although I figured she'd never say so.

"Your itinerary is on the desk by the window. I have a couple more guests who should be arriving soon, so I'll just leave you to get settled in."

She turned and looked almost right through me. For a slight moment, I thought I saw a bit of sadness or loneliness in her eyes. *Perhaps that's the reason she keeps a driver around*, I thought.

As I headed down the stairs again, I thought about myself. I didn't have many friends besides Cathy and Barb. I enjoyed church on the weekends but didn't really join in any women's events, yet I didn't ever feel lonely. I guess, as my dad used to say, I'm an introvert, which is kind of amazing for someone who decided to open a bed-and-breakfast.

Once more, I heard the front door open, and I rushed down the stairs. I knew these were my final guests, Gloria, the owner of the Tea Shoppe next door, along with her grandmother, Esther.

# CHAPTER 3

I was right. Gloria had pushed her grandmother's wheelchair from their home next door, which is also the town's only tea shop, across to my house. They actually could have decided to participate in the whole weekend and not stay in the bed-and-breakfast, but I think Gloria wanted a break from the Tea Shoppe and from pushing her grandmother's wheelchair back and forth.

Gloria was a gentle woman with soft, wavy golden-brown hair. She graduated from high school in 1977, a few years ahead of me, but I knew her back then. She was always quiet and kept to herself, except the one year she tried out for cheerleading, but the head cheerleader at the time cut her from the team. I think it was because Gloria was so pretty. I couldn't recall exactly who the head cheerleader was, but I did remember she had a bit of a reputation for wanting to be the prettiest one on the team.

Gloria's grandmother was sweet but a bit hard of hearing, so I had to shout things close to her ear when addressing her. Gloria never seemed to mind caring for the woman, and I knew she really loved her. Of course, she had been caring for her for the past three years without a break. I would have loved to have given her some time to herself, but I could already tell I was going to be busy all weekend making sure Scarlett and Mrs. Royal were happy enough.

"Hi, Gloria! And Esther!" I shouted a bit louder than I usually would, for her grandmother's benefit. "Want to follow me to your room?"

Esther nodded, so I turned and walked toward the back of the house. There are actually two rooms there. One is the accessible room. The other is the room I'd given Monica so she had easy access to the kitchen. Of course, that room isn't one I advertise, so I only hoped Mrs. Royal didn't find out about it.

"Tabi, this is really charming," Gloria exclaimed as we came to the room. Her soft voice calmed my nerves. The room was done in a light blue and decorated with several clear and blue glass pumpkins scattered throughout. There were two twin cast-iron beds with simple white lace bedspreads.

As we stood outside the door to her room, Monica opened her door and peeked out. Her eyes seemed a bit red-rimmed, as if she'd been crying.

"Hi, Monica," I said.

She cleared her throat and spoke in short, clipped sentences. "Hi, Tabi. I've got things ready for dinner. The pumpkin pie is about ready to come out of the oven."

I smiled. I could already smell the tantalizing aroma, and I began wondering if I could afford to hire Monica for all my weekends.

When I stepped back, I was looking at Monica and saw her face grow even more pale than before. She quickly tucked back into the room and slammed the door, making me jump.

I turned around to see the reaction on Gloria's face at such rudeness, but her face was screwed into an angry scowl, something

I'd never seen before.

"What is *she* doing here?" Gloria hissed.

"Monica? She's the cook for the weekend. Why? Do you know her?"

Gloria nodded, gulped, then straightened up. Esther pointed at Monica's door. "Who was that?" Her voice was loud and crackled.

Gloria stepped over to block her grandmother's view, grabbed her wheelchair, and pushed it into the room.

"Is there a problem, Gloria?" I stood, facing her back and worrying that this weekend was already having a few too many bumps.

"No!" Gloria actually shouted. Then she seemed to calm down. "I mean, no." She turned back to face me. She still looked unhappy, but the initial anger was gone.

I eyed her for a moment then turned to head to the front room. "Okay then, I won't push you for information. I'm always available if you need to talk. Go ahead and check your itinerary. I'll see you later." I gave a quick swish of my hair and left the room. Whatever Gloria's problem with Monica was, she wasn't in the mood for sharing. I only hoped it didn't ruin her weekend.

Once I reached the front room, I glanced around with a nod. Everything was set up. Each table had a brand-new Alphabet Puzzle opened and ready to go. More than likely, each group would start with the border pieces tonight.

As I reviewed the guest list, I realized most of the women here had all gone to the local high school. Most of them graduated between 1977 and the year I graduated, 1980. I wasn't sure about the ladies from church. They were a bit older. I'd ask them later.

I stepped to the bookshelf and ran my hand along one of the rows. There were several old high school yearbooks I'd picked up at local garage sales. They were actually a favorite with some of my out-of-town guests.

I pulled out the 1977, 1978, 1979, and 1980 books and spread them out on the coffee table. Maybe later we could all do some reminiscing. At that moment, I heard some scuffling on the floor. I looked up, and two brown heads popped around the corner. Bonnie and Clyde must've escaped from Monica's room.

"Well, hello there." I smiled, sat on the couch, and put my hand out. The two dogs flopped across the room, their ears too big for their bodies. Before I knew it, they were jumping up on my legs, and I was patting their heads.

I do love dogs, but I'd never considered owning one because I was busy working at the Piggly Wiggly for years. Looking at the two charming faces in front of me, I wondered if it was time for me to get a dog of my own. Pets don't seem to deter guests these days. In fact, many of my guests bring their dogs with them. Most are well groomed and well behaved.

Just then Clyde jumped up, sniffed at the yearbooks on the table, and made a little growling noise. He slid his nose under one of the yearbooks and flipped it off the table.

"No, Clyde," I reprimanded. "That's not nice."

The dog looked at me for a moment. He must've determined I wasn't threatening, because he gave a little howl then casually strolled out of the room. In the meantime, Bonnie sniffed the book on the floor, pushed at it with her paw until it was hidden under the end table, then she too gave a short woof and left the room.

I had no idea what that was all about. I pulled the book out from under the table, sniffed it, then picked up the others one by one and sniffed them. Nothing seemed different about this book, but somehow the dogs smelled something I didn't. All the books were equally musty.

"Oh well, that was a stinky year," I said to an empty room, noting it was the 1977 yearbook. I remembered how difficult my freshman year had been. I set it back on the coffee table, stood, and stretched. My guests would be coming down for dinner soon. I moved to the front window and looked out. There were a few snowflakes falling, which meant we might get a nice covering before morning, always lovely to see. The forecast hadn't predicted any bad storms, so I wasn't worried about losing electricity or water.

I hugged my arms across my chest, thinking how comfortable I was in my flannel shirt. I hated to change, but there was no doubt the others were probably going to dress up a bit, so I headed for my room to find something a bit fancier but still practical.

I peeked into the kitchen first. Monica was pulling the pie from the oven. Bonnie and Clyde sat innocently at her feet.

"Everything okay?" I asked.

As Monica stood up, a chain necklace with a ring hanging on it swayed back and forth. She tucked it into her blouse. "Yes, why?"

I was recalling the way Gloria had reacted to Monica being here. "No reason. Bonnie and Clyde were just helping me arrange some books in the front room." I snickered and glared at the two dogs. In unison, they turned their heads away from me.

Monica watched the whole thing but said nothing. I think she realized the dogs had done something a bit naughty, but she wasn't about to say anything. I decided to let it drop. Unless they became a problem, the dogs were so cute, I didn't have the heart to tell on them.

# CHAPTER 4

I'd chosen to convert the very first room at the top of the stairs into my room. With the door ajar, I can hear almost everything in the house, except the private conversations inside the guests' rooms, of course. If any guests start wandering around the house looking for something, I can hear the creaking floorboards. If anyone shows up later than nine and forgets how to unlock the front door, I can hear them too.

It's rare for me to sleep very deeply, so I don't worry too much about missing something. All the guests are given a map of the house that indicates which room is mine. If they simply knock on my door, I'll definitely hear that.

Before I redecorated, mine was actually two rooms, connected by a shower-bath combo. I use the front as a bedroom and the back as my office, which allows me to keep all my messy work completely away from any nosy guests. I hide miniature candy bars around the house, in cupboards, drawers, behind pumpkins, for the real snoops. They never last more than two months.

When I slipped my flannel shirt off and hung it on the back of my chair, I gave a big sigh. "I'll put you on again later," I promised and pulled out a pair of black slacks with a silver filigree shirt, the outfit I usually wear when I host special evenings like Valentine's.

When I stepped out of my closet, dressed in the flattering but uncomfortable clothes, I heard a whimpering noise. I turned toward the sound.

"Bonnie? Clyde? What are you brutes doing on my bed?" My door was standing wide open. The dogs must've been adventuring away from the kitchen again. Bonnie had already done a few circles and dropped into a sweet sleep, but Clyde stood on the bed, staring at me.

"So, it's a battle of wills, is it?" I asked. He actually hopped up and down, as if he understood what I said. My lips twerked into a smile.

Clyde took that as a win and plopped down beside Bonnie then closed his eyes. However, until I slipped out of the room, I'm not sure he actually went to sleep.

The large dining table was set in true elegance. I like to serve dinners on the good china Mrs. Adams left behind whether we dress up for a special occasion or not. However, her china is pretty simple—all white with a little strand of gold running around the edges. I usually add to the overall ambience of the house by adding transparent orange plates, water glasses, and serving platters. They were a steal at a local auction. Along with the long centerpiece, which boasts lovely greenery, white roses, and small pumpkins, the table setting is charming.

One chair was missing at the end of the table for Esther's wheelchair to fit. I was happy to see Gloria and Esther heading into the dining room before the others. This way we could get Esther settled in nicely.

"Did you get a little rest?" I asked, noting a bit of gray tinge under Gloria's eyes. Had she been crying? Was this going to be a sad weekend instead of a fun one?

"Grandmother did. I just lay on the bed relaxing. It's not something I do much at home. Whenever Grandmother rests, I'm usually cleaning or getting things prepared at the Tea Shoppe. I'm not complaining though. You know I love the Tea Shoppe, but it's nice to have a bit of a rest."

She wheeled Esther over to her spot then sat beside her. From their places, they could see everyone as they entered from the front room or from the kitchen. I noted Gloria's eyes flashing back and forth warily.

"Listen, Gloria. Please tell me if there's a problem with Monica. I don't want you to be uncomfortable the whole weekend."

Gloria's cheeks turned pink. "It's nothing really. Just something that happened in high school. . ."

I believe Gloria would've said more, but just then, we heard footfalls coming down the stairs. When I turned, Cathy, Barb, Dawn, and Jennifer all entered together.

"Hello, ladies." I pointed out the chairs, and they all sat down, chitchatting with one another as they did. Gloria introduced herself and her grandmother to them when there was a break in the conversation. I was a bit surprised that Cathy didn't know Gloria already. Barb, as always, sat quietly beside Cathy, but I thought she looked unusually pale tonight. The redness around her eyes made me think she'd been crying too.

*Maybe it's the lighting*, I thought. Surely not everyone in the house spent the last hour crying.

A few minutes later, Scarlett Star strolled into the room, dressed in the most outlandish red silk dress. She looked as if she were a saloon girl who just stepped out of an old Western movie. She even had a red boa wrapped around her neck.

She paused at the doorway then spoke in a strange singsong voice. "Well, now isn't this the cutest little get-together. I'm just as excited as can be to get at those mystery puzzles." She glanced around the room and finally stopped on Cathy. "Oh, I remember some of you. Weren't y'all in my high school? I think you were younger than me. You know, I graduated in 1978 and went right on out to Hollywood."

Dawn's and Jennifer's faces were blank. They didn't know Scarlett at all, but I could see that Cathy, Barb, and Gloria all knew her. The myriad of emotions that passed over each of their faces was actually a bit comical. I grabbed Scarlett's arm and propelled her to her chair, hoping Monica would serve the meal soon.

I heard the clicking of shoes on the stairwell again, thinking I'd have carpets put over the wood in the near future.

Mrs. Royal entered the room just as the kitchen door opened and Monica stepped in carrying a tureen of pumpkin soup.

The chaos of sounds erupting at that moment caught me off guard. Mrs. Royal blurted out, "What is *she* doing here?"

Cathy gasped out loud.

Scarlett Star proclaimed, "Well, I never—"

Gloria, who had been taking a sip of water, choked and spit the water all over the table in front of her.

Esther held a hand up to her ear and shouted, "What's everyone saying?"

Dawn, Jennifer, and Barb didn't react at all.

I wasn't able to tell if Mrs. Royal's entrance had disturbed everyone, or was it Monica's? I determined to have a word with the cook later and find out if she knew any of my guests and if there was a reason they would be upset.

Monica set the tureen on the table. I noticed the ring on the chain around her neck swaying again. Once more, she tucked it into her blouse and slipped out of the room, but no one moved. I finally tried to break the ice by leading Mrs. Royal to the table and asking her if we could call her by her first name.

"Yes, my name is Linda." She glared around the table as if defying anyone to disagree with her.

"Linda Marsol," Barb stated.

"Linda Marsol?" I repeated.

Linda nodded.

"Didn't you date Rog—" Cathy's voice faded and her mouth formed an *O*. Whatever she was going to say, she quickly looked away and grabbed the soup tureen. "Goodness, Tabi. This pumpkin soup looks wonderful."

That seemed to ease the tension in the room, and everyone began eating. There was a little bit of chitchat between the guests. Whenever Monica entered the room, however, everyone grew silent. She'd done a splendid job with both the soup and the roasted pumpkin salad. The loaf of pumpkin bread disappeared quickly as well.

When the plates were empty, I announced we would all adjourn to the front room. Barb and Cathy were the first to leave the dining room. Dawn and Jennifer, lovely ladies that they were, offered to help clear the table, but I shook my head. They headed toward the front room next.

Gloria was waiting for everyone to leave so she would have

room to pull out Esther's wheelchair. I think Scarlett and Linda were eyeing each other, hoping the other would go first. I was sure they both just wanted a chance to make their dramatic entrance for the others.

"Come on, ladies," I encouraged. "Let's get going. We have puzzles to begin." I stood, and both ladies rose. Scarlett tossed her boa around her neck and glided away while Linda sniffed, lifted her head, and followed.

I turned around to face Monica. "We can have pie and coffee in about an hour, but I'd really like you to join us this weekend at the puzzle tables. We need an extra."

Monica's brows drew together. "I don't think that's a very good idea, Tabi."

I was in a hurry to get things moving along, so I didn't pay very close attention to her. "Never mind the dishes. Just join us." Monica dropped her towel and followed.

In the front room, I found everyone sitting on the sofas and straight-backed chairs. No one had chosen a puzzle table to sit at, which made me happy. I wanted to assign seating. I noted Cathy was glancing through one of the yearbooks. I scanned the table and did a quick count. One of the books was gone. I wondered if Bonnie and Clyde had been playing hide-and-go-seek with them again.

"I never got a copy of my high school yearbook," Cathy said. "Someone told me there was a picture of me talking to Roger Steubing in it." She pointed to the table. "You don't have a 1977 yearbook?"

I wasn't about to go into the details of the naughty dogs' behavior, so I just didn't answer. Instead, I began to explain the evening's events, hoping to take Cathy's mind off the yearbook.

"All right, everyone. Tonight, I'll be matching you up with a partner. The two of you will be partnered all weekend when we work on the puzzles. Usually, people put the border together first, but that might not be your style. Some sort the pieces, some don't. As long as you work together with your partner, you can complete it however you want. No one can read the mystery in your puzzle box until Sunday morning. You'll have until Sunday at one o'clock to finish the puzzle and solve the mystery. The main rule is that no one can work on their puzzle except in the allotted time, when we are all in here together." I looked around, hoping to get a feel for their reactions. Everyone was looking at me and seemed interested.

I held up a box. I'd put slips of paper with their names on them in it. "This is how we will choose partners."

Gloria frowned. I knew this would take her out of her comfort zone, but I'd already planned to pull Esther's name and pair it with mine to mix things up a little. I wasn't concerned about winning.

"Okay, here we go. First two names, Dawn and Monica." Several heads swerved around, and I could feel them glaring at Monica. They probably hadn't expected the cook to join in the activities, but Dawn only smiled at her.

"Next is Cathy and Mrs. Royal—I mean Linda." The two eyed one another, but neither spoke.

"Next is Gloria and Jennifer." Gloria gasped.

"But what about Grandmother?"

Gloria was sitting beside me. I patted her hand. "Don't worry. She'll have a partner."

I held the box up again and pulled out two more names. "Okay, Scarlett and Barb," I stated. Neither of them seemed to have a problem, so I rushed on. "And finally, Esther and Tabi."

I quickly put all the names back in the box. I didn't want anyone to see that I hadn't actually pulled names for the last two. I looked at Gloria again. She mouthed, "Thank you."

Each pair chose a table and sat back down. I wheeled Esther to a table in the corner then turned once more to make my final announcement.

"We have one hour. When we have finished for the night, you are all welcome to use your free time as you wish. You can visit with one another here, read a book, watch television in your room, go out for the evening. I'm pretty sure there is some kind of movie playing at the theater. I know there isn't a play this weekend at the playhouse." All eyes turned to Scarlett.

"Yes, but there will be next weekend." She smiled. "I expect to see you all there."

I cleared my throat, glad most everyone here understood Scarlett's ways. Strangers might've felt they'd just been threatened.

I held up a kitchen timer, twisted it to sixty minutes, then did a ten-second count down. "Ten, nine, eight, seven, six, five, four, three, two, one! Open your puzzle boxes, ladies." I rang a small bell I kept around for games then sat down across from Esther.

I reached out and pulled the lid off the box, noting everyone else doing the same.

Esther leaned forward, glanced into the box, and smiled. "Did I ever tell you I won a jigsaw puzzle speed contest for putting together a two-thousand-piece puzzle faster than over a hundred other puzzlers?"

My eyes opened wide in surprise. Here I thought I'd taken on the one person who would be slowest, only to find out she was probably going to be better at this than I was.

# CHAPTER 5

For the next hour, the room was quiet except for the occasional cough or sneeze. The puzzles were new, which meant they had what appeared to be sawdust in them, though it was really only cardboard dust, or "puzzle dust," as it's commonly known.

I was fascinated, watching Esther's hands flying through the pieces. Before I could hardly get accustomed to my chair, she was making a nice pile of the outside pieces with their flat edges. Our puzzle was titled "C is for Calico," so I assumed our mystery would have something to do with a cat.

At one point, Cathy called out, "Tabi, the pieces aren't the same colors as the picture on the box."

"The puzzles are all mystery puzzles. You can't rely on the top of the box," I answered. If she had read the itinerary closer, she would have known that, but I wasn't surprised. Cathy was fun-loving and carefree but often missed the details. From the reaction in the room, I guessed Cathy wasn't the only one who hadn't read the instructions carefully.

From where I was sitting, I could see everyone else in the room. Because Esther was so adept at puzzles, I found myself just watching the others. Dawn seemed very intrigued by the puzzle, but Monica kept lifting her eyes and glancing around the room. Once, her eyes met Scarlett's, and Monica's cheeks flushed pink. It was as if she was embarrassed about something. Scarlett, on the other hand, only glared at Monica.

Jennifer yawned a few times, making me wonder if she'd actually wanted to be here this weekend or if Dawn had dragged her kicking and screaming. Gloria kept her eyes down and worked silently on the puzzle, but once I noticed her flash a look of hatred at Monica.

*I'm never going to host a friendly hometown gathering here again,* I decided, especially if this was the way people were going to act.

Once or twice, I noticed Linda staring at Monica. She seemed to have her eyes fixed on Monica's hand instead of her face. I looked at Monica's hand and couldn't see anything out of the ordinary about it, except she had no wedding ring, which only made sense. She told me she'd never been married when I interviewed her.

Scarlett kept whispering to Barb. I think she was scolding her for not being fast enough. Barb's face was definitely pale the whole evening. However, I wasn't too worried about it. If Barb even thought for a moment that Cathy was upset, Barb would let it ruin her own evening. She was very devoted to Cathy.

Esther had just set the last edge piece into place when the timer rang, causing almost everyone to jump.

"That's it. Everyone has to stop." I looked around. Several ladies stuck a few more pieces together, but then they pulled their hands back.

"We didn't get the outside edge finished," Scarlett complained. "It won't be fair."

"You'll have to finish it in the morning when we all get

together again. Maybe you'll be faster at the inside pieces."

She didn't seem to be pacified by my words.

Monica stood, and I watched as several heads turned to stare at her. She didn't meet any of their eyes but instead slipped out of the room.

"Monica's gone to get pumpkin pie and coffee. If anyone wants to sit at the table, that's fine, but everyone needs to cover their puzzle now."

I waited while the others placed the cardboard squares I'd cut to the dimensions of the puzzles over their pieces. I could almost feel their hands itching to put in a few more pieces. From what I could tell, Esther and I were the only ones who'd finished the outer edge completely.

The next few minutes, everyone rose and began to move around the room. A few headed straight to the table and sat waiting for their pie. I noticed Cathy looking around the coffee table.

"Tabi, you never answered my question," she said. "Do you have a 1977 yearbook?" I realized she wasn't going to let the question drop.

"Yes, it was on the table earlier." I started to head toward the end table, thinking that Bonnie and Clyde had somehow gotten the book and pushed it under the table again, but just then, the two dogs bounded into the room.

Monica came in behind them, pie in one hand and a carafe in another. "I'm sorry, Tabi. They just wanted to meet everyone."

I laughed. It was obvious these two dogs had minds of their own. They must've slipped out of my room and come downstairs while we were working on the puzzles.

The dogs jumped up and down, their ears flopping. Everyone

seemed to think they were adorable.

Dawn actually squealed, "Oh, Monica, these two are precious. What sweethearts!"

Monica flushed a bit. "Yes, they're my babies. I had two older beagles, but they passed away a few years ago, so I finally decided to adopt another dog. When I found these two together, though, I just had to adopt them both." She'd placed the pie on the table and was cutting nice-sized slices and setting them on plates.

"Your babies?" Gloria's normal sweet voice sounded harsh. "What about your own child?"

Monica looked like she'd been slapped. Her head dropped. "I've never had any children."

Someone gasped.

Monica called Bonnie and Clyde to follow her, and the dogs wiggled their way behind her back to the kitchen.

I wanted to reprimand someone but didn't know who. I just knew we all needed to mind our own business.

As I sat down at the table beside Gloria, I heard Cathy mutter something that sounded like, "But Roger said—" She didn't finish her sentence because the kitchen door opened again, and Monica came out with a pitcher of cream.

When she left the room again, Jennifer said, "She's a good cook." Then her eyes popped wide. "I remember her now. Didn't she work at a small diner outside of town?"

Dawn nodded.

I glanced up at Jennifer in wonder. She knew Monica too.

"Remember the time we went on that double date, Dawn? Both our husbands kept talking about what a great cook she was and how we should take lessons from her."

I watched the red roll onto Dawn's cheeks. She leaned

forward and actually hissed, "That was a long time ago. No need to bring it up now."

Jennifer placed a hand over her mouth then slowly slipped it away and whispered, "I'm sorry. I forgot. She's not the one. . ."

Dawn's head shook back and forth vigorously.

A memory of something I'd heard once niggled my mind. There'd been a rumor that Dawn's husband had an affair, but no one could ever give exact details. The desire to hear more gossip rose up in me.

*Lord, this is one of the moments I need Your help.*

The next twenty minutes were quiet. Everyone ate their pie, drank their coffee, then one by one gave a reason for leaving the room. Dawn and Jennifer were going upstairs to do a Bible study together. Gloria wanted to get her grandmother settled for the night. Scarlett announced she was making it an early evening to get her beauty sleep, and Linda simply left the room.

Only Cathy and Barb were left at the table. They waited until Monica had cleared all the dishes and was in the kitchen running water. Then Cathy leaned over and whispered, "You know, Tabi, Monica left school because she was pregnant."

Immediately, my interest was piqued. "Really? Who was the father?"

Barb reached out and laid a hand on Cathy's arm. Cathy looked at her friend then clamped her mouth shut.

I wanted to slap my head. Here I was, just minutes ago asking God to help me, and I was literally begging for gossip. It was good that Barb was such a stable force.

Barb stood. "I'm tired. I thought about going out to a movie, but I think I'll take a sleeping pill and go to bed early. How about you, Cathy?"

Cathy stood and nodded. Her lips were pressed together in a grim line. I wondered if she was mad at Barb for stopping her from talking.

"I'll just get a glass of water," Barb said. She pushed open the door and stepped into the kitchen.

Cathy turned to face me. "Sorry for bringing that up. I guess it's not my place to talk about Monica."

"I understand." My shoulders dropped. I realized I'd been hoping Cathy would tell me more when Barb left the room, and I was disappointed she wasn't going to. Once again, shame filled my soul. I'd been hoping to hear gossip. I shook my head at my own failings. Was I ever going to learn?

I reached over and took Cathy's hand, tucked it into the crook of my arm, and led her to the stairwell. We didn't say anything more. I watched as she made her way up the stairs. Barb wasn't far behind. She held a glass of water in her hand.

"Good night, Barb," I said as she made her way up the steps.

She turned and looked back at me. "Yes, I think it will be. Anyway, I hope so. I've needed a good night's sleep for a long time."

After helping Monica clean the kitchen, I was pretty tired, but I needed to find out if whatever was going on with her and the other women was going to be an ongoing problem.

"Monica, I noticed some tension between you and some guests. Are there any issues we need to deal with?"

She set down the last water glass she'd been drying with the cute dishtowel with Halloween pumpkin faces all over it.

"I don't think so. I mean, high school was a long time ago. I was a different person then, but I left school my senior year because my father got sick. I had to take care of him. I was the head cheerleader, dating a guy named Roger Steubing. I've heard rumors through the years about me and Roger. None of them are true, but I was surprised by the way a few of the ladies reacted to me. I haven't seen any of them since the day I left school."

I smiled. "Okay, well I hope now that the initial meeting is over, everyone will let bygones be bygones. I'm not going to push you for any more information, but if anyone makes you feel uncomfortable, let me know." I wondered if she was the head cheerleader who had cut Gloria from the team.

She nodded slowly. I thought she looked as if she had something more to tell me, then she dropped the towel on the counter.

"Has someone already given you a hard time?" I felt obligated to ask, although I didn't see how anyone would've had time to even speak to Monica for more than a few seconds.

Monica stared at me then shook her head. "No, I guess it's all good."

"By the way, that pumpkin pie was as good as any Mrs. Adams used to serve. Did you use her recipe?"

Monica flipped open a recipe book on the counter, which had been handwritten by Mrs. Adams. She pointed at one of the pages. "Yep, used this recipe right here. I followed it to a *T*. She was very detailed in her recipes. You have to pay attention to the little notes she jotted along the edges of the pages. Sometimes there's a special tweak."

I leaned over and glanced at the book, wondering if I would ever be able to make sense of the recipes. Once more, I thought about offering to hire Monica on a more regular basis, but I decided to wait until this weekend was over. There was always Bonnie and Clyde to consider. So far, they weren't the perfect little angels Monica had assured me they would be.

Monica left the kitchen, and I turned off the lights and moved toward the front room through the dining room then turned at the stairwell. The downstairs was very dark, but I didn't consider turning on a light. I was pretty sure everyone would sleep the whole night through. If anyone needed a drink, there were bottled waters in the rooms. Unless someone felt the need to raid my refrigerator, the kitchen would remain dark and closed.

With one last glance into the front room, I remembered the 1977 yearbook, which was missing from the coffee table. I was pretty sure Bonnie and Clyde had done their hiding trick again, but I was too exhausted to spend time looking for it. I decided it could wait until morning.

After slipping into my nightgown, I looked around my room for my robe. I usually kept it on the foot of my bed, but it wasn't there. I tried to remember if I'd tossed it in the laundry recently.

Finally, I climbed into bed and turned out the light, hoping to fall asleep quickly. My bedroom door was ajar, as usual. My last thought was that I needed to talk to each of the ladies privately to find out how we could resolve the problem with Monica.

# CHAPTER 6

Sometime in the middle of the night, two thuds on the end of my bed woke me up. I sat up in surprise. My room was pretty dark, and I could just make out the shape of two dogs.

"Bonnie, Clyde? What are you doing here?"

Their eyes were shining in the dark. They eyed me warily. Clyde leaned over and dropped something on the floor with a thud, then they both sprawled out on the end of the bed. Obviously, they were planning to spend the night in my room. I wasn't in the mood to drag them down the stairs nor search my floor to find out what they'd dropped, so I just shrugged and reached over to pet them.

"You two are going to be in big trouble tomorrow," I whispered.

Clyde's paw was a bit wet. I assumed Monica had let them outside to potty, and when they came back in, they'd hightailed it up the stairs instead of back to her room.

I didn't think she would have chased them, and since my door was the only one open on the second floor, it only made sense they chose to come in. I lay back, closed my eyes, and determined to set more ground rules about the dogs with Monica in the morning.

A piercing scream broke into my dreams and woke me again. I opened my eyes then lifted my head and glanced at the doorway, where the scream was coming from.

Scarlett Star was standing outside my room shrieking in an extremely irritating tone. She was pointing at my bed, and her arm was shaking. I slowly allowed my eyes to adjust to the morning light and followed her finger to the end of my bed where Bonnie and Clyde lay peacefully sleeping.

I sat up. "What's going on?"

Scarlett stopped the screeching. "I don't know, but there's bloody shoe prints out here in the hallway. Her eyes grew wide, and she screeched again and pointed again. "And look at your bed!"

I looked past the dogs and saw that the bottom of my comforter was stained with a rusty red color.

I heard more doors in the hallway opening, and several women joined Scarlett outside my door.

I slipped out of bed, trying not to disturb the dogs. If one of them had cut their paw on something, the last thing I needed was for them to start running around the house. I took a step, and my foot kicked something. I looked down. It was one of the old wooden-handled steak knives from the kitchen. The blade was covered in the same rusty color that was on the bed.

I stared at it in confusion. The dogs must have carried it into my room, but how did they get a knife from the kitchen counter? Had one of them cut their mouth on it? I started toward the dogs, pity surging through me, then I stopped when I noticed the carpet.

There were definitely some faint bloody prints on the carpet—although not clear, there seemed to be three sets. Two belonged to Bonnie and Clyde and the other set looked like they were from my house shoes, which were nearby and also stained.

"Don't move!" I shouted to Cathy, Dawn, and Scarlett, although they all seemed to be frozen in one spot, just staring into the room. I was surprised not to see Barb, although she did say she was going to take a sleeping pill last night, so that was probably why she was able to sleep through the hullabaloo.

I realized I was going to have to take things in hand. I automatically reached out and picked up my house robe. I slipped my arms into the sleeves then turned to face the women. Scarlett's mouth opened and closed, but no words came out as she crumpled into a heap on the floor.

Cathy's eyes were wider than I'd ever seen, but her lips were clamped closed. Dawn squinted at me. She leaned into the room and with a hoarse voice said, "Tabi, your robe!"

I looked down at the robe, which was a silky white with a yellow rose pattern all over it. It too was splattered with the same stains as the carpet and bedspread. With trembling hands, I untied the sash and laid the garment back on the bed carefully then stepped away, remembering how I'd not been able to find the robe the previous night.

There was no blood anywhere else I could see, so I rushed to my closet, pulled out an older robe, tied it around my waist, and moved back into the room.

Dawn and Cathy were trying to revive Scarlett. I wondered if it was a real faint or just a staged one. Would she be so crass as to put on an act at a moment like this? They seemed to be having trouble getting her to wake up.

I moved closer, staring at the footprints the whole time. I looked out into the hallway and followed the prints with my eyes. They ended at the stairwell, but I couldn't see the steps, so I wasn't sure if there were more.

I lifted my foot up high to step over Scarlett and moved to the stairs. The bloody prints were on the steps as well. I gulped, turned back to the women, and said, "Stay upstairs."

Shakily, I made my way down the steps, avoiding the prints, yet at the same time wondering if they would come out of the woodwork with my regular pine cleaner. Probably not the thought to be having, but hey, one can't always control their mind.

As I followed the bloody prints, they became more defined, so I knew I was almost to their source. I walked through the front room. Nothing was out of place. I stepped into the dining room and found nothing out of order there either. I stopped at the kitchen door. By this time, my entire body was shaking uncontrollably. Why hadn't I asked one of the others to come down with me? What was I thinking?

"Monica?" My voice wavered. I put my ear against the door but heard nothing.

Just then I remembered we were serving turkey for dinner. Perhaps the pan in the refrigerator with the thawing bird had somehow spilled, and Bonnie and Clyde had walked through the blood. Trying to avoid thinking about the knife, I stood up straight, a bit less worried, and pushed open the kitchen door, hoping to find myself laughing about the whole situation.

One step in, I held my hand up to my mouth to cover my scream. I could see a pair of legs sticking out from behind the counter. I hurried forward until I could see the whole body then

I turned, put my head down on the counter, and started gasping for air.

It was Monica. There was no question she was dead.

As I tried to get my breath and my bearings, the other kitchen door opened, and Gloria strolled in.

"Hi, Tabi, Grandmother and I slept wonderfully—" She stopped speaking when she noticed Monica's body sprawled on the floor. Her hand flew to her heart and she began stuttering, "Wh-wh-what happened? What is she doing there?"

For a moment, a fit of some type came over me. I wanted to cry and laugh all at the same time. I clamped my teeth together to keep either from happening. This wasn't the time for hysterics. Three more deep breaths, and I felt more in control.

I looked up at Gloria. "Can you call the police, please? Monica's been murdered."

Gloria turned and stumbled out of the room. I could hear her making the call. I couldn't look at Monica again, but I didn't move. I wasn't sure what to do, so I closed my eyes and prayed. In a few moments, my sanity seemed to have returned.

I knew from watching detective shows that I needed to make sure the body and crime scene weren't disturbed. I looked around. Besides the footprints going away from Monica's body and leading to my bed, I didn't see anything out of the ordinary. I walked over and latched the kitchen door that led to the two back bedrooms. Gloria and Esther would have to come around the other way.

Suddenly, I realized what I had done. Touching the kitchen

latch was a mistake. I could have smudged a vital fingerprint. Oh well, what was done was done. I wanted to cover Monica with a blanket, perhaps to give her some comfort or a sense of dignity, but I knew the police would frown on that, so I made my way back to the front room. I stood by the bottom steps and listened.

Scarlett had obviously been revived and was still carrying on quite a bit. I heard several other voices murmuring. By now, Jennifer and Barb were probably awake.

"Dawn! Dawn?" I called up the stairs. Her face appeared.

"Yes?"

"Can you make sure no one goes into my room? I'm sure the police will want to see it."

She nodded vigorously, but her eyes were filled with questions.

"Get Scarlett calmed down then gather all the women and bring them down to the front room. Tell them not to step on the footprints on the stairs."

"What is it?" Dawn asked.

"I'll tell everyone together."

She slipped away, and I leaned against the wall, blinking back tears. I could hear the faint sound of police sirens growing louder. I stepped over to the wall mirror in the front hallway and ran my fingers through my hair to try and look presentable.

Gloria appeared from the other end of the hall. She walked over and took my hand in hers.

"Tabi, why do you think Monica was murdered? Maybe she just fell and hit her head? Did you take her pulse?"

I shook my head, wondering if Gloria was just blocking out the image of Monica's bloody chest.

My teeth were chattering. "There's a bloody knife, and footprints. . ." I leaned my head on her shoulder. "It's pretty obvious."

"Where is the knife?" she asked.

I looked up at her. "It's in my room, along with my shoes, which are bloodstained."

I felt Gloria grow stiff. She pushed me back so she could look into my eyes.

"I didn't kill her." The words tumbled from my mouth. "But someone went to a lot of trouble to make it look like I did."

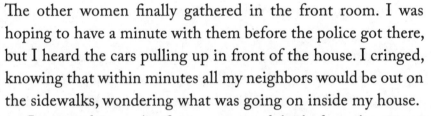

The other women finally gathered in the front room. I was hoping to have a minute with them before the police got there, but I heard the cars pulling up in front of the house. I cringed, knowing that within minutes all my neighbors would be out on the sidewalks, wondering what was going on inside my house.

I stepped into the front room and looked at the group. "Listen, I don't have very long to tell you what's going on, but Monica is dead."

The gasps around the room indicated their surprise. I wanted to watch the reaction on each of their faces, but the doorbell was ringing and I knew the police wouldn't wait.

"Everyone, stay in here, please." I rushed to the front door, grabbed the knob, twisted, and pulled. The door opened. As I suspected, there were about ten police officers in my front yard. Our whole town's force.

None of them moved at first. Then I noticed them parting and allowing one officer to make his way to the front. When he reached the door, his familiar smile caused my heart to drop. Why did it have to be Officer Jace Miller?

The man stepped inside, filling the doorway with his height. "Hello." He smiled at me, which, even though at the moment it seemed ludicrous, sent a little shiver of warmth through my insides.

"Hello." I couldn't think of anything else to say. What do you say to the man you've only just been getting to know and suddenly he's at your door because there's a murdered woman in your kitchen?

I looked up at him. He smiled again, and tears burst from my eyes.

He reached out, took my hand in his, and gave it a gentle squeeze. I tried to speak, to tell him what was going on, but the words kept catching in my throat and nothing could pass my lips. Finally, the one thing I needed to hold on to was able to slip out.

"I didn't murder her."

He leaned closer to me. "Of course you didn't, Tabi." His words were like a soft breath on my cheek.

I felt my cheeks flush pink, a ridiculous thing to happen at a time like this. I pulled back.

"Why are you so sure I didn't murder Monica? You haven't even seen the crime scene, and the blood, and it all leads to my bedroom. . ." I took a shuddering breath.

Jace swished his hair back with a quick nod.

"It's been my experience that good Christian women are not murderers, as a general rule. That's not to say they can't be."

He leaned closer and met my eyes. "Are you sure you aren't the murderer?"

Tears continued to leak from my eyes. "I'm sure I'm not. I barely knew the woman. She only came here to cook. She did go to my high school. . ."

Jace patted my hand. "Listen, we'll have plenty of time to talk about all this. For now I need to start my investigation." He dropped my hand. I felt alone and vulnerable.

I really wasn't sure what was happening the next half hour. Jace led me into the front room and asked me to sit on one of the chairs. He patted my shoulder and told me to leave everything to him. By then, the reality of the situation was setting in, and I felt rather numb.

*Who killed Monica? Why did they try to make it look like I did it?*

My shoulders dropped, and I felt a wave of weariness. If anyone would let me, I'd like to curl up in my bed and go to sleep.

I noticed the other women all huddled close to one another. None of them were speaking, but most of them were pale, with large frightened eyes.

Finally, I sat up, remembering my position as hostess. There wasn't much I could do right now, but at least I could act as if everything was going to be all right. I turned my head, trying to see what the officers were doing. Jace was in the kitchen, but others were taking pictures of the footprints and dusting for fingerprints on the stairwell. Then I saw two young officers carrying Bonnie and Clyde down the stairs. The dogs' feet were wrapped in plastic baggies.

I jumped up and met the men at the bottom of the steps. "What are you going to do with the dogs?"

"Gotta get some blood samples from their paws, then I guess wash them off. Do they belong to you?"

I shook my head. "No, Monica. . .that is, the woman who was killed, she owned the dogs."

"Okay, want us to call the animal shelter? They can keep the dogs until someone comes to claim them."

I looked at Clyde's face. He seemed frightened, and Bonnie was literally shaking in the other officer's arms.

"No. Why don't you get the samples you need, then I'll wash them off in the back bathroom." I pointed toward the door at the end of the hall, which led to the rooms Gloria and Monica had been staying in. I wasn't sure what I would do with the dogs, but as upset as they were, the last thing they needed was to be put into a cold cage at the animal shelter.

The officers agreed and headed toward the back bathroom. They assured me they'd call me when they were done getting their samples, so I sat back down to wait.

Scarlett waited until the officers were gone then leaned over and asked, "Tabi, what is going on here? Is Monica really dead? And why were those footprints and blood all over your room?"

She'd spoken loud enough for the women to hear, and they all turned their heads and stared at me.

"Yes, Monica really is dead. I have no idea why the footprints were in my room. The blood on the bed was from the dogs' paws. I assume they either saw Monica get killed or discovered her body after the fact. They must've found the knife and carried it to my room."

I spoke clearly and with determination. I wanted them to

know I had nothing to do with Monica's death, but the unspoken question on everyone's face was, *If not you then who?*

As I scrubbed Bonnie and Clyde, they sat quietly in the bathtub, enjoying the warm water. I watched as the red water disappeared down the drain, but I tried not to think of it as Monica's blood.

I leaned over the bathtub, took Clyde's head in my hands, and whispered, "Did you see who did that terrible thing to Monica?" He licked my face. A few moments later, as I held them both in my arms, rubbing them dry with some old towels, I wondered if there was anyone in Monica's life to take charge of the dogs.

She mentioned she'd never had children, but I didn't know if she had ever been married or if she had siblings. I supposed that was something Jace would find out.

The main thing on my mind now was trying to find out who actually killed Monica. Even the most inept police officer would soon figure out that the bloodstained shoes in my room, the robe, and the knife were all meant to frame me. A sudden thought hit me. *The murderer must be one of the women here for the Mystery Puzzle Weekend!* Who else could it have been? The police hadn't found any forced entry. The front and back doors were still locked, and I had the only keys to them. My stomach clenched at the thought of one of those women committing murder.

*Lord, which of the women here hated Monica enough to kill her and perhaps dislikes me as well?*

The only women I didn't really know very well were Scarlett and Linda Royal. I can't say I was on very intimate terms with Dawn or Jennifer, but by their reactions to everything that had happened with Monica so far, they didn't seem to know her at all.

Cathy, Barb, and Gloria had all gone to school at the same time as Monica, although from what Monica told me, she left school in 1977, which was the year Gloria and Linda graduated. Scarlett graduated in 1978. Cathy, Barb, and I graduated in 1980.

I tried to remember anything I could about my freshman year, but nothing significant came to mind, at least nothing that any of my classmates would've killed Monica for.

As I finished brushing out the dogs with one of my best hairbrushes, someone knocked on the bathroom door then opened it after I called softly, "Come in."

I was sitting on the floor, still in my bathrobe. I looked up. Jace was standing there with a quirky smile on his face. "I see you've taken my two best witnesses into your confidence."

I gave Bonnie a final pat on the head then stood up. "Yep, but I think they're more likely to be the innocent bystanders than the witnesses. When they came to my room last night, they were a bit shaky, but I didn't get the impression they'd just witnessed their owner being killed. I think Monica must've gone out to the kitchen, was killed, and the dogs came along a while later. Clyde must've found the knife and carried it up to my room."

The sequence made sense to me. I only hoped Jace thought so too.

"Did you know Monica very well?" he asked.

I shook my head. "She was a senior when I was a freshman and left before the end of the year. I don't remember ever seeing her at school again, and I've definitely never seen her since. I was looking for a cook for the weekend, and someone recommended her to me."

"Hmm," Jace murmured. "Did you recognize her when she

showed up for the job?"

I nodded. "I remembered her vaguely from high school but not her name. I had never talked to her before our interview a few weeks ago." I placed my hands on my hips and glared at him. "Look, if I had any issue with her, I don't see why I'd wait until the middle of the night to murder her, then traipse all the way up to my room in bloody shoes, and allow anyone to see the prints the next day. Please tell me you know a setup when you see one?"

Jace ran a hand through his blond hair, his blue eyes seeming to twinkle at me. "It does look like a pretty obvious frame job, but murderers have been known to create blatant setups to throw the police off their trail."

I sat down on the edge of the bathtub with a huff. Clyde moved closer to me and growled at Jace. I reached down and patted his head.

"Well, all I can tell you is I've never met Monica before, and I had no reason to kill her. If I ever do decide I want to kill someone, I won't do it in my own bed-and-breakfast. Do you know what this will do to the reputation of the place?"

Jace backed out of the bathroom. "I see your point. I really don't think you did it, but I do have to keep an open mind. We've finished in the kitchen, and we've gathered all the evidence we need. The only thing I want is for all your guests to stay here through the weekend. We will be coming back to take everyone's statements, but I'm not sure when. I plan to leave an officer outside for now."

"Okay," I answered. "Can I. . ." I gulped. "Clean the bloodstains? It will be pretty difficult for the women to feel comfortable with those still here."

"Yes, we've gotten photos and samples of everything. I think the officers cleaned the kitchen already, and we've taken Monica's body to the morgue. You don't know who we should contact about her death?"

"No. But when you do find out anything, let me know if they plan to take Bonnie and Clyde." I pointed at the duo sitting at my feet.

"I will." Jace turned and walked away.

I realized I'd been holding my breath most of the time he was in the bathroom with me. Not out of fear of being arrested but out of pure attraction. The man made my heart beat double time, but this was not the time to let him see my feelings. I glanced down at the fur babies.

"Are you two hungry?"

Both dogs gave a little bark, so I headed toward the room Monica had been staying in. I knew she had their food and water bowls in her room.

Before I entered the room, another officer stopped me. "We've done a preliminary on the room, but we'll want to go through all of her belongings, so don't disturb anything."

I assured him I wouldn't and entered the room. I found the bowls and bag of food against the wall and bent over to pick them up. Something shimmered by the foot of the bed. I reached out and grabbed the item. When I opened my hand, I found myself looking at a high school class ring, much like the one I owned. The only difference was this one was too big for a woman's finger.

I held it up to the light and noticed something was engraved inside. I moved closer to the window and squinted. The engraving was easy to read. *Roger Steubing.*

Shaking my head at my own stupidity for touching the ring, I walked over and set it on the desk next to the bed. I'd have to tell

Jace about the ring later on. Even though Monica had told me the nasty rumors about her and Roger weren't true, she must've cared for him a great deal to be carrying around his class ring for so many years.

# CHAPTER 7

When I got to the kitchen, I set the bowls on the floor and filled them with food and water. Bonnie and Clyde seemed happy and began eating.

Gloria came into the kitchen, a bit hesitant. She was carrying a tray with empty coffee cups. "The police officer said they cleared the kitchen."

"Yes, they've taken Monica's body to the morgue, and they cleaned up a bit. I want to do a thorough scrubbing, but I need to talk to the whole group first."

Gloria nodded and set the tray on the counter.

"Gloria, yesterday you were going to tell me something about Monica and high school. Can you tell me now?"

Gloria's facial features changed. She looked very serious and a bit angry. "I don't like to remember it, but I suppose I can tell you."

She stepped closer and lowered her voice. "You know, I've always been a quiet person."

I nodded.

"There was only once in my whole life I wanted to do something, shall we say, not so quiet."

I leaned closer. "Yes?"

"I wanted to be a cheerleader."

I nodded again.

"I know I'm not the type, but believe me, I worked hard, and I was really good. Everyone said so, but Monica's vote was more powerful than anybody else's. She voted against me being on the team, so I never got to be a cheerleader."

"Why did she vote against you?" I was afraid I already knew the answer.

"Because I was pretty. Monica only wanted girls on the squad who were not as pretty as she was."

"You must've hated her for that." The words just slipped out, and I could see I'd upset Gloria.

"That was a long time ago. In fact, once I found out I wasn't going to be a cheerleader, I joined the cooking club. That's how I learned to make such good scones. I was very happy and made some really good friends."

I felt she was telling the truth. "Why did you react so strangely when you first saw Monica then?"

Gloria shrugged. "To tell you the truth, I'm not sure. Monica left school that year, and I never saw her again. I guess I was just surprised. When I saw her, the memory of her keeping me from the team upset me."

Just then, Esther called out for Gloria, who turned and rushed out of the kitchen. I followed. When I entered the front room behind her, the other women were gathered there. They all looked at me.

"Officer Miller has informed me that he wants all of you to stay here the entire weekend. He will be coming back to take personal statements from everyone later on."

Scarlett threw her arms up in the air. "What, in a house where there's been a murder? How can he expect us. . . What does he expect us to do?"

"Well, I know it may seem a bit callous, but I think we should try to follow the itinerary as planned to the best of our ability. It will keep our minds off this tragedy."

Linda spoke up. "I agree. Isn't that what we all came here for? I for one don't want the death of that upstart to interfere any further with my weekend. But who will take her part?" She looked at Dawn. "Wasn't she partners with you?"

I was a bit surprised by the woman's heartless words. "I plan to drop out and let Dawn partner with Esther."

I knew it could take hours to scrub the prints off the stairs and my bedroom carpet. I wondered if they'd taken my shoes, robe, and comforter as evidence. I had forgotten to tell Jace about not being able to find my robe the night before. Someone must've snuck into my room and taken my shoes and robe to wear while murdering Monica.

The thought shocked me because that also meant it was a premeditated murder. One of these innocent-looking women had planned it all out and killed Monica.

"Why don't you all get started on your puzzles? This afternoon you can probably get quite a lot done. Remember, no reading the mystery yet," I admonished.

The women all stood and moved around the room, taking their places at the tables where they'd sat the night before, except for Dawn, who took my place across from Esther. I set the timer for an hour and rang the school bell.

"If you need to use the restroom, there is one down the back hallway. For now, however, please don't go into the room Monica used."

No one commented, but they all gave an acknowledging nod. They began working on the puzzles, and I slipped back into the kitchen.

The first thing I did was look in the refrigerator. The women were going to get hungry, and I wasn't sure if Monica had prepared anything. I was happy to find a tray filled with pumpkin-stuffed deviled eggs and another tray of finger sandwiches. There was also a bowl with more of the pumpkin soup from the evening before. This was surely enough to serve for lunch, and I could think about dinner later on.

I ran upstairs and quickly changed into some real clothes. I'd been wearing my old ratty bathrobe long enough. Back in the kitchen, I got out a mop and filled the sink with Pine-Sol. In minutes, I was scrubbing the floor and all the cabinets around the area where Monica had been killed. Each time I found a splatter of blood, my stomach twisted. As upset as my insides felt, I wasn't going to be able to eat more than a few crackers today.

I'd just finished rinsing out the mop and hanging it up to dry when Linda made her way into the kitchen.

"Can I get you something?" I asked.

"Yes, do you have a soda of any kind?"

I nodded and pulled open the fridge door. "Sprite or Coke?" I asked.

"Anything diet? I have to watch my weight."

I handed her a Diet Coke then asked, "Mrs. Royal...Linda. What did you mean when you called Monica an upstart?"

Her eyes flashed angrily. "Don't you remember? Weren't you a freshman that year?"

I automatically stepped back at her onslaught. "In 1977, I was."

"Then I'm sure you remember my humiliation." Her cheeks were turning red now.

"No, not really."

"I was dating Roger Steubing. We'd been together two years. I was sure he was going to ask me to marry him at the end of the year, but then he met Monica, and he broke up with me right there in the middle of the school cafeteria. Everyone saw it. I was so humiliated."

I didn't speak, but I noticed a tear dripping slowly down her cheek. She was obviously still very hurt over this.

"I had to watch him, all year long, with Monica. He didn't really love her, though, not like he loved me."

I leaned closer and dropped my voice. "What makes you so sure?"

"Because Monica wasn't the only one he was dating. There were several other girls. When we were together, there was only me. It had to be Monica who changed him."

"I'm so sorry that happened to you. Have you hated her all these years?" I slid the question in, hoping she wouldn't notice my attempt at sleuthing.

Suddenly, she stopped speaking and wiped the tears off her face. "Hated her? Well, at first, perhaps. But then I graduated and went away to college, something I wouldn't have done if Roger and I had married."

She stood straighter. "At college, I met Stan. He was one of my college professors and a very wealthy man. We got married when I graduated and have lived happily together ever since. So, you see, in a way, I owed Monica my gratitude. I don't know whatever became of Roger Steubing, but I seriously doubt he ever amounted to anything beyond a college football player. He wasn't very smart."

I didn't say any more. From what I could tell, she was being truthful. Perhaps the police would be able to find a chink in her story, but I believed her. Even if she'd hated Monica, it hadn't lasted long enough for her to want to murder the woman.

Linda took her Diet Coke and returned to the front room. I walked over to the kitchen desk and pulled out a pad of paper. I wrote each woman's name in one column. Next to Linda's name, I jotted down her story. Then I added Gloria's story beside her name.

Perhaps if I was able to talk to all of the women, I could help Jace find out which one had the best motive for murder. I wondered if he would be pleased or not. I glanced down at Bonnie and Clyde. They had finished eating and were sitting at my feet, staring up at me with what I can only say was a look of true adoration.

*If only Jace Miller would look at me that way.*

I peeked in to see how the jigsaw puzzles were going. It looked like Esther and Dawn weren't in first place any longer. Most of the puzzles were a bit dark in my opinion, without much detail, making the puzzles even harder to put together, and with no photo to follow all the more so.

I had been really looking forward to participating in this event, but making sure I wasn't accused of murder seemed to be more important.

I worked vigorously on the stairs, washing the bloodstains away. When I heard the timer go off, I removed my rubber gloves, washed up, and moved into the front room. I walked from table to table looking at the puzzles. If we had another session tonight, I realized most everyone would finish their puzzles, and the next day could be spent on reading and trying to solve the mysteries. The women seemed to be enjoying the puzzles in spite of the circumstances. From the way they were acting, I couldn't believe any one of them was guilty of murder.

Usually on Saturday afternoons, my guests go into town to shop in the quaint old town square, but no one was allowed to leave the house this weekend. I racked my brain to come up with an activity for them but wasn't sure what to do. Then I remembered my box of rubber stamps and notecards.

I stood in front of the ladies. "How would you all feel about making some greeting cards for the local nursing home residents?"

Their eyes brightened and heads nodded, except Scarlett's. "Why would we want to do that?"

"I thought it would keep us busy since we aren't allowed to leave the house. If you prefer to read a book or take a rest, that's fine too."

Scarlett stood up. "I'll opt for a rest. I don't want this murder to take its toll on my health. I have a performance next Friday."

Scarlett left the room and made her way up the stairs. I think everyone was too shocked at her callous words to say anything.

I asked Dawn to help me. She followed me to my hall closet. I rummaged around a bit and finally found the box.

"This is a good idea, Tabi. It will help keep our minds off the murder."

"That's what I was thinking. I can't imagine anyone here having a reason to murder Monica."

Dawn picked up the box. "Well, Linda didn't like her, and I felt a lot of strange waves at the table last night."

"Did you know her? Monica?" I asked.

"Nope. From what everyone has been saying, we went to the same high school, but she must have been there a few years after I graduated. Jennifer thinks we saw her once, working at a diner. I don't remember. . ." Her voice faded away.

"Who else do you think recognized her?"

Dawn squinted her eyes in thought. "Hmm, I'm trying to remember the scene. I know Linda knew her, but I thought I saw a few others with an angry look in their eyes. Scarlett, Cathy, Barb. . ."

"Gloria?"

She shook her head. "I don't remember."

We carried the box to the front room. I suggested everyone gather at the dining room table again, where I laid out the stamps and cards. I was glad to see I still had colored pencils and markers.

Once they got started, I walked back into the front room just as Bonnie and Clyde came pouncing in. I'd almost forgotten about them. They'd had breakfast and a nap. Now, they wanted some attention.

I guess I wasn't surprised to see them both head straight for the end table and start sniffing there. I'd forgotten about the yearbook. I knelt down and began searching under a sofa when the front door opened, and Officer Miller stepped into the front hall.

# CHAPTER 8

M y cheeks flushed pink. He'd come in when I was on my knees with my backside stuck up in the air. Not quite the side of me I wanted him to see. At least I wasn't in pajamas and a robe any longer. I quickly stood and tried to walk toward him casually.

"Hi." I smiled.

"Hi." He smiled back. "How is everyone holding up?"

My shoulders dropped. For a minute there I'd almost forgotten the only reason this gorgeous man was here was because Monica had been murdered.

*Lord, what kind of person am I?*

"I think they're doing okay. There are a few things I want to tell you." I wondered if he'd be glad that I was able to find out some things from a few of the guests or if he'd think I was just interfering.

Clyde started growling. I turned to look at him. He was pawing under the end table.

"What's wrong with him?" Jace asked.

"One of the yearbooks fell under the table. I'm not sure why Bonnie and Clyde are so interested in that one book."

Jace cocked his head. "Dogs have really great senses. Maybe

you should take a close look at that book. If you find anything, let me know."

I nodded. "I'm glad you said that because I had the chance to talk to a couple of the women alone. I think I found out some things you might want to know." I looked up at him innocently.

He leaned forward. "So, you're one of those?"

"One of what?"

"I could call it a nosy neighbor, a busybody. In your case, I'll just call you a sleuth." He stared at me, a serious look on his face.

I bit my bottom lip but giggled. "Sort of a Nancy Drew."

His smile spread over his face. "Since we understand what you're doing, let's set some guidelines. You can ask questions in a friendly way, but don't put yourself into any dangerous positions. You know, don't go into a room with the door closed with any of the women. Always make sure others are near, and don't accuse anyone of anything. We don't need to cause the murderer to feel desperate enough to harm you."

I was really surprised by Jace's attitude. I've watched enough crime shows to know that usually the police don't want any help from the public.

"I'll be careful. Do you want to set up in the room where Monica was sleeping to interview the guests? It's pretty private."

Jace nodded. "Sounds good."

I led the way to the room, even though I was sure he'd already searched the room earlier. On the way, I told him what I knew about Linda's public humiliation in high school and how Gloria had been barred from being a cheerleader. "The only thing is, they seem to think it worked out for the best. I think they were both angry at Monica at one time, but not anymore, and definitely not enough to resort to violence."

When we reached the door, I stopped. "By the way, I was in here earlier, and I found a class ring on the floor. It belonged to Roger Steubing, a boy in high school I think may have something to do with this."

Jace looked in the room. "What did you do with the ring?"

"I put it on the desk over there." I pointed, but when I looked, I saw that the table was empty. Pushing Jace out of the way, I rushed across the room. I searched the desk, dropped on my knees again, and felt all over the carpet. I even looked under the bed, but the ring was gone.

"I put it on the desk. I have no idea what happened to it. Do you think whoever murdered Monica took it?"

Jace ran a hand through his hair. "I don't know. Maybe one of the dogs got hold of it. Or maybe one of the other women grabbed it. Don't mention it to anyone. I'll bring it up during my interviews."

I left Jace to set up the room however he needed. I headed back to the dining room. The women were actually making some really nice cards. I noticed each of them had a soda, which meant one or more of them had been out of this room at some time while I was cleaning the stairs. Any one of them could've slipped back to Monica's room and taken the ring. Even Scarlett could've slipped down the stairs and gone around the back way.

I wondered where Bonnie and Clyde were, so I started to look around. It didn't take long to find them in the front room, sitting by the small end table. It was obvious they weren't going to give up until I pulled that yearbook out, so I knelt down and ran my fingers under the table. It was a tight squeeze.

"What are you doing?" Cathy called from the other room. She was leaning back in her chair so she could see me.

"Nothing much. One of the yearbooks must've fallen off the coffee table. I think it's under this end table."

Cathy and Barb strolled into the front room and watched as I pulled the book from under the table. Bonnie and Clyde both started growling. Whatever this book smelled like, these dogs did not like it.

Barb moved closer and said, "Why don't you take these cuties and put them in the room where Monica was staying? Maybe being in there will give them some comfort. I'm sure they're feeling a bit confused by all this."

I was totally surprised. Honestly, Barb usually didn't give her opinion on things. I didn't realize she was such a dog lover.

I put the book on the table then grabbed the two dogs around their stomachs and lifted. "Can one of you help me?"

Cathy nodded and followed me down the hall. When I reached the room, I stopped.

"Oops, I forgot Officer Miller is setting up to interview everyone in Monica's room. I guess the dogs will just have to handle the smell of that yearbook." I turned and carried the dogs back to the front room.

Barb was at the dining room table again, laughing and joking with the other women. Cathy sat down and picked up the yearbook. "This is the 1977 book?"

"Yep." I set the two dogs down. They rushed straight across the room and started growling again. This time not at the book but at the table. "Hmm, I guess it wasn't the book bothering them after all. Maybe that table has some unfriendly cat smell or something."

Just then I heard Jace calling me. I turned on my heel and moved back down the hall. When I reached the door, I peeked in. "You rang?" I joked.

"Yes, you can start to send the women in to visit with me, one at a time." I noticed he had a recorder on the desk, official-looking papers, and several pens. Definitely ready to take their statements.

"Anyone you want to see first?"

He tapped his head. "Send in Linda Royal first. Let's see if her story lines up with what she told you. Then Scarlett Star."

"Sure thing." I gave a little salute and turned away.

I traipsed down the hallway and through the front room, noting Cathy had set the yearbook back on the coffee table. As I slipped past, my leg hit the book and pushed it onto the floor. I sighed. Seemed like this book almost *wanted* to be on the floor. I didn't pick it up right away, but Clyde rushed over and started sniffing it again.

With a hand on my hip, I stared at the dog. "You are a weirdo." He looked up at me, gave a little "woof," and placed his paw on the yearbook.

I turned away from him and walked into the dining room. It seemed the women were done with making cards, so I suggested they all take a short rest. No one objected. As they stood and filtered out of the room, I asked Linda if I could speak with her. She stopped.

"Yes?"

"Officer Miller is going to take everyone's statement. I thought you might like to go first and get it over with."

She glared at me. "Well, I'm not sure I needed to be first, but I suppose I'd rather get it over with so I can rest uninterrupted." She turned and glided out of the room as only a rich woman knows how to do.

Bonnie was barking so I hurried out to the front room again.

Somehow Clyde had pushed open the yearbook, and Bonnie was sniffing and barking at it. I walked over and picked the book up. The only way to solve this problem with the dogs was to put the book way up on a shelf. I was getting ready to close it when I noticed a ragged edge inside. I held it closer and realized that a page had been torn out of it.

I slammed the book shut. "Bonnie, Clyde, did you rip this page out?" I glanced around the room but didn't see any paper on the floor. The dogs didn't seem to cower at my voice. Actually, they both looked very happy and sat with their tongues hanging out of their mouths. I had to admit to myself, they had already stolen my heart.

"Well, you two better hope I don't get accused of murder. Because if I do, you won't have a home."

# CHAPTER 9

I decided to let Scarlett know Officer Miller would want to see her next. I set the book on a shelf but knew I needed to show it to Jace as soon as possible.

Climbing up the stairs, I scanned the floor, making sure there were no blood spots left. I peeked in my room. There were still the prints on the floor in there, but my sheets and comforter were gone, along with my robe.

I frowned. It was going to be hard to sleep in there tonight, even with all of the evidence gone.

I moved down the hall and knocked on Scarlett's door. A sleepy voice called out, "Come in."

I opened the door and stepped into the room. "Scarlett, Officer Miller wants to speak to you next."

Scarlett was standing in front of the window, looking out. She turned in surprise, her makeup streaked from tears. "Next? I can't."

I moved across the room. "What's wrong, Scarlett?"

"Oh, Tabi, this is such a mess. That officer is going to think I killed Monica if I tell him the truth." Her shoulders shook as tears flooded her face.

I patted her arm. "Scarlett, relax. Tell me all about it. I'm sure if you didn't kill Monica and you explain things in a calm way, Officer Miller won't jump to any conclusions."

Scarlett stared at me. I didn't think she was going to tell me anything, but then she collapsed onto the bed with a heavy sigh.

"Maybe that's a good idea." She looked up at me. "You know I went to school with Monica."

I nodded.

"Linda was dating Roger Steubing. He was captain of the football team. Everyone in school wanted to date him, but he broke up with Linda to start dating Monica."

So far this lined up with what others had shared with me.

"Well, not too many people know that Roger was voted prom king and I was voted queen."

I cocked my head. "That's nice."

I noticed her clench her hands. "Nice, yes. It was a dream come true, but then Roger left school right before prom. I heard that Monica was pregnant, and he was going to marry her."

My eyes must've registered confusion.

"They canceled the whole king and queen part of the prom. I was devastated."

Now I understood. Someone like Scarlett, who needs an audience, must've felt completely betrayed by Roger. I could understand if she hated Monica.

"Did Roger tell you he was going to marry Monica?"

Scarlett blinked. "No, I can't remember who told me that."

I couldn't imagine Scarlett killing Monica because she didn't get to be high school prom queen, but I'd seen more unusual things on detective shows.

"I think you should share all of this with Officer Miller. I don't see how it will make him think you are the murderer." I tried to assure her, hoping I was right. I also hoped if I was wrong, Jace would be able to figure the whole thing out.

I left Scarlett to freshen her face and headed back down the stairs. I decided to show the yearbook to Jace before he had to face Scarlett. I slipped into the front room, grabbed the book, and carried it down the hall. Outside the room where Jace was doing the interviews, I leaned in.

"Officer Miller, may I have a word with you?"

He looked up, swished his hair back, and gave me a smile. He stood up. "Mrs. Royal, I think I've got everything I need from you for the moment." He held out a hand, and she lifted hers gingerly and allowed him to shake it. Then she also stood.

As she glided out of the room, her eyes met mine. I was a bit shocked at the angry glare she gave me.

Jace waited a minute, looked down the hall to make sure Linda was gone, then turned around. "Honestly, I think she was really enjoying the interview. Odd."

"Oh, that's why she gave me such a look." I giggled.

"Did you need something? Not that it wasn't perfect timing. I wasn't sure how to get her to leave."

I held up the yearbook. "This book has something to do with Monica's death. I'm almost sure of it."

Jace stepped nearer. "Set it on the desk and tell me why."

I placed the book down and opened it to the missing page. "I have no idea what was on this page, but it wasn't missing before."

Jace scrutinized the book. "Hmm. Know anyone who has another copy?"

"Some of the other women here might."

Jace shook his head. "In a group this small, it should be easier to find the killer than it has been." He stared at me, an odd smile on his lips.

"Are you back to thinking I did it?"

He reached over and took my hand. "You know, Tabi, I've been watching you."

"Watching me? Why? Where?"

"At church. You know the ladies' society has made it their goal to find me a wife. You were highly recommended and, honestly, the only one I found interesting."

I could feel my cheeks flushing. I clenched my hands. "Those women should be. . ." I couldn't think of a nice way to say what I was thinking, so I clamped my lips shut.

Jace cleared his throat. "Anyway, not in a stalker kind of way or anything, I've been watching you, and I'm a pretty good judge of character. You may be a bit sassy from time to time but not a killer."

"Sassy?"

He held his hands up as if warding off an onslaught. "Okay, okay. I'm only kidding."

Just then an idea flashed through my mind. "The library has a copy of the yearbook. They have one for every class going back fifty years."

Jace's eyes lit up. "I'll call and ask what's on the missing page."

I flounced down the hallway and flopped onto a couch in the front room. Four eyes looked up at me. Bonnie and Clyde were there, still lying beside the end table.

"Seriously, what is it with you two?" My voice wasn't as sweet as it could've been, and I noticed both dogs seemed to withdraw from me.

*What am I doing, Lord? Taking my frustration out on two helpless animals.*

I felt guilty, so I reached out my hand. "I'm sorry."

The dogs lifted weary eyes, rose, and moved closer to me. I needed to remember these two sweethearts just lost their owner. Surely they were confused. I picked up Bonnie and snuggled her close to my face. They were really cute dogs.

Just then, Jace entered the room.

"I called the library."

I set Bonnie down and gave Jace my attention. "Did you find out what was on that page?"

He nodded and lowered his voice. "It was a picture of Roger Steubing and Cathy."

My mouth opened wide. "Does that mean that Cathy. . . ?"

Jace shook his head. "It's not definite proof, but it's pretty strange for only that page to be ripped out."

I slumped a bit. "But when she first saw the yearbooks on my table, Cathy mentioned there was a picture of her and Roger in one of the books."

Jace blinked. "Really?"

"Yes."

He moved closer to a shelf and tapped his finger on it. "That is strange. Maybe she didn't mean to say it out loud. I don't want to arrest the wrong person, and from what you've told me, most of the women here didn't even know Monica and certainly wouldn't be holding a long-lasting grudge against her. I guess I need to speak to Cathy as soon as possible."

"What about Barb? You haven't interviewed her yet."

"No one has mentioned that she knew Roger."

I stood to my feet, hoping I wasn't covered in dog fur. "Well, Barb has always been Cathy's sidekick. If Cathy and Roger were dating, Barb had to be around. She might know things no one else does."

Jace moved closer to me. "You know, Tabi, I shouldn't be allowing you to investigate at all. I wouldn't want anyone to hurt you."

"I'm being very careful. I've only asked basic questions." I didn't tell him how much of a gossip I'd been in the past. That was something I hoped God was helping to change in me. "Why don't you talk to Cathy as soon as you can, see if you can get anything out of her?"

Jace nodded. "I will."

Just then, Scarlett appeared. She had redone all her makeup and looked as if she'd never shed a tear in her life. I wondered if she would cry in front of Jace at all, even just for effect.

Jace turned and led Scarlett down the hallway to the interview room. I continued petting the dogs. "So, did Cathy hurt your Mommy?" I whispered. But both dogs just sat quietly, allowing me to comfort them.

I sat thinking, trying to make sense of everything.

# CHAPTER 10

I wandered around the room, looking at the mystery jigsaw puzzles. Several were starting to take form. It was amazing how the ladies were able to put them together without a picture. I love jigsaw puzzles, but I like to have a picture to follow.

I lifted the box of the calico one I'd worked on the first night. What a crazy weekend it had been so far! It was a real letdown, because I'd hoped this would become a yearly event, perhaps even quarterly. Once word got out a murder took place here, it was going to be hard enough to get guests to visit except, of course, for Halloween. Every ghost hunter would beg to stay in a house where someone was murdered, which was not the reputation I wanted for my sweet bed-and-breakfast.

I heard footsteps on the stairwell, and I looked toward the archway. Cathy, followed by Barb, entered the front room.

"So, what's the plan?" Cathy plopped onto a sofa near Bonnie and Clyde. Barb followed but sat more gingerly.

I was surprised to see the dogs get up and move away from the table, because they hadn't ventured from it all day. I wondered if they were afraid of Cathy.

"I'm hoping we can all work on the puzzles again in a while. I need to get us some food." My mind started running with ideas. What could I get delivered that would satisfy the women and not seem too cheap? Chinese, sushi? Those sounded too exotic, but would pizza be all right?

I noticed Cathy reach out and try to pet Bonnie, but Clyde bared his teeth. Cathy pulled her hand back.

"Dogs never like me," she stated.

I wondered. So far, I hadn't noticed Bonnie or Clyde growling at anyone else, but not many of the guests had actually come into direct contact with them. I decided to try and quiz Cathy a bit before Jace spoke with her.

"Cathy, there's a page missing from my yearbook," I said casually.

She glanced at me. "I didn't notice."

"Officer Miller wondered about it. I think someone tore it out of the book today." I needed to tread carefully here. I was doing just what Jace worried about—detective work that could get me hurt. I watched Cathy's face, but her attitude didn't change.

"But don't you think that's weird? Why would someone want to rip a page out of a yearbook? Do you know what was on the page?"

I was just about to answer when Barb interrupted. "Tabi, why are you asking Cathy about the book? I've noticed you asking a lot of questions. Are you trying to be a junior detective or what? That's sort of silly, isn't it?"

Cathy nodded.

"I'm not trying to be anything. I was just wondering about my book. Do you have any idea how it got ripped?"

"No, and I'm pretty sure Cathy wouldn't go around ripping pages out of books." Barb's voice rose as she tried to defend her friend. This was rather typical behavior on her part, always defending Cathy.

I decided to try one more thing with Cathy.

"Officer Miller is wondering about a ring Monica had. It was on the desk in her room this morning, but now it's gone." I watched Cathy's eyes.

She blinked, but it seemed natural.

"Ring?"

"Yes, it was a ring that Roger Steubing gave to Monica."

Now Cathy's eyes opened wide. "His. . .his class ring?" Her voice dropped. I thought her tone sounded hurt but not angry. She seemed genuinely surprised. "I always wondered. . ." She didn't finish her statement because Barb stood up, startling her.

For a moment, I wondered if Cathy would say anything more, but suddenly her eyes squinted at me. "Tabi, really? Are you trying to accuse me of something? All these questions about the yearbook and about Roger's ring?"

Oops. I'd gone too far.

"No. That is, I'm not accusing you of anything. I guess Barb's right, I'm just doing a bit of detective work myself. You know, this whole thing might ruin the reputation of the Pumpkin Patch."

Cathy's eyes were wide open in shock. "I never would've imagined you could think that of me. Everyone knows I dated Roger, but he left school before prom. I never saw him again. It was high school, for goodness' sake, such a long time ago."

"Why do you think he left school?"

Cathy bit her bottom lip. "There were rumors he left to marry Monica because she was pregnant. I never believed it." She turned and looked in Barb's direction. "Right, Barb?"

Barb nodded noncommittally. "It was the rumor," she stated

emphatically, but her voice dropped in empathy for Cathy.

Cathy shook her head vigorously. "No way. Roger *was* a bit of a playboy. Everyone knew he was dating more than one girl, but getting one pregnant? I don't think so."

Barb patted Cathy's shoulder. "Shh, Cathy. Everyone said it was true."

"Everyone may've been saying it, but did Roger ever tell anyone that's why he was leaving school? Did Monica ever tell anyone she was pregnant? Did they get married?"

Barb seemed taken aback by Cathy's outburst.

I was surprised too. She seemed to be standing up for him and in a sense for Monica as well, which didn't line up with the idea that she would've killed Monica because of Roger.

I sat back, taking a deep breath.

*Lord, help me make sense of all this. We need to know who killed Monica.*

The room was silent. Cathy and Barb were staring at one another. I'm not sure Cathy had ever spoken to Barb like that before, and as far as I knew, Barb had never gone against Cathy before. All I could think was that Roger must've been quite a ladies' man, stringing along so many girls, and there may have been more...

Just as the thought entered my mind, Clyde began digging at the end table again, and Bonnie suddenly rushed across the room and stood in front of Cathy and Barb, barking. I wasn't sure what to do, but I decided to see what was bothering Clyde, so I bent over, reached under the table, and felt around.

Bonnie continued barking, and I watched as Cathy took three steps away from the dog.

My hand came in contact with a piece of paper. I slid it from under the table and straightened with it in my hand.

Bonnie turned away from Cathy and began jumping on Barb's leg and barking louder.

Jace rushed into the room to see what was going on just as Barb lifted her foot to kick at the dog, but Jace rushed to her, and she changed her mind. My eyes fell on the paper in my hand. It was the page torn out of the yearbook, a picture of Cathy and Roger together, smiling. I noticed someone in the background of the picture and squinted at it. There was definitely someone else in the photo, someone in the background, and she wasn't smiling.

My head lifted and my mouth dropped open just as Bonnie sank her teeth into Barb's pants at her pocket level, tearing a hole in the material large enough for a single object to fall out of the pocket and onto the floor.

*Roger's ring.*

Barb met my eyes, no longer a gentleness in them. Instead, they were full of pain, hate, and fury.

Jace leaned over and picked up the ring. I held the paper out for him. "Barb? Is that you in the picture? In the background?"

"That's right." The words seethed through her teeth.

Cathy's brow furrowed. "What does that mean? What are you trying to say? Of course Barb was in the picture. She was always with me." She grabbed the paper from my hand before Jace could take it and scanned the picture.

"Barb, why do you look so angry? This was before I knew Roger was leaving school. I was happy then. You should've been..." Her words faded as realization hit her. She lifted tear-filled eyes and stared at her best friend.

"That's right, Cathy. I was angry. Roger wasn't supposed to show up for that photo. He promised me he wouldn't, but he couldn't resist."

"Why wasn't he supposed to show up? Why did he promise you. . . ?" Cathy seemed genuinely confused.

Barb stomped her foot. "Don't you get it? I was dating Roger too. I thought we were keeping it from you until he could think of a gentle way of telling you he was breaking up with you for me."

Cathy sat down, tears flowing now.

"But it was all a lie. I heard the story that day, in the girls' bathroom, about how Monica was leaving school because she was pregnant with Roger's baby. When I confronted him, he denied it, but he also laughed at me. He told me he wasn't really going to break up with you, that he'd only been using me for the excitement of getting away with it behind your back." Barb was screaming at this point.

I heard feet rushing on the upstairs hallway. The other women must've heard the commotion and were heading down the stairs to see what was going on. When they reached the archway, I held my hand up, and they all stopped, standing and staring into the front room. Even Scarlett remained silent.

Cathy shook her head, trying to reject what she was hearing. "Barb, how could you?"

"How could I? Did you ever even think I might've wanted a boyfriend?"

Cathy stared at her friend. "You had boyfriends—"

"Sure, but think about them. Were any of them good-looking? Popular? Of course not. You got all those guys. With you around, no one ever looked at me. But Roger did, at least I thought he did. I was a fool. I *loved* him. I thought he loved me."

Cathy lifted her hand. "I'm sorry, Barb. Why didn't you tell me? I'm your friend."

Barb turned away. "No, Cathy. I'm *your* friend. I do things for you. I take care of things for you. You're never there for me." She glared at Cathy. "Tell me, if I'd told you I was seeing Roger behind your back, what would you have done? Would you have continued to let me hang around with you?"

A red flush went over Cathy's cheeks, and she closed her eyes.

"I knew that would be your reaction. I couldn't tell you or anyone about it. When I realized Roger wasn't being true to me, I couldn't stand to see you and him together anymore, and I wasn't going to let Monica have him either."

Cathy's eyes flew open.

I gasped and took a step back, almost falling over Bonnie, who was now lying in a cozy ball behind me.

"What. Did. You. Do?" The words sounded as if they were being ripped out of Cathy's soul.

"Well, all I can say is, Roger didn't get a chance to marry Monica." Barb's words were flowing now, laced in hatred.

Jace was slowly moving up behind Barb, readying his handcuffs. Suddenly, he grabbed her and slapped the cuffs on her wrists. I thought she would fight. Instead, she dropped down on the floor, exhausted.

Cathy ran from the room, up the stairs. I heard a door slam.

Barb looked up at me. "You just couldn't mind your own business!"

I felt a deep sadness sweep over me. Barb, Cathy, and I had been such good friends. I could never have imagined she'd do something so horrific and be able to hide it all these years.

"Barb, are you saying you killed Roger?" I spoke in an even tone, not wanting to upset her.

She nodded.

"And Monica?"

"Yes."

"If you hated Monica so badly, why did you wait. . .well, until now to do anything about it?"

Barb took in a ragged breath and exhaled. "After I. . .killed Roger, I couldn't feel a thing for a long time. I actually buried it all in my mind, trying to forget. Cathy and I went to college. I dated a nice guy. Then when Cathy dropped out, I broke up with him and followed her. I think I turned my love for Roger into a love for Cathy. I've been the best friend anyone could ever ask for. The memory of Roger was gone, and I never saw Monica again."

Looking at Barb now was like looking at a total stranger. Even in her exhausted position, I could see the bitterness and hatred flowing from her.

"When Cathy and I got here, I saw Monica in the kitchen. I remembered everything. I started thinking about how her being pregnant with Roger's baby had caused me to murder him, and all that old anger resurfaced. Seeing Roger's ring around Monica's neck was the final straw. I went crazy."

Jace pulled Barb onto her feet, led her to a chair, then pressed her down. He pulled out his cell phone and dialed for backup.

I moved across the room and knelt in front of Barb.

"I planned it as quickly as I could. When I went in to get a glass of water, I asked Monica to meet me in the kitchen at midnight. I told her I knew where Roger was and would tell her all about it when everyone else was in bed. Then I stole your shoes and your robe. . ." She looked down at me, regret etched in her brow. "Sorry, Tabi. I'm not sure I would've really let you take the blame for it."

I placed a hand on her knee and gave a little pat. "Monica

wasn't pregnant, Barb. She left school because her father was ill."

Barb's expression changed. She glared at me. "Who told you that?"

"Monica told me. She never saw Roger again. She did love him though. That's why she still wore his ring."

"So, I killed him, her, both of them, for no reason?" The light in Barb's eyes seemed to dim.

I rubbed her knee gently. "I'm sorry, Barb."

"Well, I always knew someday I would pay for my sin. I've carried this burden for so long. I'm tired and just want it all to be over. Do you think God will forgive me, Tabi?"

A part of me wanted to comfort Barb, the sad girl who'd always been in Cathy's shadow. Still, another part of me wanted to yell at her, punish her for the crimes she committed. I sat back, silently waiting for Jace to finish his call.

When he slipped his phone into his pocket and pulled Barb to a standing position, I stood up as well, praying for courage.

"Barb, God can forgive anything, but you'll have to pay man's price for what you've done."

She gave a weak smile. "Thanks, Tabi. You were always a true friend."

Jace led Barb to the hallway, where the other women were all clustered together, staring at them.

Everyone heard the sirens as two other police cars arrived. Jace opened the front door and directed Barb to one of the cruisers.

I closed the front door behind them then turned to face

what I expected to be an onslaught of questions. For once, all the women seemed unable to speak. Not sure what to do, I simply smiled and said, "Why don't we finish our mystery puzzles now?"

# CHAPTER 11

The rest of the weekend was uneventful. The women finished their jigsaw puzzles, and every team was able to solve the mystery that went along with the puzzle. Cathy asked to just stay in her room as she was too upset to return to normal activities. Esther and Dawn worked together and actually ended up the first to finish and solve the mystery, so I gave them the prize, which was a basket filled with chocolates, tea, bath soaps, and a few other little gifts.

No one lingered long after we finished with the puzzles. Cathy left, agreeing to call if she needed anything. Scarlett made us all promise to be there on Friday for her opening, and Gloria invited everyone to stop by on Wednesday for tea and scones.

I don't think Dawn or Jennifer planned to go to tea or to the play, but they were too polite to say so. I wondered if any of the ladies would ever attend another Jigsaw Puzzle Mystery Weekend at the Pumpkin Patch Bed-and-Breakfast or anywhere else for that matter.

The women had been gone for about an hour when the doorbell rang. I moved lethargically toward it, realizing I was exhausted from the events of the weekend.

Jace was standing on the porch, his gorgeous blue eyes lit up and a smile on his face. "Hi. Just stopped by to check on you."

I opened the door wider and indicated for him to come in.

We sat on the sofa together. He scooted closer and swung an arm behind me. "Are you doing all right?" he asked.

I wanted to lay my head back on his shoulder, maybe have a good cry, but instead I just nodded. "Do you think this murder will ruin my business?"

"No. In fact, it will probably bring you more business: you know the morbidly curious. I'd say as long as it doesn't become a common occurrence, you're safe."

I glared at him. "Well, I hope not."

Just then, Bonnie and Clyde came trotting into the front room. They ran right over to Jace and sat at his feet like perfect little angels.

"What are you going to do about these two?" Jace asked, bending over and giving them each a pat on the head.

I glanced at the dogs.

They looked at me, eyes pleading.

"If Monica didn't have any family or friends who have a claim on them, I'll be keeping the darling duo. I mean, they did figure out the whole puzzling case before anyone else."

Jace opened his mouth to object then let his eyes fall on the two beagles again. He patted Clyde's head and gave a hearty laugh.

"I guess they did."

I picked Bonnie up and gave her a gentle hug, and Clyde flopped down on my foot with a contented sigh.

Jace leaned over and pressed a gentle kiss on my cheek.

"I hope the only mysteries you ever have to solve again are mystery jigsaw puzzles."

I smiled. "Amen, Officer Miller. Amen."

**TERESA IVES LILLY** has been writing for over twenty years. Her articles have appeared in a variety of magazines including *Turtle, Vette, Corvette Fever,* and more. She has written and published over twenty-five novellas with publishing companies Lovely Christian Romance and Forget Me Not Romance. At one point, her novel *Orphan Train Bride* was a number-one bestseller on Amazon.

# Puzzle Me This

By Janice Thompson

# CHAPTER 1

I've often felt that my life is like a giant jigsaw puzzle, one where several pieces are randomly missing from the box. I mean, it's one thing to only see bits and pieces of your life story, another thing to feel like you're walking around with blinders on most of the time. (Hello, adventure! I can't see what's coming around the next bend! Are you tormenting me on purpose?)

That's kind of how I felt that first Thursday night in July as I set up puzzles on my display table at our city's famed opera house. I'd signed up as a vendor for Camden's annual Jigsaw Puzzle Show, my first time out of the gate. And I didn't mind admitting, I was plenty nervous. I would turn thirty soon—the next week, in fact—and needed clarity on where my life was headed. If you asked my one-time boyfriend, Walter, he would say nowheresville. Then again, Walter prided himself on being the best CPA around. My lackadaisical approach to all-things-financial probably irritated him more than he'd let on during our three-year courtship. Maybe that's why he took off for NYC on the very day I'd hoped for a proposal. Who knew?

But, as I unloaded boxes of puzzles from bins on the third floor of the Camden Opera House, I felt my life playing out in

front of me like a B-rated movie. Only, instead of being the heroine, I felt like a tepid subcharacter. All around me, local vendors
with more chutzpah and finesse set up their tables with enticing
displays. I did my best to stack my puzzles in a way that made
them look moderately appealing. Or, at the very least, less tacky.

If this weekend didn't turn a profit, I'd be looking for another
job. Or, as my mother was prone to say, a "real" job. Apparently,
she and Walter were in agreement on that point. Selling jigsaw
puzzles wasn't going to make me rich anytime soon. I'd already
figured that out with my flailing online store, which was what
brought me here today. In person. To an event that made my
knees knock and my voice quiver. One where I was surrounded
by people who knew a lot more than I did—about puzzles and
about business, in general. Would I come out of this looking like
a complete goober?

Maybe. Unless I sold the Grindle Point, the puzzle that had
started it all for me. If I could actually get someone to take a
serious interest in my one item of great value, I could prove the
Walters of this world wrong. And my mother might even see me as
something other than "that daughter who can't seem to figure out
her life."

The beautiful 2,000-piece replica of one of the most famous
lighthouses in our area had already garnered some interest from
our town councilman, Harvey Bates. For weeks he'd dropped
hints that he wanted to buy the pricey antique. But had he?
Nope. Not one offer. Nothing. Nada. Zilch.

Even now, as I watched him from across the crowded gallery,
I silently prayed that he would be drawn in my direction.

Perhaps this weekend's event would seal the deal, once and
for all. Would he take the bait?

"Hey, you made it!"

A jovial voice sounded, and I turned to discover my friend Amber had joined me at my table, all smiles as usual. With that amazing ensemble and impeccable makeup job, she looked like a cover model. Nothing new there. Some gals just have the knack. And the genes. Me, on the other hand? I'd twisted my funky red hair up into fairy sprouts on top of my head. They went perfectly with my red-and-white-striped blouse and shiny teal slacks. Hey, no one can accuse me of being boring. What I lack in genetics I more than make up for in color.

I managed a quick, "Hey, girl," then reached for another bin, determined to stay focused.

"Need help unloading?"

Relief flooded over me as I gazed up into her calm face. How did she do it? The woman was all grace and ease, even on the busiest of days. And she still managed to look completely put together.

"Do you mind?" I dropped another puzzle box onto the table. "Are you all done with yours?"

"Yeah, you know how particular Charlie is."

"Yep." I knew her hubby, all right. Great guy. Über-left-brained.

"He made sure we came early. We've been done awhile. He's hanging out with the other vendors, visiting." Her nose wrinkled and that joyous smile faded. "Well, complaining, really. Apparently, there's a big brouhaha involving one of them."

"Brouhaha?" I cringed at that proclamation. "If something bad is happening, please don't tell me. This is one of those days where I'm hoping all of the news is good."

"All righty then." She swiped a loose blond hair off of that perfectly made-up face and grinned. "So, what can I do to help?"

"Can you make sense of my mess?" I gestured to the puzzles I'd stacked on the table. "You're more artistic than I am, Amber. Work your magic?"

"Gladly." She dove in and before long had several of the items displayed in whimsical fashion. I wasn't sure how she did it, but boy was I glad she had that gift. I might be able to pull off an eclectic outfit and hairdo, but table decoration? No way.

As Amber worked, I paused to take in my surroundings. With fifty-plus participants jammed into the gallery area encircling the elevator, I felt a little claustrophobic. . .but intrigued. Nearby products ranged from modern to traditional. I knew a handful of the vendors, but most hailed from other areas around coastal Maine and nearby Cape Cod. They were completely unfamiliar to me. Including the guy directly to my right, though the name of his company was catchy. Puzzle Me This. Cute.

The strains of a familiar jazz tune flitted up from the main stage below, where the musicians rehearsed in preparation for the weekend's big event, which would begin tomorrow morning. I took a couple steps over to where the gallery opened onto the balcony seating area. From there, I had a bird's-eye view of the stage below. And what—er, who—I saw made beads of sweat pop up on my brow.

Roland White. The best bass player in town and the one guy—short of my ex-almost-fiancé—who caused my heart to flutter. Not that he knew. Oh no. I wasn't quite ready to spill the beans on those feelings just yet, though I swooned every time I saw him playing with the worship team at church on Sundays.

Even now I felt a little dizzy as I watched him play his heart out on the stage below. Did he have any idea how good he was? Should I tell him? Nope, scratch that. My mind trailed back to a recent encounter with Roland at the supermarket, one where I'd stumbled all over myself. No doubt I'd left a lasting impression, babbling on about broccoli.

I watched as the musicians wrapped up their rehearsal and then stood. Was it my imagination, or was Roland gazing up at me? Yes, he was definitely staring up at the balcony. *Be still, my heart!* I felt heat rise to my cheeks and offered a little wave, which he returned. Could this day get any better?

"How many puzzles did you bring with you, Mariah?" From my table several feet away, Amber's voice rang out, shattering the dreamy Roland-esque images flitting through my brain. "A hundred?"

"Hmm?" I turned away from my view of the stage and took a few steps toward my friend, who had emptied the remainder of my bins.

"You have a lot, girl. Way more than us. And I love your new logo. 'Solve it!' Very cute."

"Thanks. I don't do anything small. I've got a hundred and twenty puzzles." And, if I had my way, I'd sell most of them this weekend. That was the plan, anyway, especially after investing so much money in them and then paying to rent my booth as well. Living in the garage apartment above my sister's place was getting old. Maybe, if this weekend went well, I could do the grown-up thing and get a place of my own.

Aw, who was I kidding?

Harvey Bates happened by at that very moment and paused in front of my table, his eyes widening as he took in my offerings.

*Please, Harvey. Please.*

"The Grindle Point." A smile tugged at the edges of his lips as he reached out to touch the box holding my most prized possession. I wanted to slap his hand away, to say, "Don't touch that unless you're serious about buying it this time." But I didn't. Instead, I flashed an over-the-top smile and said, "Wait till you see the new price."

"Finally coming down, eh?" Those manicured gray brows of his elevated slightly. "Gonna make it worth my wait?"

I wanted to sing at those words. I wanted to dance. I wanted to throw back my head and laugh with glee. Only, I didn't. Instead, I decided to play it cool.

"Mm-hmm." Another rehearsed smile followed on my end. "I think you'll be happy."

"I like happy."

I did too. And right now, I was plenty happy. My excitement grew as the vendor from Puzzle Me This joined us. He seemed intrigued by my Grindle Point puzzle too. In fact, I had to wonder if he might be interested in buying it. Maybe these guys would end up in a bidding war. Wouldn't that be terrific?

Before I could give it much thought, the fellow led Harvey away from my table and toward his. Ugh. The two were soon engaged in a lively conversation. I felt the edges of my lips shift downward as they carried on about the Puzzle Me This products, which the vendor pulled from boxes and placed on his table. Really? I squinted to have a closer look at the items on display. Was it just my imagination, or did the price tags on those puzzles seem ridiculously low?

I eased myself in Amber's direction and whispered, "You know that guy?" then gestured to the attractive young man who now held Harvey spellbound. With those squared-off glasses, he looked a bit like Clark Kent. Handsome but serious. Only, the spiked hair seemed to contradict that notion. So did the effervescent personality, which ballooned large in front of me. He had a way of commanding a crowd, as was evidenced by the sheer number of vendors now gathering around him as he carried on, box-cutter in hand, opening more cardboard boxes and presenting his offerings.

Amber groaned. "Yeah, Brandon Craig. Don't get me started or I'll have to tell you about that brouhaha I mentioned earlier. Charlie and the others aren't happy he's here. Let's just leave it at that."

"Why not?"

She balled her fists and planted them on her hips. "They've only been around a few months. We met them at the spring swap on Martha's Vineyard back in April. But they're already outselling all of us by undercutting everyone."

"They?"

"Yeah." She gestured with her head. "Check out the fiancée. Her name is Cheyenne. Former runway model from New York."

My gaze shifted to the tall, slender woman with the gorgeous mane of auburn hair, which was beautifully styled in waves around her face. Her skin was like porcelain, and I'd never seen such riveting brown eyes. And that expensive outfit. Wow. "Oh, my stars and garters."

"Right?"

Some people have all the luck.

Amber clucked her tongue. "I don't know how he does it, but Brandon offers his puzzles at a fraction of the cost. Come with me and I'll show you."

She led the way to the Puzzle Me This table, and it only took a minute or two to realize we were all in trouble. Sure enough, this guy had a ton of products at rock-bottom prices. Okay, so most of them weren't antiques, like the ones the majority of the other vendors carried. But he seemed to have a plethora of items...and all for a song. Ugh. How in the world did he manage that? Were these puzzles manufactured in a sweatshop overseas, perhaps?

Amber dove into an animated conversation about how unfair all of this was, and I suspected Brandon could overhear her. So I nudged my friend in the direction of the windows on the far side of the room to see if I could calm her down. This spot usually offers a lovely view of Camden's village green, but with dusk settling in, I could barely make out the goings-on below.

I had always loved this view from the gallery windows. But right now I wasn't thinking about all of that. No, I couldn't stop worrying about my competition, especially as Amber carried on about him. With this guy Brandon in the mix, our higher-priced puzzles wouldn't stand a chance. Ugh. So much for getting my own place.

Charlie joined us for a quick pow-wow, and another local, Tristan Woodhouse, showed up moments later. I'd known Tristan since elementary school. He was a bit odd as a child. Okay, a *lot* odd. Those oddities had only blossomed as he'd grown and not in a good way. Now, at thirty-one, he owned The Camden Curiosity Shop, a quirky building filled with eccentric items no one much cared for. Still, I wanted to remain upbeat around him. He too had expressed an interest in the Grindle Point at our last meeting. Maybe today would be the day.

"He's low-balling us!" Tristan raked his fingers through that dirty blond hair and then crossed his arms at his chest. "That's what happened last time too. On the Vineyard. We've got to stop him before he puts us all out of business!"

"Yeah, deliberately undercutting us to get the upper hand."

Charlie's eyes narrowed to slits. "I don't get it."

I didn't get it either. But I couldn't respond because my tongue didn't seem to want to cooperate. Out of the corner of my eye I caught a glimpse of my favorite bass player entering the gallery. Roland. Mr. Practically-Perfect-in-Every-Way. Oh, my. Had my friendly wave served as a siren's call, perhaps?

He glanced my way, creases forming around those gorgeous blue eyes of his.

Oh, help.

*Did I put on lipstick? Is my hair a mess? Is he about to head my way?*

No, Roland seemed distracted by someone else entirely—Brandon Craig's fiancée, Cheyenne. The gorgeous young woman turned his way, and I felt my heart deflate like a balloon drifting to the ground. Cheyenne's smile faded too. But why? And why did Brandon storm toward Roland with anger blazing in his eyes?

Yikes. Things were about to get heated in here. And where there's smoke, well. . . Let's just say I love a good fire. So I meandered back to my table, hoping to eavesdrop on their conversation. Apparently, Tristan wanted in on the action too. He followed me to my table and then eased closer to Brandon and Roland. He reached for the Grindle Point, running his finger over the cover as he leaned in to listen to the conversation at the next table. His gaze shifted back to my puzzle.

"Oh, wow. The Grindle Point. I remember this one. You were asking $2,500?"

"Yep. I've come down though."

"Good to know. Keep a close eye on it, Mariah." He gave me a knowing look. "You can never be too careful in a crowd like this."

He had a good point.

The argument at the next table carried on. Tristan glanced at his watch and then headed to his table to finish setting up.

Much to my relief, Roland eventually calmed down. He took a few steps away from Brandon and Cheyenne, and his gaze shifted to me. A relaxed smile lit his face, squelching the afore-mentioned tension in the room. "Hey, Mariah. I thought I saw you up here earlier."

"Hey," I managed. *Say something brilliant, Mariah.* "I heard you playing down there. Sounded good. Can't wait for tomorrow."

"Yeah. I'm excited too." He took a couple steps to my table and rested his hand on The Grindle Point. "Oh, wow. My favor-ite lighthouse."

"Mine too." Was it my imagination, or was Brandon easing his way toward us? Ugh. Hopefully, he wouldn't create another scene. I tried to make my voice sound as normal as possible as I switched to sales-y mode. "This puzzle's an antique, designed in 1914, during WWI."

"Wow." Roland picked up the box and tipped it over to look at the back. "Must be worth a fortune."

"It is."

*Don't drop it. Don't drop it!*

I took it from him. "It belonged to my great-grandfather. From there it went to my grandmother, who passed it to my dad, who gave it to me."

"And you're *selling* it?"

Why did those words sound like an accusation?

"I am. It's always been kind of a sore spot in our family." I did my best not to sigh aloud as I set the puzzle back in place at the center of my table. "See, my great-grandfather was what my granny always called a 'rounder.'"

"A rounder?" Creases formed between Roland's eyes.

"Yeah." I cleared my throat. "He got around. And it turns out he had a whole other family my great-grandmother didn't know about. So they split in the '30s when the story broke. My grandmother never really knew her dad but was always bitter about the pain he caused the family."

"So she got the puzzle as an offering?"

"I'm pretty sure he just left it behind, along with most of his other possessions. Of course, it wasn't worth much then. It's worth $2,500 now."

"Whoa."

"Right? My dad didn't realize it when he passed it to me. But a little research turned up the truth, and here we are today. Trust me when I say that my dad's not interested in anything that belonged to his grandfather. So he's happy I'm selling it."

I waited for Brandon to respond, but instead his gaze darted to the next table, to Cheyenne. I couldn't help but notice that she gave him a quick glance in return. Was that fear in her eyes, or was I imagining things?

Moments later I lost Roland altogether. He ended up at the Puzzle Me This table once more, where he attempted a conversation with Cheyenne. Next thing I knew, Brandon was in the thick of it, demanding Roland leave. . .or else.

"Or else what?" Amber whispered from behind me. I turned to discover she had rejoined me at my table.

"No idea, but this is getting a little scary."

Brandon's voice continued to rise, and he threatened to call security. But why? What had Roland done to deserve that? He was just standing there, after all.

Just about the time I thought the opera house's elderly security guard might emerge from the elevator, Roland stormed off in the direction of the balcony.

"Whoa." Amber shook her head as she shot a glance my way. "Do you think it's going to be like this all weekend? I'm not sure my nerves can take it, if so."

"I sure hope not. There's nothing like an argument to put people out of the mood to shop."

"Agreed."

The whole thing left me with a bad taste in my mouth. No matter how perfect Roland might be, he wasn't worth the kind of off-stage drama I'd just witnessed. No thanks.

Before I could give the notion another thought, a rapid-fire succession of ear-splitting *pops* split the air. A collective gasp went up from the crowd as several more shots rang out from the village green below. I grabbed hold of Amber's hand, and we stampeded toward the windows like Spanish bulls barreling toward a fight.

# CHAPTER 2

"What in the world?" I stared out the window into the darkness below. All around me, voices rang out in dissonant chorus as the vendors tried to figure out what we'd just heard. Now that the sun had set, our view of the green was limited to shadows and lamplight. Certainly not enough visual cues to determine the cause or effect of the shots. Was anyone injured? Or. . .worse?

Before I could give it another thought, the elderly security guard entered the gallery. Known to all in our community simply as Mr. Purvis, the tiny man had to be at least a hundred and six. Okay, seventy-six. But the years had not been kind to him. I couldn't figure out why he'd been kept on as head of security at the opera house, but right now he looked like a superhero blazing into the room. Hunched over or not. Trembling or not.

"Everyone away from that window! We're headed down to the main stage where it's more secure." He gestured with a shaky finger to the stairway. "No one leaves the building until we're sure it's safe to go outside. The police are on their way!"

The lights flickered, adding to the chaos.

"Amber?" I called out her name, frantic as the blinking lights continued and the room finally faded to black. Ugh.

"I'm right here, Mariah." She latched on to my hand and gave it a squeeze.

I wanted to rush to my table, to grab the items that meant the most to me. But with the crowd pushing me from behind, I wasn't able to take any steps in that direction. Besides, I couldn't see much of anything at this point. My purse would have to wait. The Grindle Point would have to wait. I ushered up a silent prayer that both would remain safe in my absence.

Harvey Bates took charge of the room, aiding the security guard by guiding us in groups to the stairwell and using a flashlight to lead the way. He'd never been a favorite of mine—blame it on the way he bragged on his own accomplishments in the third person—but right now he felt 100 percent trustworthy. I appreciated his confidence and his schmoozy charm. He patted me on the arm as I passed by and said, "Don't you worry now, Mariah. I'll keep a close eye on your stuff. Everything will be fine."

And I believed it would be.

Well, until we were all crammed into the stairwell, where the darkness felt exaggerated against the echoes of the voices, which now sounded hollow against the concrete steps. My heart began to thump-thump-thump in painful but steady rhythm. Amber and Charlie flanked me—he led the way and she pushed me from behind. I felt like a slice of bologna wedged between two slices of bread. Surrounded by fifty-plus other slices of bread.

The vendors' voices overlapped in chaos as we traveled en masse downward to the first floor and then into the large auditorium. Moments later we found ourselves on the pitch-dark stage. Just about the time my eyes adjusted, the lights popped on. And I mean all the lights, including those over-the-top stage lights that actors always complain about. Now I realized what they meant. Blinding!

I blinked several times and then looked around, wondering where Roland had landed. Was he still up on the third-floor balcony, or had he come down with the rest of us? I looked around but couldn't find him in the crowd. Of course, there were a great many people I couldn't find at the moment, including Amber, who had somehow lost her grip on my hand in the darkness. In spite of being surrounded on every side, I suddenly felt very, very alone.

My mind wandered to the goings-on outside, and I whispered a prayer that no one was hurt. Then I took several deep breaths and shifted my gaze to the auditorium.

"Whoa." So this was what it looked like from the actor's point of view. Interesting. My gaze swept the grand auditorium, and I took in the seats, all 489 of them. I still had the number memorized from my youth when my drama teacher brought us on a field trip to the opera house. Weird, how that number came back to me now.

"There you are." Amber eased her way into the spot next to me. "Thought I lost you."

"That would be easy to do in this crowd."

"Right? Charlie's looking for Tristan. He can't find him. But he's more worried about that Puzzle Me This guy. Have you seen him?"

"Nope." I glanced around to be sure. "Why are you worried?"

She rubbed at the back of her neck. "I'm overly suspicious, since we don't know him. You don't suppose he's up there rummaging through our stuff, do you?"

Well, that didn't exactly instill confidence. Still, I had to respond with encouraging words or I'd get her even more worked up. "I'm pretty sure he wouldn't risk his life to stay behind for something like that. Those were gunshots we heard, after all."

Okay, so not exactly a positive, upbeat speech, but I got my point across.

"You're probably right." Still, she didn't look convinced.

Charlie approached, looking equally as glum. "No sign of Tristan."

"Do you think he's okay?" Amber brushed her hair out of her face. "You don't suppose he headed down to the green, do you?" As she voiced that possibility, she looked a bit nauseated. In fact, she looked downright ill all of a sudden. Oh dear.

"I'm sure he's fine. Maybe he's up there with Harvey and the security guard, helping out."

From above, a cry rang out. My gaze traveled to the balcony. Had Harvey or Mr. Purvis fallen in the dark? I did my best to shift gears, to keep the conversation light.

A few minutes later, Harvey arrived on the scene. He looked winded, and that usually slicked-back hair of his was somewhat erratic. Still, he seemed in control. Nothing new there.

"Everything okay upstairs?" I asked.

"Hmm? Upstairs?" He looked confused.

"I thought I heard a noise."

"Oh, I don't know what's happening in the gallery. I went outside to check things out. The police have arrived. They'll come in as soon as they have definitive answers."

Definitive answers. Sounded like a ten-dollar statement meant to cover up a two-dollar problem. At least I hoped it was a two-dollar problem and not a murder.

Ack.

No, surely not.

I shifted my gaze to the back door of the auditorium, hoping it would swing open and Brandon and Cheyenne would come walking through. Then Amber could rest easy. Right now her nerves were getting the best of her. And she was usually the calm one.

The door did eventually open, and two officers—one male and one female—pressed their way inside with Mr. Purvis hobbling along behind them. They made their way up the left aisle of the theater to the foot of the stage, where they commanded our full, undivided attention. The guy—a burly fellow with a thick mustache and bald head—spoke first.

"Folks, we're still doing a sweep of the exterior perimeter of the building, but right now we can tell you that the noise you heard came from fireworks not a gun."

A collective sigh of relief went up from the throng of people gathered around me.

"Fireworks?" Charlie rubbed his brow as if to ward off a headache. "Sure didn't sound like it."

"We caught a bunch of college kids with fireworks," the female officer explained. "They set them off in the dumpster behind the building, which is why they sounded like explosions."

"Really?" Amber groaned. "All that drama over some *fireworks*? Don't they realize the Fourth is behind us?"

"Only by a few days," I reminded her.

A call came through on the first officer's radio, and moments later he released us to finish setting up our tables, so we headed back upstairs.

I entered the gallery area once again, my gaze shifting at once to the balcony, where I searched for Roland. No sign of him anywhere. No sign of Tristan either. He had mysteriously disappeared.

Not that I had time to fret over such things. With so much stirring around me, I was more determined than ever to check my table to make sure the Grindle Point was okay. Something in my gut told me otherwise.

I raced to the table and scanned the puzzles until my gaze landed on the spot where the puzzle had been.

Gone.

"No!" I tugged at several other puzzles, flipping them over, searching through the piles for the Grindle Point. I had to be imagining this.

The truth settled over me like a dark, ominous cloud and my hands began to tremble. Someone had stolen my most prized possession.

"You okay?" Amber said as she walked my way. "You look scared to death."

"Amber?" I fought to steady my breathing. "The Grindle Point. . ."

"Front and center, place of honor." She pointed to the location where Harvey and Roland had both reached for it a short while ago. "Oh, Mariah!"

"I know."

"I'll help you look." She flew into action, sorting through the various puzzles and making a mess of things on my table. In the end, we both had to conclude it wasn't there.

This had to be a mistake. Surely I'd set it down in a random spot was all.

Amber rested her hand on my arm. "Stay calm. Retrace your steps. When did you last see it?"

"Tristan looked at it. We talked about its value. After that, I showed it to Harvey then set it back down front and center, just as you said. After that, Roland came by and picked it up."

"And he put it back down?"

"I set it down myself. I took it from him. Put it right back down."

"And then..."

"Then the shots rang out. And we all went downstairs."

"Did we *all* go down, though?" Amber's gaze narrowed. "I knew that Brandon guy couldn't be trusted! My instincts were right. Oh, I hate it when I'm right!"

My gaze shifted to the Puzzle Me This table, still loaded with merchandise. Only, the proprietors were missing. Hmm.

I felt like kicking myself for not grabbing the puzzle—and my purse—before heading downstairs. "My purse!" Was it gone too? No, a quick glance behind the table revealed that my purse was still right there, as well as all of my credit cards and cash, along with a ton of receipts and other scraps of paper that I should probably clear out. Whew.

But without the Grindle Point, what chance did I stand of making any real money this weekend? I was doomed! My mother was right. I needed a real job.

*Deep breath, Mariah. Deep breath.*

Three people had shown an interest in the masterpiece. Well, four, if you counted Brandon. But his appearance at my table was likely just a diversion to get his hooks into Harvey Bates. Ugh.

Harvey Bates. He'd led us to the stairwell but hadn't appeared on the main stage until later. Sure, he claimed to be outside, but was he really up here, stealing my puzzle? Then again, it could be Tristan. He was a savvy businessman, shrewd and observant.

No, it had to be Brandon and that girlfriend of his. Why else would they be missing from the room right now? They must have snatched the Grindle Point in the darkness and headed out.

I wanted to scream. I wanted to cry. I wanted to holler, "Who let those imposters into this event, anyway?" But I didn't. Instead, I took several steps over to the Puzzle Me This table to tear through his stash of puzzles. Maybe he had buried it.

As I drew near his table, something caught my eye. There, on the floor, sticking out from under the table. . .what was that?

Oh. My. Stars.

"Um, Amber?" My hands trembled as I realized the truth of what I was looking at. "Someone call the cops. There's a body under the table!"

# CHAPTER 3

"A body?" Amber let out a squeal, and within seconds all the vendors were gathered around me, staring down at the leg poking out from under the table.

I felt dizzy all of a sudden. I saw stars. Or maybe that was just the beam from Mr. Purvis's flashlight as he hobbled our way. As he got closer, the smell of hot sauce caused my nostrils to flare. Someone had just eaten Mexican food.

He hollered, "Step back, everybody!" then pulled back the tablecloth to reveal Brandon's lifeless body underneath. I let out a gasp as I saw the pool of blood under his chest. I began to feel dizzy. This time I saw stars for real.

Before I could give any serious thought to passing out, Amber took care of that for both of us. She hit the floor with a thud, and Charlie came running.

I couldn't really give a full accounting of what happened next, because it was all such a blur. I remember Harvey Bates showing up and taking charge of the room, pressing Mr. Purvis to the side. Then the two cops from downstairs made a reappearance. And then a half dozen or so paramedics arrived on the scene. A couple of them tended to Amber, but the rest were hyperfocused on Brandon, who was pronounced dead soon after their arrival. After that, more police officers filled the room and pressed the rest of us to a far corner to wait.

At this point, panic set in. The man I'd suspected of stealing my puzzle wasn't the bad guy, after all. Someone wanted him dead. . .but who? And why?

I began to tremble. I couldn't stop thinking about the Grindle Point, wondering if it had somehow played a role in Brandon's death. Why hadn't I just stayed home this weekend and streamed mind-numbing shows? What sort of pipe dream had led me here, to this chaos?

*Mama, I'm sorry! I'll never work another puzzle as long as I live!*

I kept a watchful eye on the paramedics as they worked on my best friend. Amber revived quickly from her fainting spell but still looked plenty green around the gills, even after the paramedics freed her to go back to her booth. Charlie slipped his arm over her shoulders and led her that way. I followed closely behind, hovering as she took a seat at their table.

"You okay?" I asked after giving her a moment to catch her breath.

"Mm-hmm." She shifted her gaze to Charlie then back to me. "We weren't going to tell anyone just yet, but I guess the cat's out of the bag now." A slight smile tipped up the edges of her lips and she hollered, "Surprise!"

"Surprise?" The realization hit me hard and fast. "Oh, Amber! You're. . .*pregnant!?*"

Nothing like a little squeal from an over-the-top drama queen like myself to turn a room full of otherwise engaged puzzle vendors into fervid spectators. Before Amber could do anything but nod, several of the locals rushed our way to offer congratulations.

No doubt she would murder me later.

Murder.

Brandon.

My gaze shifted back to where the police were taping off the crime scene, just yards away.

Nausea kicked in as I remembered the argument between Brandon and Roland. Where was Roland, anyway? I turned my gaze back to the balcony area, the last place I'd seen him. And what about Cheyenne? Had she run off with Roland? Had the two of them planned this, perhaps?

No, it had to be Tristan. He was plenty angry with Brandon for undercutting us, after all. Maybe he did the deed and then snagged my puzzle before leaving.

Or had Harvey stolen the puzzle? Perhaps Brandon and Cheyenne witnessed the thievery and tried to stop him, so Harvey turned on them.

No, that would mean Cheyenne's body would be here too. Right? Why had she disappeared?

As terrible as I am at financial matters, it turned out I was even worse at crime solving. This was all just too much for me.

I turned back to face the table just as the coroner arrived. Moments later, a hysterical Cheyenne bounded from the elevator, flanked by police officers. She rushed to the table in time to watch the coroner load Brandon's body onto a stretcher. Her ear-piercing wails filled the room, adding a whole new layer to the frenzy. The shrieking dissolved into quiet sobs as the coroner nudged the stretcher in the direction of the elevator. Minutes later, they disappeared from view, Cheyenne included. She refused—quite vocally—to be parted from her beloved.

The room came alive as soon as the elevator doors shut, this time in frantic conversation as we all tried to figure out what we had just witnessed.

Harvey took charge, as always. "I *knew* there was something strange about that guy," he proclaimed for all to hear. "I felt it in my gut."

Should I remind him that he had allowed Brandon to schmooze him earlier in the evening? Nah, no point.

At that moment, a call came through on my cell phone. Oh, great. Mom.

I answered, hoping to put her off with a quick, "Can't chat right now," but those are fighting words where my mother is concerned. She lit into a lengthy response, one intended to make me feel guilty for never having time for her.

She finally paused for breath and released a slow, exaggerated groan. "I suppose you're with those *puzzle* people, playing around again."

"Not playing, Mother. I can assure you of that."

"When are you going to get a *real* job, Mariah? Your father and I are worried about you."

From the background I heard my dad call out, "I'm not worried, honey."

I wasn't sure if "honey" referred to Mom or to me, but it did help to know he wasn't fretting over my life choices. Then again, he might worry if he realized his unemployed daughter was in the middle of a crime scene at the moment. Should I tell him?

"Mom, I hate to do this, but I really have to—"

"Ladies and gentlemen, we're going to have to ask you to clear the room!" the female officer called out, her voice shrill. "Let's load up these puzzles then vacate the room the same way you left earlier, down the stairwell to your left."

"Mariah, what in the world is all that noise?" Mama asked. "Can't they see you're on a call? Can you ask them to be quiet?"

"Yes, Mother, I know. They're asking us to leave the room and head back down to the main stage."

"Well, why?"

"Because, I, well. . ." I paused to listen to the instructions they were giving us. "They say we're not going to be able to use the gallery for tomorrow's event after all. We have to transfer our displays downstairs."

"Why in the world would they say that? I love that gallery. It's got a terrific view of the green and it's perfect for a gathering."

"I know, Mother, but it's now a crime scene."

"A. . .what?" Her high-pitched squeal caused me to pull the phone away from my ear. I put it back in time to hear her say, "All of this because of that horrible puzzle your great-grandfather left behind. There's a curse on that stupid thing, I tell you. Just throw it in the trash and be rid of it once and for all."

I lowered my voice so as not to share too much information with the other vendors, who were now pressed in around me like sardines. "Oh, it's gone, but not in the way you think."

"Gone?"

"Stolen."

"And *that's* why the police are there? The crime scene is all about you?"

"Well, no. They don't know about the puzzle yet. I'll tell them in a minute. They've been pretty busy hauling out the body."

"B-body?"

"Yes. Body. A young man was murdered. His table was right next to mine."

"Mariah Elizabeth Jamison, you leave that place immediately and come home!"

Would this be a good time to remind her that I no longer lived at her house?

"I'm fine, Mama. Really."

"Thank God you're okay!" She took to weeping, and before long my dad was on the phone in her place.

I managed to convince him I was safe then ended the call.

I turned to Amber, who was hard at work shoving her puzzles into boxes. She glanced my way and groaned. "Looks like we're headed downstairs. I'll help you as soon as I'm done with our stuff."

"No, I'll help her." Harvey stepped into place, this time in the role of hero, and reached for one of my empty bins. Moments later, he was helping me stack puzzles in them. I didn't know whether to thank him or grill him about the missing puzzle.

"Are they really sending us down to the main stage?" I asked.

"Yeah, this room is now a crime scene. The sooner they can clear it, the better. You know?"

I didn't know. I'd never actually been in a room where someone was murdered before. And would this be a good time to mention the missing puzzle?

Moments later, Charlie arrived to help us. He and Harvey had my table packed up within a few minutes. Harvey began the process of hauling my bins to the stage while Charlie carried his boxes down. When all the vendors had transferred their puzzles downstairs, the task of carrying down the tables began.

"So what about the musicians?" I asked as we placed my table on the main stage a short while later.

"We'll put them in the lobby," Harvey explained. "People will get serenaded the moment they come in. No one will be any the wiser."

"You don't really think the public will show up tomorrow oblivious to the fact that a murder took place here tonight, do you?"

He shrugged. "I hope they'll still come. We've put a lot of work into this weekend's event. And you guys will be on the main stage, far away from where it happened. Out of sight, out of mind."

"What about Brandon's puzzles?"

"That stuff will remain just as it is, Mariah. Police won't want to interfere with any DNA evidence."

Out of the corner of my eye, I caught a glimpse of Tristan heading up the steps leading to the stage. He came right toward us.

Charlie and Amber rushed our way, but Charlie did not look happy. "Tristan. Dude, you scared me to death. Were you down here the whole time?"

"Sort of." Tristan shrugged. "I heard there were some kids outside with fireworks, so I went out to confront them. I gave them a piece of my mind for getting everyone so worked up. Threatened to call their parents. Kids these days. . .you know?"

"Well, I guess you heard what you missed up in the gallery." Charlie got busy unloading my bins, placing the puzzles on the table. "Crazy."

Tristan pursed his lips. "Mr. Purvis filled me in. Horrible. Do they know who did it?"

I shook my head. "No."

He leaned my way and lowered his voice. "I'm guessing it was the fiancée. Did you see her earlier? They were fighting."

"No, she and Brandon were both upset at Roland," I interjected. "Not each other."

"But why?" Tristan's brows arched. "I still say she's our number one suspect."

"Well, while we're talking about suspects. . ." I paused from unloading my bins to make the necessary announcement. "Add another crime to the mix. The Grindle Point is missing, folks."

"Missing?" Either Harvey was a terrific actor or he was genuinely shocked. "Mariah, I hope you're kidding."

"Nope. Not kidding. When we got back up to the gallery, it was gone."

"See?" Tristan's eyes blazed with anger. "I *told* you those people couldn't be trusted!"

Would this be a good time to mention that one of "those people" was DOA?

"It's got to be that girlfriend." Tristan's eyes narrowed to slits. "She took the puzzle and then did him in."

"Or vice-versa," Harvey said.

"But why?" Amber posed the question on my mind. "I mean, I get why she would steal a valuable antique, but why kill her boyfriend at the same time? You know? It makes no sense."

Harvey's jaw flinched. "Could be a scheme."

My thoughts exactly. One involving a certain bass player who had once looked like Prince Charming to me. Right now? He was looking more like a viable suspect. One who happened to be missing in action.

# CHAPTER 4

On Friday morning I arose with the sun, worrisome thoughts ping-ponging around in my head like loose change at the bottom of the dryer. I wanted to pull the covers over my head, to pretend last night's chaos was nothing but a bad dream. Could I just stay in bed today and forget all about the madness of last night? Unfortunately, a string of text messages from my mother dinged in rapid succession on my phone. She was worried about her little girl going back up to the opera house.

Frankly, I didn't blame her. But with 119 puzzles left to sell, I needed to make every penny I could, especially since the Grindle Point was out of the picture.

I made a call to the police station and filled them in on the missing puzzle. In all of the confusion last night, I hadn't found the perfect moment to do that. They took a report over the phone and said someone would come to the event to meet with me in person later in the day. Great. Nothing like drawing even more attention to myself.

I dressed in a more conservative outfit than usual, hoping to attract the right kind of buyer, someone with a lot of cash. Or several someones with moderate amounts of cash. Really, at this point I would settle for a poor man with a few pennies in his pocket, as long as he planned to spend them on puzzle pieces.

After doing my best to fashion my hair in a sensible style, I drove up to the opera house, praying all the way that today would be smooth sailing.

Smooth sailing.

Those words made me think of Martha's Vineyard. And that made me think of Brandon. Hadn't Amber and Tristan both said that their first contact with the man was on the Vineyard back in May? Was that his stomping ground, perhaps?

I tried to press images of him out of my brain but kept reliving that horrible moment when I'd seen his leg sticking out from under his table. And, worse. . .when Mr. Purvis pulled back the tablecloth to reveal the bloody truth hiding underneath.

*Please, God. . .let that image go away!*

Only, it didn't. It stuck with me as I made the fifteen-minute drive to the opera house. I arrived at nine-thirty, parked my VW bug, then entered through the front door. The band was seated in the lobby, warming up. And in his normal spot, my favorite bass player. Roland. Just sitting there as if nothing had happened last night. As if he hadn't gone MIA during a crime scene. With—or without—the victim's girlfriend.

Okay then. Maybe there was some reasonable explanation for why he'd disappeared on us last night. Perhaps he'd just gone home for the evening and missed the whole thing. Yes, surely that was it. Maybe he was still clueless.

I tried to compress my suspicions into a slot in my brain, but they slipped back out again when Cheyenne walked through the front door. Roland immediately stopped playing and stared bug-eyed at her. She froze in place and stared back, her swollen eyes still red and glistening from what must've been a recent cry.

Tears of despair, or something more suspicious? I couldn't be sure. Not that any of this was my business, of course. Why, oh why, couldn't I stop my crazy imagination from working overtime?

Oh, right. Because I'd witnessed a murder.

Well, not witnessed, exactly. . .but almost.

"Hey, you!" Amber sidled up next to me, looking as pretty as a picture in her jeans and blue flowy chiffon top.

"Hey. Please tell me you got some rest."

"I did. I slept like a baby." She giggled. "Oops. That just slipped out."

When we arrived at the foot of the stage, I was pleasantly surprised to see everything still as we'd left it. Nothing else appeared to be stolen, thank goodness. No doubt Mr. Purvis had stayed through the night to ensure that.

Wait. One thing was different. The Puzzle Me This table now sat center stage, in a place of prominence, loaded with merchandise.

Tristan joined us, releasing an exaggerated groan. "Really? I thought their stuff was considered evidence now. Why is it down here—and smack-dab in the center, no less? Aren't things bad enough?"

"I guess it's not evidence." I spoke in a controlled tone to keep things from escalating. "I mean, the victim was found *under* the table not on it. So maybe they were okay to let Cheyenne forge ahead? Looks like it, anyway."

A sheen of sweat dampened Tristan's forehead, and he swiped it with his palm. "What kind of a girlfriend moves forward with an event like this on the day after her boyfriend is murdered?"

"The kind who fronted the money for her now-deceased

fiancé's dream of getting rich quick selling stupid, cheap puzzles." The cranky female voice sounded from behind us, and we all turned at once, kind of like animated characters in a video game, to discover Cheyenne standing there with her hands on her hips, looking completely disheveled. "Now, if you don't mind, I have work to do. Could I get through, please?" She gestured for us to part the waters and then walked up the aisle toward the stage after pressing through our little group.

Amber shook her head. "I sure wish she hadn't heard that. I'm so embarrassed."

I shrugged. "I'm not sure I feel so bad for her anymore. Wouldn't you say she was a little..."

"Catty?" Amber offered then nodded. "Yeah."

"I'm telling you, it was Miss Cheyenne in the gallery with the box cutter." Tristan gave us a knowing look, as if he had this all figured out.

Still, one thing he'd said puzzled me.

Puzzled.

Ha.

Until now, no one had mentioned a box cutter. Was Brandon stabbed with a box cutter and not a knife? If so, how did Tristan happen to know that little detail?

Before I could give it much thought, Harvey Bates came in and took control of the room like a director coaching his actors before a big show. Always the leader of the pack, this one.

Mr. Purvis interrupted him to give us a lecture about not going into the stage right wings due to some kind of construction issue. No problem. I would stay on the stage where I belonged.

Ten o'clock rolled around, and the event went into full swing. Patrons flooded the auditorium, streaming down the aisles

PUZZLE ME THIS

toward us. Standing up on the stage under those bright lights, I felt like Pavarotti, about to sing an Italian aria. Or my swan song, at the very least. Without the Grindle Point. . .

No, I wouldn't think about that. I'd remain positive. If I sold most of the others, I'd still be okay.

I hoped.

*Please, God, let them sell.*

The next hour was spent acclimating myself to the sheer noise level. With so many people crammed onto the stage, I could barely hear myself think, let alone speak calmly and clearly to potential buyers. I managed to holler, "Thanks for stopping by!" to several who made purchases, but that was about it.

Speaking of loud, Tristan was something else. I'd never seen him so animated. His effervescent style matched his over-the-top ensemble. Really? A vest with red, white, and blue sequins on it? When had he donned that number? Who showed up at an event dressed like Uncle Sam?

Oh, right. The owner of the curiosity shop. And what was up with that flamboyant top hat? Regardless, it seemed to do the trick. Folks flooded to his table for lots of chatter and quirky products. They seemed to enjoy the Puzzle Me This table as well. If anyone picked up on the fact that a man had died underneath that table less than fourteen hours ago, they didn't say so. Neither did Cheyenne. She kept her business face on as she made sale after sale.

I did my best not to watch her too closely, but she did seem to be doing well with the customers, especially the guys. Go figure.

Harvey happened by my table around noon, just before we were set to take a lunch break.

"Tough news about the Grindle Point." His lips curled

363

downward in a pout. "I was seriously going to buy it, Mariah. I really was."

"Really?"

"Yeah." Those silver brows of his slanted into a frown. "I put you off too long. Now it's gone forever."

"Don't say that, Harvey. I'd like to think I'll get it back."

"Maybe." His eyes took on a faraway look. "I've always had a fascination with it. That lighthouse sits on my grandparents' property, you know. I remember playing on the stairs as a kid. And I loved to draw when I was young. I have a sketchbook filled with images of the lighthouse from various angles. I'll have to find it someday and show you."

"No way. I had no idea." That explained a lot but made the pain of the missing puzzle even more pronounced.

Still, something about his expression made me question his sincerity. Was all of this to throw me off track? A diversion to keep me from realizing he'd snagged the puzzle while the rest of us were on the main stage last night? Was he really outdoors talking to the police, or was that all a ruse?

Who knew?

The crowd continued to press in around us, and I happily sold puzzle after puzzle, including some of my higher-priced ones. By the time we took a break for lunch at noon, I was starting to feel more hopeful. Maybe God had a bigger plan for my life, one that didn't involve the Grindle Point.

Or maybe Mama was right and I needed to look for a real job. The convenience store around the corner from my sister's house was hiring. I'd always been pretty chatty. Maybe I could make a career out of selling gasoline and lottery tickets to the locals.

Nope. I just couldn't see it.

I could almost hear my third-grade Sunday school teacher's voice ringing in my ears: "Just trust God, Mariah."

I do. Or at least, I try to. He is, for sure, the biggest piece of my life-puzzle these days. Not that I've always given Him room. I can remember a time when I pushed Him out, thinking the picture was complete without Him.

Then I finally figured it out. I had everything I needed—but the one thing I needed most. I was avoiding a relationship with the Creator of the universe. So I plugged in that piece, and the others came into focus.

If God could bring them into focus back then, He could do it again. And would, if I'd just give Him time and space to do so.

At ten minutes after twelve, a handful of vendors converged on the small café on the far side of the lobby while the others manned the booths. I took a few bites of a ham sandwich and nibbled on a couple of stale chips, then chugged down several swigs of my diet soda.

Cheyenne took the spot to my right and opened the lid on a prepackaged salad. She shot a glance my way and said, "You know those artificial sweeteners are going to kill you, right?"

So many things I could say. . .but didn't. Instead, I flashed a warm smile and said, "We've all gotta go somehow."

Good grief. Talk about insensitive. What was wrong with me?

Still, I couldn't figure out why she would be so snarky, today of all days. I'd think she would be subdued. Or medicated. She was acting more like a spoiled rich girl and less like a grieving widow.

Not that she and Brandon were married yet, but still. . .

Amber slid into the spot to my left with a sandwich and

chips in her hand. "Mariah, you're going to want to see this."

"What?"

Judging from the worry lines creasing themselves into her forehead, she wasn't about to share good news. Amber opened her phone and pointed to an online store, one I'd never heard of—Out of Time.

"I follow this antique shop on Martha's Vineyard and get notifications when they post something that might be of interest to me. You're not going to believe what just popped up."

"What?"

She turned the phone so I could have a better view. My breath caught in my throat as I laid eyes on the picture in front of me.

"Um, what?" I stared at the site, unable to believe my eyes. There, in plain view...my Grindle Point. With a price tag of $3500.

# CHAPTER 5

"Wait. What?" I snatched the phone from Amber's hand and stared at the image. "No way!"

"Yeah, I couldn't believe it either, but there it is, plain as day."

I squinted to get a better look at the box in the picture. Mine had a little pink sticker on it with my *Solve It!* logo. It was noticeably absent on this box, but then again, it would be. If someone stole it, they would pull off my sticker in a hurry.

I wanted to stop everything, for time to freeze so that I could figure this out. . .but I couldn't. We had work to do. After wrapping up our lunch, we made our way back to the main stage to dive back in.

Only, I couldn't stop thinking about that puzzle. Even if it meant I lost a couple of customers, I had to check this out myself. I pulled up the site on my own phone and stared at the picture. Yep. The Grindle Point, in all of her glory. Same faded box. Same. . .everything. Well, except for that little dent in the corner. Someone must've rushed while stealing it.

I did a quick search for the Out of Time phone number then stepped into the wings to make the necessary call. The owner—a man who introduced himself as Mr. Mulligan—picked up on the other end, and I dove in with a full explanation of who I was and why I was calling.

"So, my puzzle was stolen last night in Camden, Maine," I explained after pausing to snag a breath. "And now it's sitting in your shop. I need to know who brought it to you. . .and when. What did they look like? Male or female? Tall? Short? Suspicious looking? Any distinguishing birthmarks or other characteristics?"

"Well, actually, I—"

"And just so you know, the police have already been notified that you're in possession of my property."

Okay, that last part wasn't a hundred percent true, but I would be calling them as soon as this call ended. So there.

I must've sounded a little too accusatory, because he interrupted with great fervor in his voice. "Whoa, Nellie. Slow down!" A nervous chuckle followed on his end. "You're quite a live wire, aren't you?"

"Yes, a live wire who's about to hop on a ferry and plant herself on Martha's Vineyard so she can get her puzzle back."

"Well, before you make that trip, maybe you should know that this particular Grindle Point puzzle has been in my shop for over three years. I bought it from a family who lost their elderly aunt, who lived in Maine. They passed it to me, and I've been trying to sell it ever since. . .without much luck, I should add."

All the air went out of my proverbial balloon at that explanation.

"We've got lighthouses of our own here on the island, and my customers are more inclined to be interested in those. So, I guess you could say I made a mistake, investing money in the Grindle Point. It's probably never going to sell. Unless you want to take it off my hands, I mean. Then we could both be happy."

"I see." Suddenly, I felt like a heel, making assumptions like I had.

"I've got the receipt from the purchase three years ago if you'd like to look at it." His voice was all business now. "I'd even be happy to connect you with the family, if you still have doubts. But I can absolutely assure you that the puzzle you lost last night is not the one sitting in my shop right now."

I sighed. Loudly. For effect.

Amber walked my way, looking more than a little concerned. "Everything okay?"

"Yeah, everything's fine."

Mr. Mulligan must've assumed that last part was meant for him because he came back with, "So, we're good now?"

"Yeah, we're good. I'm sorry I bothered you."

"You didn't bother me. My life is pretty boring, if I'm being honest. I needed a little adventure, and you provided enough to last for days." He paused. "But hey. . .if you happen to know anyone who might want to take this puzzle off my hands, I'm about to cut the price in half. That's why I pushed it up to the front of my list, to prep for the sale."

"I might, actually." Oh, but how it pained me to speak those words. All these months I'd counted on selling my puzzle to Harvey Bates. Would I really send him to a competitor now?

Yeah. Probably.

Man, that job at the convenience store was looking better and better.

"I know someone who will buy the Grindle Point from you, and he'll be thrilled at that price. Would you like his contact information?"

"Would I!"

I scrolled around on my phone until I came up with Harvey's number, which I shared with Mr. Mulligan. It was the right thing to do. And if there's one thing Mama—and all of my Sunday school teachers over the years—have taught me to do, it's the right thing.

"Do unto others," Mama always says.

To which I usually respond, "Before they do unto you."

But today I passed off all chances of a sale to a man I'd never met before, a Mr. Mulligan from Martha's Vineyard. And somehow it felt good. Right.

Okay, so I might not be moving to my own place anytime soon.

Mr. Mulligan could hardly believe my generosity. He kept gushing, thanking me over and over again as I told him about Harvey's interest in the Grindle Point.

"I'm sure you would do the same for me," I managed to eke out.

"I would," he assured me.

And I believed him.

After I ended the call, I released an exaggerated groan, hoping to release all the angst of the day in one long breath.

"Bad news?" Amber looked genuinely concerned.

"It wasn't my Grindle Point. He's had his for three years. Bought it from a local family." I fussed with the remaining puzzles on my table, rearranging them as best I could.

"Really?" Her nose wrinkled. "Wonder why the notification came up on my phone today, of all days?"

"He's about to put it on sale and just moved it to the front of his list. He hasn't been able to find a buyer."

"Really?" She snapped her fingers. "Hey, hasn't Harvey Bates wanted to buy that—"

"Yeah. And he's about to get a call. I gave the guy his name and number."

Compassion filled Amber's eyes, and she rested her hand on my arm. "You're a good Christian woman, Mariah Jamison."

"Some days. Other days, not so much."

"Harvey will be thrilled."

"More than you know. This guy's price is way lower than mine ever was." I paused, my thoughts in a whirl.

"That's great news!"

"For Harvey." I couldn't think clearly about what to do next. "Give me a minute, Amber. I still have to process all this. Five minutes ago I thought my puzzle was back within reach. Now it's gone again."

I walked to my table and did my best to plaster on a smile, especially when Cheyenne cast a concerned glance my way. If I didn't know any better, I'd say she was worried about me.

Then again, I probably looked pretty defeated right now.

A few tables over, Tristan carried on, making an absolute spectacle of himself. I felt a headache coming on and reached for my purse to grab a pain reliever. I opened it and fished around—past the receipts, the gum wrappers, the keys, and the busted eye shadow container—to the bottle of pills.

When I pulled it up, something else came with it. A scrap of paper. Another receipt, probably. No, this one was baby blue. With something scribbled on it. I pressed out the wrinkles on the paper to read the text. My breath caught in my throat as it came into view:

*Puzzle me this. What do the Grindle Point, the puzzle show, and a greedy business owner all have in common?*

I let out a gasp, and the paper floated out of my hand.

Cheyenne looked my way, head tilted forward. I must've looked as shaky as I suddenly felt, because she bolted my way.

"Are you okay?"

"N-no." I shook my head.

"You're not. . .you know?"

"No, that's my friend, Amber. She's the one who's expecting. I'm just. . ." My gaze shifted to the floor to the tiny piece of blue paper. I needed to snag it before Cheyenne noticed.

Too late. She noticed.

She leaned down, picked it up, and read the text. Her jaw tightened, and the pitch of her voice rose. "What. Is. This?"

"I promise, I don't know. I just found it in my purse, Cheyenne."

If I'd been writing this scene as a TV police drama, I would bring the police in right about now. They had promised to come at some point today, after all, to take my statement about the missing puzzle.

Only, they were nowhere in sight when I needed them most.

So, I had to settle for Mr. Purvis. I made my way past the stage left wings, along a dark, narrow hallway, down some steps, and up to the door of his tiny, dank office. I found the poor old soul asleep in his chair, his head on his cluttered desk. The overpowering scent of spicy food filled the minuscule room.

When I opened his door, he startled to attention. "Yes? Can I help you?"

"I've got something to show you." I lowered my voice. "It might be related to the murder!"

"You'll have to speak up." He pointed to his right ear. "I've lost fifty percent of my hearing on the right and eighty on the left."

Well, wasn't this sleeping beauty just the perfect specimen to stand guard over a murder scene?

He pushed aside a stack of items on his desk, and I took note of the fast-food taco bag. Taco-Mia. Yum. One of my personal favorites.

But man! That desk was a cluttered mess. I'd never seen so much stuff piled into one space except, perhaps, a *Hoarders* episode—everything from stacks of books to notepads to pens. Crazy.

"I opened my purse just now to get something out and found this." I pressed the paper into his shaky hand.

He squinted and held it close then adjusted his glasses for a closer look.

"Where did you say you found this?"

"In my purse. Which, by the way, was left at my booth last night when the murderer was doing his thing."

"By 'doing his thing' I assume you mean murdering Brandon Craig with a box cutter."

"Ah ha! So it *was* a box cutter!"

"How did you know that?" A muscle clenched along his jawline.

"Well, *you* just told me." I crossed my arms at my chest, determined to keep going. "But someone else mentioned it earlier today too. Tristan Woodhouse. And I happen to know for a fact that he was noticeably absent while the rest of us were on the stage last night. We were all looking for him. He was very worked up about Brandon just prior to the murder. Said the guy was trying to undercut the rest of us."

"I see."

Did he though? The poor old guy looked like he might doze

off again at any moment. I convinced him that he needed to call the police ASAP, and he agreed to do that as I stepped out of his room and back into the creepy narrow hallway, where shadows swallowed me whole. Honestly? I had to wonder if Mr. Purvis might end up taking a nap instead.

I returned to my table and discovered it was surrounded by customers. I rushed toward them, ready to get back to work. When I got closer, I realized Cheyenne was in my spot, taking care of them.

No way. The grieving widow was standing behind *my* table, taking care of *my* customers?

*Oh no you don't, girl. Don't even think about stealing my business!*

I buzzed over there, a forced smile on my face. As I stepped into my spot, I did my best not to knock her down while gently nudging her out of my way.

"This lady right here"—she pointed to an elderly woman in a red blouse—"is interested in your shipyard puzzle. And this gentleman"—she gestured to a blond teenager dressed in basketball shorts and a Bunker Hill Community College T-shirt—"has his eye on the Mariners one. Oh, and the thousand-piece Green Bay Packers puzzle. He liked it too."

I didn't know whether to thank her or worry about the fact that she'd been schmoozing my customers, but I opted to thank her. She nodded and disappeared back to her booth, where she faced a bevy of people to wait on.

I turned my attention to my customers but caught a glimpse of Tristan out of the corner of my eye. Good gravy, the guy had the lion's share of the customers at his table. What in the world was his draw? Why did they all adore him so much?

Because he was effervescent, fun, and colorful.

I, on the other hand? I'd already forgotten which puzzle the woman in the red blouse was interested in.

So had she, apparently. She turned from my table and headed straight to Tristan's, where he spontaneously burst into a rousing rendition of "Oh, What a Beautiful Morning."

Should I remind everyone it wasn't morning? It was midafternoon?

No, I'd let it go.

His song dragged on, and the crowd around him grew. The boy in the Bunker Hill T-shirt headed that way and started singing, filming it on his phone. Well, terrific. Tristan was probably going to go viral and be a global superstar by day's end.

Before long, several others joined in his song, a few singing harmony. By the time they finished, a reporter and cameraman from the local news channel showed up.

Go figure.

They caught the tail end of the performance on camera then asked for a live interview from Tristan.

Some guys have all the luck.

Me? All I had was a headache. A really, really bad headache.

# CHAPTER 6

Turned out the guys from the news channel had come to the puzzle show hoping for a scoop on last night's murder. Should I tell them about the note I'd found in my purse? Probably not. I hadn't even talked to the police about it yet. I couldn't exactly share evidence publicly, anyway.

Still, I couldn't help but notice that Tristan was happy to share what he knew.

Wait, how could he know anything? He was gone from the building during the murder. Right? He was outside, chewing out the teens who had set off the fireworks. That's what he said, anyway.

Yes, I remembered his words clearly: *"I gave them a piece of my mind."*

Still, that didn't stop him from carrying on as if he'd been right here on the stage with us last night. As he spoke, I kept a watchful eye on Amber and Charlie, who stood just a few feet away from him. I could tell they weren't happy with his on-screen performance. No doubt they would lay into him about embellishing the story once the reporter left the room.

Only, he didn't appear to be leaving anytime soon. Turned

out, the guy was looking for more volunteers to appear on the evening news. I took several steps back, putting great distance between myself and the crowd growing around the reporter. If they started asking me questions, I would probably blurt out something about that note. I never can control my impulses when I'm nervous.

Harvey Bates—never one to miss an opportunity—offered to go on camera next. He straightened his tie, fussed with his perfectly sculpted silver hair, and flashed a broad smile as he carried on about the role he had played in ushering us all to safety when the supposed shots rang out.

*Wait, you're taking credit for our safety? Really?*

I mean, he had guided us toward the stairwell last night, but that was about it. A few steps in the dark did not a hero make.

Harvey continued to sing his own praises. He was a great talker, that one. The reporter seemed captivated. So did the cameraman, who zoomed in on the councilman's face then shifted his angle to focus on Harvey's profile.

The patrons and vendors all gathered close, hanging on his every word. Nothing new there. Harvey has that way about him. He knows how to attract a crowd. That's probably how he ended up being elected councilman. Mama would call it charisma. I call it phony baloney. But I couldn't be *too* hard on the man. He was almost my best customer.

Almost.

The Grindle Point. My heart suddenly felt as heavy as lead. I replayed the moment when I'd realized the puzzle had gone missing and I felt nauseous all over again. Why hadn't I taken it downstairs with me? My whole life would be different today if I'd just listened to that nagging voice inside of me and grabbed it from my table in the dark.

Harvey's voice rose in pitch and fervor as he shifted gears and started sharing about the moment he had discovered Brandon Craig's body.

*Whoa. Wait a doggone minute here! Who discovered Brandon's body? That would be me, Harvey Bates, not you. I saw his leg poking out from under the table, remember?*

He didn't seem to remember that part. . .at all. On and on he went, taking credit for pretty much everything.

I got so distracted watching his made-for-TV performance that I almost missed the real-life scene playing out directly in front of me at center stage.

Roland. Cheyenne. In a private conversation at her table. I watched as the two of them hyperfocused on each other as if they were alone onstage in their own private scene. Maybe they thought they were. Their acting skills were stellar. Riveting, in fact.

Man, it looked intense. Was my imagination working over-time, or did she have tears in her eyes? Whoa. And what was up with him? I couldn't tell if he was angry or just fueled by some sort of internal passion, but he grew more animated as he spoke. And gracious, was he ever speaking. Roland seemed to have a lot on his mind today, and he was letting it roll. If only I could make out what they were saying.

I took a couple of tiny steps toward them then bent down and pretended to pick up something from the stage. A speck of lint. Hey, one can never be too careful about specks of lint. They can be dangerous. A person could trip.

I still couldn't hear, so I took a couple more steps toward them and shifted my gaze to Harvey, as if I'd moved in to better see his on-camera performance. Nothing could be further from the truth, of course.

Roland and Cheyenne never noticed me. In fact, they didn't appear to notice anyone, even the reporter and his crew. They were far too engaged with each other. And yes, she was definitely crying now. Oh my. Would the reporter catch a glimpse and turn his camera on her?

*Hey, folks! You're missing the real story over here!*

Only, everyone seemed blinded to it except me. Harvey kept right on singing his own praises, and the crowd clung to his every word.

All but me. I watched in rapt awe as Roland took Cheyenne by the hand and led her to the stage left wings.

If I ever needed an excuse to head stage left, it was now.

*Think, Mariah, think.*

Wait, I had the best excuse ever! Mr. Purvis's office was just beyond where they were now standing. I should probably check back in with him to make sure the police were on their way. No doubt they would want to talk with me about the note I'd found in my purse.

The note. What had I done with it? Did I give it to Mr. Purvis? Or did I stick it in my pocket? Suddenly, I couldn't remember.

I fished around in my pocket but came up empty. Surely I'd given it to him. Right? Why couldn't I seem to remember anything today?

Really, that job at the convenience store was looking more appealing by the minute. If I couldn't even be trusted to hold on to one simple piece of evidence, how could I ever manage running my own business? *Mama, you're right! I am a loser!* And this time I'd actually lost something important.

But enough about that. I had to get to the wings ASAP if I

wanted any clues about Roland and Cheyenne. Their conversation seemed to be intensifying. And for some reason, they were still holding hands. Yep, something was definitely up with these two, and it was far more exciting than an overzealous town councilman posing as a superhero.

I tiptoed in their direction then did my best to appear nonchalant as I eased past the side curtain in front of them.

No, not side curtains. What were these narrow velvet panels called again?

Legs. These side curtains were called legs.

*Thank you, Mr. Cook!* My ninth-grade drama teacher would be so impressed that I remembered.

Roland and Cheyenne stood directly behind the first leg, so I took up residence directly in front of it. Once situated, I paused and strained to hear their conversation from behind the velvet fabric.

I couldn't hear a thing. Then again, these curtains were meant to block noise from backstage. Apparently, they worked really well.

"Speak up, you guys," I whispered.

As if they'd heard my command, Roland's volume elevated. "Chey, you know how I feel. You've always known. What else do I need to do to convince you?"

What else? Good question. Had he already proven his affections by getting rid of the man standing in his way? That would explain his disappearing act last night while the rest of us were heading to the main stage in the dark.

"Well, yes, but. . ." Cheyenne's voice drifted off then got louder. "Why did you do it, Roland? Why?"

*Why, indeed! Inquiring minds want to know.*

"I've made a lot of mistakes, Chey. But I'm asking you to give me another chance. We can pick up where we left off. Start over."

"It's not that easy, and you know it."

*Whoa. No kidding.*

"I never said it would be easy, but it'll be worth it. We've made mistakes, but we can fix them now. It's not too late." His words faded as the noise from the stage escalated. Was someone singing? Again?

"Tristan, you've really got to stop," I whispered.

He didn't. This time the quirky curiosity shop owner had the crowd going with a rousing rendition of "If I Were a Rich Man." Good grief. He was singing my life song. Under ordinary circumstances, I would have joined in, but not today.

The song eventually came to an end, and I eased back a few steps to see if I could pick up on any more of Roland and Cheyenne's conversation. They had gone silent. Ugh. Now what?

I decided to brave it, to march past them as if I had a perfect right to be there. Which, of course, I did. I needed to see a man about a note, after all. I took several bold steps toward the far wall to get a better view of the couple.

And what I saw took my breath away.

There, in the shadows, Roland and Cheyenne were—*Wait, are my eyes deceiving me?*—kissing.

Um. No. My eyes were definitely *not* deceiving me. These two were going at it like two teenagers on steroids.

Heavens to Murgatroyd. What in the world was going on here? I felt like I was watching an opera house theatrical. Only, I couldn't make sense of the plot.

I half-expected the cameraman to turn toward us, to catch the whole thing on film. That would've been something for the evening news: *Fiancée of murder victim caught making out with bass player. Details at six o'clock!*

But he didn't. No one seemed to notice the goings-on in the shadows. Except me.

I moved to lean against the wall to give myself a moment to think things through, but I missed. Instead of hitting the wall, I smashed into some sort of set piece. Oh, great. . .a Roman column. It tilted to the right and almost fell into another set piece, an Italian fountain. Good gravy.

I somehow managed to get the column righted and kept the fountain from getting damaged. Once that was done, I attempted to ease my way back to the wall, where I could hide in the shadows. But I tripped. Over what, I couldn't be sure, but definitely not a piece of lint.

I went sailing over something on the floor below. It propelled me forward and I careened toward the wall, where I reached out to grab hold of something—anything—to keep me from face-planting against the bricks.

In desperation, I grabbed hold of some ropes. The moment my hands latched onto them, the painted backdrop for the opera society's recent production of *The Marriage of Figaro* came slamming down across the back of the stage.

And wouldn't you know it? It took out the cameraman and Harvey Bates, all in one fell swoop.

# CHAPTER 7

I didn't mean to knock Harvey out with the Figaro backdrop, but there he was, upstage center, out like a light.

The cameraman, God bless him, took a hard hit on the head but kept on filming. I had to give the man props. He was worth his weight in gold.

Speaking of props, I worked my way past the one that had tripped me up—a faux stone piece—and rushed onto the stage to make my apologies. In the heat of the moment, no one seemed to realize I was the one who had caused the fiasco. And, as hard as I tried to convince them, they seemed oblivious to my cries of guilt.

Apparently, my crime-solving abilities come in second to my lousy confessional skills, though somewhere in the middle of it all, I remembered that I had, indeed, given the note to Mr. Purvis while in his office. At least I could stop worrying about that.

*See, Mama? I'm not a total loser!*

In the midst of the chaos, I caught a glimpse of Cheyenne, heading back to her table. Roland took off down the center aisle of the auditorium toward the door leading to the foyer.

I worked my way to the middle of the crowd and babbled incoherently about how I'd accidentally tugged on the ropes and caused the backdrop to fall, but everyone seemed too focused on Harvey to pay much attention to me.

Mr. Purvis appeared out of the stage right wings looking wide awake. Man, this guy always seemed to be in the shadows, waiting for something to go wrong. Right now, he was all business, taking care of Harvey and calling 911.

Great. Just what we needed. . .more sirens in the distance.

I'd never seen the reporter so giddy. He perched himself center stage, just behind Cheyenne's table, and gestured for the cameraman to keep filming. The poor guy looked a little discombobulated but did what he was told.

The paramedics arrived in short order, but by then Harvey was up and moving and proclaimed himself to be in tip-top shape. I felt horrible for what I'd done, but no one seemed to notice or care that I'd caused the chaos.

I scooted back to my table and Amber rushed my way. "Girl. What a mess."

"You did hear the part where I caused this, right?"

"Something about falling into a wall and grabbing some ropes?"

I nodded and pointed to the wings. "Yeah. Far left there are ropes that control all of the backdrops. When I fell, I reached out to grab hold of what I thought was the wall and—"

"You missed?"

"I missed."

"Man." She sighed. "This day has more subplots than a soap opera."

"Oh, you're right about that. And boy, do I have a story for you. You're not going to believe it. But I think I might've solved the riddle of who killed Brandon Craig last night."

"Mariah, really?" She stared at me, bug-eyed. "Who?"

"Let's just say I'll never look at bass players and fiancées the same way again."

"I'll have to figure out what you mean later."

"Yep."

The paramedics checked Harvey out and proclaimed him fit as a fiddle. He hopped up and smiled and waved at the people then headed straight for me.

"Mariah. . ."

"I know, I know. But I promise, it was a mistake. I fell and I grabbed some ropes."

"Oh." Curiosity registered in his eyes. "You caused all of that? I was just coming over to tell you that I found another copy of the Grindle Point. A guy from a shop in Martha's Vineyard called me just before the reporter got here and said that you—"

"Yeah." I sighed. "I gave him your name and number. I hope you don't mind."

"Don't mind a bit. But it doesn't seem right, buying it from someone other than you. I put you off for so long and led you on, hoping you would lower the price. Now I feel bad."

"After what I just did to you, Harvey? I'd say it's the least I can do. If you're willing to forgive me for the bump on the head, I'll forgive you for not buying my puzzle sooner." I stuck out my hand.

He grabbed it and gave it a firm shake. "Deal."

Somehow, the vendors all got back to work. We were a resilient bunch. We'd survived a murder, a backdrop incident, and two choruses of "If I Were a Rich Man." Nothing could take us down.

The police finally arrived and pulled me aside for a statement about the missing puzzle. They grilled me on when, where, and how I'd connected with the shop owner on Martha's Vineyard, and I did my best to give the right details.

They left a short while later, and I felt like kicking myself when I realized I'd been so scattered that I had forgotten to ask them if they had any leads related to the note I'd found in my purse. Surely Mr. Purvis had given it to them by now. I would have to call them later for that. Right now I had puzzles to sell.

Still, I felt uneasy as the afternoon progressed. By the time eight o'clock rolled around, I was wiped off my feet. I threw a sheet over my table and called it a day. We would be back tomorrow for the final day of the show, but for now I had one thing on my mind: food. And sleep.

Okay, two things.

"Hey, want to grab some dinner?" Amber asked as she walked my way. "I'm starved."

"I thought you'd never ask."

We settled on the fifties diner on the opposite side of the green. They had terrible food, and the service wasn't much better, but tonight none of that mattered. I just needed to sit and eat and put the events of the past twenty-four hours behind me.

We entered to the scent of something burning. Lovely. Not that I cared. Right now they could char my food and I'd still eat it.

It took a while to be seated. The place was more crowded than usual. Many of the vendors converged on the popular eatery, including Tristan, who sat with a couple of the others at a table on the far side of the room. The blond kid in the Bunker Hill T-shirt who'd been at my table earlier headed to a booth near the door. He must've recognized me, because he offered a little wave, which I returned.

The hostess finally got around to finding a table for us, just behind the teens. Finally. We sat for some time before the waitress brought our glasses of water.

"I'm so sorry!" She tossed a couple of menus our way and reached for her pad and pen. "It's been a night. We're short one cook and I've been pinch-hitting. Trust me when I say you don't want me cooking your food."

"What happened to your real cook?" Charlie opened the menu and stared down at it.

"Ugh. Don't ask. Liam's just a kid, college sophomore, but he's good at what he does. Unfortunately, he got himself into a little bit of trouble last night, and our manager is making him take a few days off without pay to teach him a lesson."

"Trouble, eh?" Charlie glanced back up.

"Yeah." Her gaze shot to the window and she gestured to the green. "You might recall a little story about some fireworks."

"Oh, I do." I remembered, all right.

"He and his buddies used the dumpster behind the opera house." She lowered her voice and gestured to the boys at the table behind me. "Rough bunch."

"Ack." Now I saw why the manager was upset.

"Yeah, tell me about it. Scared us to death in here. We thought someone had been shot."

"Welcome to the crowd." Amber laughed as she passed the remaining menu my way. "We were on the third floor of the opera house thinking the very same thing."

"Oh, the gallery!" The waitress leaned in close. "I heard what happened up there. Terrible!"

"Horrible," we all agreed.

She got called away, and we scanned the menus in search of something to eat. I settled on a burger and fries. Through the window I caught a glimpse of something startling—Roland rushing across the parking lot to meet up with Cheyenne. Whoa.

"You okay, Mariah?" Amber asked.

"Maybe. I'm not sure." I spent the next couple minutes filling her in on what had happened in the stage left wings earlier today, and she and Charlie both looked shocked.

"Are you sure?" Charlie asked. "I mean, it was dark over there."

"Oh, I'm sure. They were making out."

"Kind of looks like they're arguing right now," Amber observed.

I gave the duo another glance. Sure enough, Cheyenne stormed off, leaving Roland alone in the parking lot.

So. Weird.

The boys behind us got more animated as time went on, to the point where we couldn't hear ourselves think. The waitress returned, glared at the boys, and then took our order, hollering over them. I decided to start with a chocolate shake and go backward from there.

Amber and Charlie lit into a conversation about the backdrop incident, and I buried my face in my hands. "Really, guys? Do we have to go there? Haven't I been humiliated enough?"

Behind me, the boys got louder and louder. One of them, in particular, seemed overly animated. I was pretty sure I recognized that voice as the Bunker Hill T-shirt kid.

"What did you guys think of our fireworks last night?" He let out a peal of laughter. "We called it 'the Big Bang Theory'!"

"I heard about that. . .on the news," another one responded.

I tried not to look obvious as I dropped my napkin on the floor and then leaned down to pick it up so that I could angle myself toward them.

Yep. Bunker Hill was definitely the loud one. "Not just me," he said. "Liam was with us."

"You know the cops thought someone was shot, right?" the other boy said.

"Yeah." His tone shifted. Now he sounded more worried than excited. "Probably the whole dumpster thing. But it wasn't our idea."

*It wasn't?* I wanted to ask. Then who suggested it?

"That guy who gave us the fireworks was something else." Blond boy offered a nervous laugh.

"Wait." Now I couldn't resist. I stood and faced them, hands planted on my hips. "Someone gave you those fireworks last night?" This had to be more than a coincidence. "Do you know who it was?"

Blond boy suddenly looked startled and embarrassed that he'd been overheard. "Nah. No idea."

"Tall? Short? Young? Old? If you saw him in a lineup, would you recognize him?"

"A lineup? Really?" He shrugged. "It was dark out and we were in the alley behind the diner. Just messing around. No big deal."

"The alley?"

"Yeah. Liam goes out there to smoke on his breaks. I brought him a pack of cigarettes."

"And this guy just happened along and offered you some fireworks." I must've increased my tone, because the other boy at the table suddenly looked nervous.

"Yeah, he said they were left over from the Fourth. Why the third degree?"

"Call me a curious bystander."

Blond boy shrugged. "He was just a nice guy. Told us the best places to pop them and the perfect time of day."

"I'm sure he did." I took a seat and reached for my chocolate shake, my headache intensifying.

"I heard." Amber rapped her fingers against the table. "Just a coincidence or. . ."

"Someone set us up with those fireworks. No doubt about it. The timing. The dumpster. All of it."

"A diversion to empty the room so that he—whoever he was—could kill Brandon Craig?" Charlie asked.

"Yep. That's my guess. And steal my puzzle too." Though I still couldn't figure out what one had to do with the other.

I leaned in for another sip of my chocolate shake but felt a little woozy. Man, I needed some sleep.

Out of the corner of my eye, I watched as Tristan carried on with the other vendors at his table on the far side of the room. Before long, Mr. Purvis joined them. That man really was like a phantom. He kept turning up everywhere.

A couple of minutes later, I heard another familiar voice behind me, even louder than the others. I turned to discover Harvey Bates had joined the boys at their table. Before long, they were laughing and chatting.

One thing was becoming abundantly clear as my thoughts twisted from suspect to suspect: I really needed to give up on crime-solving and take that job at the convenience store.

# CHAPTER 8

My phone rang early Saturday morning. I reached to grab it from the bedside table and flinched when I saw the word "Mama" on the screen. . .not because I didn't love to talk to my mother but because I knew her well enough to know that she was probably worried. That seemed to be her job these days.

Before I could even say "Hello," she spit out the words, "We're worried about you, Mariah."

Okay, then. Mama always seems to lead with those words. In a kinder, gentler world, she would have ended up with a daughter who didn't cause so much anxiety and strife. Someone with a normal life.

But she was stuck with me.

"I'm fine, Mama." The words came out sounding a little too rehearsed.

"You always say that, Mariah, but are you?"

"I am. I promise. I sold a bunch of puzzles yesterday, had dinner with friends, and got a good night's sleep."

Okay, so I conveniently left out the part where I'd knocked out Harvey Bates with the Figaro backdrop, but that would be a story for another day. I did my best to sound cheerful as I added,

"Now I'm headed back up there for what I hope will be another stellar day."

"Hopefully, one with no dead bodies in it," she countered.

"Did the police figure out who killed that man, honey?" My dad's voice sounded from the background.

"Nope. But the note in my purse might help them solve the case. I hope. They're probably checking it for prints as we speak."

"What note in your purse?"

Oh. Oops. Hadn't meant to let that slip out. Now Mama really sounded troubled.

"The murderer touched your purse?"

It took about five minutes to unpack that story. Then another five to share my thoughts on all of the viable suspects. Mama decided right away that Roland and Cheyenne had done the deed. Daddy wasn't so sure.

"I never trusted that Harvey Bates," he explained. "He's a little *too* perfect, if you know what I mean."

I knew exactly what he meant. The sculpted hair. The firm handshake. The confident voice. The way he talked about himself in the third person, saying things like, "You'll love Harvey Bates! A vote for Harvey Bates is a vote for a winner!" The guy was a little too car salesman-y. But, then again, he was *almost* my best customer.

Mama asked some pointed questions about Tristan Woodhouse. Where was he during all of this? Did I see him as suspect material? I explained that his over-the-top vocal performance placed him center stage during the latest goings-on.

"He's always been an odd duck," my father said.

"That's putting it mildly." I bit my tongue before shifting into gossip. Odd people usually couldn't help their quirkiness, after all. And he did seem to be a nice guy. When he wasn't angry at the other vendors.

After I hung up from talking to my parents, I hit the road. As I drove to the opera house, my thoughts went on a continual loop that revolved around Harvey Bates. He might be a showboat, but he was no murderer. Right now, I considered him more friend than foe, especially since I put him in touch with Mr. Mulligan. If my puzzle business took off, he might be the perfect advocate. Or...

My mind reeled back to the moment when I'd heard Harvey's voice in the booth behind me last night at the diner. How did he know those boys? Was he, by chance, the one who had given them the fireworks? They seemed pretty comfortable around each other.

The more I thought about it, the more nervous I got. Had he set up that fireworks thing and then joined us in the gallery, ready to step into the hero role at just the right moment?

Ugh. Suddenly Roland and Cheyenne weren't looking so guilty after all.

If Harvey was behind this, then surely he had taken my puzzle too. He of all people knew its value.

But if he *had* taken my puzzle, why was he so excited and grateful to buy the one on Martha's Vineyard? That part didn't make sense. Then again, none of this really made sense, did it?

My imagination threatened to run away with me as I headed inside the opera house for the final day's events. I sailed right past the musicians in the lobby and took note of the fact that Roland wasn't among them. My heart did that crazy little flip-flop thing, and I did my best not to sigh aloud at the idea that I'd lost him completely to a real-life competitor.

Strange, how I could miss someone who barely realized I existed. No doubt his lingering gaze up at the balcony that first night was because of Cheyenne not me.

*Sayonara, Mr. Practically Perfect in Every Way. You were never meant for me.*

Oh well.

I'd find Mr. Right-for-Me soon enough, but he wouldn't be a bass player.

Or a CPA.

Or a curiosity shop owner.

Ick. Where had *that* idea come from? A shiver ran down my spine as visions of Tristan singing "If I Were a Rich Man" raced through my memory bank.

I landed on the stage at five minutes till ten, just in time to pull the sheet off of my merchandise and check to make sure nothing else was missing. Everything seemed fine.

Mr. Purvis happened by and paused when he saw me. He looked even more weary-worn than the day before, if such a thing were possible. Did the man stay here all night?

He leaned close and spoke in hushed tones. "I heard from the police."

"You did?"

"About that awful note you found in your purse." He nodded. "The only fingerprints they found on the note were yours." A little shrug followed on his end. "Well, and mine."

My heart quickened. "Please tell me I'm not a suspect."

"No." He looked startled at this suggestion. "You have over fifty witnesses who can testify to your whereabouts that night. You're perfectly safe and so am I."

"So, no clue who dropped that note in my purse. . .or why?"

He shook his head. "None. But I'm thinking it was someone on the outside who set us all up. He—or she—slipped in when we weren't looking and did the deed. That note was meant to scare you."

"It certainly did."

"Whoever put it there must have been wearing gloves, so this crime was well thought out." He rested his hand on my arm. "You've got to be safe, Mariah. I would suggest you back away from all this and leave it to those of us who are trained. We'll figure out who did the deed."

"Did the deed." Sounded like something from a made-for-TV movie.

"I feel sick about it." The edges of his lips tugged downward, and I could read the defeat in his expression. "I was on the job that night. I must've missed something, for this to happen. After all these years, I end my career with a dark cloud hanging over my head."

"Whoever did this was sly, Mr. Purvis." Now I rested my hand on his arm, hoping to bring some degree of comfort. "Don't blame yourself."

"I'll try." He offered a compassionate nod. "And *you* try not to worry. If I hear anything else from the police, I'll let you know, I promise."

I thanked him and then turned to greet my first customers of the day, a family with three little kids who were—according to the mother—puzzle aficionados. We had a wonderful chat, and I sold them five puzzles, one for each member of the family. After that, several more customers ventured in and made purchases. By noon, I'd sold over thirty puzzles. With the ones I'd sold yesterday, I'd almost cut my inventory in half.

Maybe I wouldn't end up selling gasoline and lottery tickets, after all.

*See there, Mama? I'm not the failure you think I am!*

I kept shifting my attention to the Puzzle Me This table at center stage. It sat empty. Someone had cleared it of all its merchandise. And Cheyenne was noticeably absent today. Weird.

My thoughts trailed back to Roland, who was also MIA. Ack. For that matter, I hadn't seen Harvey either.

Before I could give it much thought, more customers arrived. Like the last batch, these folks seemed genuinely interested in my puzzles. Should I take a picture to send my mother?

Nope. No time for that right now. I had to stay focused on the people in front of me.

The Saturday crowd picked up even more, making it impossible to contemplate a lunch break. When I did finally manage to sneak away to the café around one-thirty, I checked my phone and realized I'd missed a couple of calls from the shopkeeper on Martha's Vineyard.

I decided to call him back while I had a moment to myself. He seemed a little out of sorts, and it didn't take long to figure out why.

"Hey, I wanted to let you know I reached out to that guy you told me about—Harvey something-or-other."

"Bates." I did my best not to sigh aloud as I thought about the sale I'd lost. "He told me that you and he spoke. I'm sad to be losing his business but happy for you guys."

"Yeah, I was too. . .until he called me back this morning. Turns out, he's found another Grindle Point at a better price."

"Wait. . .what?"

"Exactly. I thought you'd want to know. He said he found it

online late last night so I did a little digging, and sure enough, he's right. It's a brand-new listing, selling for nine hundred, from an individual owner not a company."

"Nine hundred dollars?" Good grief. "Can you send me the link?"

"Yep. As soon as we hang up. But I thought I should let you know on the off chance that it might be your puzzle floating around out there."

"I'm grateful. And I'm sorry you lost the sale. But thanks, Mr. Mulligan."

"You're welcome. I sure hope this story has a happy ending, if not for me then you."

"For both of us would be nice."

"Yes. Thank you."

His text message came through less than a minute after we ended our call, and I followed the link to the website. Sure enough, a Grindle Point photo appeared with the word SOLD next to it. I zoomed in and noticed the remnants of the tiny pink *Solve It!* logo. Whoever tore it off didn't quite get all of it. I grabbed a quick screenshot on my phone so that I could enlarge the photo later for a closer look to see if I could decipher any clues.

This was definitely my puzzle. I started trembling as anger gripped me. This thief had some serious nerve! I read the description of the puzzle, and it matched, almost word for word, the way I'd always described it on the website of my online store.

When I had an online store.

The most telling sign of all—the person who posted it said the puzzle had a value of $2,500. My original asking price.

Harvey knew that I planned to sell the puzzle for $2,500, didn't he?

For that matter, Tristan knew too.

Honestly? Half of Camden knew.

But why would Harvey steal the puzzle then pretend to buy it himself? None of this made any sense.

Unless it was all part of his master plan to throw me off course.

Yes, perhaps this was all a ruse to make it look like someone else had stolen the puzzle. He posted it online as part of his act, then pretended to buy it before anyone else could make an offer.

If Harvey didn't steal the puzzle, that didn't let him off the hook. Buying it from the thief made him a rat! He knew it was stolen, after all. Did he think I wouldn't figure it out? Why not just tell me about it instead of buying it at the thief's cut rate? Ugh.

I didn't have a clue how to resolve this, but maybe the police would. So I bypassed Mr. Purvis this time and decided to take matters into my own hands. I placed a call to the Camden police station and five minutes later was in a hot and heavy discussion with a detective by the name of James Durham.

"You think the missing puzzle is linked to the murder?" he asked me when I finally paused for breath.

It made me feel a little nauseous to admit it, but I did. And told him so.

He asked me to forward the link to the site where Harvey purchased the puzzle, which I promised to do once we ended the call.

"We'll trace that web account and see if it turns up anyone local," he said. "But you have to consider the fact that the puzzle Mr. Bates purchased actually belongs to someone other than you."

"I'm telling you there were remnants of my logo sticker still on the box, so I'm sure it's mine. If Harvey shows up today, I'm going to watch him like a hawk."

"We would prefer you not do that, ma'am. Leave the investigating to us."

Why did detectives always say things like that? Oh, right. Because they were trained, and folks like me were just ordinary people.

Well, I might be ordinary, but right now this ordinary gal had a bee in her bonnet. I was more than a little irritated that someone had already turned a profit on my one item of great value. And I wouldn't stop until I figured out who that someone was.

# CHAPTER 9

Sometime around three o'clock on Saturday afternoon, I decided to take a little break to run to the ladies' room. Amber agreed to watch over my table—which was now down to only twenty-four puzzles—while I disappeared for a few minutes.

I went sailing down the aisle toward the lobby then past the spot where the band normally sat. They were already gone for the day, but I did find one person seated there—in Roland's seat.

Cheyenne.

Crying.

Whoa.

I eased my way past her and went to the restroom, my thoughts tumbling around in my head. As I washed my hands, I couldn't stop thinking about Cheyenne. Sitting there in the lobby, tears flowing, she looked so. . .innocent.

Maybe she was. Maybe I'd misjudged her from the get-go.

My heart went out to her, but what could I do? No doubt she would be gone by the time I got back out there. I hoped. I gave it a couple of minutes then headed back through the lobby once more, toward the auditorium door.

She hadn't moved an inch, and this time there was no escaping her. The somber young woman glanced my way, eyes filled with tears, so I slowed my pace and gave her a sympathetic smile.

"I'm sorry," I managed. "Didn't mean to disturb you."

"You didn't. I just. . ." She leaned forward and rested her head in her hands.

Because Cheyenne left off midsentence, I felt compelled to stick around for whatever she might say next.

*If* she said something.

It took a moment. An awkward moment. Cheyenne finally sat up and swiped at her tear-filled eyes. "I don't know what I'm doing here, if I'm being perfectly honest. I really don't. I didn't plan to come today. . .at all. I cleared out my stuff—Brandon's stuff—last night after. . ." She shook her head. "Anyway, I didn't plan to come back."

"And yet you did."

"And yet I did." She looked up and sighed. "Have you ever been so confused, so mixed up, that you didn't know what to do? Like nothing made sense?"

I couldn't help but laugh. Was she kidding? "Only every day of my life. My mother thinks I'm the flightiest person on the planet, and I've proven her right more times than I can count."

"I think I might've just stolen that title from you." She offered a faint smile. "Does it come with a crown?"

"Yeah, but you're not going to like it. It's made out of pipe cleaners."

Okay, that got a laugh out of her, which was good because it broke the tension in the room, which we needed.

She gestured for me to take the seat next to her, and I did. Cheyenne turned to me, stuck out her hand, and said, "Hi. I'm Cheyenne."

"Hi." I shook her hand and offered a smile. "I'm Mariah."

"Nice to meet you."

"You too."

"I should've done that the first day, but to be honest, I was so preoccupied." She reached in her purse and came out with a tissue, which she used to dab her nose. "I didn't know Roland was going to be here. If I had known, I never would have agreed to come."

"Ah, I see."

But I didn't. Not really. I didn't fully comprehend her back-story with Roland.

"So I showed up on Thursday night and had to come face-to-face with him. And then, on top of all that, I lost my best friend." She dissolved into tears, and I sat in strained silence. All I could do at that point was whisper a little prayer that she would be okay.

"I'm so sorry about your fiancé, Cheyenne," I said when she finally calmed down. "It's horrible what happened to him. Horrible."

"Yes, it was." She sniffled. "But if I'm being totally honest. . ." Her eyes flitted shut and she shook her head. "He wasn't my fiancé."

"Huh?"

Her eyes popped open. "I can't believe I'm actually admit-ting it to someone, but it's true. Brandon and I were never really engaged."

"But. . ." Okay, now she had my full, undivided attention. "Everyone said—"

"Yeah, I know what they said. That's what we wanted them to think. But it wasn't true. It was all a plan to get back at Roland. After what he did to me. . ." Her words trailed off.

"A plan?"

She released an exaggerated breath as she looked my way. "It sounds so ridiculous saying it out loud like that. Brandon was my best friend in college, my strongest ally. He always hated Roland, thought he wasn't good enough for me."

"Ouch."

"Let's just say that Brandon had his reasons," she added. "Roland broke my heart about seven months ago. I caught him hitting on someone else." She sighed. "It happened at my family's annual Christmas party on my dad's yacht."

"Yacht?" That got my attention.

"Yeah. And, man, I fell hard. Sometimes you can tell right away that you're going to be a good fit with someone. You know?"

"Yes." I didn't mean to release a sigh, but there it was. Roland was pretty dreamy, after all.

"Anyway, we were a couple for a year and a half before the night of that infamous Christmas party. That evening, everything came crashing down. He hit on a girl I've known since junior high, one of my best friends."

"Oh. Ouch."

"I know, right?" She paused and appeared to be deep in thought. "I ditched him right away. He wanted to patch things up, said she was the one who came on to him and things weren't what they looked like. But I just couldn't get past it."

"That's understandable."

"My heart was broken. I really thought he loved me."

Based on what I'd overheard in the wings yesterday, he still did. What was it he had said? *I've made a lot of mistakes, Chey. But I'm asking you to give me another chance. We can pick up where we left off. Start over.*

So, *that's* what he meant.

Cheyenne forged ahead, oblivious to my internal ramblings. "Brandon was at the Christmas party and witnessed the whole thing, which totally confirmed to him that Roland was the wrong guy for me. And, at the time, I agreed with him. But Roland kept pursuing me, and it got harder and harder not to give in to the temptation to go back to him."

"Some people can be very persuasive."

"He was. Is." Her nose wrinkled. "And I can't trust myself to know if he's genuinely sorry or just trying to play me. You know?"

"Um, yeah. I know."

"Anyway, Brandon cooked up this idea to act like we were engaged. Figured that would push Roland away. But it didn't work."

"Apparently." I chose my next words carefully. "Cheyenne, do you think there's *any* possibility that Roland...well..."

"Killed Brandon?" She shook her head. "I can tell you without a shadow of a doubt that he did not."

"And you know this because..."

"Because I was *with* Roland when it happened." Her voice broke, and she began to cry in earnest now.

Which gave me time to think.

She and Roland were together at the moment of the murder. But this didn't mean they weren't working in tandem, right?

On the other hand, would she be sitting here, blubbering like this, if she *had* murdered her best friend?

Maybe I'd better just wait and let her explain.

Cheyenne finally got herself under control. Her tissue, on the other hand, looked like it had seen better days. She fished around in her purse for another one then turned her attention to me. "When the lights went out, I wanted to go downstairs with everyone else. I was scared there was a murderer on the loose. After hearing those shots—"

"Which turned out to be fireworks."

"Yes, but in the moment, I truly thought we had a shooter on the loose in the building, and I was scared to stay in the gallery. I tried to talk Brandon into going downstairs with the rest of you, but he wouldn't hear of it. He was worried someone would steal our stuff."

"I was worried about that too, and for good reason."

"Yeah. I mean, honestly? I could've cared less about that part, but when the lights went down. . ." Her words trailed off. "Well, I'd seen Roland go into the balcony area just before that, and he looked so heartbroken. So, when the lights started flickering, I told Brandon I was heading downstairs without him."

"But you didn't."

"I didn't. I slipped off to the balcony to see Roland." She wrung her hands. "I feel so guilty now. If I'd just stayed with Brandon, he would still be alive."

"Or you might be dead, Cheyenne. Did that occur to you?"

Her jaw dropped.

"I'd say it's a blessing you weren't with him. But someone wanted him dead." And even as I spoke those words, I realized my suspect list had just narrowed.

"Now I've lost my best friend, and things with Roland are just. . ."

"Complicated?"

"To say the least. Look, I know what people think. I've overheard some of their ugly comments, especially that Tristan guy. He thinks I'm responsible for Brandon's death."

"Ignore him. Just step away from these people. You'll probably never see most of them again anyway."

"Maybe. But can you even imagine what they would say if they found out I wasn't Brandon's fiancée? Or, worse. . .that Roland and I used to be a couple?"

She did have a point there.

"What happened when you found him in the balcony?"

"He wanted to talk." She shook her head. "But I knew Brandon would flip out, so when the lights came back up, I headed to the gallery, hoping he would just think I'd been downstairs with all of you. I couldn't find him anywhere, though."

"Oh, wow. He was already. . ." I couldn't bring myself to say the word.

"Yes. But I thought he'd left, so I took off, hoping to find him. I wanted him to know that my heart was twisted in knots after talking to Roland. Brandon would've known what to do. He always knew what to do."

"So you left the building?"

"I came here. To the lobby. I thought maybe Brandon had come downstairs after all."

"And you stayed here until after his body was found?"

"Yes. When everyone went back upstairs, I knew I'd better join them. I had no idea I was about to walk into the worst nightmare of my life."

I rested my hand on her arm.

"I know people thought I was to blame, including the police. I spent that whole night at the police station being interrogated."

"Oh, wow."

"Yeah, tell me about it. That's why I was so cranky yesterday morning when everyone first got here. I barely had time to go home, shower, and change before I had to come back up here to sell those stupid puzzles. I was exhausted and an emotional wreck."

"Man." I wanted to ask a question, one that had been bothering me since yesterday morning. "Speaking of stupid puzzles, you mentioned in passing that you funded Brandon's business. Did you mean that?"

She groaned and pushed a strand of hair out of her face. "I shouldn't have mentioned that. But yes. He needed start-up money for the puzzle company and asked me to join him. So I did. I always thought it was a goofy idea, to be honest, but he was always so good to me. How could I turn him down?"

"Do you mind if I ask where you guys get your puzzles?"

"In China. For next to nothing." She released a labored sigh. "I know, I know. It's awful. But that's another reason I want to sell off the merchandise and be done with it all. I never liked the idea in the first place, and now? Knowing that *this* business is what took his life. . ." Her eyes flooded with tears. "I'll never forgive myself."

"Hey, selling puzzles isn't a crime."

"Unless people end up dead. And hearts are broken."

"I guess this wouldn't be the best time to confess that I overheard some of your conversation with Roland in the wings yesterday."

"What?"

"Yeah." I sighed. "Right before I accidentally pulled the ropes and knocked the backdrop down. You guys were behind the side curtain. I was just in front of it. So, yeah. . .I heard a lot of what he said to you." I gave her a pensive look. "You don't know me from Adam—and I don't have the best track record with guys—but I have to say, he sounded really genuine."

"He did." She sighed. "And I got caught up in the moment. We ended up—"

"Kissing."

"You saw that too?" She cringed.

I responded with a nod.

"When the backdrop came down, I took that as a sign. I told him it was all a mistake, that I never wanted to see him again."

"Hey, don't let my slick move with the backdrop determine your love life. Maybe you should give him another chance. Maybe things really happened like he said. You know?"

Her nose wrinkled. "Maybe. I know things aren't always what they look like."

"Exactly."

"And it's not like I never made any mistakes. But can you imagine what people will say if I get back with him now?"

"You can't control any of that."

"True."

"I'm going to pray that you make the right decision so you can have peace. That's what you need right now. And by the way, Roland seems to have his life together. I mean, he plays on the worship team at my church every Sunday, so I see him on a regular basis and he seems like a standup guy."

"Roland goes to church?" She looked mesmerized by this notion.

"Every Sunday. Never misses."

"Interesting."

"I've always thought he was a great guy. Any woman would be lucky to have him."

I'd leave it at that and not confess my true feelings.

She sighed. "I've made such a mess of things. And who knows if Roland would even still want me after what I said to him yesterday."

"I still want you." A voice sounded from behind us, and I turned to discover Mr. Practically-Perfect-in-Every-Way was standing less than three feet away. How much he had heard, I couldn't say. But apparently enough to know that he stood a chance with her.

And, judging from the look of pure relief on her face, he really did.

I rose and gave Roland my chair. He took it, and Cheyenne immediately flung herself into his arms.

# CHAPTER 10

S o much for not knowing what to do.

Apparently, Cheyenne's decision was made the moment Roland spoke those magic words—*I still want you.*

I had to admit, they would've won me over too. Hey, how many years had I waited for my own Mr. Right to admit how desperately he wanted and needed me? It was nice to see things coming together for someone, even if it didn't happen to be me.

At some point those two must've forgotten I was still in the room. They did a replay of the kissing scene I'd witnessed yesterday on stage left. Then, when they came up for air, Roland took her hand and gazed into Cheyenne's eyes.

"I know your friends think I'm a total screw-up. And I know they don't think I'm good enough for you."

"It was never about that, Roland."

"Well, good. Because there's something I need to tell you." He raked his fingers through that gorgeous dark hair. "There's been a little change since last Christmas. A big change, I should say."

"What kind of change?"

I leaned in a little closer, anxious to hear whatever he was about to say.

"I...well...I've been writing some music on the side. It's kind of my passion."

"Right, I remember."

"I met an agent a while back at a band gig in New York City. And he signed me to a contract."

"Wow, that's great!" I didn't mean to say the words out loud. Oops.

"He's got great connections in the industry." Roland directed his words at both of us. "So, he pitched some of my stuff to a producer in Nashville."

"Wow!" I said. "That's so cool."

"Amazing," Cheyenne added. "I'm so proud of you, Roland. I know you've always wanted this."

He nodded. "For as long as I can remember. Anyway, the long and short of it is, my first song is going to be released in a couple of months, and the producer is looking at several others too."

"Wh-what?" She grabbed him by the arm. "Oh, Roland. I'm so happy for you."

"Thanks." His gaze shifted to the floor and then back up again. "The song is actually about you. It's a love song."

She threw her arms around his neck once more and thanked him with about ten kisses.

At some point things got really awkward, so I decided to head back to the stage. These two didn't need me horning in on their love life any more than I already had.

I got to the door leading to the auditorium, and it opened from the other side. Tristan held it to let me walk through. He glanced across the lobby at Roland and Cheyenne, and then he blinked in rapid succession, his mouth falling open.

"I *told* you there was something up with those two," he said. "I wanted to be wrong, but time has proven me right yet again."

No doubt everyone else would have the same response once they found out. *If* they found out.

I tried to interject my thoughts with a gentle, "You need to hear the backstory, and then you'll understand."

"Oh, I've seen enough to make me understand. That's for sure. But I'm not as naive as you, Mariah. My eyes are wide open."

His might be, but Mr. Purvis's were not. The poor old guy approached, looking bone tired. Tristan lit into an animated conversation with the exhausted security guard—pointing his finger at Cheyenne and Roland—and the two men disappeared across the lobby and into the café.

There was nothing I could do about all of their suspicions. But I'd heard enough to convince me that the lovebirds weren't to blame for the theft of my puzzle or Brandon's death. Not that they were paying much attention to what others were thinking. No, Roland and Cheyenne headed to the front door, ready to move on. Good for them.

Instead of bemoaning my own lack of a love life, I decided to focus on selling the rest of my puzzles. With only a few hours remaining, I needed to give it my best shot.

So, I plastered on a big smile, made my way through the throng of people coming and going in the auditorium, and then walked back to the stage. When I arrived at my table, I thanked Amber and gave her the two-minute version of what I'd just witnessed.

She stared at me, bug-eyed. "That's some story, girl."

"No kidding. Talk about twists and turns."

"Right?" Creases formed between her eyes. "Well, that's good for them, I suppose, but we still don't know who killed Brandon."

"Or who stole the Grindle Point. I told the detective that I felt the two were linked."

"Detective?"

"Yeah. I called the police yesterday when I saw Roland and Cheyenne kissing."

"Tell a person! But you might want to call him back now that you know their. . ." She paused and a reflective look came over her. "What did you call it again?"

"Backstory. We all have one. And yes, I'll call him. Good idea. But I've figured out one thing, for sure. It's undeniable."

"What's that?"

"I. Stink. At. Crime. Solving."

A ripple of laughter followed from Amber. "Why do you say that?"

"Because. . ." I paused to choose my words with care. "I suspect *everyone*. And then, in the same breath, I want to believe everyone. Mama would say I'm gullible. Or flighty."

"There are worse things to be, Mariah. I mean, we *are* at a puzzle show, after all, and this whole murder mystery has been like a puzzle of its own."

"One with half the pieces missing."

"Exactly. But you know how it goes. Puzzles always eventually come together. And then you can see the whole picture. Right now, we just can't. But one day, we will. That's life. You know?"

Yeah, I knew all right. I felt the sting of tears in my eyes because she'd struck a nerve without even realizing it.

She must have sensed the emotional volcano stirring inside of me because she gestured for Charlie to take over at my table while still keeping an eye on his own. Thank goodness, he seemed willing. He stepped into her spot and gave us a thumbs-up, then she dragged me to the wings, to the very spot where I'd stood yesterday afternoon to listen to the love scene play out behind the curtains. Well, perfect. Just what I needed—another reminder that some people had a love life and others didn't.

"Did I upset you?" Amber asked once we were at a safe distance from the crowd onstage.

"No, not at all." I shook my head. "Well, not intentionally anyway. It's what you said about seeing the whole picture. I'm starting to think I'll never see all of it in time to have a normal life."

"Normal life?"

"Yes, normal. Like you and Charlie have. I'm worried my puzzle's crazy pieces aren't going to come together in time."

"Time for what? And whose time are you referring to anyway?" She crossed her arms at her chest and gave me a pensive look. "Yours. . .or God's?"

"Ouch."

"Sorry. Just curious. You don't want to get ahead of Him."

*That's easy for you to say when you're married and have a baby on the way.*

Okay, so I didn't say the words out loud, but I wanted to. "I'm just saying, I'm about to turn thirty years old. Everyone else my age has it all together."

At this point she snorted. The girl actually snorted.

"I'm just saying, I'm not like everyone else. And that's making me think my box came with a ton of missing pieces. Maybe I'm never going to find them. I have to face that possibility."

There. I'd said it. And I meant it.

"Mariah!" She looked genuinely shocked by my proclamation. "We *all* have missing pieces. That's part of the adventure of being a Christian. We have to learn to trust God to see what we can't see. He's working things out behind the scenes, even when we can't see it. And I'm sorry I laughed earlier, but girl. . .tell me you don't really think Charlie and I have it all together. I forgot to pay the electric bill last week, and they almost shut us off."

Great example, but she still didn't get it. Not really. "You know what I mean though. I want things when I want them. Like, now. I'm not very patient."

"Welcome to the club." She laughed and placed her hands on her belly. "I'm about to become your most impatient friend. For the next several months, anyway."

"I'll be here for you," I said.

"And I'll be here for you too, Mariah. Whether you see tiny glimpses of your story or the whole picture. Charlie and I will be right here. We promise."

Ugh. She said the "we" word. Tears sprang to my eyes once again before I could stop them.

"Go on, spit it out," she said after observing me for a moment. "You've got something else on your mind."

"Well, yeah. The guy thing." I offered an exaggerated sigh. "I'm wondering where that piece of my puzzle is."

"If it's part of your story then God will make it wonderful in His time. And if it's not. . ." She gave me a compassionate look. "Then He will make you content in your singleness. I truly believe He will."

"I guess." Would another exaggerated sigh be too obvious?

She leaned in close and whispered, "But girl, at least you don't have to deal with the toilet seat being up in the middle of the night. You'll never know how cold that rim is until you sit down on it in the middle of January."

"Amber!"

A giggle followed. "And don't even get me started on the stinky socks in the hallway and the open containers in the refrigerator."

"Stop it. Now you're just making me more jealous. I'd love to find socks in the hallway and someone else's food containers in the refrigerator."

"Filled with leftover Chinese food that's three weeks old, buried behind a container of moldy cottage cheese?"

"Well, when you put it like that. . ." I laughed. "I get it. I should stop complaining."

"Oh, I wasn't saying that." She looked to her right and left, as if making sure no one else could hear, then tilted her head in my direction. "Complain all you like. But enjoy this season as much as you can. Once God does bring Mr. Right into your life—and I tend to think He will—things will change. They'll get more. . . complicated."

"And more wonderful?"

"Sure." She smiled. "More wonderful. And more complicated. And. . ." She leaned forward to whisper the rest. "More smelly. But that's a story for another day. In the meantime, don't give up on the idea of romance just yet."

"I won't. And maybe this whole Cheyenne and Roland thing will bring me hope. He was her missing puzzle piece, after all. I mean, he went missing for a while then showed up again. Her picture wouldn't have been complete without him."

"True."

"If God can do that, then maybe that's a sign for me to hang on until I can see the rest of the picture."

"True. He's given you enough beautiful glimpses of the picture to know that He's up to something good, Mariah. And He's never let you down in the past, so I have no doubt He'll eventually slide those missing pieces into place—in His time and His way."

Deep thoughts.

"And by the way. . ." She paused and her nose wrinkled. "I'm not sure if this is the appropriate moment to make this confession, but I've always been überjealous of you, so thank you for letting me get that off my chest."

"Wait, what?" Surely I had misunderstood.

"Well, yeah. You're so fun. Easygoing." She pointed at my outfit. "And look at you! You have such a quirky sense of style."

"Quirky? Like Tristan?"

"Um, no." She laughed. "Not even close. He's too over the top. Fake. But, you're. . .you. And everyone adores the real you. Don't you see that?"

I didn't, actually.

"And it goes without saying that you've got the best figure in town. Don't even get me started on how annoying *that* is, especially now that I'm about to lose mine completely."

Okay, when had I slipped off into the twilight zone? Surely she was talking about someone else. I glanced to my right and then my left. Nope. We were still alone.

Amber gave me a pensive look. "You don't get it, do you, girl? You don't see your own value, do you?"

Ouch.

"You're perfect just as you are, Mariah. God made you... you. And don't you dare go changing anything about yourself.

When the right guy comes along—if he comes along—well, you'll know. And you won't have to hunt him down. God's really good at bringing you what you need." She glanced at Charlie and shrugged. "Even if he is a little stinky."

Okay, I had to laugh at that.

We walked back to my table, the mood much lighter than before. When we got there, I took one look at Charlie and started laughing. I don't know if it was the story of the moldy cottage cheese or the one about the stinky socks, but something had me tickled.

"What?" He glanced our way, brow furrowed. "What did I do?"

"Nothing, honey." Amber walked his way and gave him a kiss on the cheek.

The crowd around us thinned, and I realized my table was now almost empty. Charlie had sold several more puzzles while we chatted.

"Wow." I gave him an admiring look. "You're a super salesman."

"Nope, you've just got great product. People love it."

"And they love you," Amber added. "Just like I said. That's how I know you're going to do great at this business. And another thing. You keep saying that your Grindle Point was your 'one item of great value,' but that's not true."

"What do you mean? None of my other puzzles even come close."

"Girl, your greatest asset is *you*. You've got the personality. You've got the gumption. You've got the likability. You were born for this."

"You think?"

"I do."

"Try telling that to my mama."

"Okay, I will." She pointed over my shoulder, and I turned to discover my parents climbing the stairs leading up to the stage. "And it looks like I won't have to wait very long either."

# CHAPTER 11

"Mama? Dad? What are you guys doing here?"

"Well, that's a fine welcome." My mother leaned forward to give me a little peck on the cheek. "A person can visit her daughter at work, can't she?"

"Well, of course. I just didn't realize you were coming."

"We weren't." My father lifted his palms. "And then we were."

"We're headed out to dinner, and I thought this would be a nice stop on the way." My mother glanced down at my table. "For pity's sake, I thought you were here to sell puzzles, Mariah. Your table is empty."

"I am. I mean, I did. I sold all but these two." I pointed to the ones left on the corner of my table.

"You sold all of them?" She fussed with the strap of her purse, which threatened to slip off her shoulder. "Well, that's wonderful news."

"Thank you."

"Did you hear that, Herb?" Mama reached to take hold of my father's hand. "She actually sold all of those puzzles. Who would've believed it?"

Not her, obviously. But my dad's smile convinced me that he

had higher hopes than Mama.

"Mariah's got a knack for this," Amber chimed in.

"Oh?" My mother did not look convinced.

"People love her." Amber slipped an arm around my shoulders. "And she's got a great eye when it comes to the puzzle market. Some people buy too high, and their puzzles are out of reach. Some buy too cheap and offer an inferior product. But Mariah?" Amber squared her shoulders as if ready to take down an opponent. "She knows just what the customers want."

I would have to thank her later for her kindness. I could tell from the warmth in her eyes that she meant every word, and that touched my heart.

"Well, this customer wants to buy these last two." My father reached to grab the two remaining puzzles.

"Why ever would you do that, Herb?" Mama asked. "You don't even like puzzles. The last time I tried to get you to work one you said they were too hard on your eyes."

"Did I? I can't remember." He offered me a little wink and pulled out his wallet.

"Dad, you don't seriously think I'm going to let you pay for those, do you?" I argued.

"You'd better do as you're told, Mariah Elizabeth Jamison." His stern words were followed by a chuckle. "Or else."

"Or else you'll send me to my room?" I tried.

He laughed again. "No. Or else I'll put your mother to work as your helper."

She slugged him on the arm. "That's not nice."

He paid for the puzzles, and I bagged them and passed them his way. We all stared down at my empty table. I offered a contented sigh. Maybe I wasn't a failure, after all. What I lacked in sleuthing skills I made up for in puzzle sales.

Sleuthing skills. Ugh.

I still needed to figure out how my Grindle Point had ended up online. That would require a visit with Harvey Bates, one I wasn't looking forward to. I searched the stage but couldn't find him. Weird. He always seemed to be hovering.

A commotion upstage right drew our attention. I turned to discover Tristan had reentered the stage and donned another crazy outfit.

"Who is that very strange man in the feather boa and large sunglasses?" Mama asked.

Well, terrific. My mother really would think puzzle people were a bunch of kooks now.

"That's the guy we were talking about earlier on the phone. I went to school with him. His name is Tristan."

"Oh, the Woodhouse boy. Yes." My mother's eyes widened as she focused on him. "He was always such an odd duck."

*Be nice, Mother.*

"For that matter, so were the parents. I graduated with his mother."

"They're the ones who started that shop in town, aren't they?" my father asked. "The one that looks like a junk heap."

"Yes." I watched Tristan as he reached for a fake microphone. Oh boy. Was another song coming? *Please, God...no.* "Tristan is... different."

Mr. Purvis approached Tristan's table, and I had a flashback to last night, at the diner. I'd seen them both together there. And the night before, when they had remained behind in the gallery. And half an hour ago, when they disappeared into the café together.

These two really *were* very chummy, weren't they?

Indeed. Based on the hot and heavy conversation going on between them now, I had to conclude they were.

And that raised my antennae. It made me want to take a closer look at something that had been bothering me since Thursday night, something I still hadn't settled in my mind.

"Mama, can you excuse me for a minute? There's something I need to take care of."

Before she could respond, I sprinted to the wings on stage left then into the back hallway. With Mr. Purvis on the main stage, I had a couple of minutes to take a peek at his desk. Maybe—just maybe—I would find a few clues there.

Unfortunately, I found the door to his office locked. And when he showed up in the hallway a couple of minutes later, I fumbled around for an excuse for being there.

"I, um, wondered if the police ever found anything out about that note," I managed.

He leaned against his door, arms crossed. "Like I said earlier, the only fingerprints on the note were your own."

That wasn't exactly what he'd said before, was it? No, the last time he'd included his own prints in the story.

I forced a smile. "Well, let me know if anything changes. I want to help."

"I know you do, Mariah." He gave me a sympathetic look. "And I appreciate it, trust me. But some things are better left to the experts."

Why did people keep saying that? And did he consider himself an expert?

I turned back toward the stage but ran smack-dab into Harvey Bates standing in the shadows just past the security guard's door. What in the world was he doing back here?

My heart rate picked up and I wanted to run. Where were my mom and dad when I needed them? Oh, right. At my table with Amber and Charlie.

I managed a calm, "Sorry," then took a couple of steps back.

He put his hands up as if surrendering. "No, it's my fault. I was following you, actually."

Well, great. My trembling intensified, and I backed myself against the wall.

"Yeah." Harvey cleared his throat, and his gaze shifted to the floor then back up again. "I have something to tell you. A confession, I guess you'd call it."

"Okay." I waited, anxious to hear what he had to say.

"So, about that Grindle Point on Martha's Vineyard."

"Yes? What about it?"

"I called that guy back and told him I wouldn't be buying it after all."

*Play it cool, Mariah.* "Did you?"

"Yeah. I found another one online. And that's what I want to talk to you about. Let me show you." He reached for his phone and pulled up a link then pressed it.

It led to a dead site.

He tried again, his brow wrinkled as he pushed the link once more. "That's weird. The post was taken down."

"No way." I leaned in for a closer look. Sure enough, the site I'd visited on my own phone just a few hours ago was now a thing of the past. No reference to it at all.

He shook his head. "This is so weird. I was just on it a couple of hours ago. Someone was selling the Grindle Point for $900. I actually bought it last night. It's going to be delivered in three to five business days. That's what I wanted to tell you."

"That's why you didn't buy the one on Martha's Vineyard? Because you found a cheaper one?"

"Yeah." He groaned. "Man, I hope I didn't just waste $900. Do you think it was a scam?"

"Maybe." At this point I wasn't sure what to think. So I decided to come clean. "Harvey, I know all about that Grindle Point. I'm sure it's mine."

"Are you saying you listed it?" He looked more than a little confused.

"No. I'm saying that the person who stole it listed it. I had a call from the guy on Martha's Vineyard earlier, letting me know that you had changed your mind. He's the one who told me about this one. So I did a little scrolling online and found the site."

"So, you know."

"Yeah. I know. And so do the police."

"The police?"

Was it my imagination or did he flinch?

"I called them as soon as I got the news," I explained. "They were going to try to trace the email address, but if he—or she— took it down, they'll have nothing to go on."

"I'll have to cancel the transaction on my card right away. This is a hot mess."

"It is." And I hoped it wouldn't get any hotter. If only I could figure out who had listed the puzzle online, I'd have this case solved.

In that moment I was struck by a recollection. I pulled out my phone and went straight to my photos. "I took a screenshot of it earlier so I would remember to go back to it later." I opened the photo and gave it a close look then pressed my phone in Harvey's direction. "Any idea who this is?"

"No, that screen name isn't familiar to me. I remember him—or her—saying they were an individual not a shop."

"Right." But who?

"Here's the crazy part—I didn't go looking for this. I got an email from the owner. He seemed to know I was looking for one."

"And you fell for that?" Time to speak my mind, to give this guy my opinion on how he'd handled this mess. "You didn't once think it might be mine? Shouldn't you have gone to the police, Harvey?"

His eyes reflected a level of emotional intensity I hadn't expected, and I wondered if I had upset him with that question.

"Mariah, don't you see? I was buying it for you."

"For me?"

His eyes filled with compassion, and he rested his hand on my arm. "Yes. I did plan to go to the police. I had every intention of calling them today. But I wanted to go ahead and purchase the puzzle so that I could give it to you. I recognized the sticker and realized right away it was yours. I had to act fast before someone else bought it."

At that, all of my suspicions melted. I wanted to throw my arms around Harvey, to thank him for his kindness.

But on the other hand. . .

This could all be a ploy to confuse me. Ugh. Where was my discernment when I needed it?

*Stay focused, Mariah.*

One question still lingered, and it must be addressed.

"Harvey, last night at the diner you had dinner with a group of boys at the booth behind me."

"Right." His smile faded. "Oh, were we too noisy for you? I

know Josh can get a little rowdy."

So that was the blond boy's name. Josh.

"It's not that. I'm just wondering how you know them." *And if you gave them fireworks on Thursday night.*

For the first time since our conversation began, a relaxed smile lit Harvey's face. "Oh, that's easy. I've been mentoring them for a couple of months now."

"Mentoring?"

"Yeah." He nodded. "I teach the college kids at my church. I've been trying to connect with this group for a while, to get them interested in coming. Finally got to know Josh, so he was a good in to connect with the others."

"Oh, wow."

"They showed up for our Fourth of July event but didn't stick around long." He seemed to lose himself to his thoughts for a moment then jumped back into the conversation. "Hey, you do what you can. You know?"

I did.

"So, let me ask you a question, Harvey. Did you see those boys on the night of the murder? They were the ones with the fireworks, right?"

"Yeah, I was down there when the police arrived and caught them. That's actually why it took me so long to come back to the opera house. I had a long talk with the boys after the fact."

"Any idea where they got the fireworks?"

He looked genuinely perplexed by this question. "Never thought about it, to be honest. Just figured they had them left over."

"One would think." Only I'd heard Josh say otherwise. Someone had given him those fireworks.

And I now felt pretty sure I knew who.

I glanced down at the photo one last time before shoving my phone into my purse. This time I took note of something that had gone unnoticed before.

*Biddybum.*

The screen name for the seller contained the word *biddy-bum.*

It came swirling back over me in a flash. I knew exactly where I'd heard that word before, in musical form. Smack-dab in the middle of Tristan Woodhouse's favorite song.

# CHAPTER 12

"Mama, here's what I need you to do." I looked her square in the eye, all business. "You've got to find Mr. Purvis and keep him distracted while I wait for the police. Don't let him leave the building. Can you do that?"

"P-Police?" She shook her head and looked as if she might be ill.

"Yes." I nodded then turned to my father. "You're not gonna like this, Dad, but I need you to take on Tristan."

"Ugh."

"I know. But you can do it. Flatter him. Talk about how much you love his puzzles. Promise him you'll visit his shop. Anything."

My father's eyes bugged. "You want me to lie?"

"Well, just do what you can without offending your conscience. But keep him busy. Ask him how he got started in the business. Or. . ." The best idea hit me, and I had to grin as I thought it through. "Ask him to sing. He seems to love that."

"Well, that sounds downright painful."

"Oh, it is. But whatever you do, don't let either of them out of your sight. I need to make a quick call. Hopefully, the police will be here soon. I'm going to cut through the stage right wings and unlock the back door so they can sneak in without anyone knowing."

Amber walked up just in time to hear that last part. She shook her head. "No, Mariah. Purvis said not to go into the stage right wings. That area is under construction."

"I sincerely doubt that," I countered. "I'm guessing he lied to us."

"Why would he lie about construction?" She seemed genuinely perplexed. "That makes no sense."

Before I could say, "I'll tell you in a bit," Charlie called to her from their table and she walked his way.

I turned back to my parents, nerves mounting. "Okay, folks. Time to get this show on the road. I'll be back as soon as the police get here." Was it my imagination or did my chest tighten as I spoke those words? And why was I suddenly struggling to breathe?

*Because, Mariah. . .you've done it. You made your list, checked it twice, and figured out who's been naughty and nice.*

And the naughty one—er, ones—were just as likely to strike again if I didn't handle myself with care.

*Please, God. Give me wisdom. And protection.*

I slipped into the wings on stage right and inched my way toward the door that led to the back parking lot. My plan, if all went as I hoped, was to ease my way out of the back door—the one I still remembered from ninth grade—and wait for the police behind the building. That way they could enter unannounced.

Only, the part about the construction on stage right turned out to be true. I tripped over a metal pipe in the middle of the floor and took off like a bird in flight. Thank goodness I didn't fall, but I made enough noise to cause a stir. Before I knew what hit me, a beam of light caught me squarely in the eyes.

A familiar voice sounded from the other side of the light. "Who is that?" In the shadows I couldn't make out Mr. Purvis's face, but I certainly knew that gravelly tone.

The trembling began in earnest now, but I tried not to let it show. "It's. . .it's me, Mr. Purvis. Mariah Jamison."

"What are you doing back here?" He waved the flashlight in my face.

*Play it cool, Mariah. Play it cool.*

"No one's allowed on this side of the stage," he growled. "I told you that yesterday. It's dangerous back here."

"Right. Just found that out the hard way. But I seem to remember a bathroom back here, and I really need to—"

The light bounced up and down. Was he nervous? "No one is allowed on this side of the stage. Use the one in the lobby, and don't come back here again."

"Got it!" I flashed a forced smile, my heart now going a hundred miles an hour. Then I propelled myself back to the auditorium, up the aisle, into the lobby, and out the front door of the opera house. I would have to change my plan. I'd still meet the officers behind the building and pray the back door was unlocked. Maybe they could still enter that way without Purvis noticing.

*Please, God.*

I sprinted past the parking lot, beyond the diner, where patrons were enjoying their greasy burgers, and around the back of the building to the dumpster area. By the time I got back there, I was panting. And with the shadows of evening slowly easing their way down on me, the area felt more than a little creepy. Maybe this hadn't been my best idea.

I fidgeted with the back door and was relieved to find it unlocked. Perfect.

As quick as I could, I placed a call to Detective Durham. It took a couple minutes to relay the latest details of this ongoing story.

When I got to the part about Harvey Bates and the Grindle Point, he interrupted me. "We tried to check that online site where you said your puzzle was being sold, but the post was removed."

"Right. We figured that out. But it's okay. I know who placed the ad now."

"You do?"

"Yep."

When I told him, he responded with a rushed, "I'll be right there. But get back inside and act normal."

As if.

In the background I could hear motion. Then the dinging of a car door opening. Then the sound of an engine starting. It brought comfort to know he was on his way.

"I think it's important that you not have any lights or sirens when you come," I suggested. "I'm afraid they'll run."

"They?"

"Yes. Tristan definitely wasn't working alone. His fingerprints weren't on that slip of paper I found in my purse, remember?"

"Slip of paper?"

"Well, yeah. The blue one from the perp?"

"Blue slip of paper?"

"Mr. Purvis turned it in and you guys ran the prints and. . ."

Oh. No.

He hadn't turned it in. That note was meant to scare me, to cause me to back off. And to throw me off-track. Aw, man. Now my blood was boiling. How dare he try to pull one over on me?

On the other hand, how dare he and Tristan murder a man and steal my puzzle?

"No idea what you're talking about, Ms. Jamison. But we're headed to you now. I've got a patrol car on the way too."

"Can you come to the back? There's a door back here and it's unlocked. I just checked it. They won't suspect anything if you come in through the stage right wings. But be careful because that area is under construction."

"You've got this all worked out, haven't you?"

The laughter that wriggled up was laced with nervous energy. "Yeah, and I'd like to live through it, which is *why* I've got it all worked out."

"We'll be there in five minutes. Six, if we hit the light at Elm."

We ended the call, and I turned back toward the diner but caught another glimpse of the dumpster out of the corner of my eye. Now that I knew the truth about that note, a nagging suspicion wouldn't leave me alone. Maybe Purvis had tossed it into the trash after I gave it to him yesterday. If so, it might still be here. If I could locate it, then Durham wouldn't think I'd lost my marbles.

The side panel of the dumpster was wide open, and I peered inside. The overhead streetlight wasn't enough to illuminate the situation so I reached for my phone and turned on the flashlight then glanced inside again. I saw bags of trash down below but couldn't quite reach any of them, so I leaned in and stretched my arm to see what I could grab hold of.

Nothing.

So I tried again.

At some point my leaning became a straddling routine. I hung by my belly, the top half of my body tipped forward into the dumpster and my feet poking up into the air behind me.

Boy, wouldn't this make a lovely image for the evening news?

I pointed my flashlight at what appeared to be a piece of paper.

Nope. Some sort of paper bag. White.

My nostrils flared as a familiar icky scent gripped me. Ugh. Hot sauce. Again. Mr. Purvis and his Mexican food.

*Mr. Purvis and his Mexican food.*

*Taco-Mia.*

Had he used the bag to dispose of the note, perhaps? If I could just reach it maybe I would find my answer.

I stretched my arm forward until it ached. This position also caused terrible pain to my abdomen, but it would all be worth it, if only I could manage a couple more inches. Then I would have the bag in hand.

Or...

I'd land face-first in the dumpster and a pile of empty cardboard boxes would come tumbling down on my head, dropping leftover food from the café all over me.

# CHAPTER 13

There are those times in life when you wish you could go backward in time. This was one of those times. Sitting there, covered in lettuce and tomatoes, I felt like a ham sandwich. If only I could find my phone, I'd locate that fast-food bag and crawl out of here, hopefully with my pride intact.

I dug around until I finally found my phone. The flashlight was still beaming away, illuminating slivers of trash.

And there, just in front of me. . .a white bag with a Taco-Mia label on it. "Yes!" I reached for it, my breath in my throat. Man, it felt heavy. Clearly, Mr. Purvis didn't finish his meal.

Off in the distance, I heard cars approaching. Maybe I would end up on the evening news after all. Lovely.

With the bag in hand, I tried to right myself but tipped forward even more and almost face-planted again. I managed to keep myself from falling just as the sound of brakes caught my attention a few feet away, followed by the gravelly sound of tires coming to a halt against the pavement.

Either the police had arrived or I was in big, big trouble.

I peered through the opening to discover the police in one vehicle and an unmarked vehicle beside it. The officers got out of their patrol car and then the driver's side door opened on the other vehicle and a swoon-worthy man stepped out.

*Well hello, Detective Durham!*

Crazy. I'd pictured him to be much older. This guy was. . .wow. Maybe a couple of years older than me and quite the looker. Oh my.

*Focus, Mariah. Focus.*

I called out to him so he wouldn't be alarmed to find me in the dumpster. As if hearing a woman's voice from inside a dumpster could be comforting. Still, I gave it my best effort, leading with the words, "Detective, it's Mariah! I'm in the dumpster."

Seconds later he was peering through the opening, a high-beamed flashlight aimed straight at me. Goodness. How many times would I end up in the limelight tonight?

He and the other male officer helped me out, and seconds later I stood alongside them. Durham must've gotten a whiff of me, because he took a giant step backward.

"Sorry!" I lifted the Taco-Mia bag into the air. "But it was worth it! I found the taco bag!"

"The taco bag?"

"Yes. I haven't had a chance to look through it yet, but I'm hoping there's something in here. I think you're going to want to see it."

I passed off the bag to Durham, and he opened it then pointed the beam of his flashlight down inside.

"Um. . ." He looked back at me. "Where did you say you got this again?"

I pointed at the dumpster. "In there. I got to thinking that Purvis might've thrown that note away. I remembered he was eating Mexican food at the time, so I went digging for the bag. And I found it all right!"

"Yes, you certainly found something. But I'm going to need gloves before handling it." He grabbed some from the trunk of his car and put them on before reaching inside the bag. I gasped when he came out with—not a note but a box cutter.

"Oh. My."

"Okay, I've gotta give you props." The man flashed me an admiring look, and I felt heat rise to my sticky cheeks. "What made you think to look in the taco bag?"

"Just a hunch."

"And you crawled into the dumpster to get it."

"Crawled would be a bit of a stretch. Let's just say I landed in there. And I wasn't looking for a box cutter, by the way. Like I said, I was trying to find the note."

"The one on the blue paper. Right."

"I wanted to prove to you that it existed."

"Oh, I believe you. I'd say you're our most credible witness so far."

"Would you mind saying that in front of my mother?"

He laughed. "Sure. But I've got a little situation to take care of first, if you don't mind."

"Don't mind a bit."

Another police vehicle pulled up behind him, and the officers I'd grown familiar with over the past couple days climbed out. They put together a plan to enter through the back door, just as I had suggested. I wanted to go in with them, but they insisted I go around to the front. I made them promise not to start without me.

Five minutes later I found myself zipping across the lobby toward the auditorium. I barreled down the aisle until I got to the stairs leading to the stage.

Mama took one look at me and her eyes widened. "Mariah,

441

you've got lettuce in your hair." She clamped a hand over her nose. "And what's that smell?"

"I'll tell you later. But for now, we've got to get as many people off the stage as we can. In a discreet sort of way."

She pointed to my father, who was standing upstage center next to Tristan. They were hot and heavy into the chorus of "If I Were a Rich Man." Turned out, my dad is a decent tenor. Who knew?

I sent Mama to fetch him, knowing my scent would raise too many questions. Then I headed back into the auditorium, where I stood at a distance so as not to draw attention to myself. I ushered up as many rapid-fire prayers as I could under the circumstances and prayed my parents would make it off the stage in time.

They didn't.

What happened next felt like a scene from a movie. From the stage right wings, Detective Durham made a swift move in Mr. Purvis's direction. From the opposite wings, the other two officers startled Tristan with the phrase, "You have the right to remain silent!" halfway into the *biddy-bum* portion of his tune.

Tristan stopped cold. He turned as if attempting to escape, but my father cornered him. "Oh no you don't, buddy. Not on my watch."

"Go, Dad!"

Mama had taken to lecturing Mr. Purvis on the evils of stealing our family heirloom as Detective Durham cuffed him. I was caught somewhere between them all, unsure which way to look.

The news reporter and cameraman rushed in through the lobby door and worked their way to downstage center, where they began filming. I had to wonder who tipped them off? These two must hover close to their police radio.

As the chaos intensified, Amber and Charlie rushed my way.

"Um, Mariah? Something you want to tell me?" Amber pinched her nose and then waved her hand as she backed away. "Whoa."

"What *is* that?" Charlie asked.

"Kind of a long story," I explained. "But to answer your question, Tristan and Mr. Purvis did it. In the gallery. With a box cutter."

"Tristan?" Her eyes were like saucers now. "Tristan Woodhouse?"

"And Old Man Purvis?" Charlie looked genuinely shocked by this news.

They both shifted their gaze to the stage, where the bad guys were cuffed and being escorted out.

"Oh, one thing I have to do before they leave!" I rushed up the steps to Detective Durham, who held Purvis in a tight grip. I could barely catch my breath but managed. . . "The Grindle Point!"

"What about it?" he asked.

"I want it back. I'm going to ask Tristan what he did with it, for real."

My gaze shifted to Tristan and I started to rush his way, but Durham shook his head. "Back away, Ms. Jamison."

"But—"

"No buts." His expression shifted and I saw compassion in his eyes. "I have a feeling it won't be long before you have your puzzle back. In the meantime, we'll be in touch."

I hoped he would stay in touch, all right.

Our eyes met for what felt like a magical moment. Then I realized he was looking at the sprig of lettuce in my hair. I plucked it out and shoved it into my pocket as he headed out with Mr. Purvis arguing the whole way.

"He's a cutie," Amber said as she watched Durham head down the aisle.

"Yeah." I sighed. "Kind of wish I hadn't fallen into the dumpster on our first meeting. As Mama always says, you never get a second chance to make a first impression."

"Wait, you fell in a dumpster?" Amber laughed. "Mariah, what are we going to do with you?"

I didn't have a chance to answer because the news reporter rushed in, cameraman following not far behind. They caught a few clips of Tristan and Purvis before turning to the vendors for comments.

Turned out Mama and Dad were happy to report how their daughter had saved the day. Go figure. They carried on and on. To hear them speak, I was some sort of local hero. Harvey Bates spoke up next and shared with great enthusiasm about the role he had played in helping me solve this crime.

Some things never change.

Amber flashed a warm smile. "I told you the puzzle pieces would come together. God is good."

"All the time." But He felt particularly good right now.

A short while later, the puzzle show came to its inevitable end. My proud parents headed out to dinner, but not before pausing to share the story of their daughter, the hero, with ten or twelve people in the auditorium.

At that point the vendors kicked it into high gear, working to dismantle our tables and load up boxes with leftover puzzles. Since I'd sold all of mine, I opted to help Amber and Charlie with theirs.

"Crazy, isn't it?" Amber swiped a loose strand of hair from her face as she looked up from an open box on the floor below. "We started on Thursday night with me helping you. Now you're helping us. What goes around comes around."

"Happy to be of service." And I was, though the sticky mayonnaise in my hair was becoming problematic.

Minutes later, Charlie taped up the last box then glanced our way. "I'm starving. Can we get food?"

"Yeah, want to grab dinner, Mariah?" Amber asked.

"Sure. But someplace where my appearance doesn't matter."

"Fast food?" Amber asked.

"Sure." My mouth watered as an idea hit. "Hey, what about Taco-Mia?"

She looked a bit nauseous at this suggestion.

Before I could offer any other ideas, my phone rang. I glanced down and smiled when I saw Detective Durham's name appear on the screen. I stepped into the stage left wings to take the call, my heart thump-thumping as I heard his voice.

"Hey, Ms. Jamison."

"Mariah."

"Mariah." An awkward silence filled the space between us. "I'm Casey, by the way."

"Casey." The name suited him.

"You can stop looking for the Grindle Point," he said. "We've got it."

"Really?"

"Yep. Woodhouse and Purvis thought they had a foolproof plan, but you thwarted them. Good work, by the way."

"Did this plan include killing a man or stealing my puzzle? I'm still a little confused on that point."

"Killing a man. From what we can gather, Tristan had been stalking Brandon online for some time."

"So, stealing my puzzle was an afterthought?"

"Well, you told me yourself it was worth $2,500."

"True. Though that guy on Martha's Vineyard had his listed for $3,500."

Casey laughed. "Well, my point is, we have it now. The police found it at Tristan's place. They've marked it as evidence in the case, so it might be a while before we can get it back to you."

"I understand."

"Would you mind coming up to the station to identify it?"

"I wouldn't mind a bit."

In that moment, I wanted to sing. I wanted to dance! I wanted to rush straight to the station and thank him in person.

But I didn't do any of those things. Instead, I offered a calm word of thanks for the information and then ended the call. I begged off on my dinner plans with Amber and Charlie, opting to head home to take a shower. I would wash the lettuce out of my hair and then change into something quirky and fun before meeting up with a certain handsome detective at the Camden police station.

Because, hey. . .maybe Mama was wrong this time. Maybe I really *would* get a second chance to make a first impression.

**JANICE THOMPSON**, who lives in the Houston area, writes romantic comedies, cozy mysteries, nonfiction devotionals, and musical comedies for the stage. She is the mother of four daughters and nine feisty grandchildren. When she's not writing books or taking care of foster dogs you'll find her in the kitchen, baking up specialty cakes and cookies.

# *You Might Also Enjoy. . .*

## GONE TO THE DOGS
### Series of Cozy Mysteries

The town of Brenham, Texas, has gone to the dogs! The employees of Lone Star Veterinary Clinic link arms with animal rescue organization Second Chance Ranch to care for the area's sweetest canines. Along the way, there are mysteries a'plenty in this series of six books by authors Janice Thompson and Kathleen Y'Barbo-Turner.

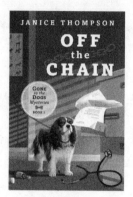

### Book 1
### OFF THE CHAIN
**by Janice Thompson**

Marigold Evans's first attempt at rescuing an abandoned pooch lands her in a drainage pipe in Brenham, Texas. . .and almost in jail, until Parker Jenson comes to her defense. Then a bad day only gets worse as the Lone Star Vet Clinic, where they both work, is vandalized, and the list of suspects starts to climb. With the help of her fellow employees, Marigold sets out to simultaneously solve the crime, rehab the rescued dog, and help more dogs in crisis. But why would anyone continue to work against all their good efforts?

**Paperback / 978-1-63609-313-0 / $14.99**